Disney

TIM BURTON'S THE NIGHTMARE BEFORE CHRISTMAS

ZERO'S JOURNEY

BOOK THREE

WRITTEN BY
D.J. MILKY

MAIN PRINTING COVER BY
KIYOSHI ARAI and JUN SUZUKI

VARIANT COVER BY
DAVID MACK

STORYBOARDS AND PENCILS BY
KEI ISHIYAMA

INKS BY
DAVID HUTCHISON

COLORS BY
DAN CONNER

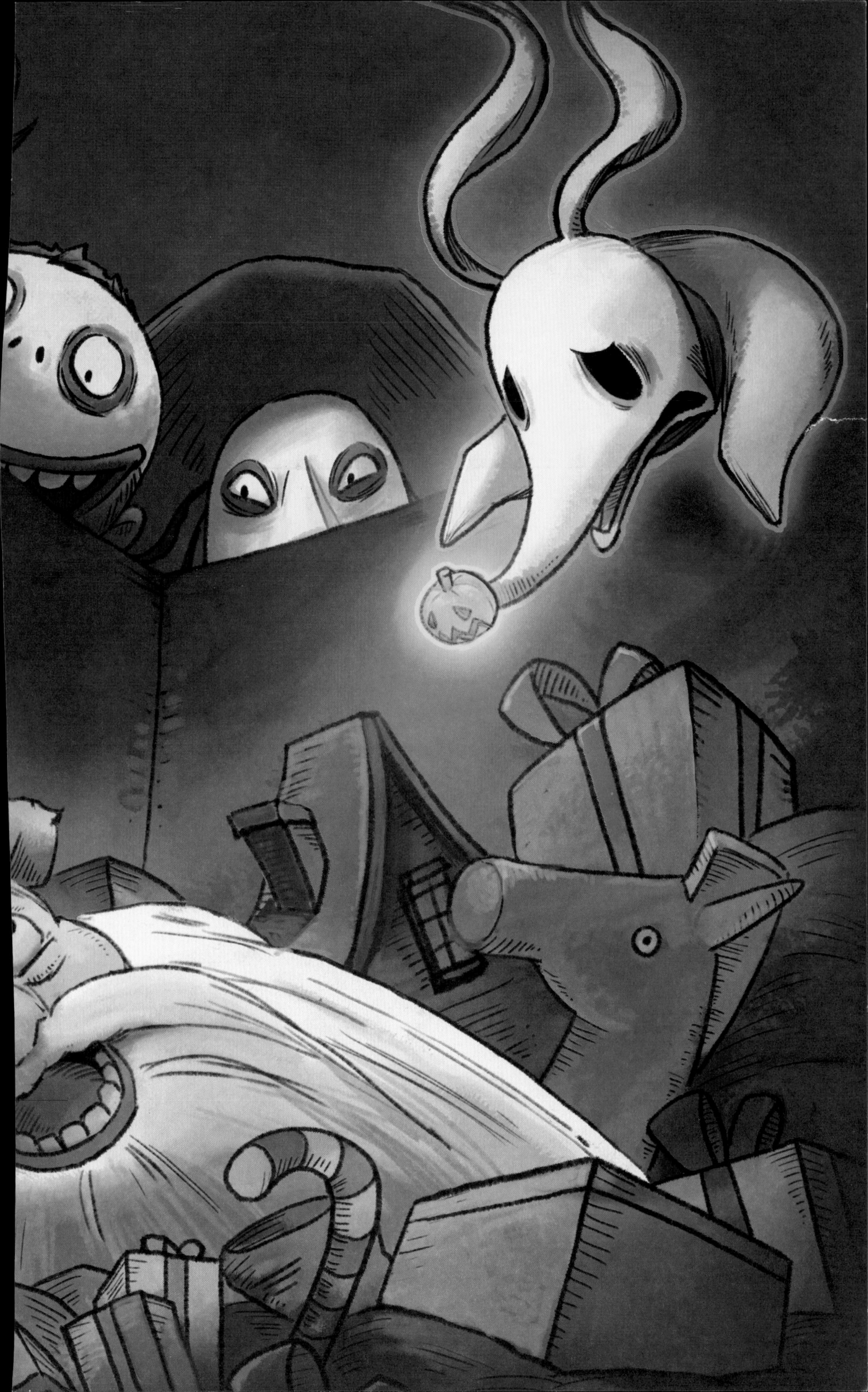

CONTENTS

◇◇◇◇◇◇◇◇◇◇◇◇◇◇◇◇◇◇◇

PREVIOUSLY ON...

ZERO'S JOURNEY

ZERO FINDS HIMSELF FACE-TO-FACE WITH
MR. MYZER, THE CRANKIEST, MOST MISERABLE OF
THE CHRISTMAS TOWN RESIDENTS. HE LEARNS ABOUT
MR. MYZER'S TRAGIC PAST, SO HE POSES AS MR. MYZER'S
DECEASED PUPPY TO TEACH MR. MYZER THE IMPORTANCE
OF CHERISHING EVEN THE SADDEST MEMORIES.

AFTER THE ADVENTURE WITH MR. MYZER AND
GINGERBREAD MAN IS OVER, ZERO, FORTUNATELY, SLAMS
INTO LOCK, SHOCK, AND BARREL! UNFORTUNATELY, LOCK,
SHOCK, AND BARREL ARE BEING CHASED BY SOME OF THE
CHRISTMAS TOWN RESIDENTS FOR WREAKING A LITTLE BIT
TOO MUCH HAVOC. ON THE RUN, LOCK, SHOCK, AND
BARREL FALL INTO A MYSTERIOUS HOLE WITH
ZERO CLOSE BEHIND.

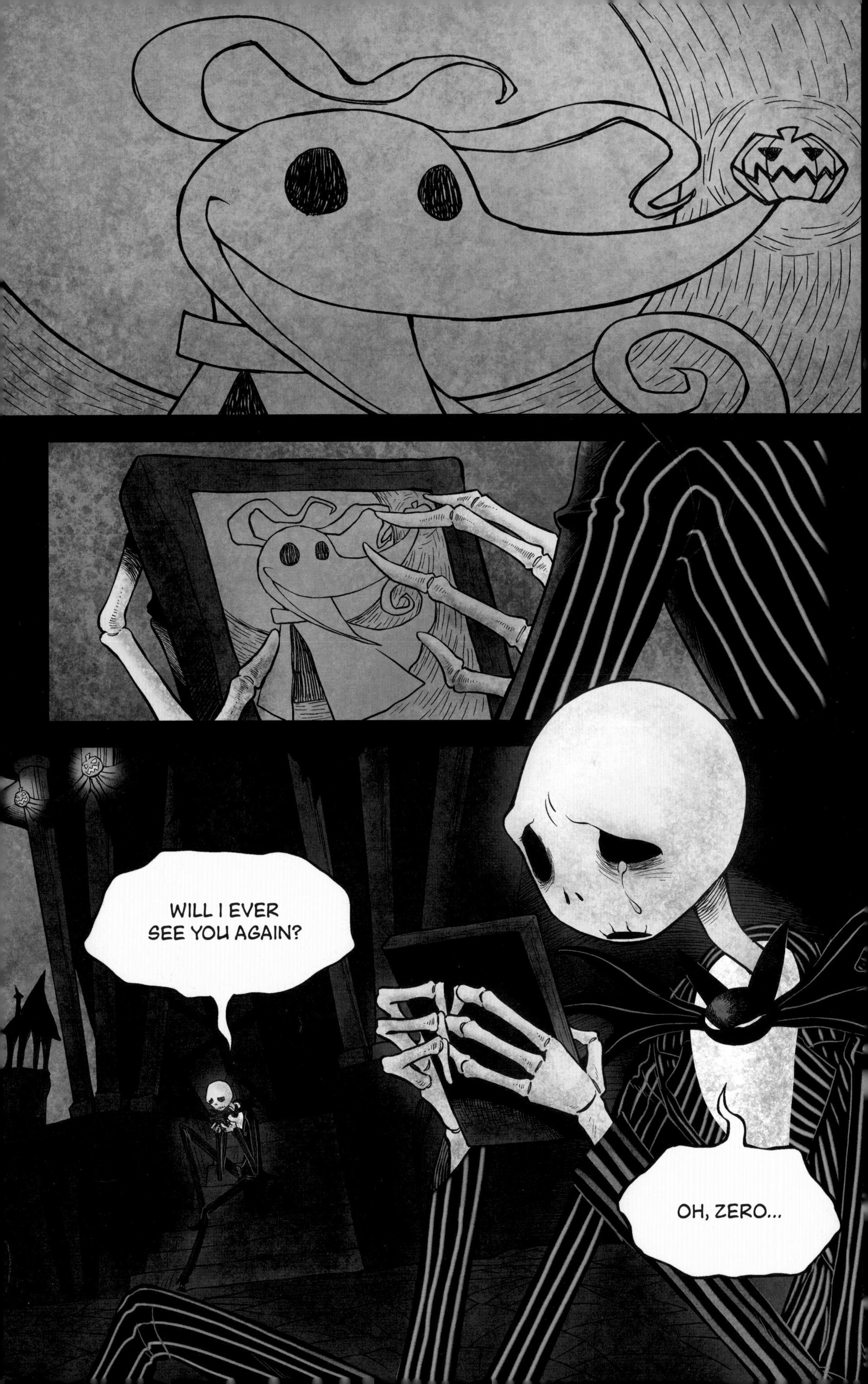
WILL I EVER SEE YOU AGAIN?
OH, ZERO...

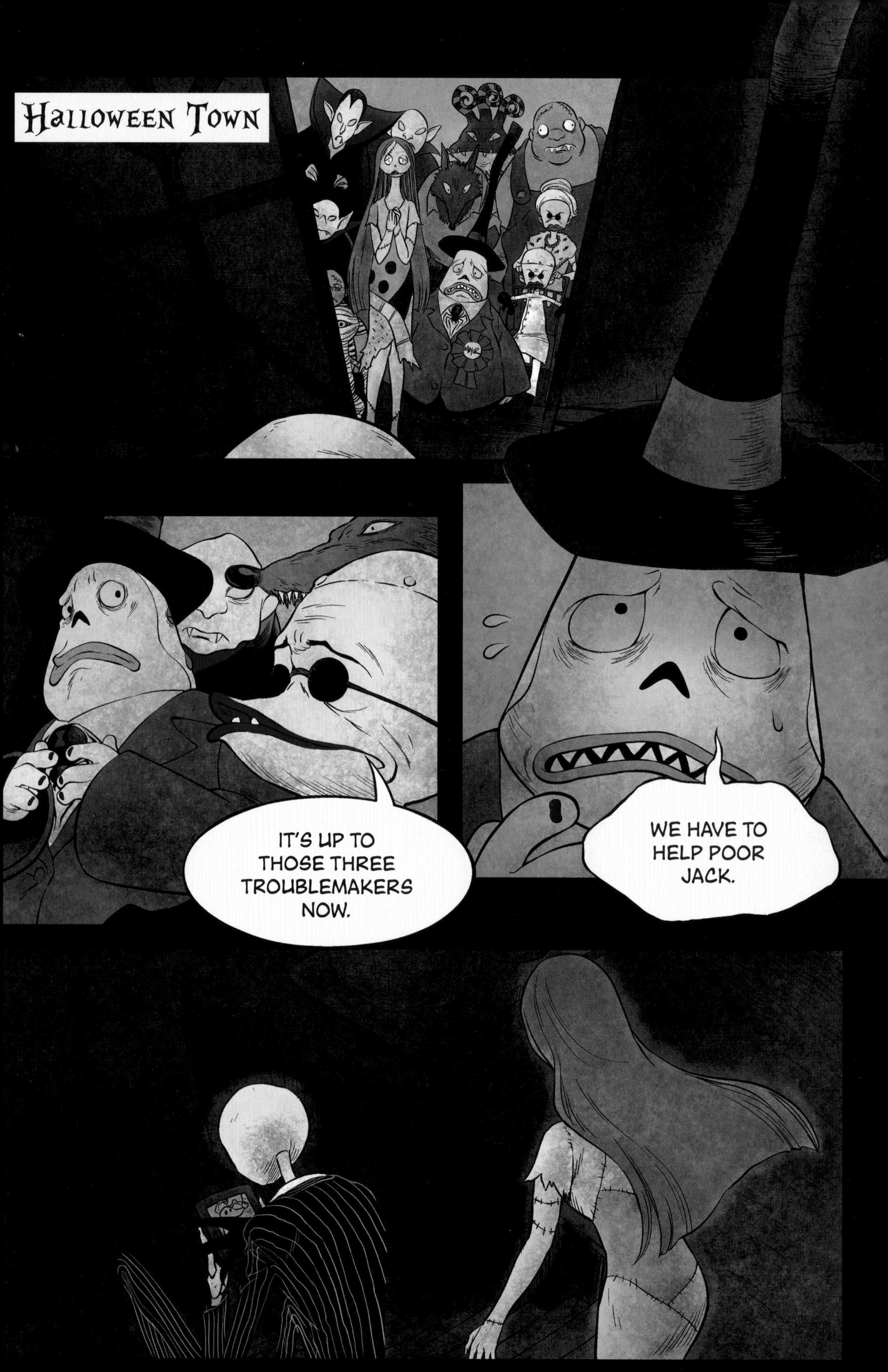
Halloween Town
WE HAVE TO HELP POOR JACK.
IT'S UP TO THOSE THREE TROUBLEMAKERS NOW.

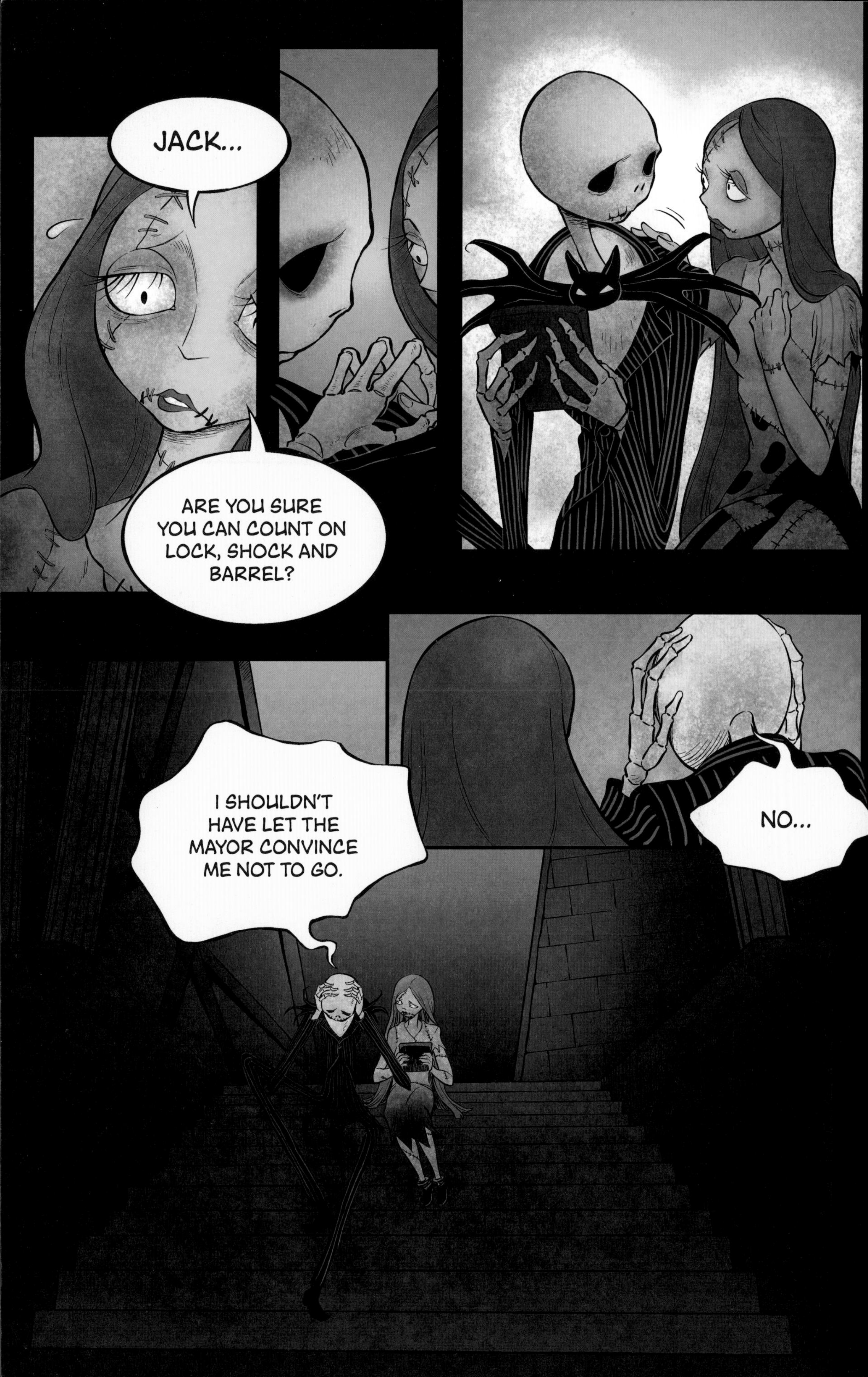
JACK...
ARE YOU SURE YOU CAN COUNT ON LOCK, SHOCK AND BARREL?
NO...
I SHOULDN'T HAVE LET THE MAYOR CONVINCE ME NOT TO GO.

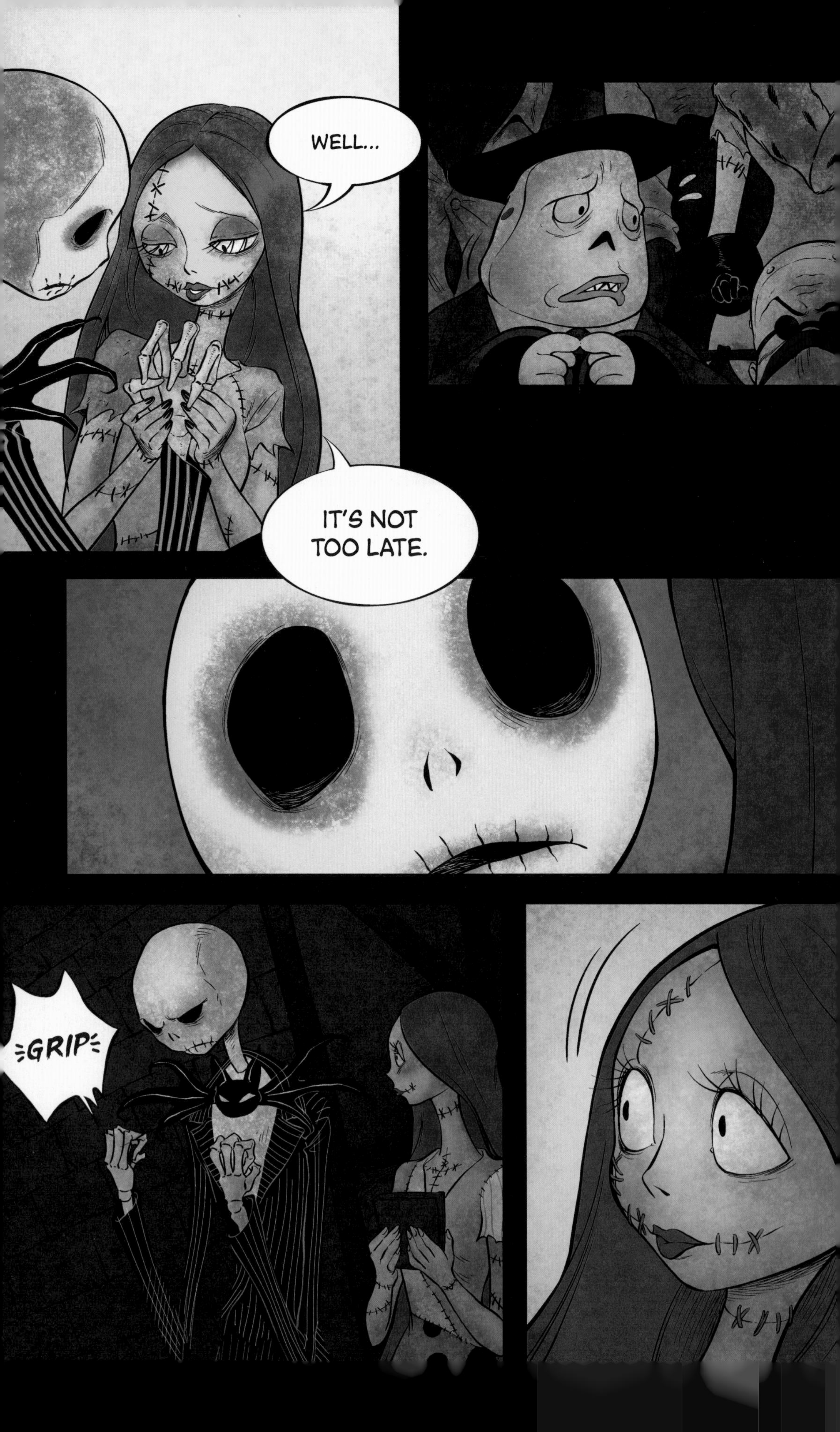
WELL...
IT'S NOT TOO LATE.
GRIP

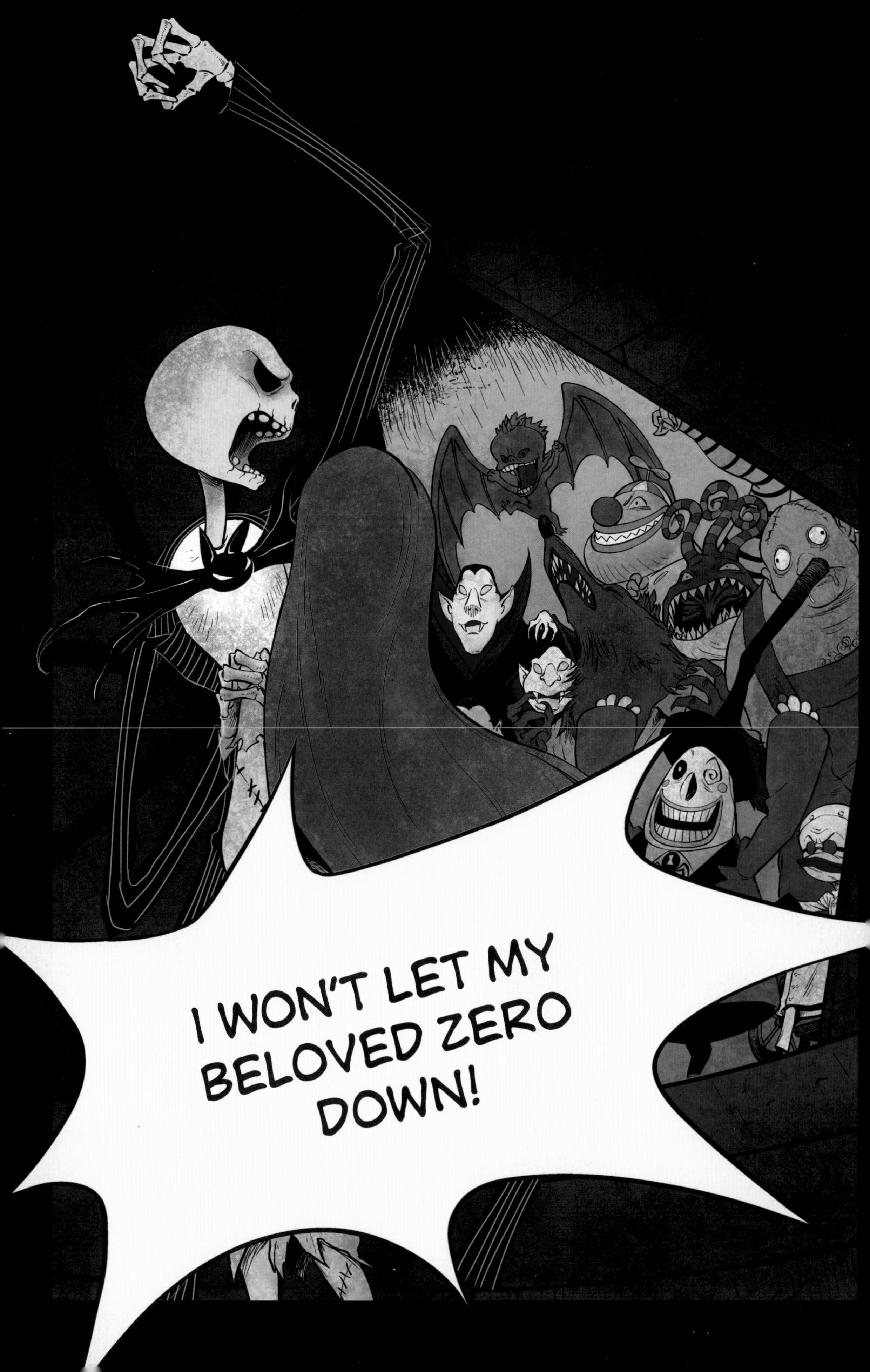
I WON'T LET MY BELOVED ZERO DOWN!

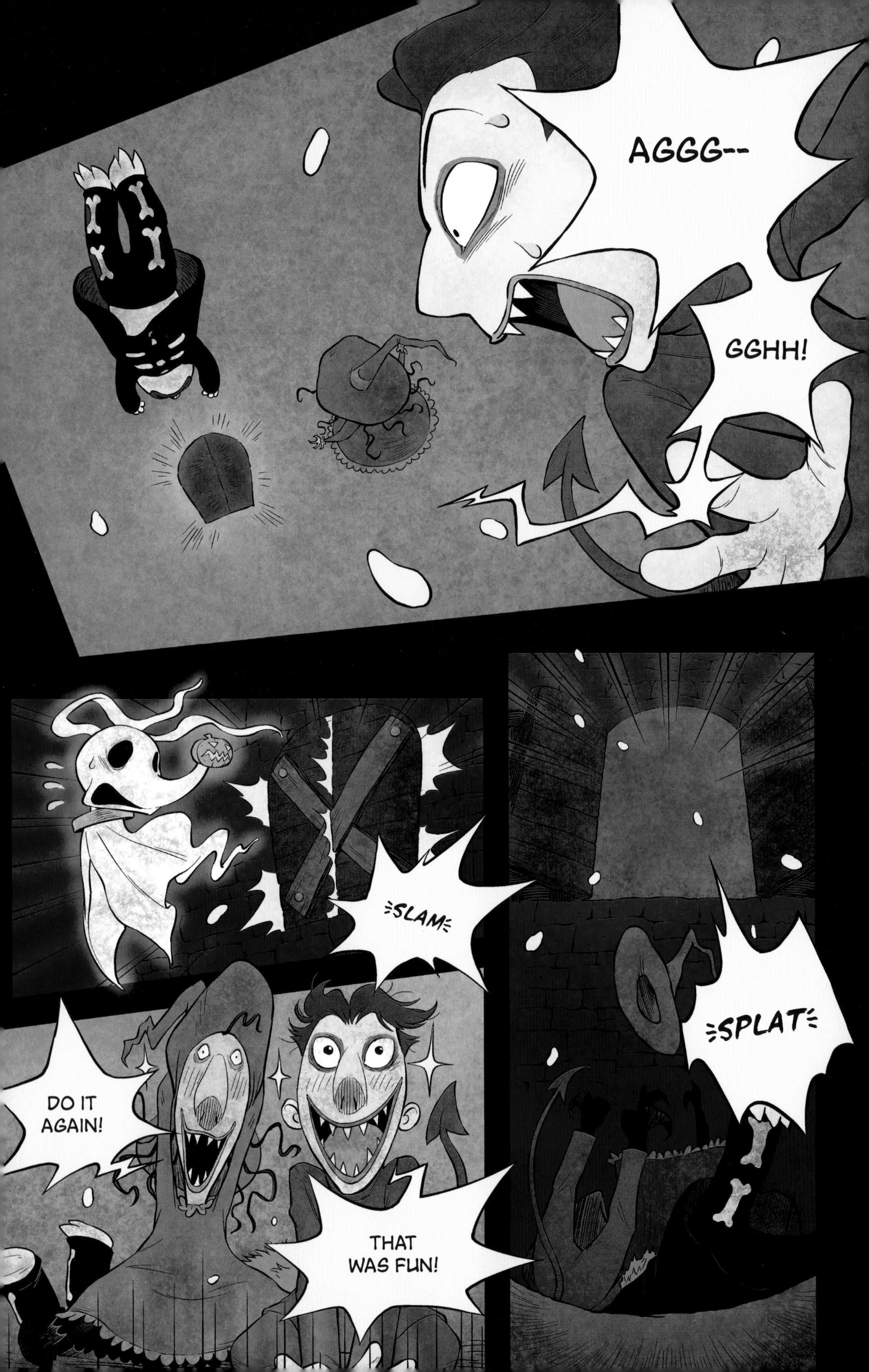
AGGG--
GGHH!
SPLAT
SLAM
DO IT AGAIN!
THAT WAS FUN!

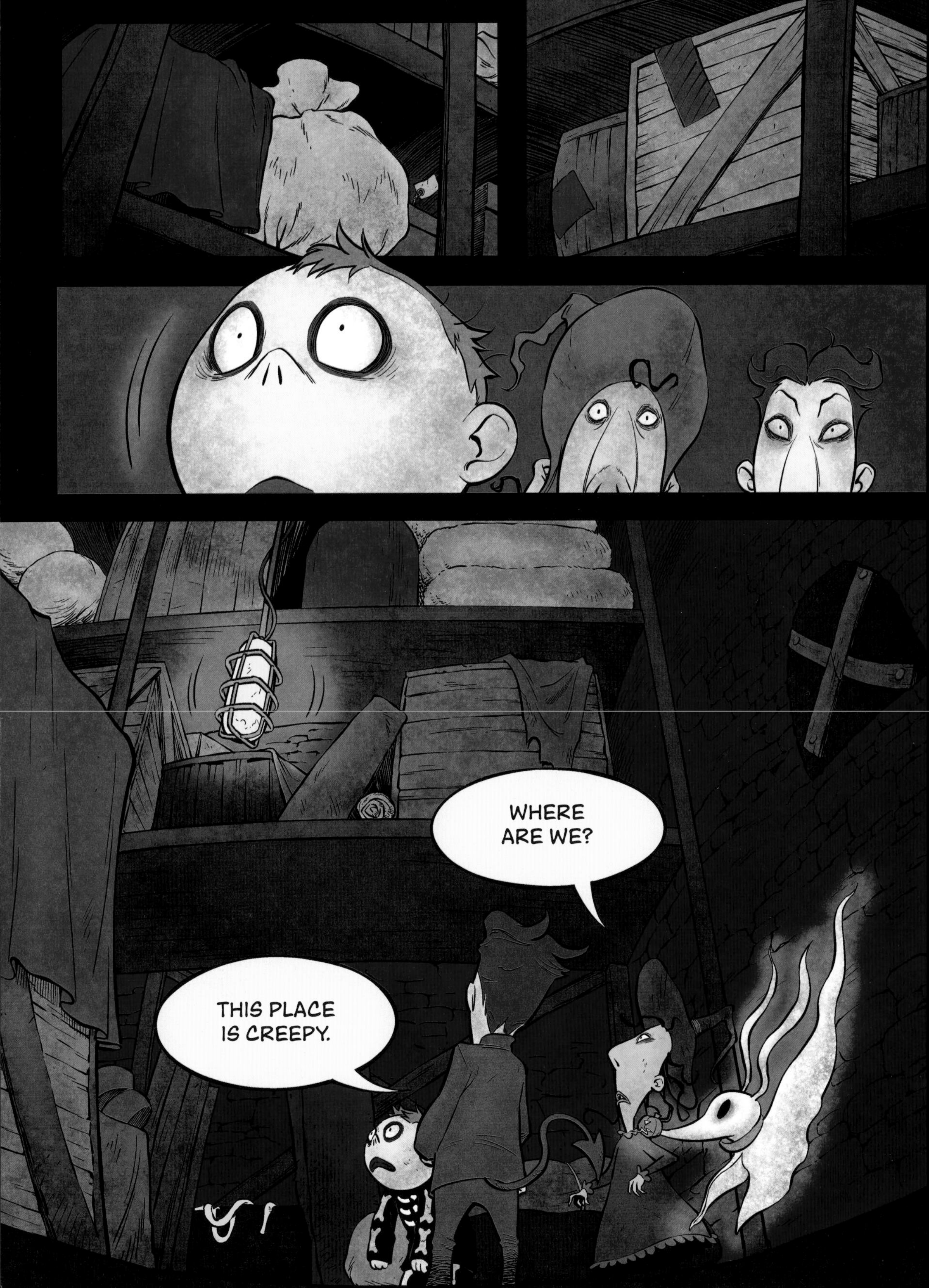
WHERE ARE WE?
THIS PLACE IS CREEPY.

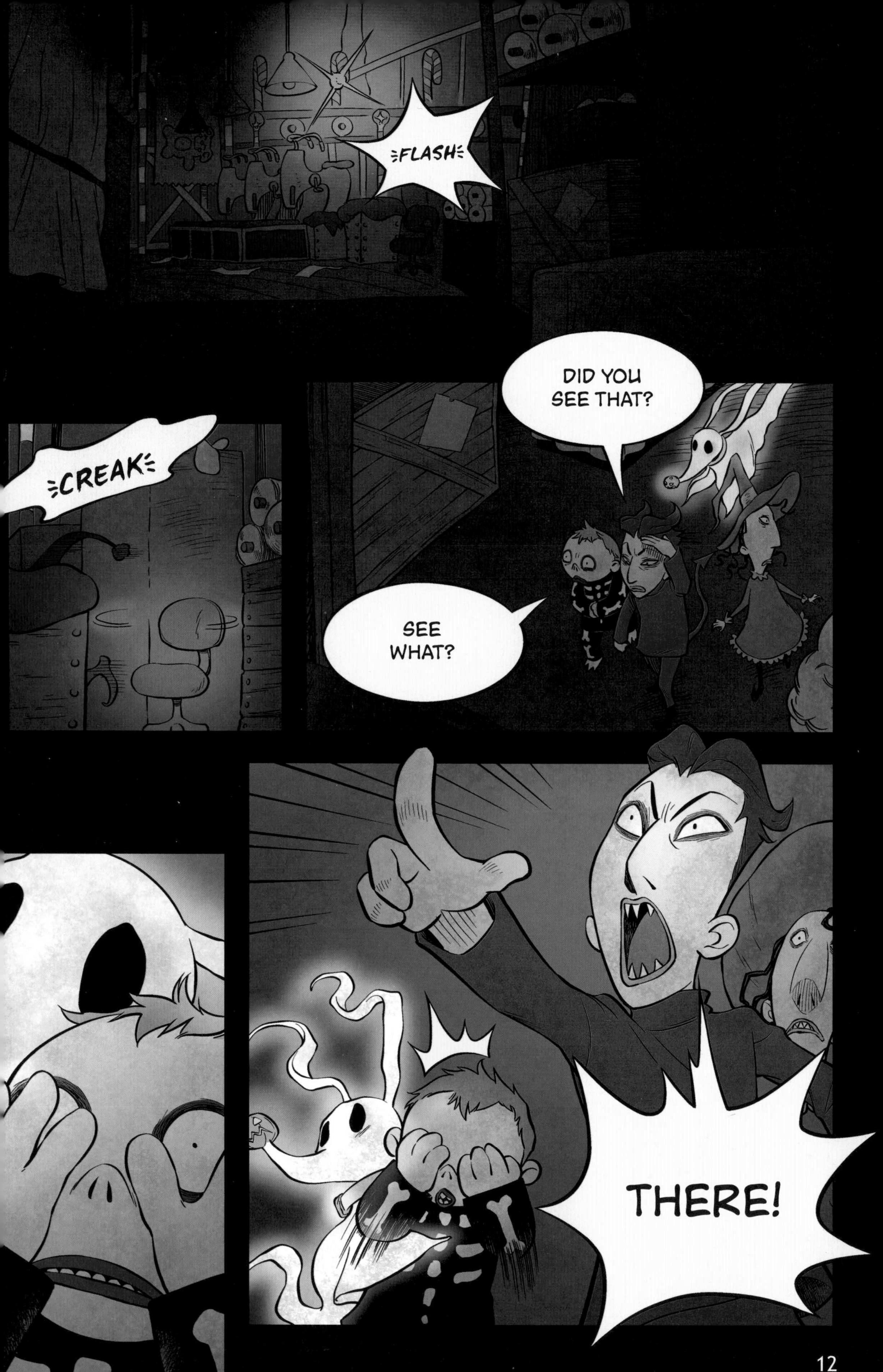
FLASH
DID YOU SEE THAT?
SEE WHAT?
CREAK
THERE!

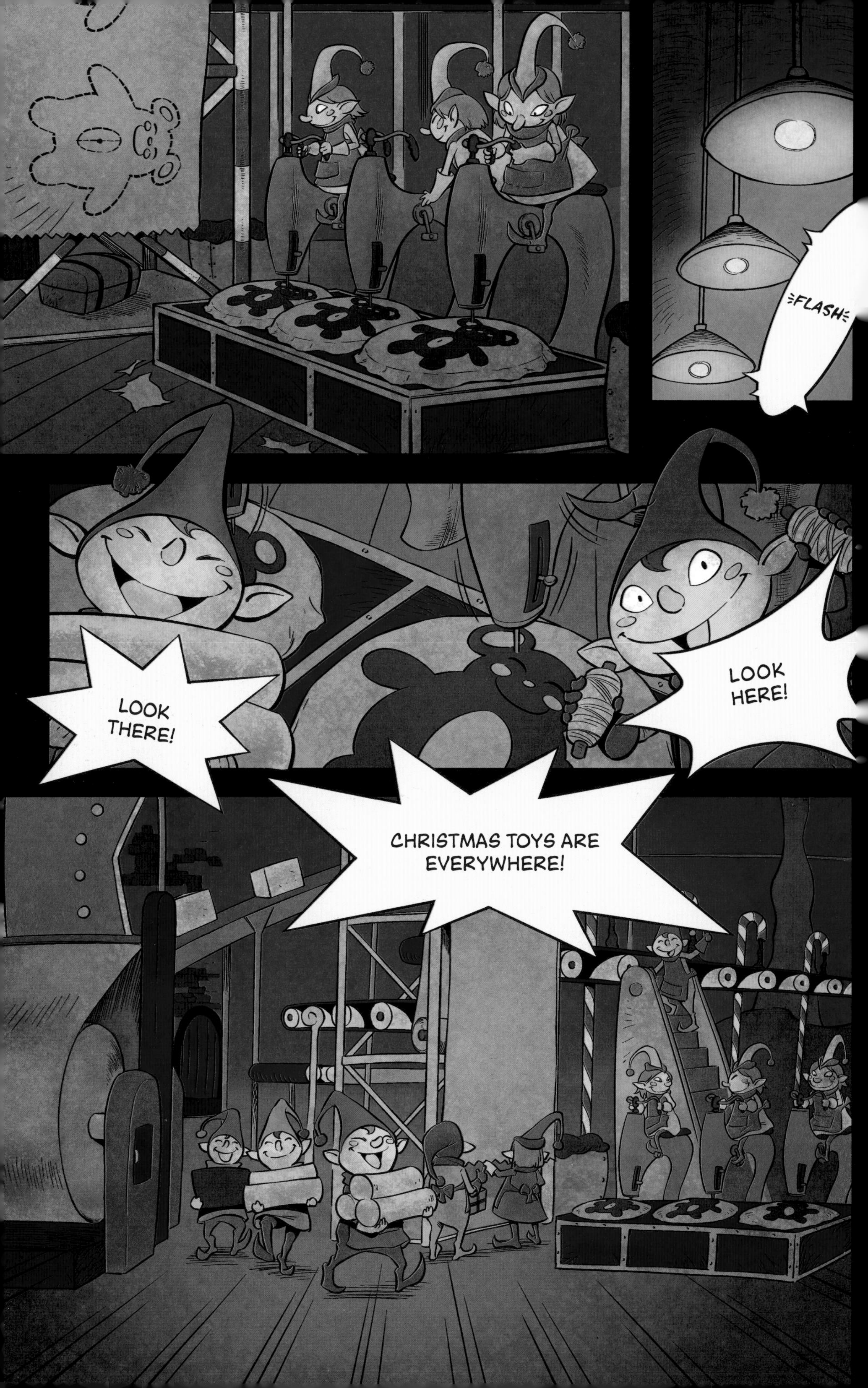
FLASH
LOOK HERE!
LOOK THERE!
CHRISTMAS TOYS ARE EVERYWHERE!

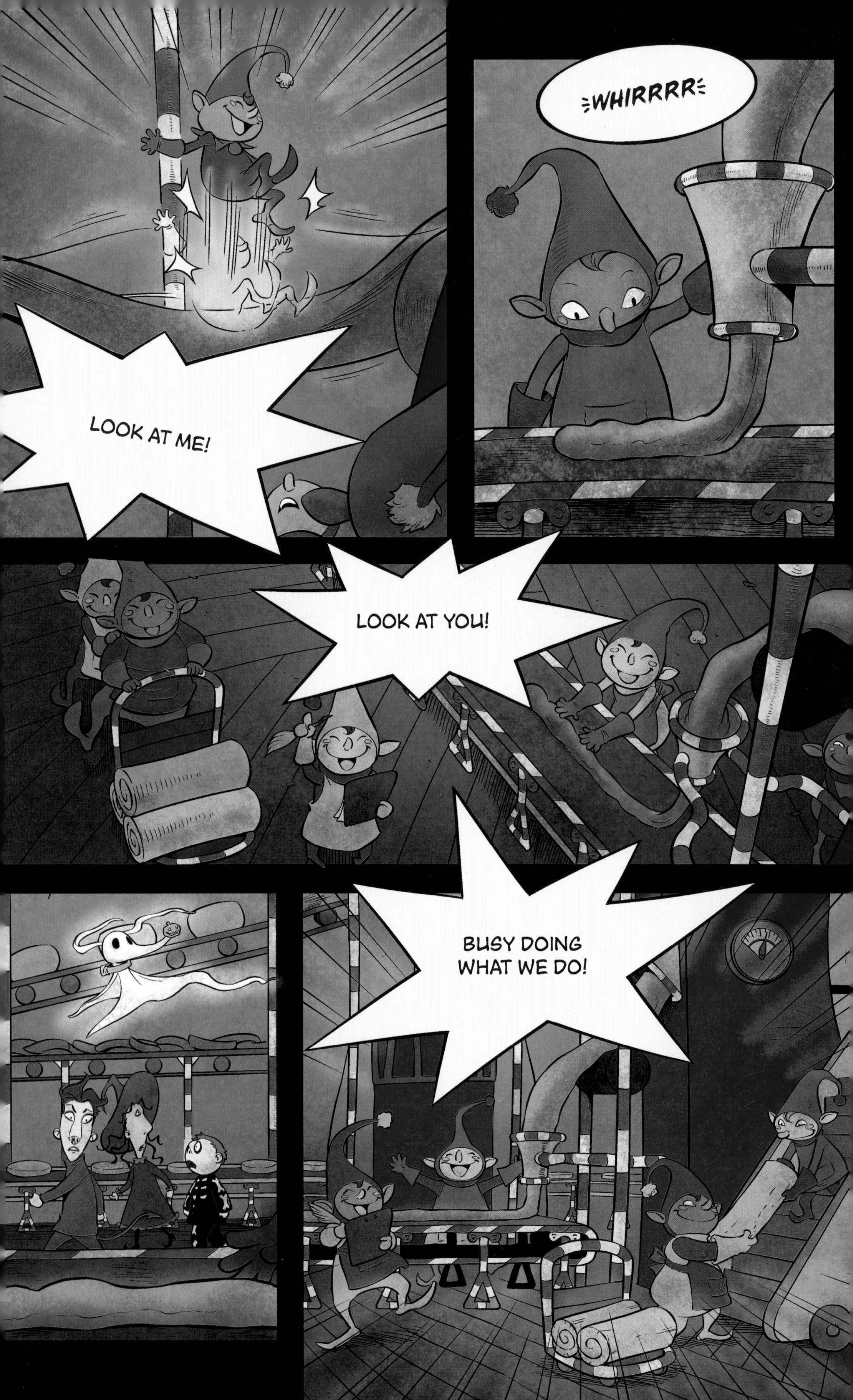
WHIRRRR
LOOK AT ME!
LOOK AT YOU!
BUSY DOING WHAT WE DO!

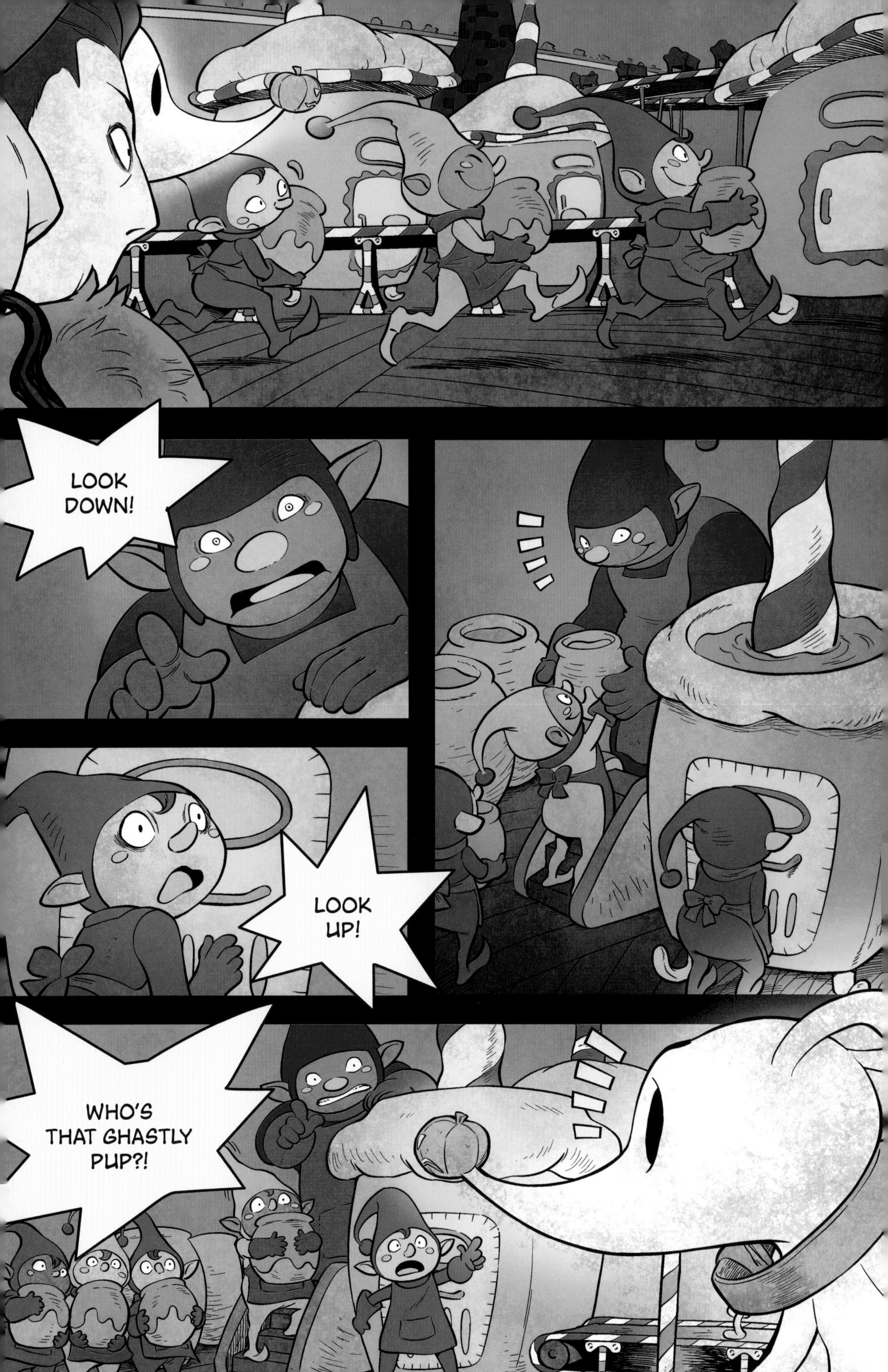
LOOK DOWN!
LOOK UP!
WHO'S THAT GHASTLY PUP?!

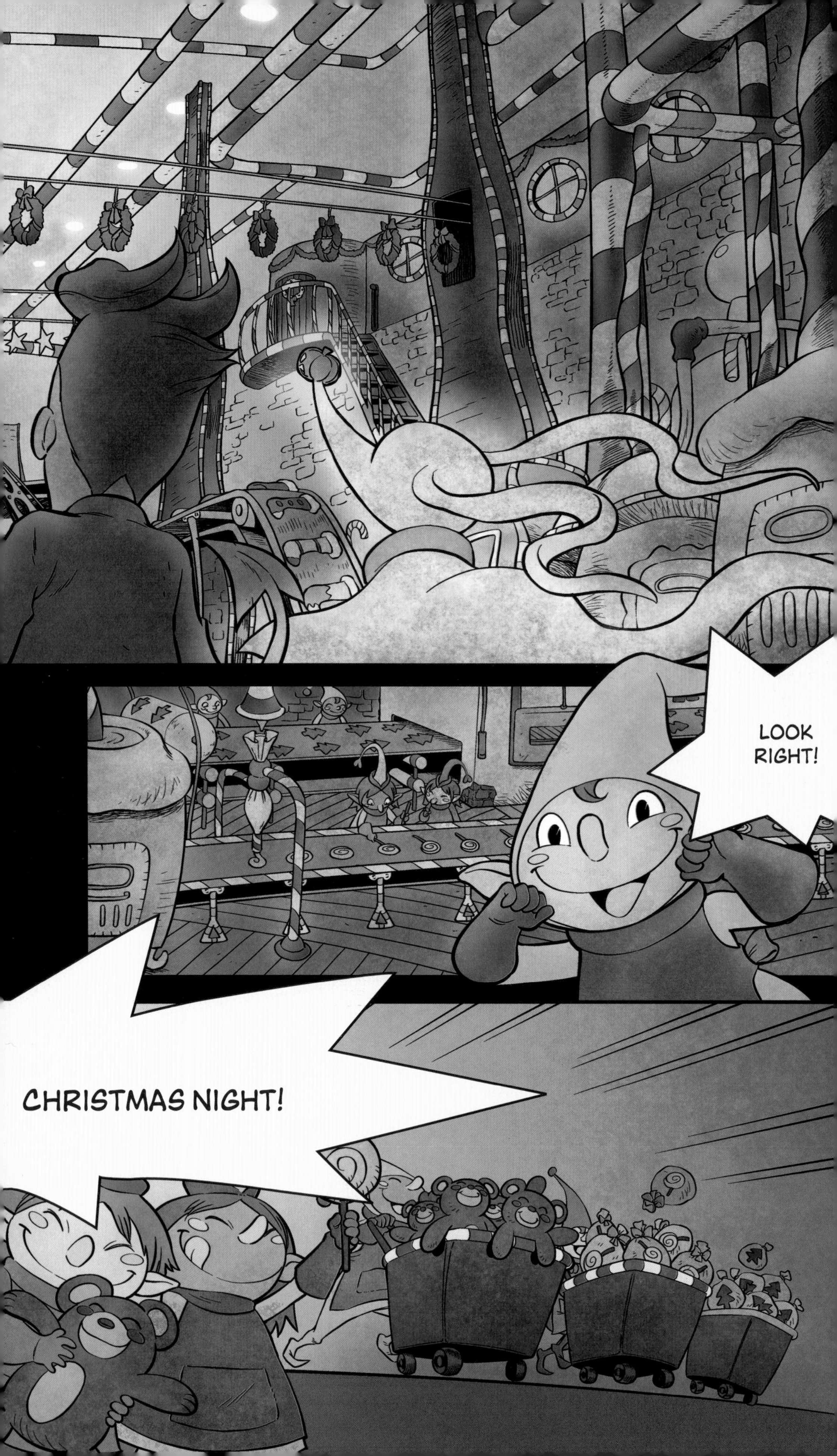
LOOK RIGHT!
CHRISTMAS NIGHT!

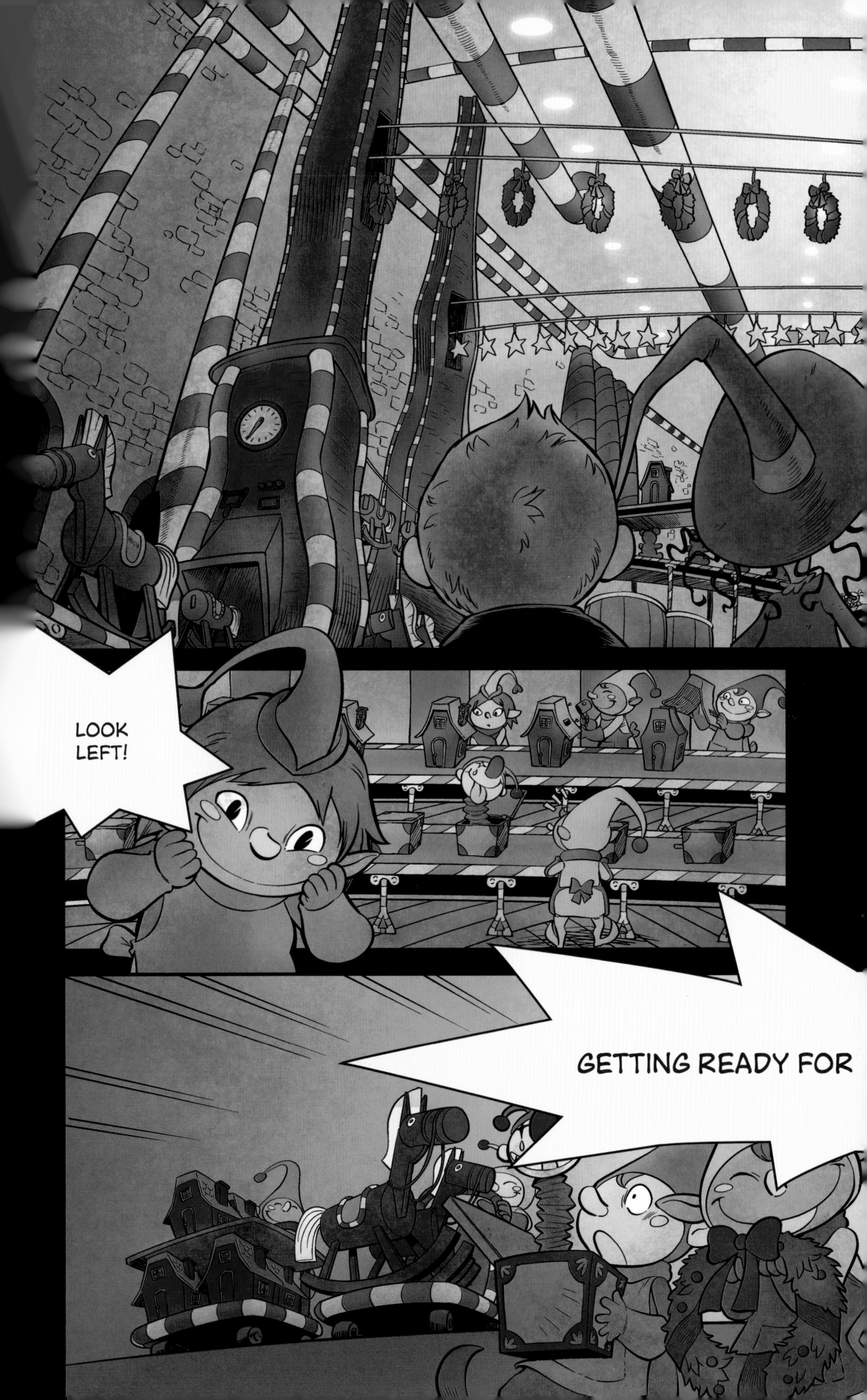
LOOK LEFT!
GETTING READY FOR

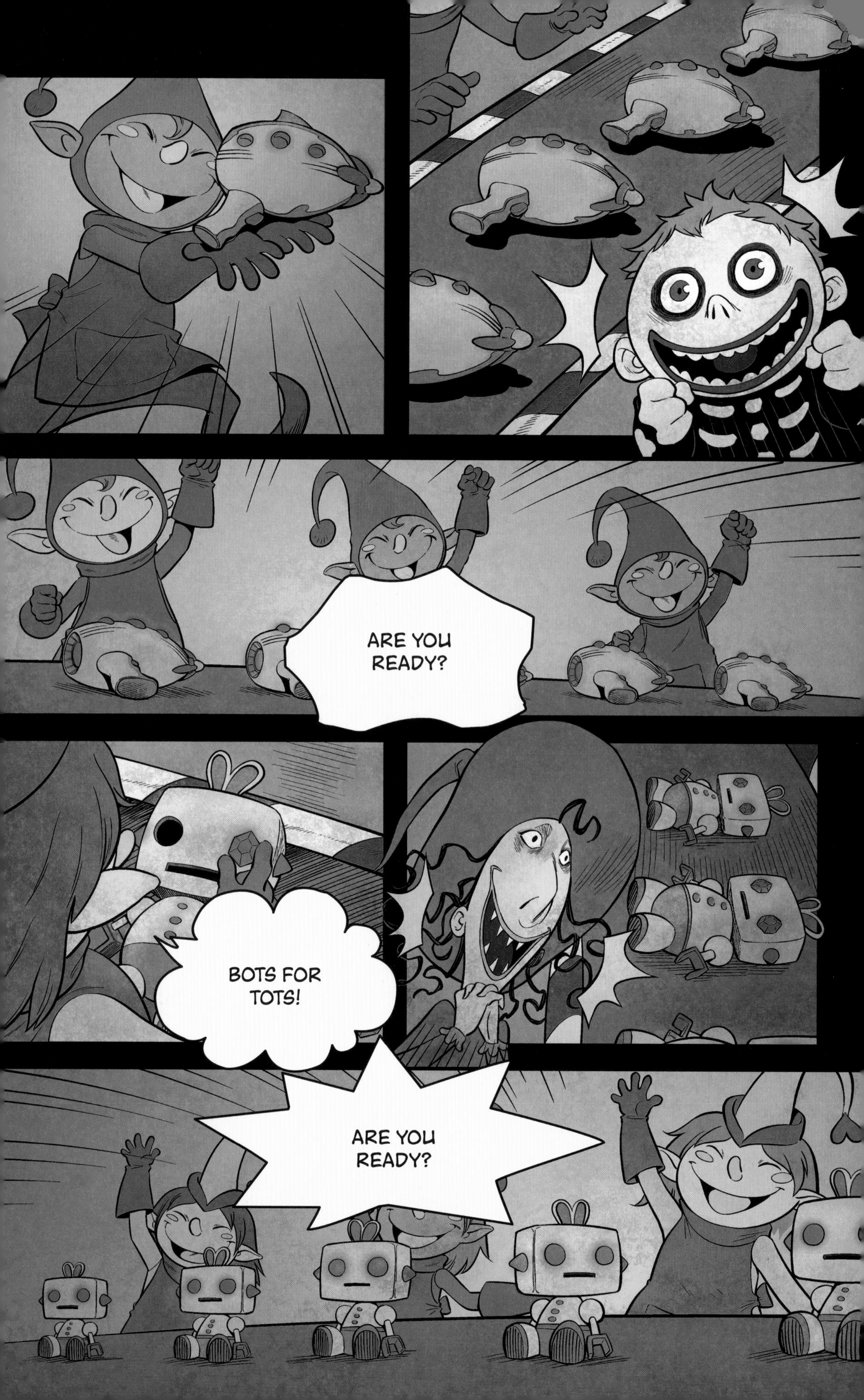
ARE YOU READY?
BOTS FOR TOTS!
ARE YOU READY?

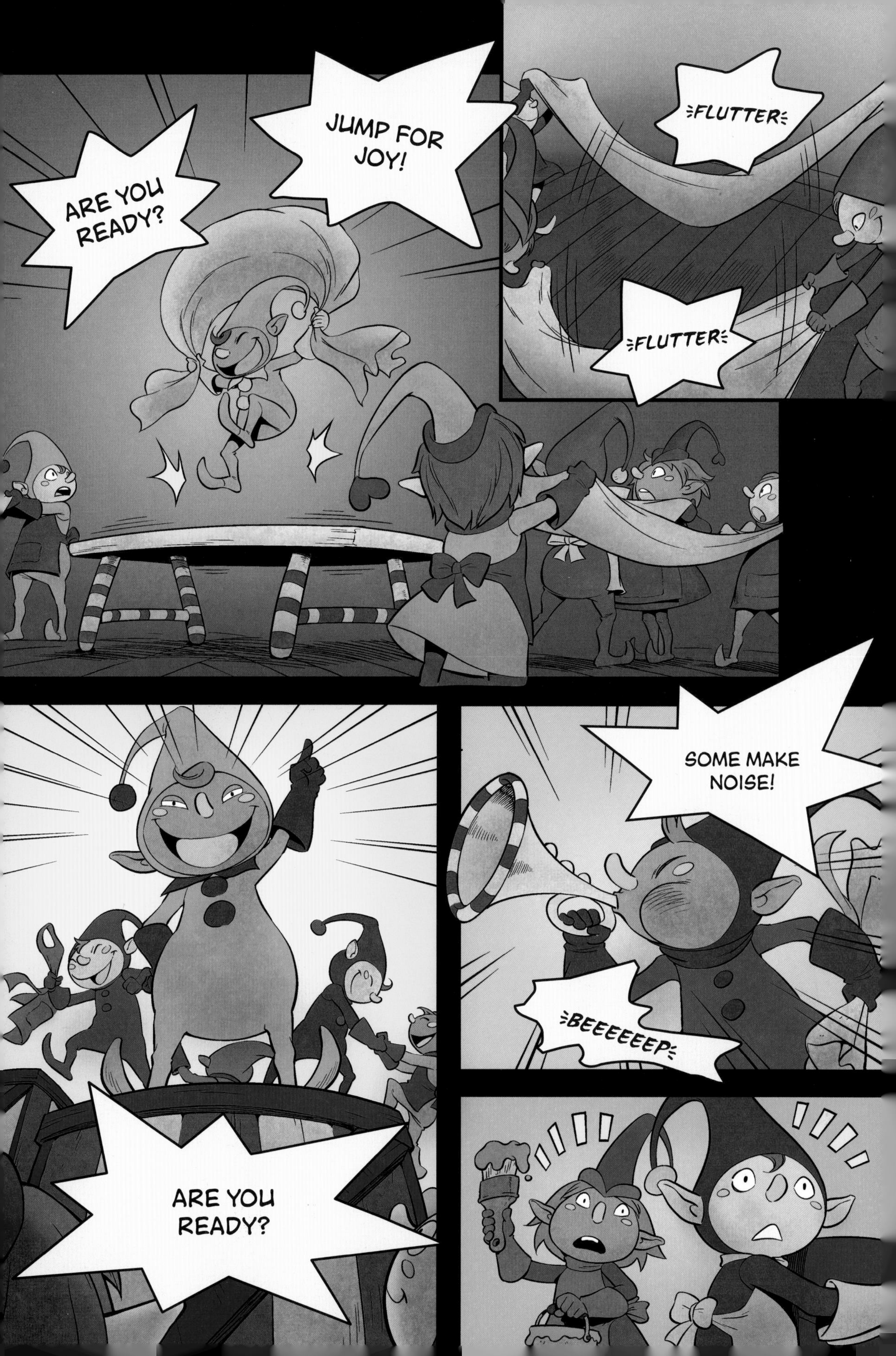

FLUTTER
FLUTTER
JUMP FOR JOY!
ARE YOU READY?
SOME MAKE NOISE!
BEEEEEEEP
ARE YOU READY?

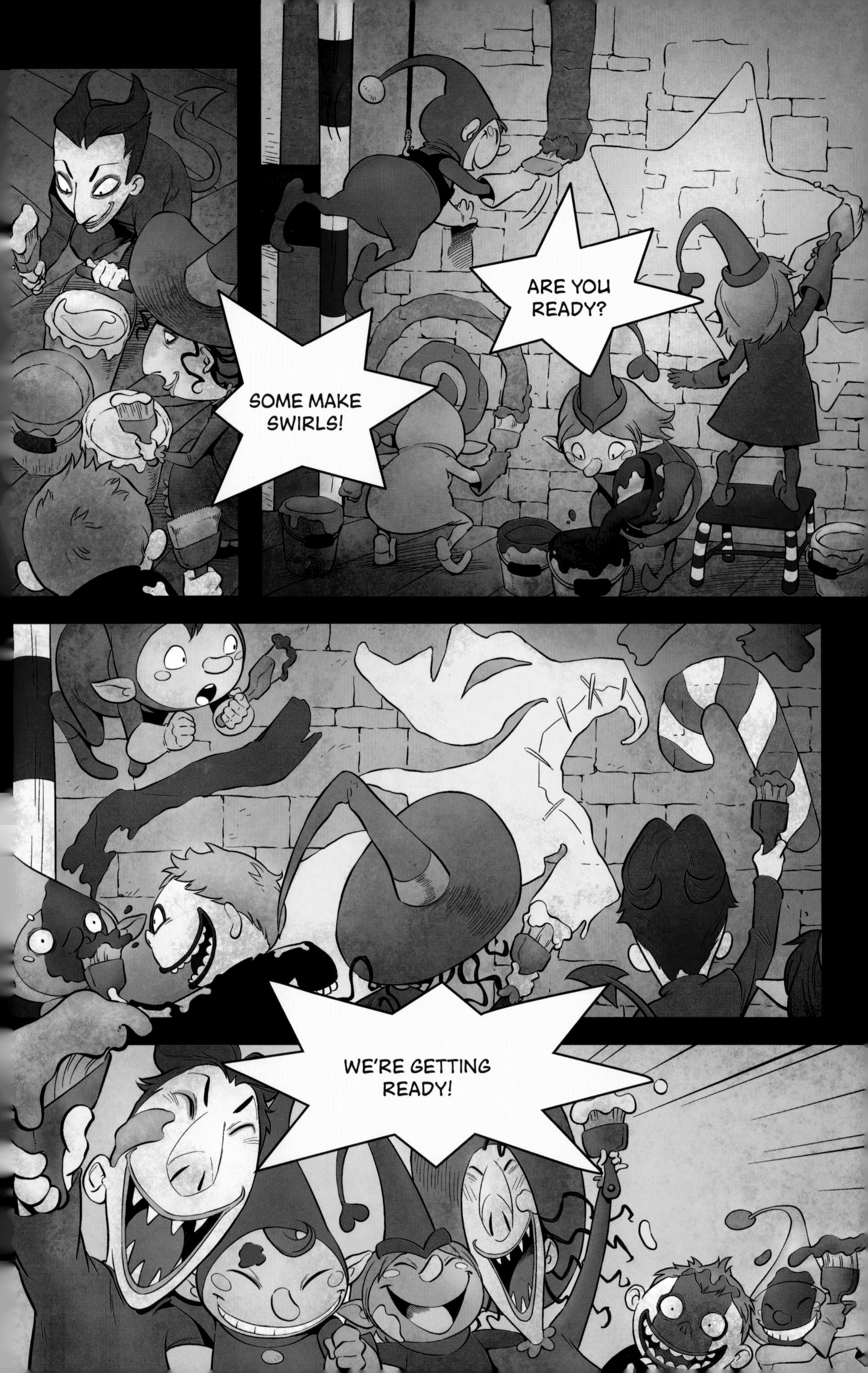
ARE YOU READY?
SOME MAKE SWIRLS!
WE'RE GETTING READY!

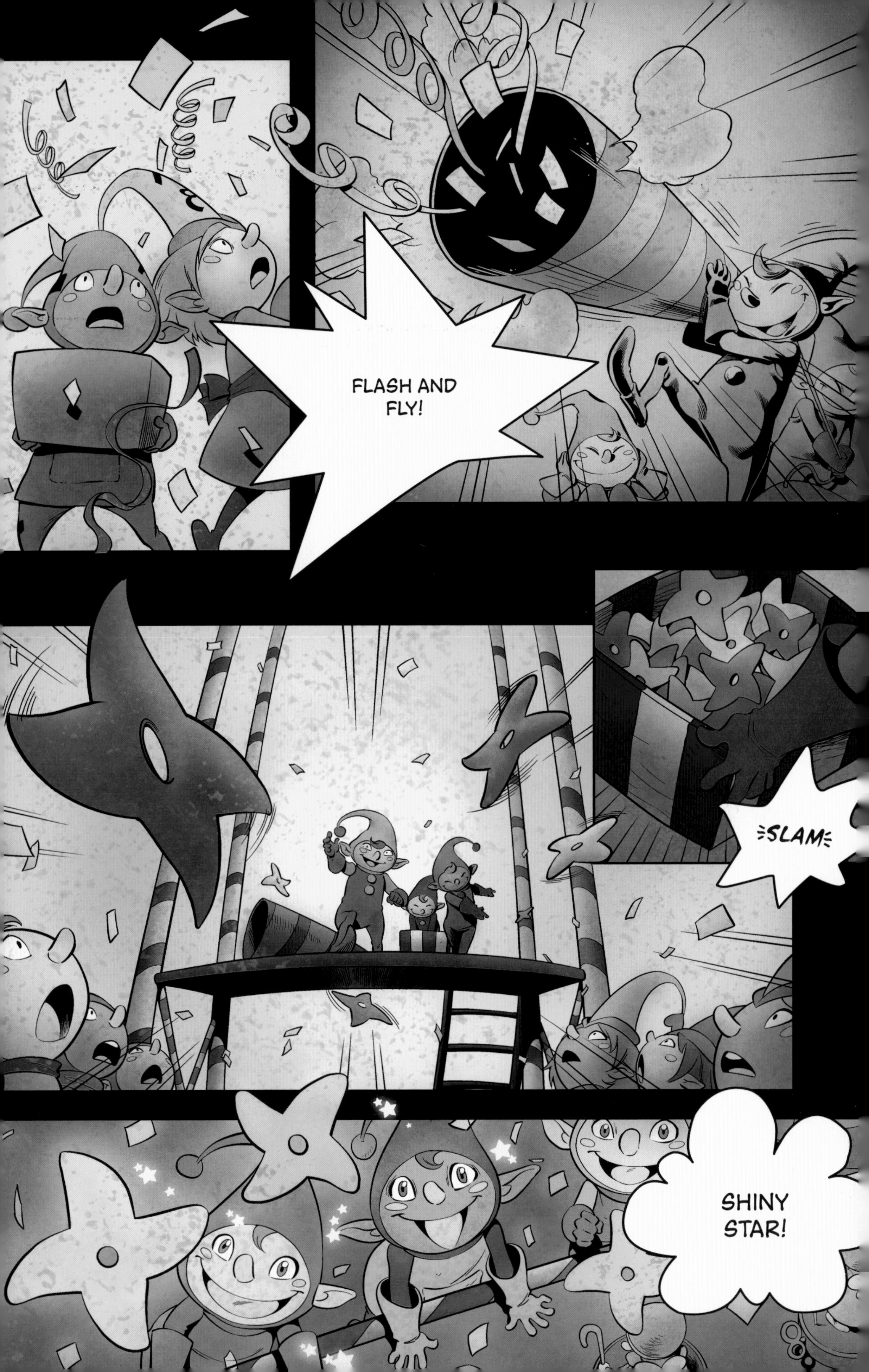
FLASH AND FLY!
SLAM
SHINY STAR!

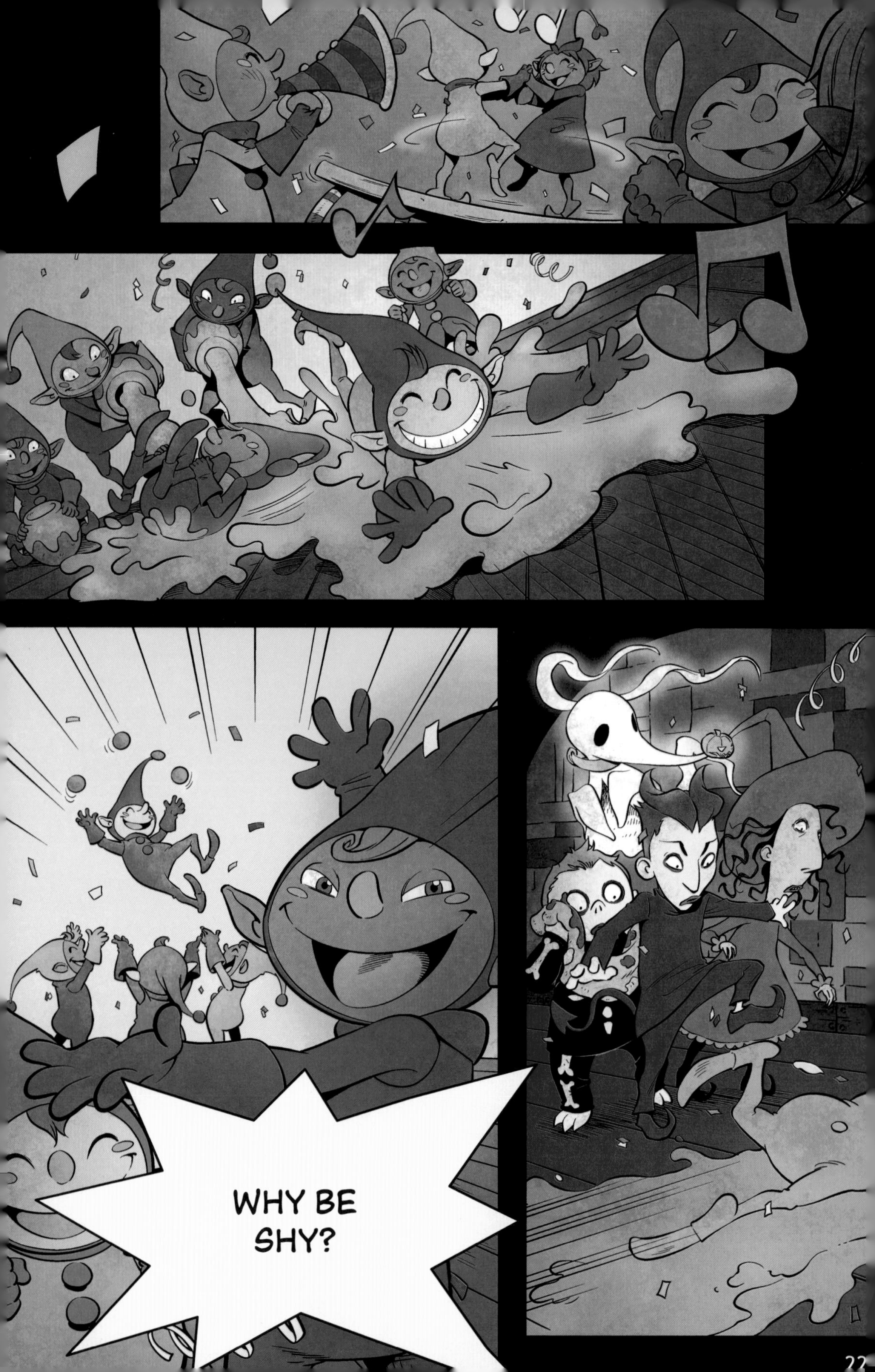
WHY BE SHY?

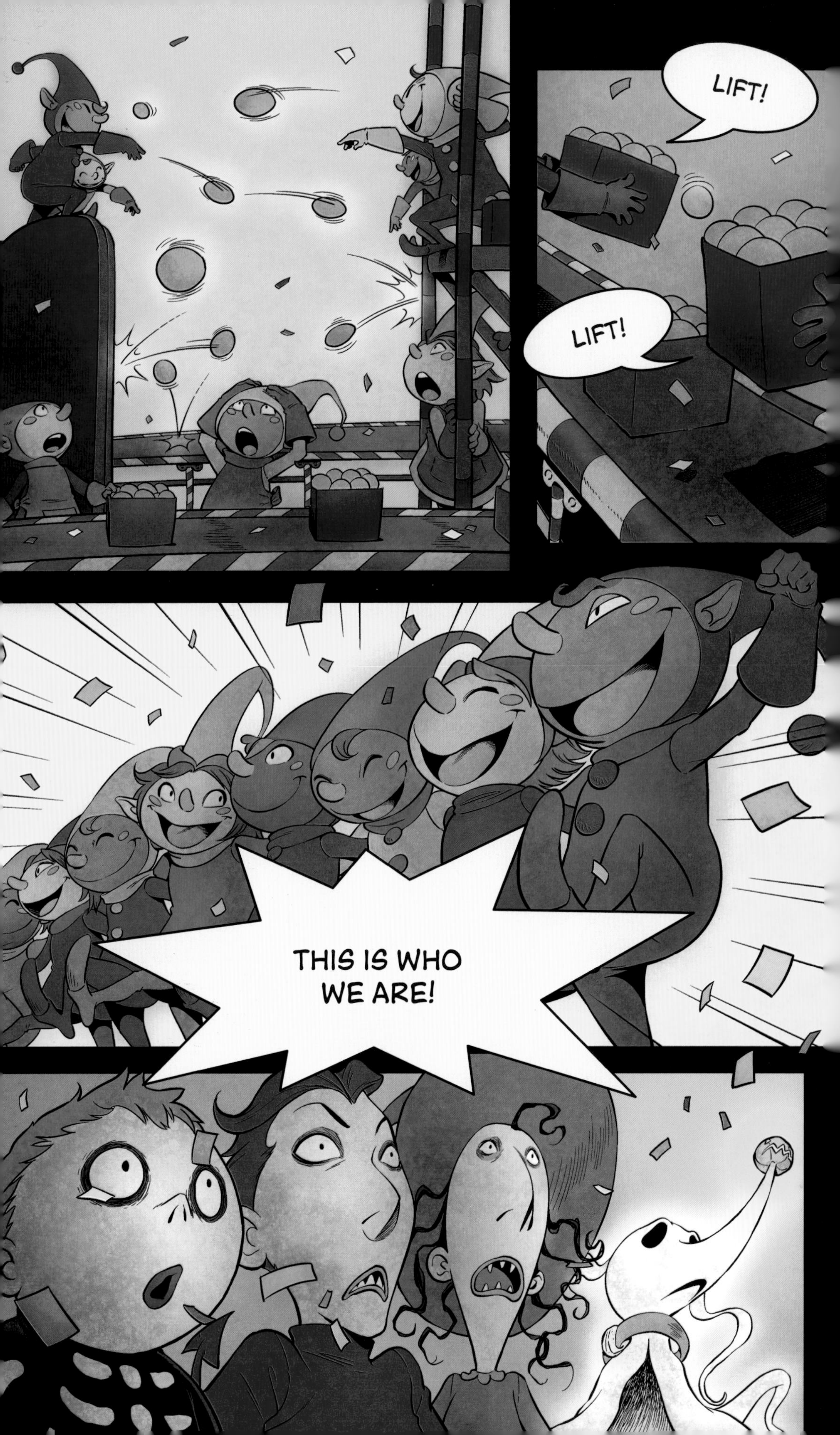
LIFT!
LIFT!
THIS IS WHO WE ARE!

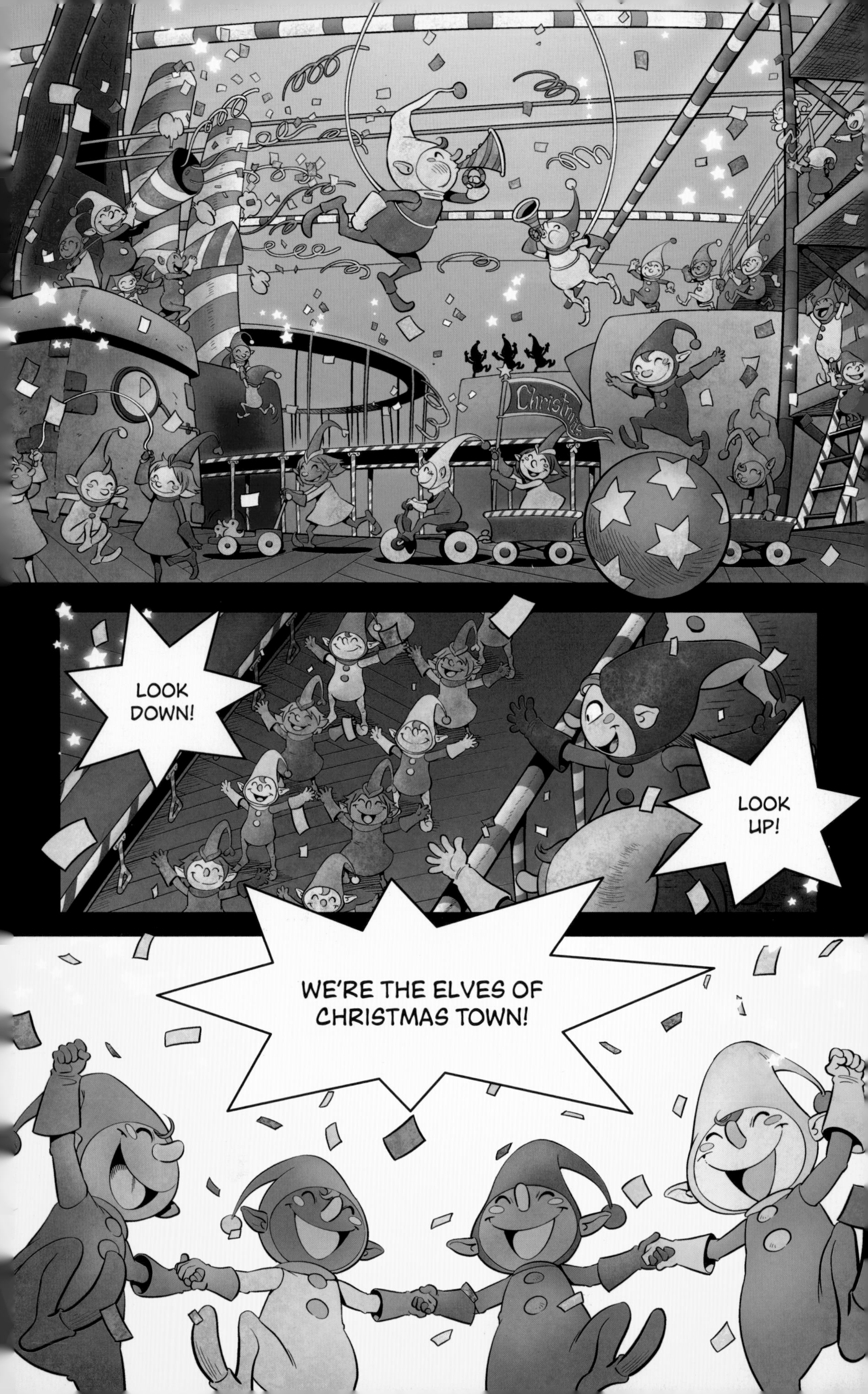
Christmas
LOOK UP!
LOOK DOWN!
WE'RE THE ELVES OF CHRISTMAS TOWN!

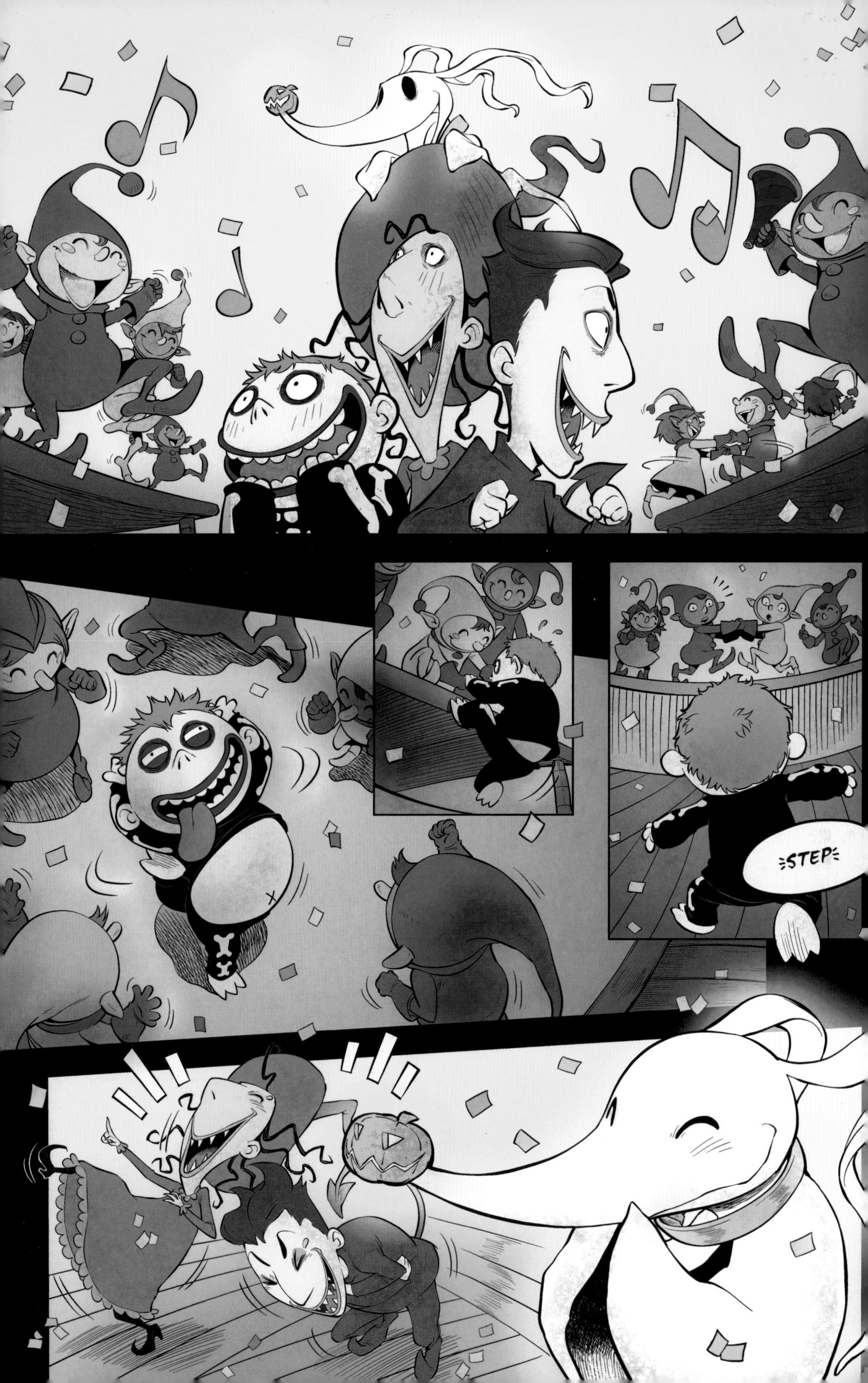
STEP

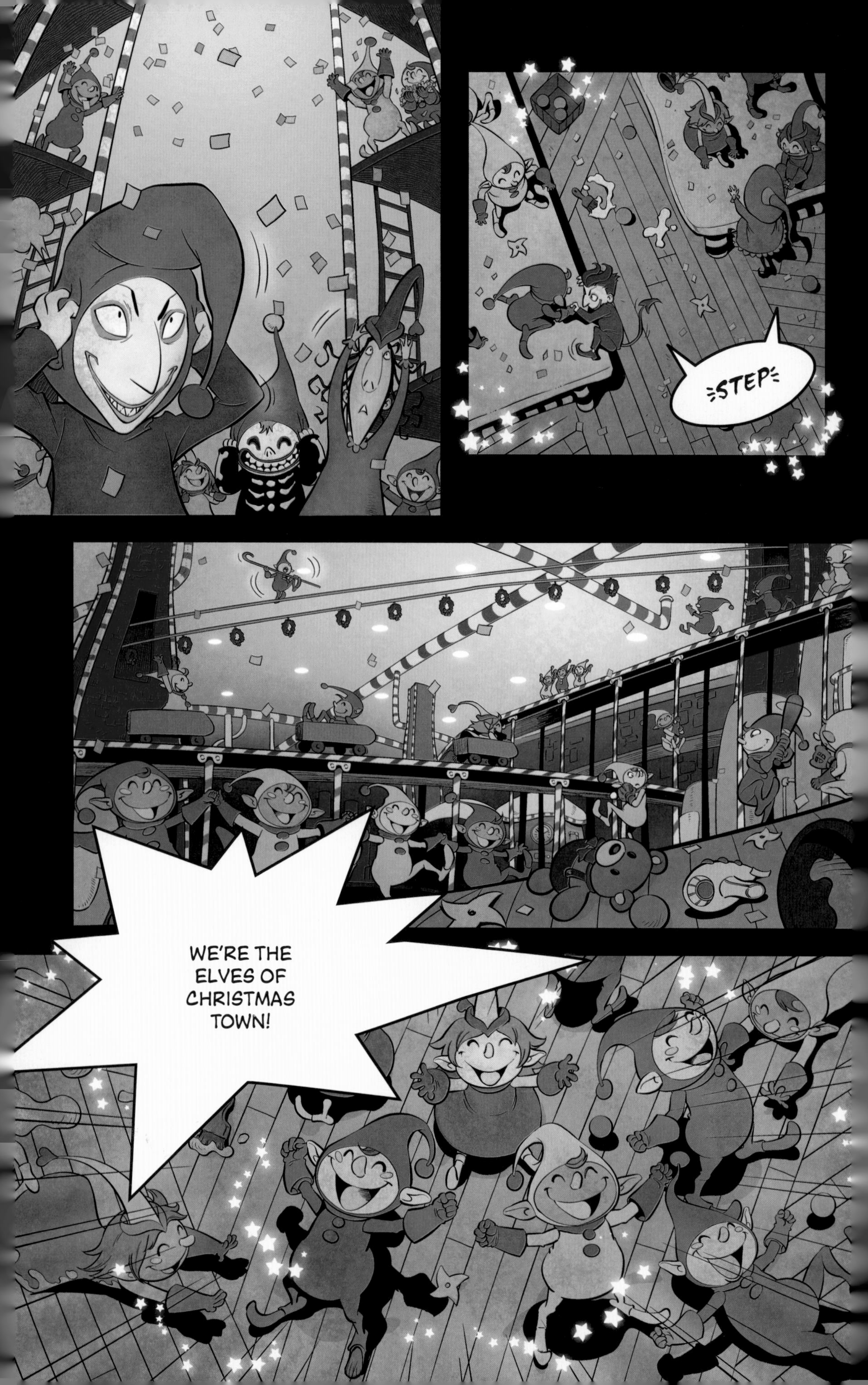
STEP
WE'RE THE ELVES OF CHRISTMAS TOWN!

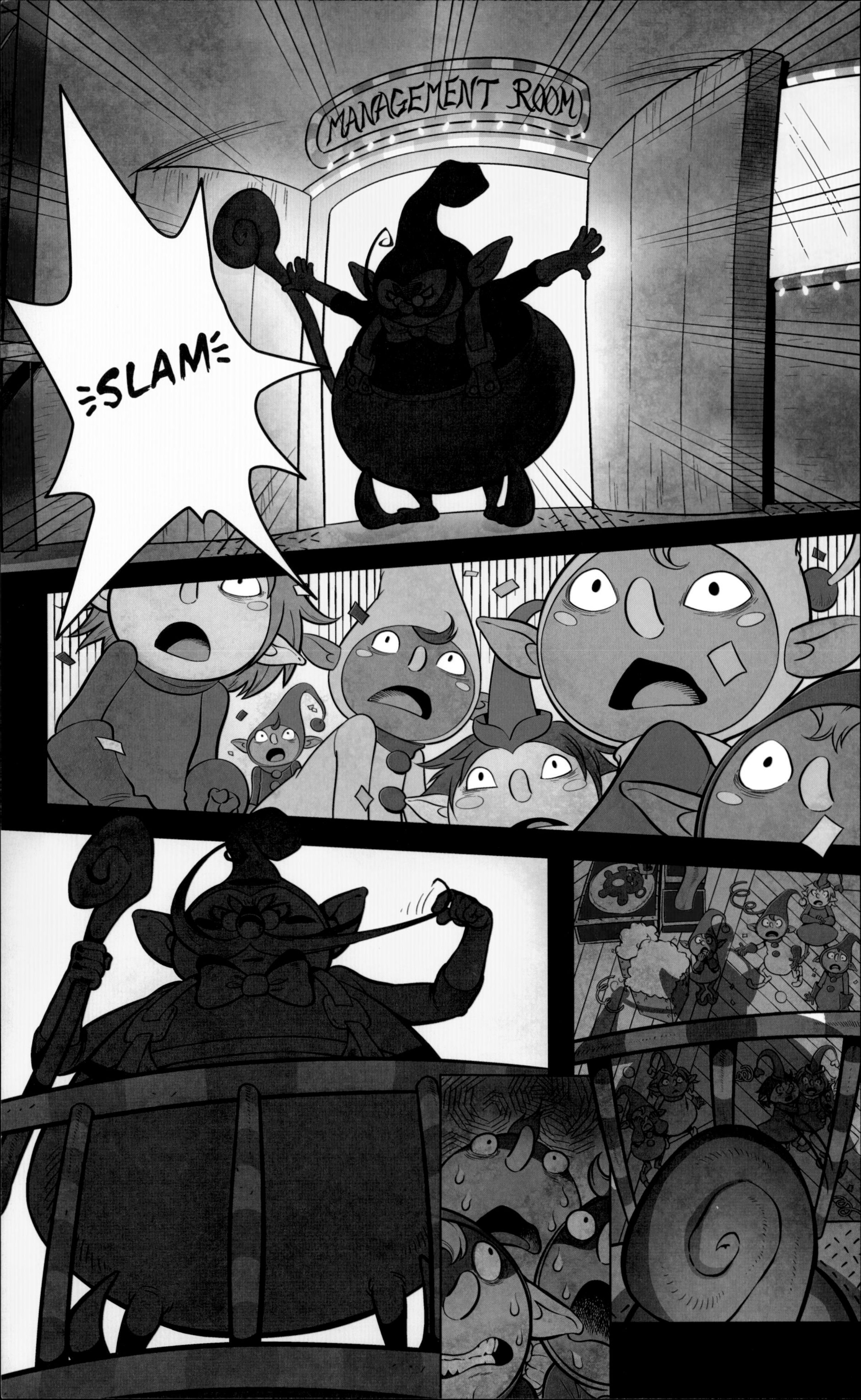
MANAGEMENT ROOM
SLAM

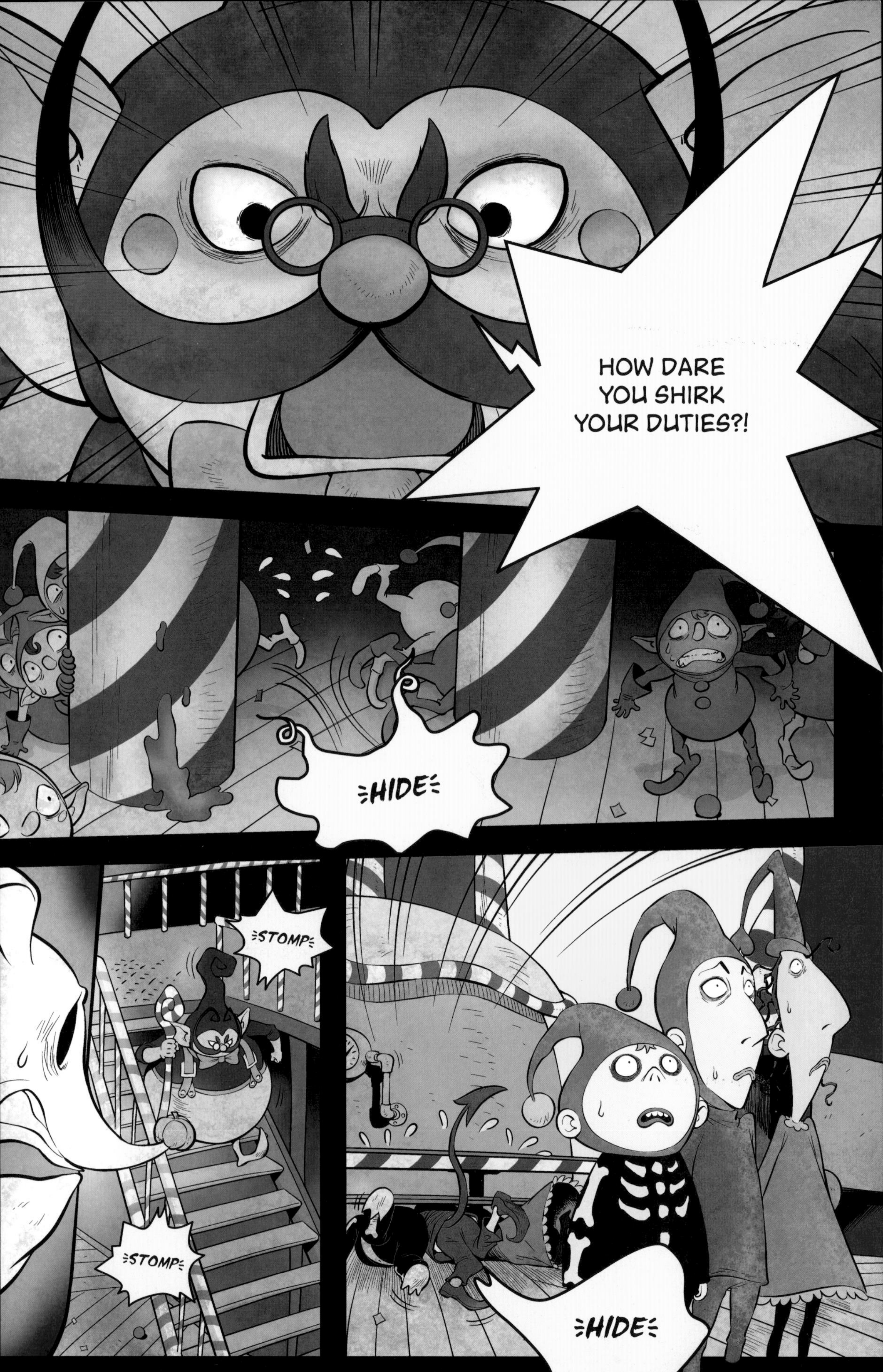
HOW DARE YOU SHIRK YOUR DUTIES?!
HIDE
HIDE
STOMP
STOMP

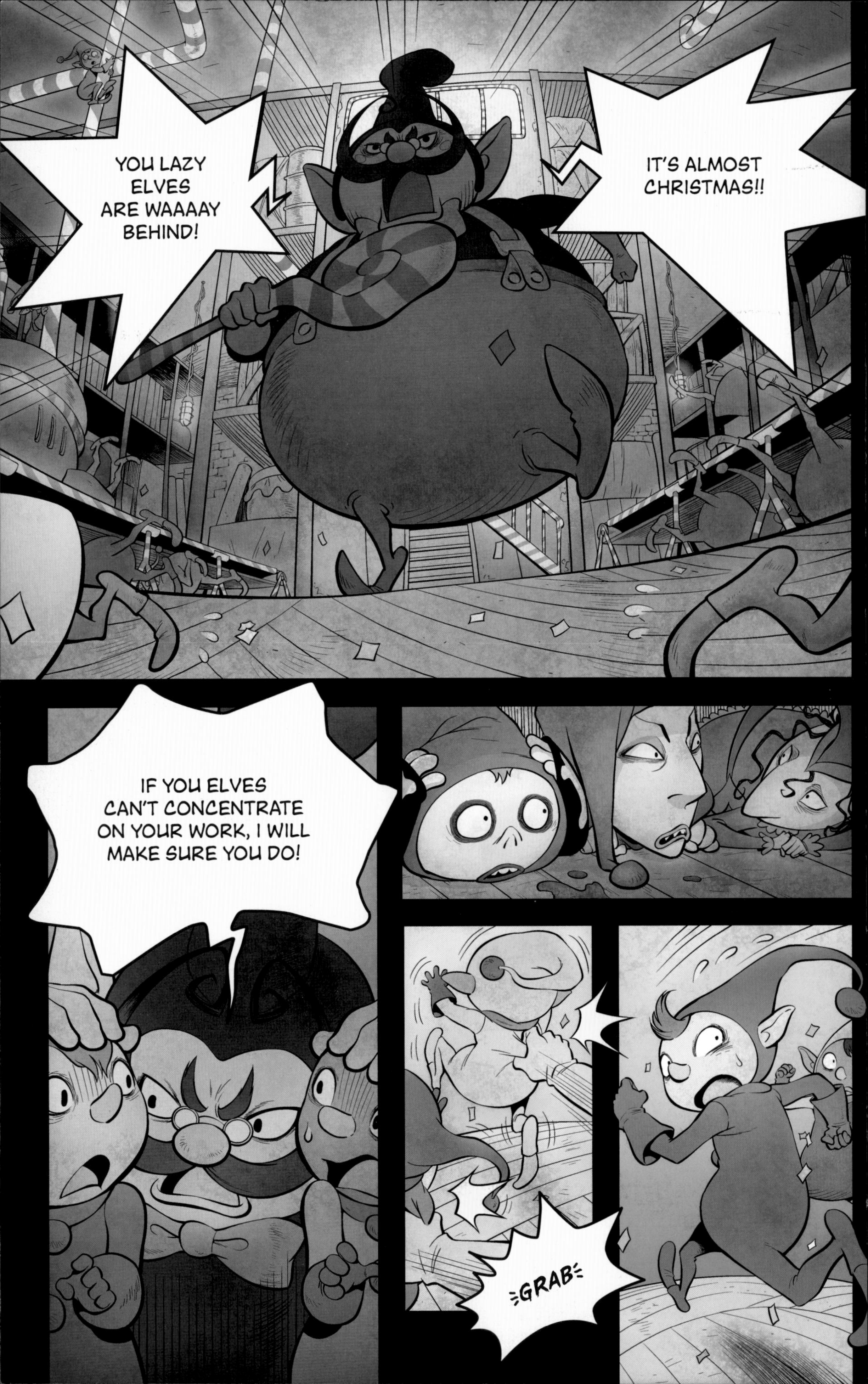
IT'S ALMOST CHRISTMAS!!
YOU LAZY ELVES ARE WAAAAY BEHIND!
GRAB
IF YOU ELVES CAN'T CONCENTRATE ON YOUR WORK, I WILL MAKE SURE YOU DO!

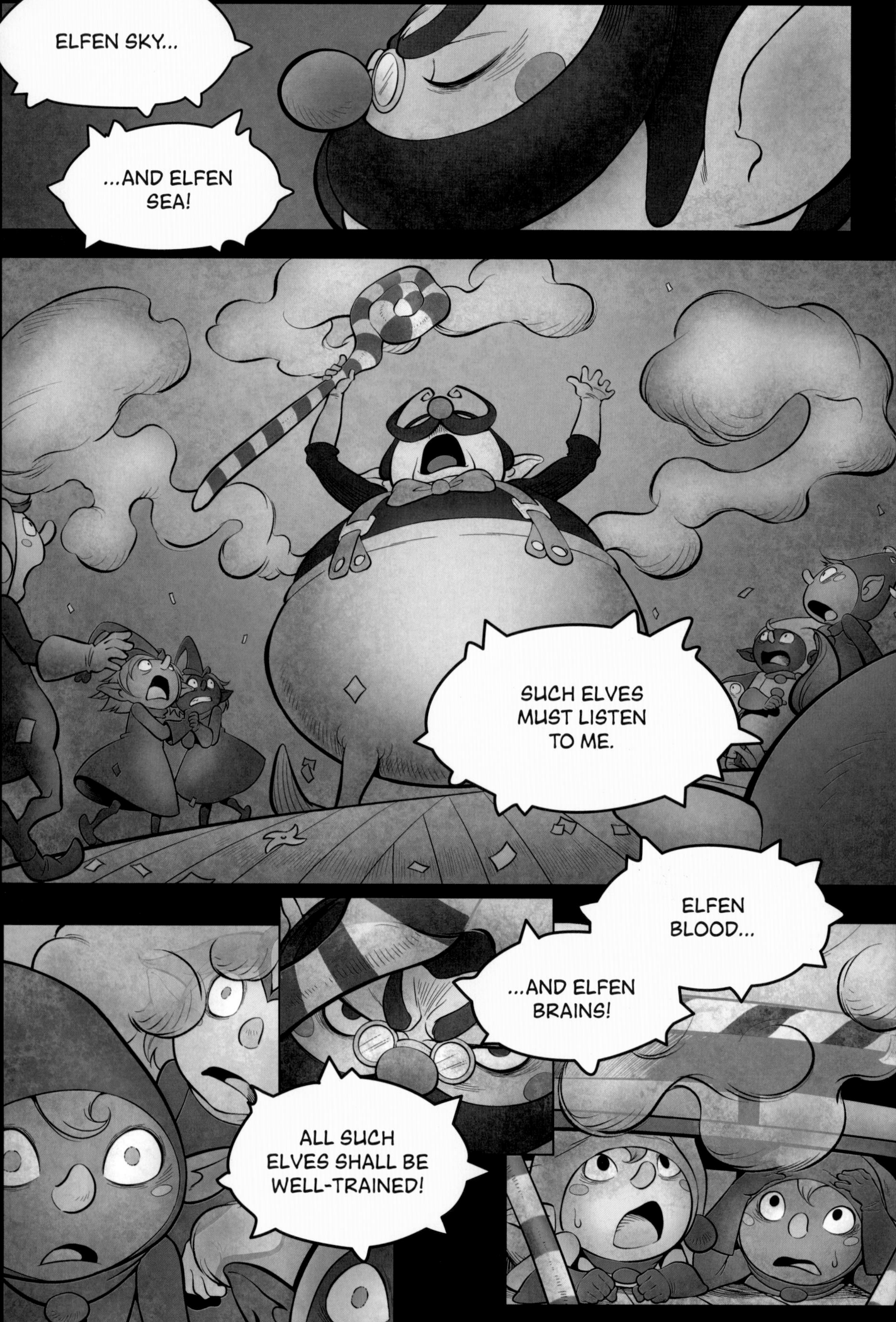
ELFEN SKY...
...AND ELFEN SEA!
SUCH ELVES MUST LISTEN TO ME.
ELFEN BLOOD...
...AND ELFEN BRAINS!
ALL SUCH ELVES SHALL BE WELL-TRAINED!

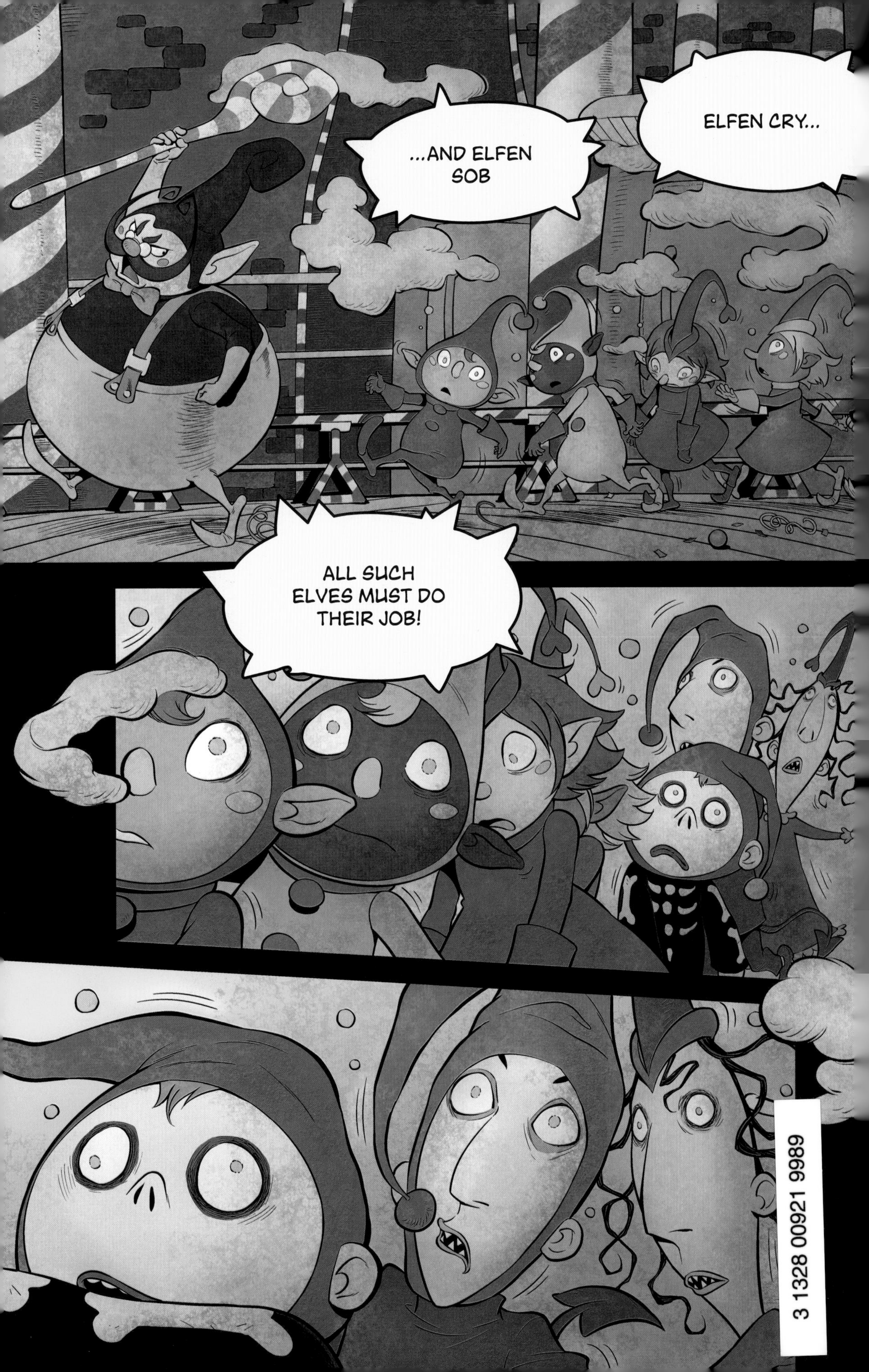
ELFEN CRY...
...AND ELFEN SOB
ALL SUCH ELVES MUST DO THEIR JOB!

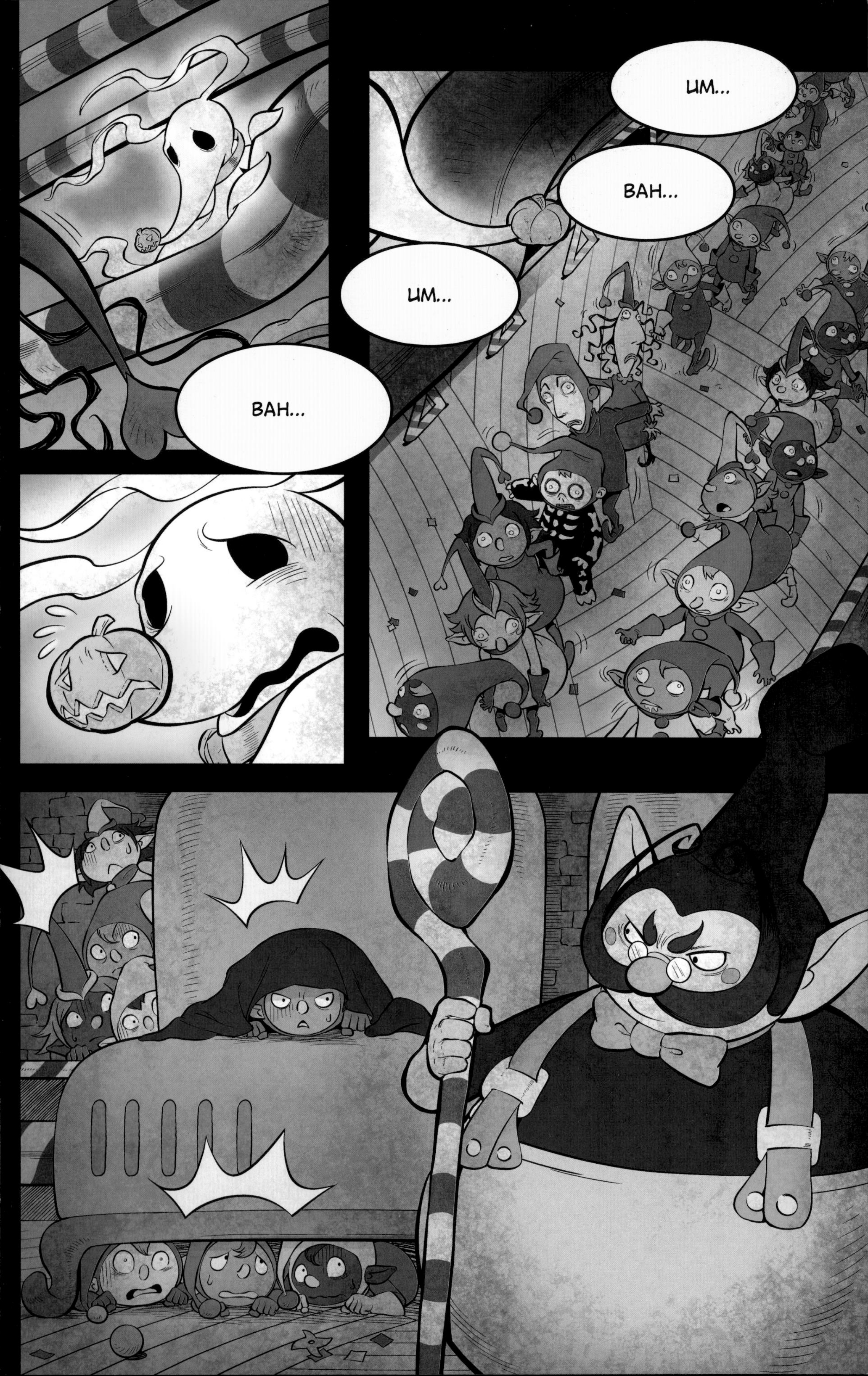
UM...
BAH...
UM...
BAH...

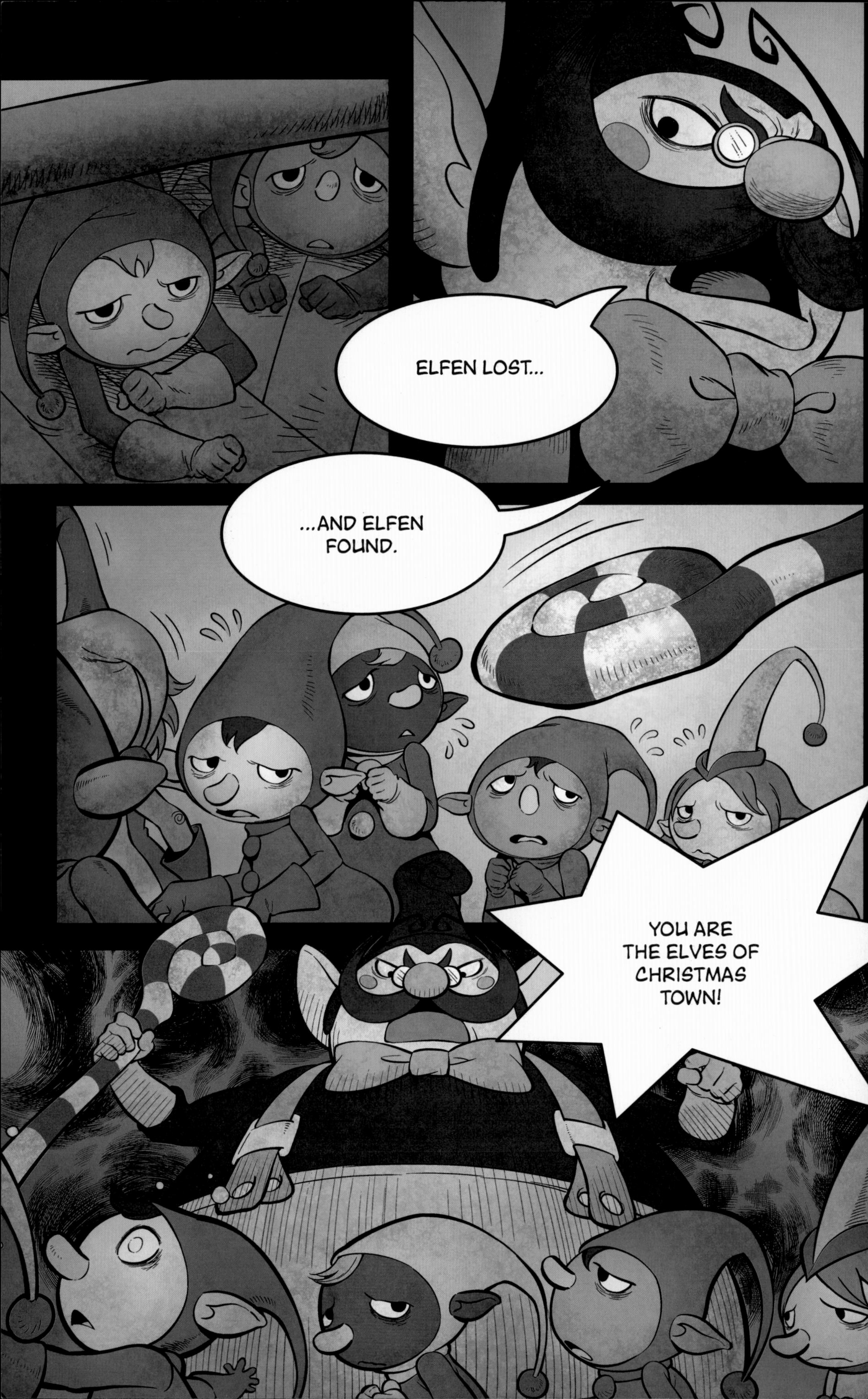
ELFEN LOST...
...AND ELFEN FOUND.
YOU ARE THE ELVES OF CHRISTMAS TOWN!

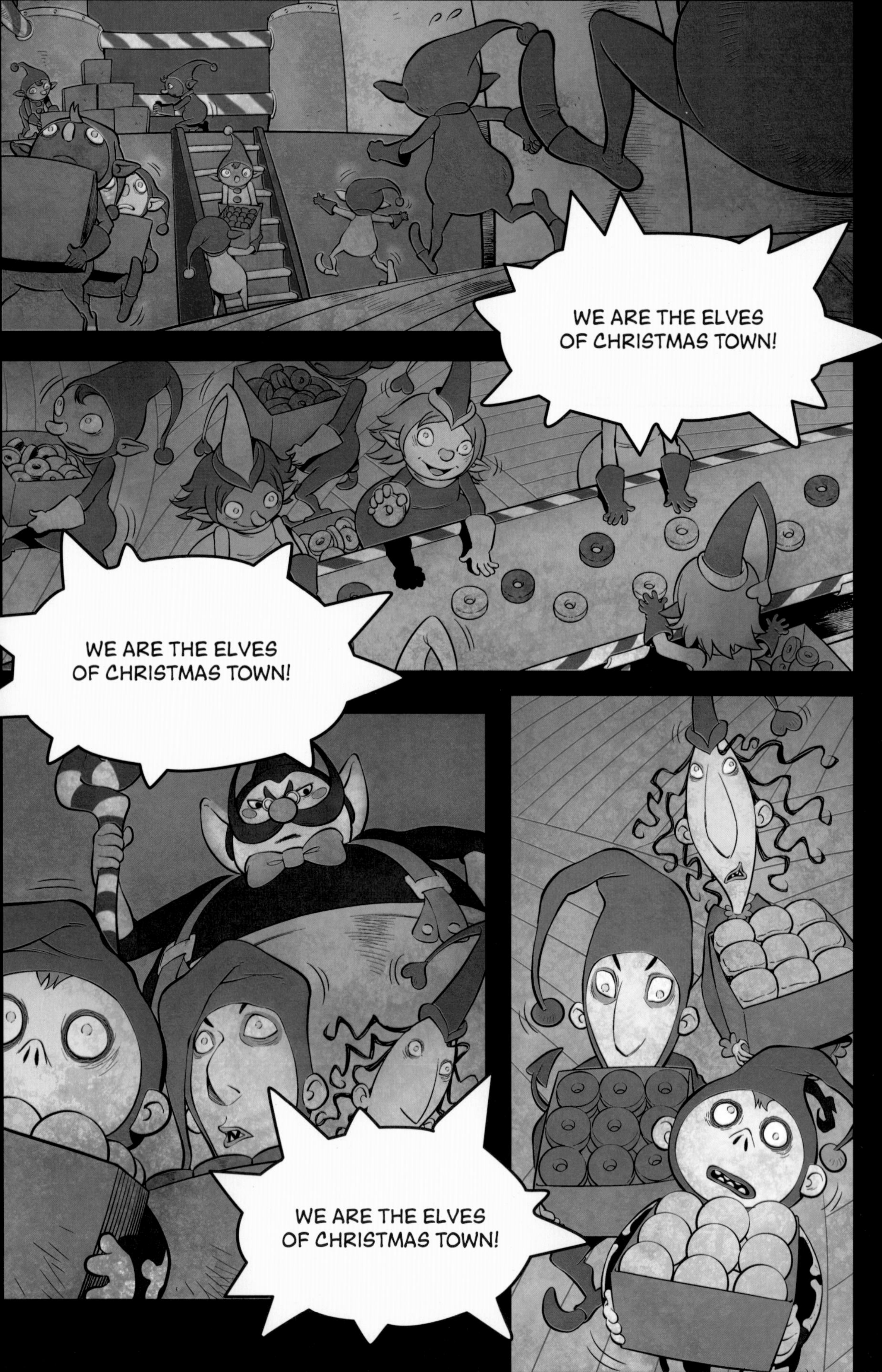
WE ARE THE ELVES OF CHRISTMAS TOWN!
WE ARE THE ELVES OF CHRISTMAS TOWN!
WE ARE THE ELVES OF CHRISTMAS TOWN!

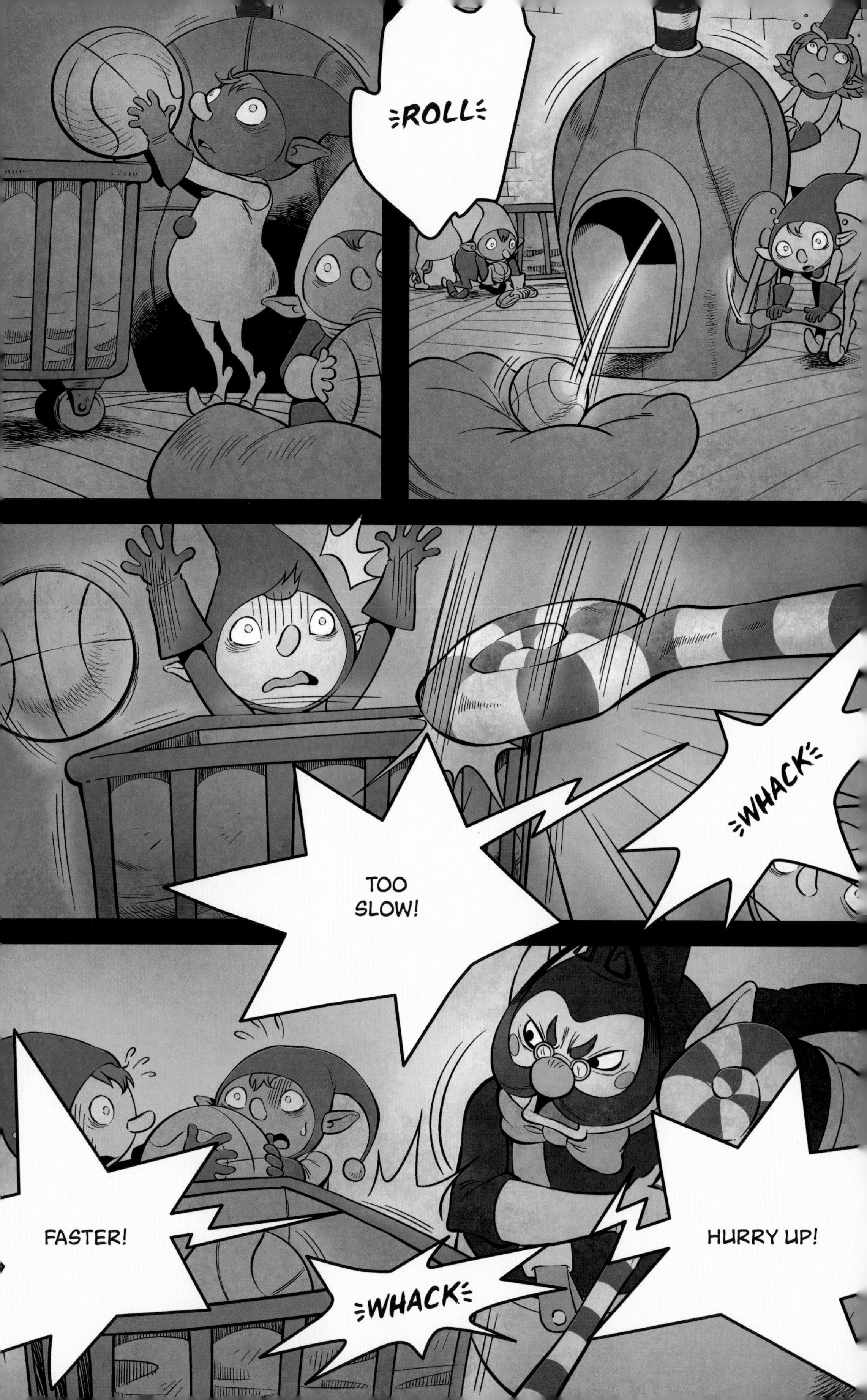
ROLL
WHACK
TOO SLOW!
HURRY UP!
WHACK
FASTER!

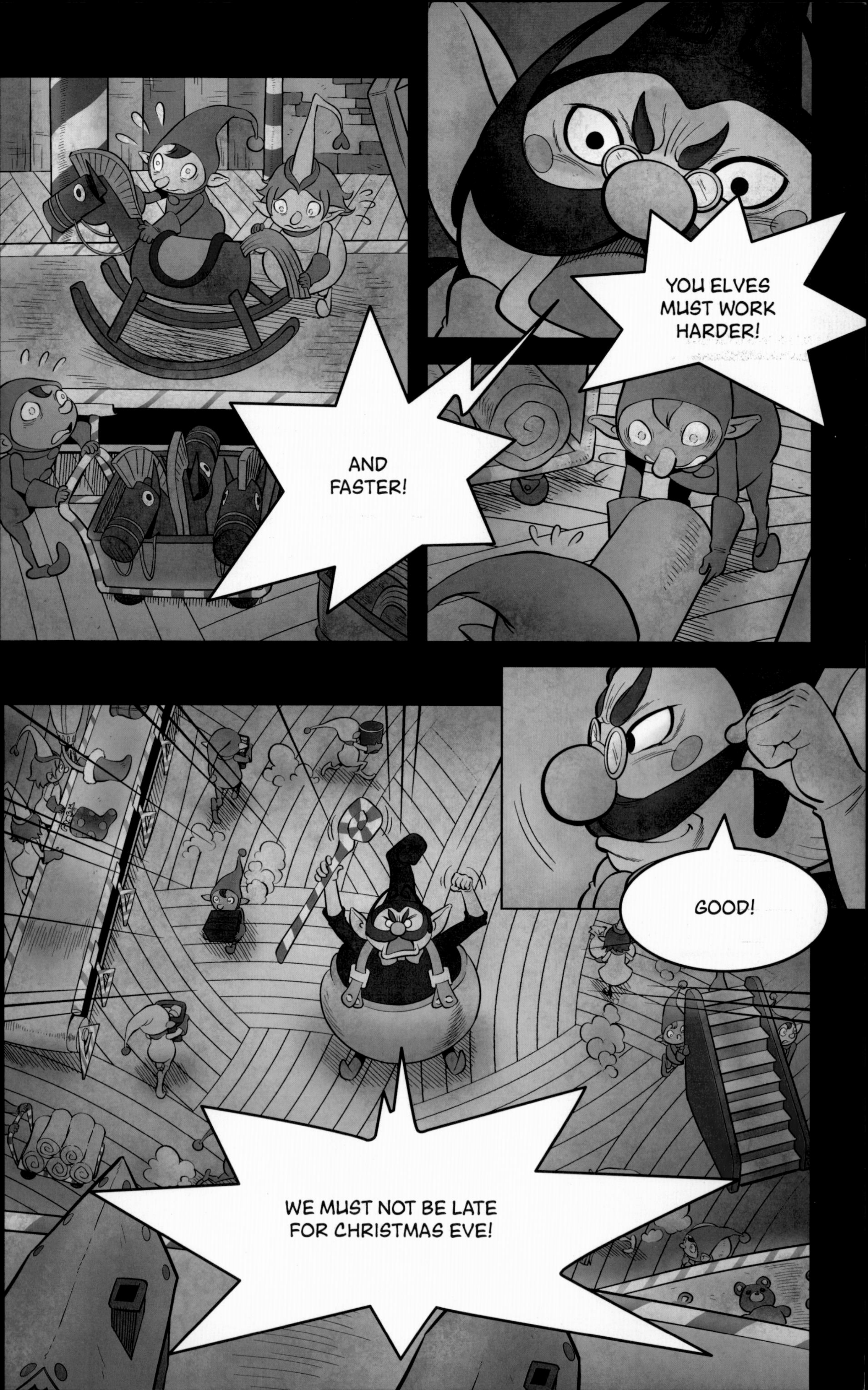
YOU ELVES MUST WORK HARDER!
AND FASTER!
GOOD!
WE MUST NOT BE LATE FOR CHRISTMAS EVE!

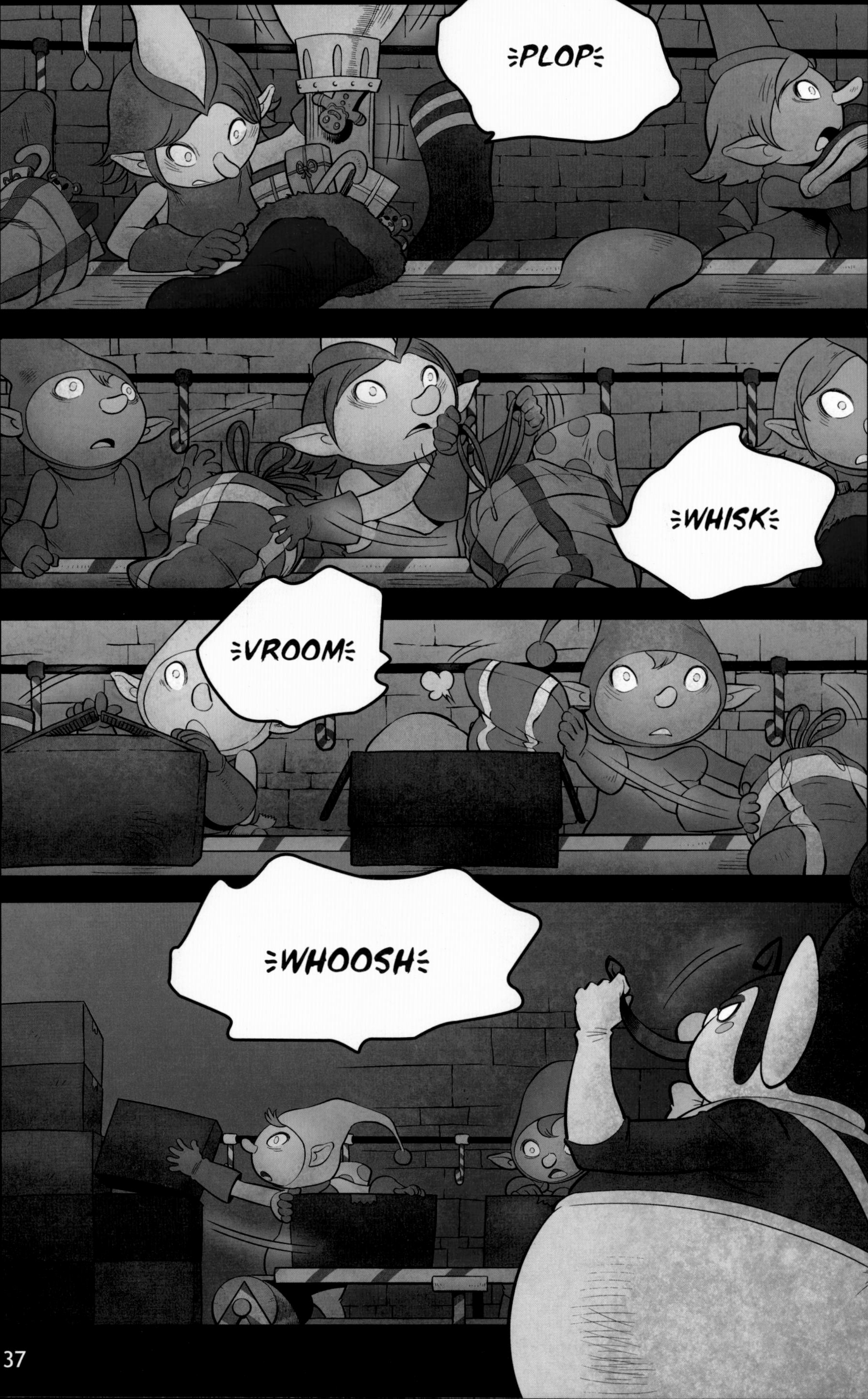
PLOP
WHISK
VROOM
WHOOSH

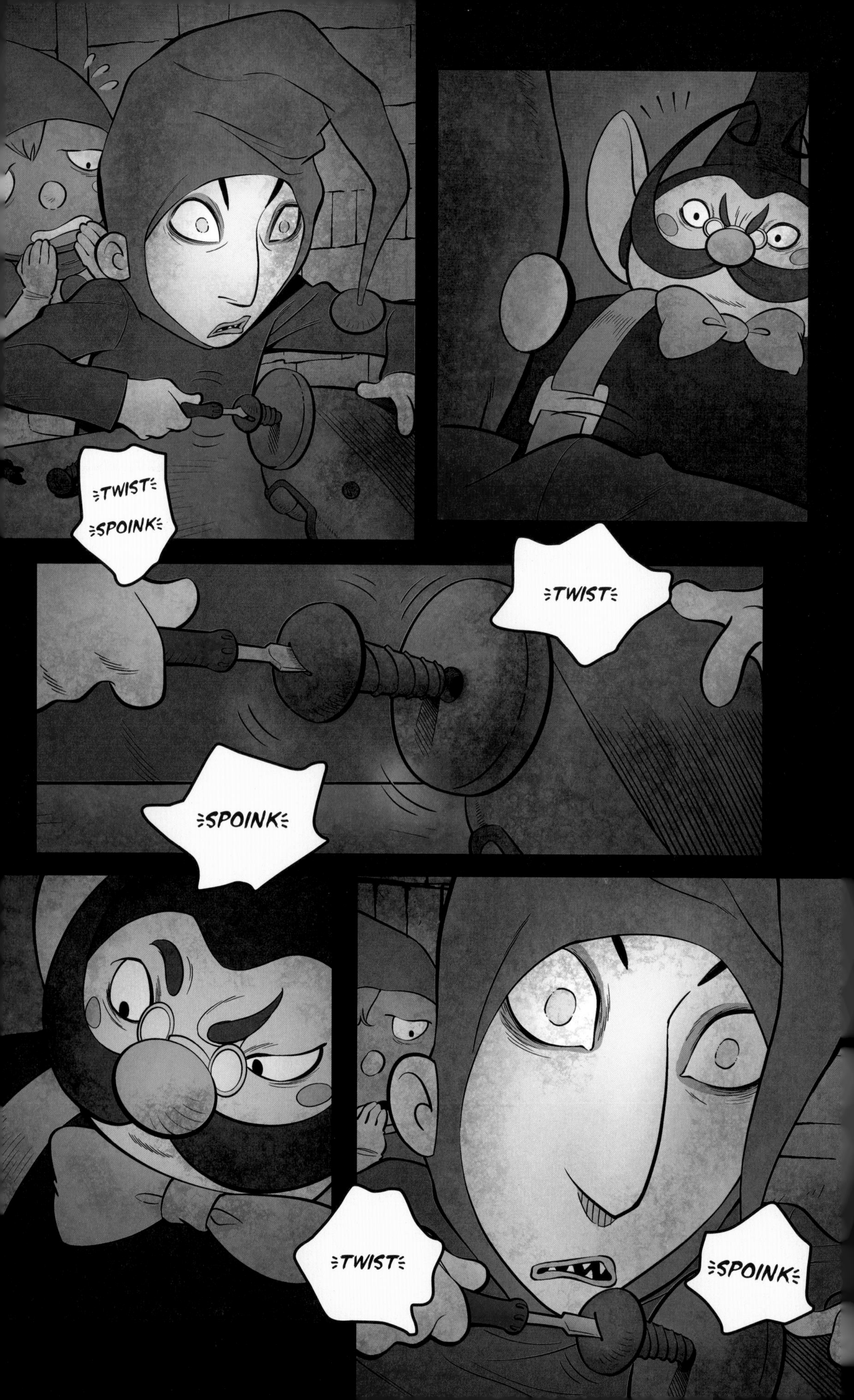
TWIST
SPOINK
TWIST
SPOINK
SPOINK
TWIST

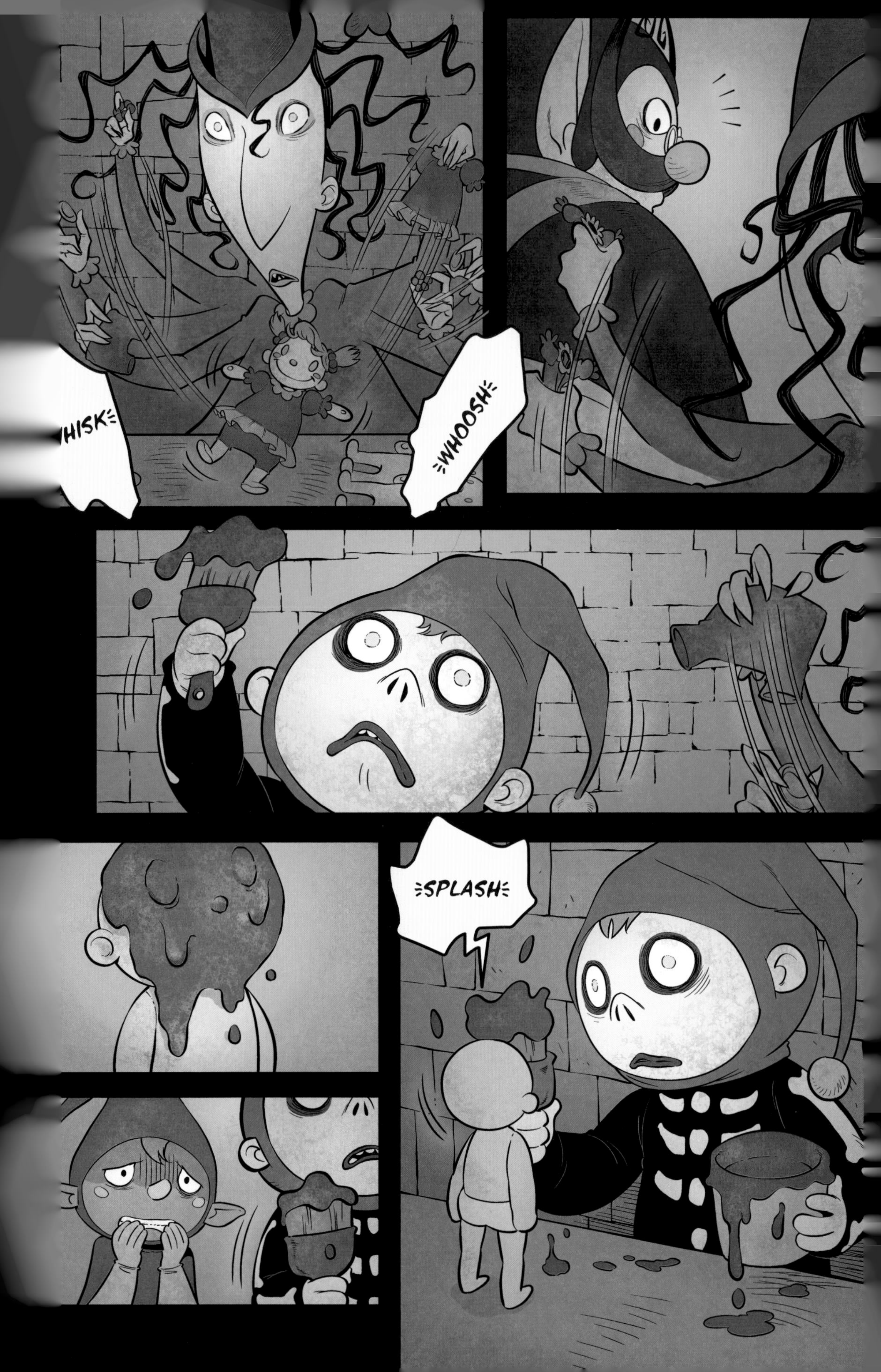
WHOOSH
WHISK
SPLASH

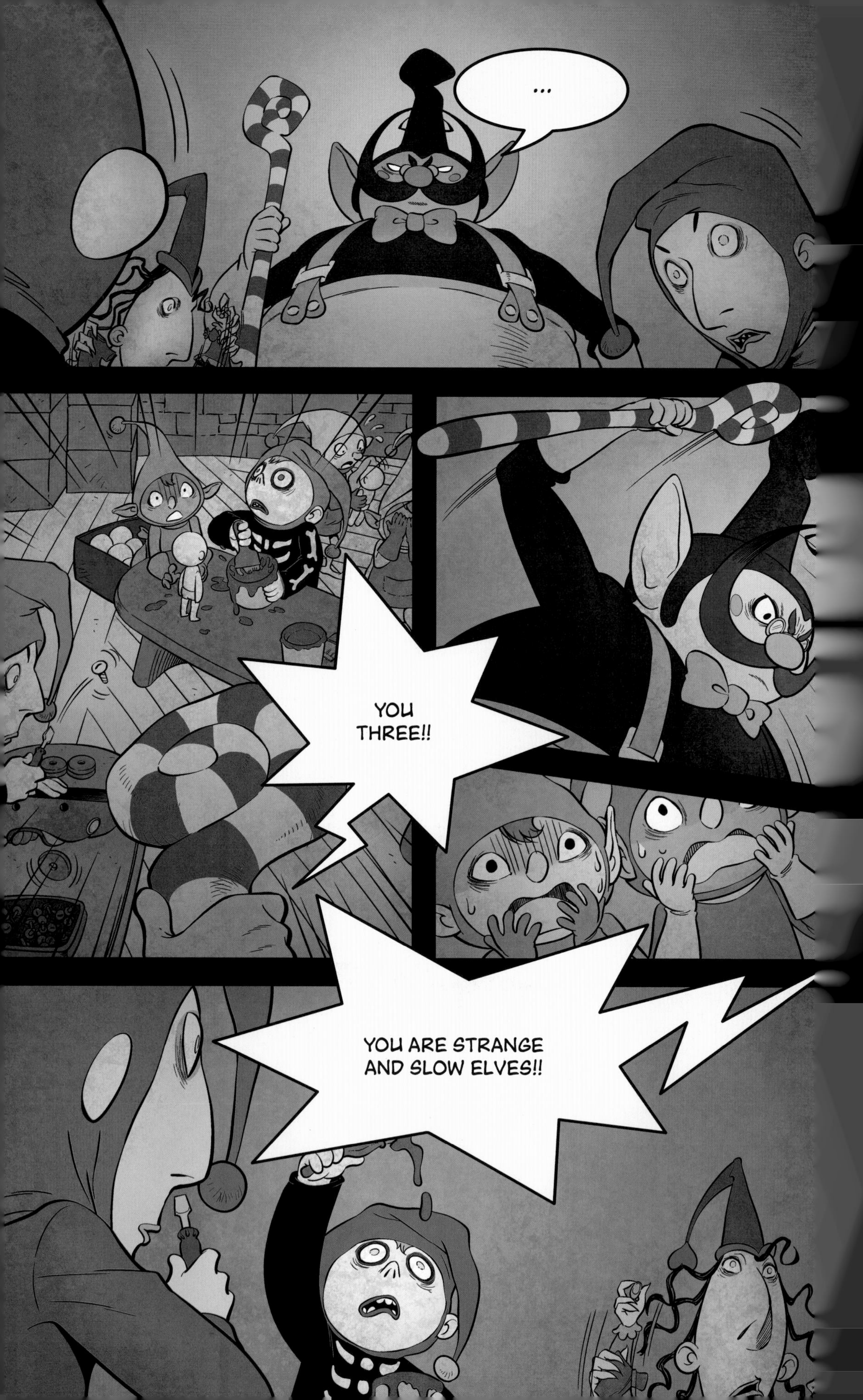
...
YOU THREE!!
YOU ARE STRANGE AND SLOW ELVES!!

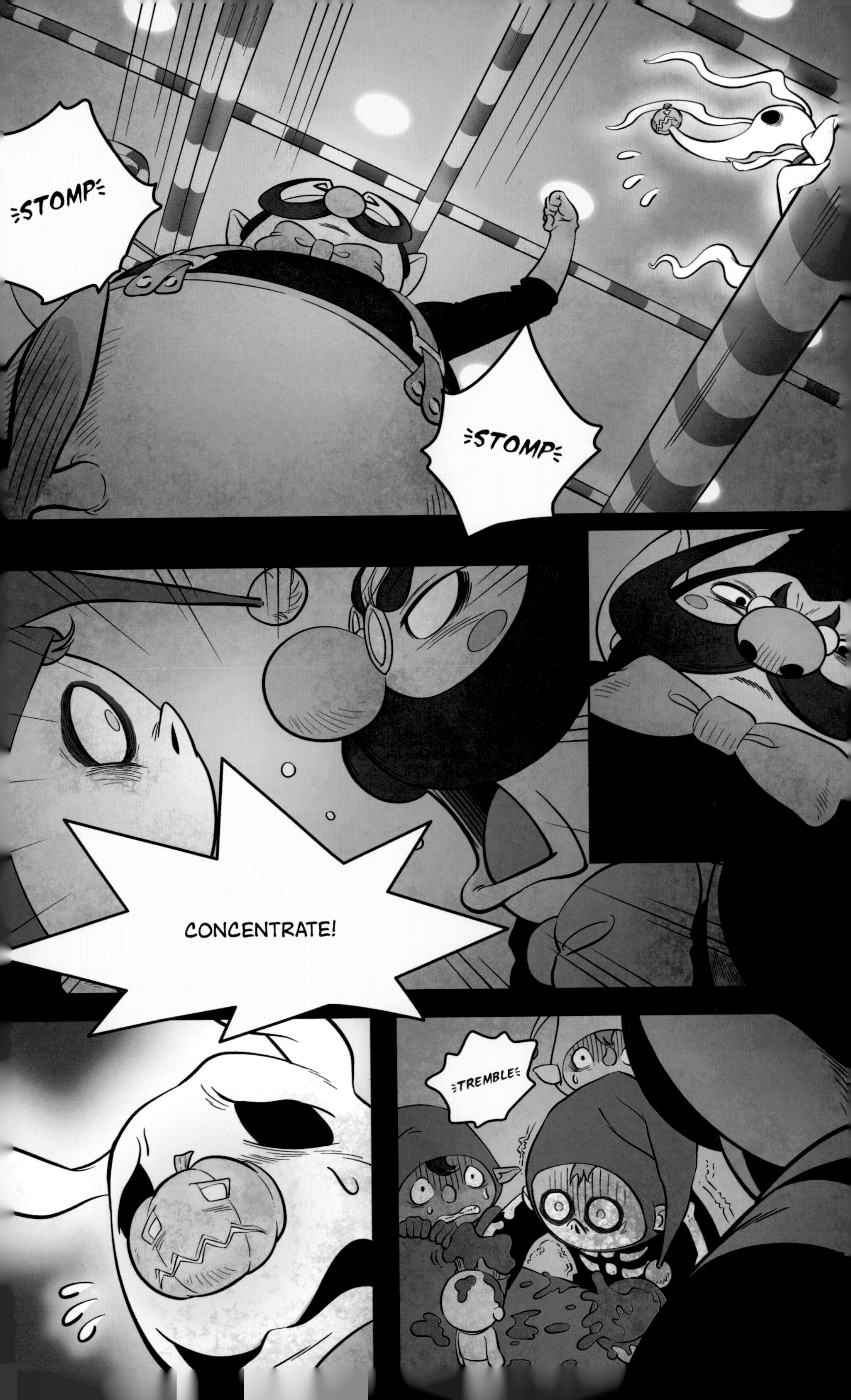
STOMP
STOMP
CONCENTRATE!
TREMBLE

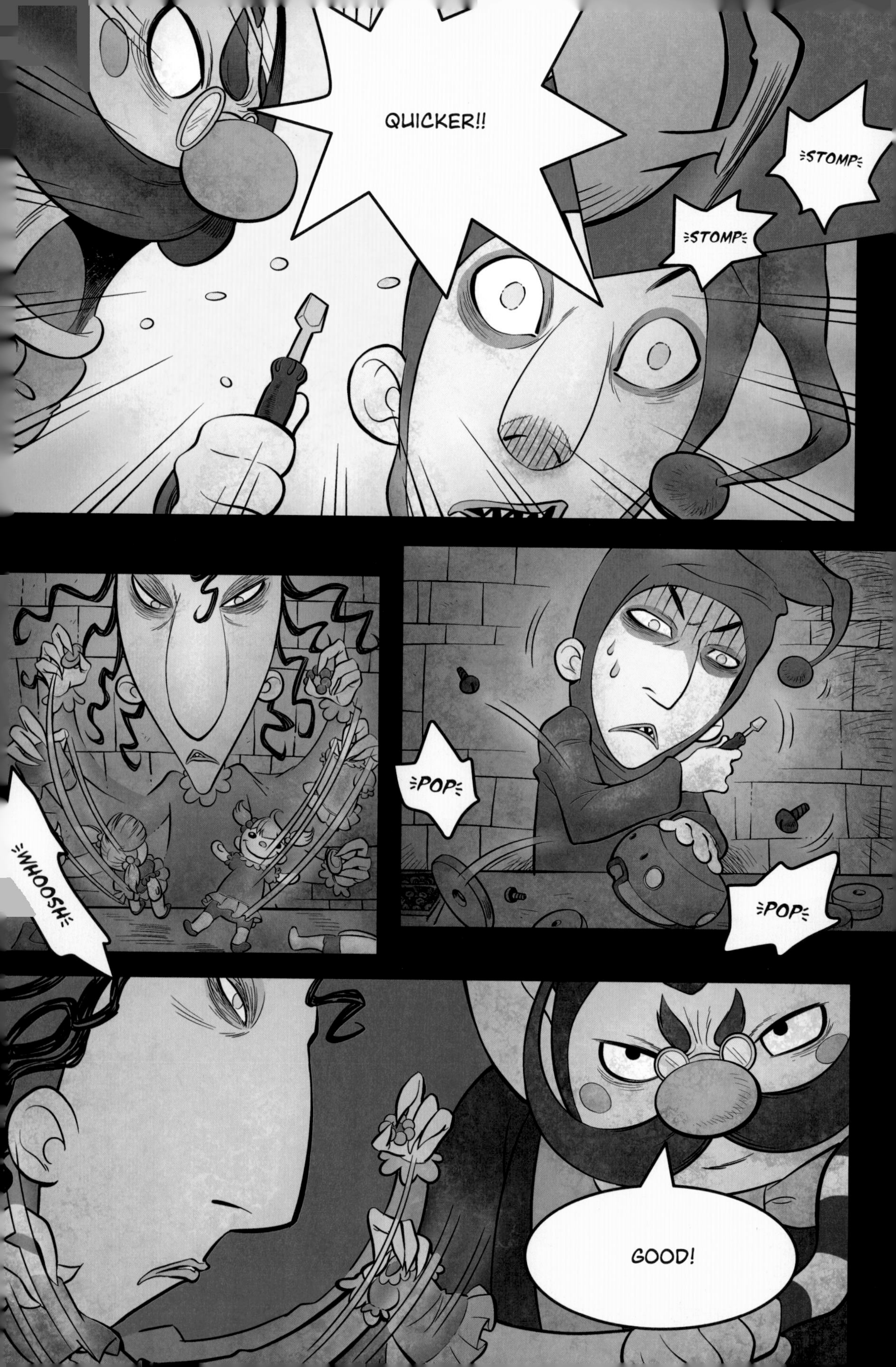
QUICKER!!
STOMP
STOMP
POP
POP
WHOOSH
GOOD!

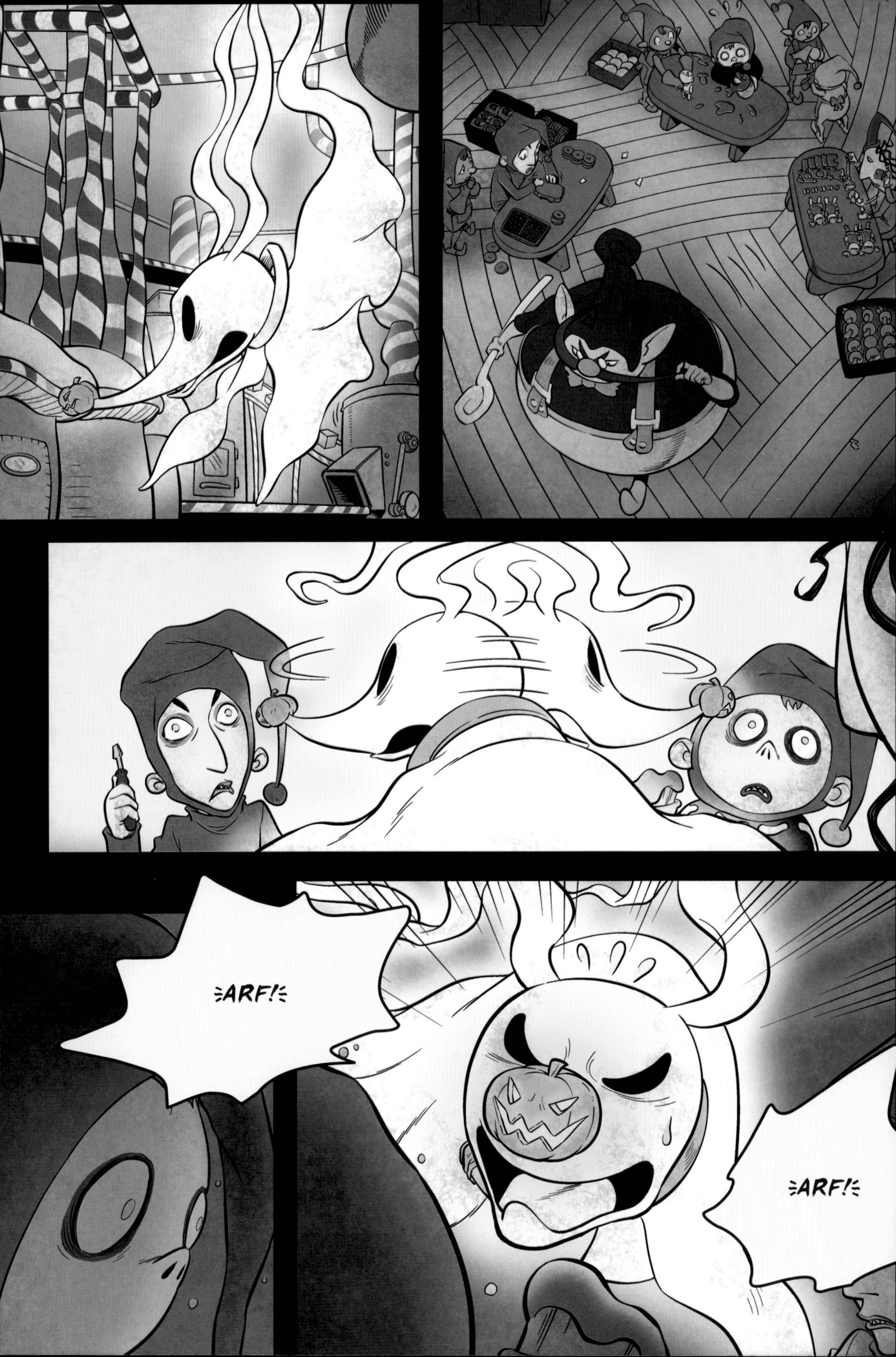
ARF!
ARF!

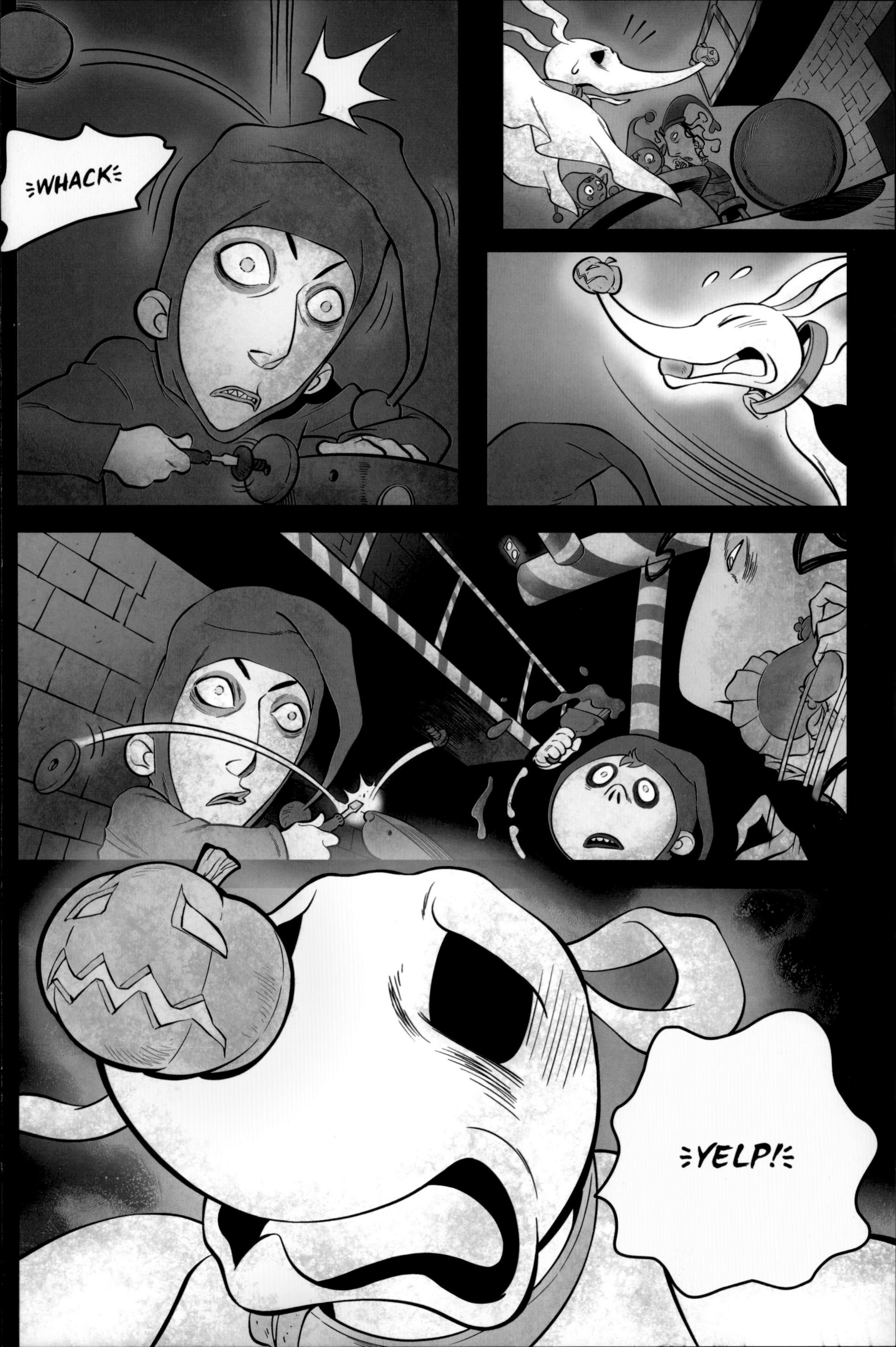
WHACK
YELP!

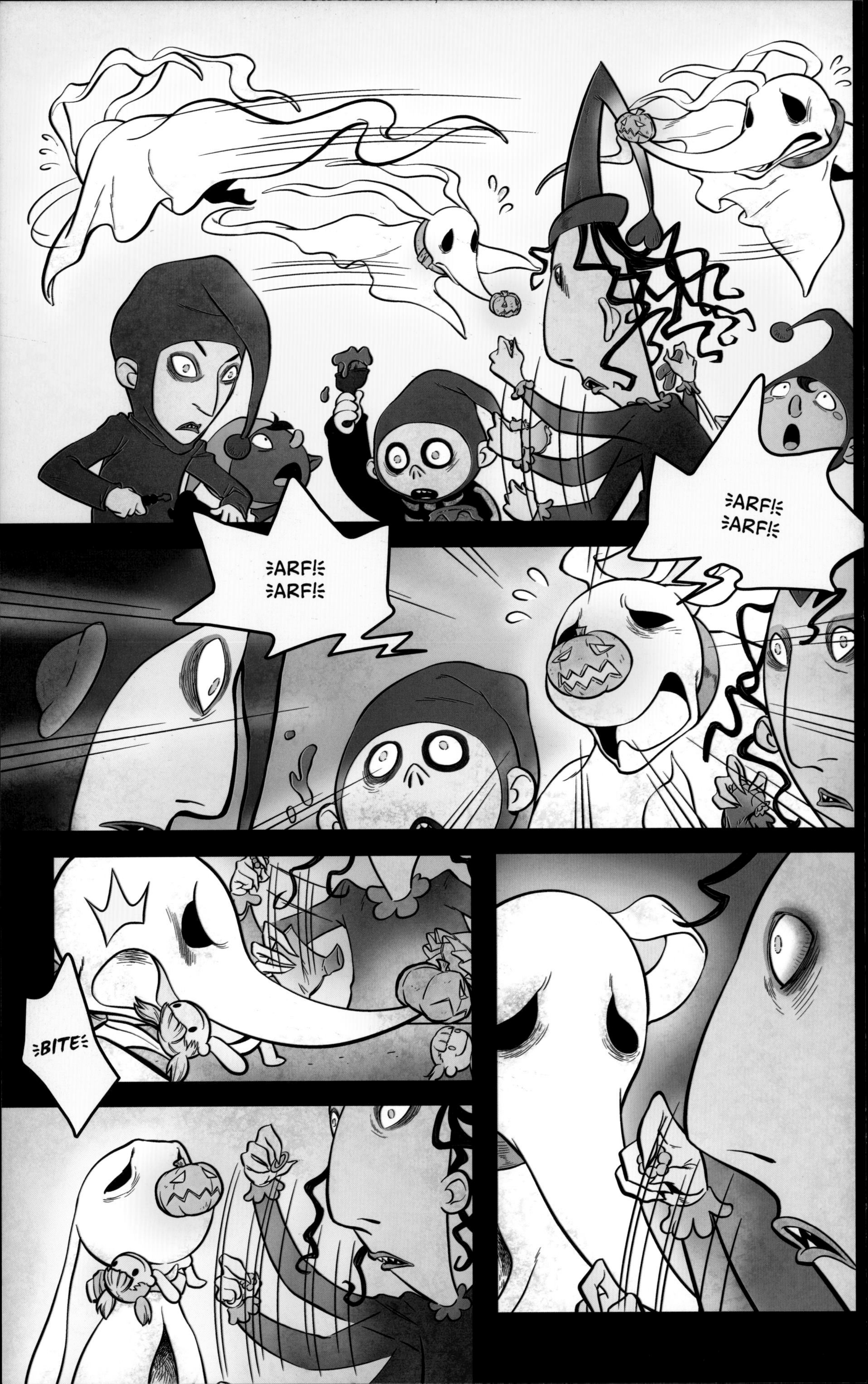
ARF! ARF!
ARF! ARF!
BITE

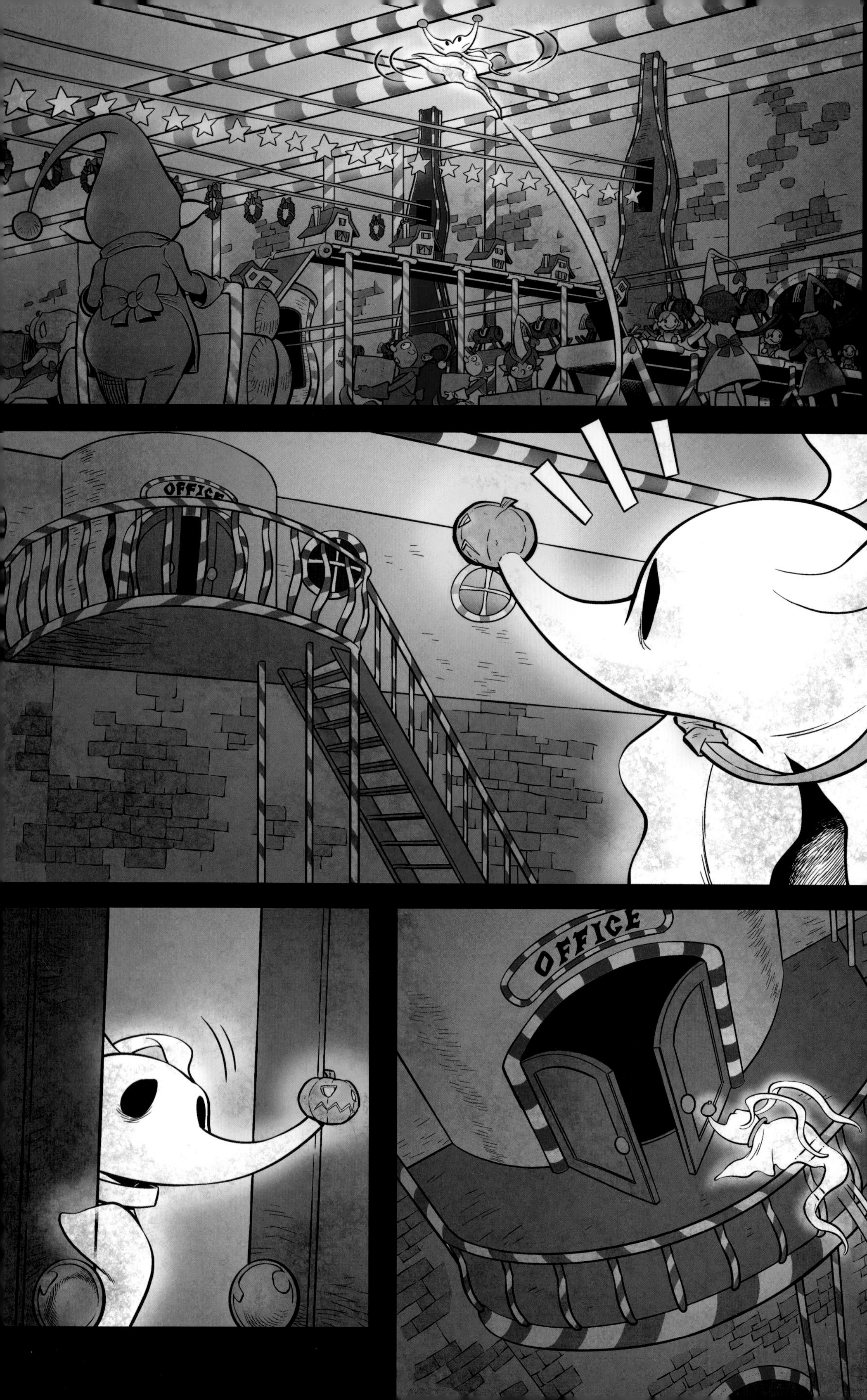
OFFICE
OFFICE

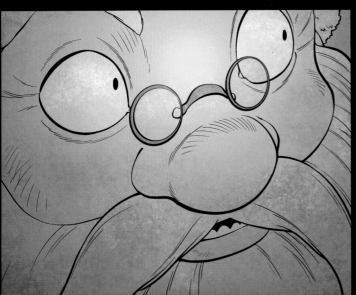

ARF!

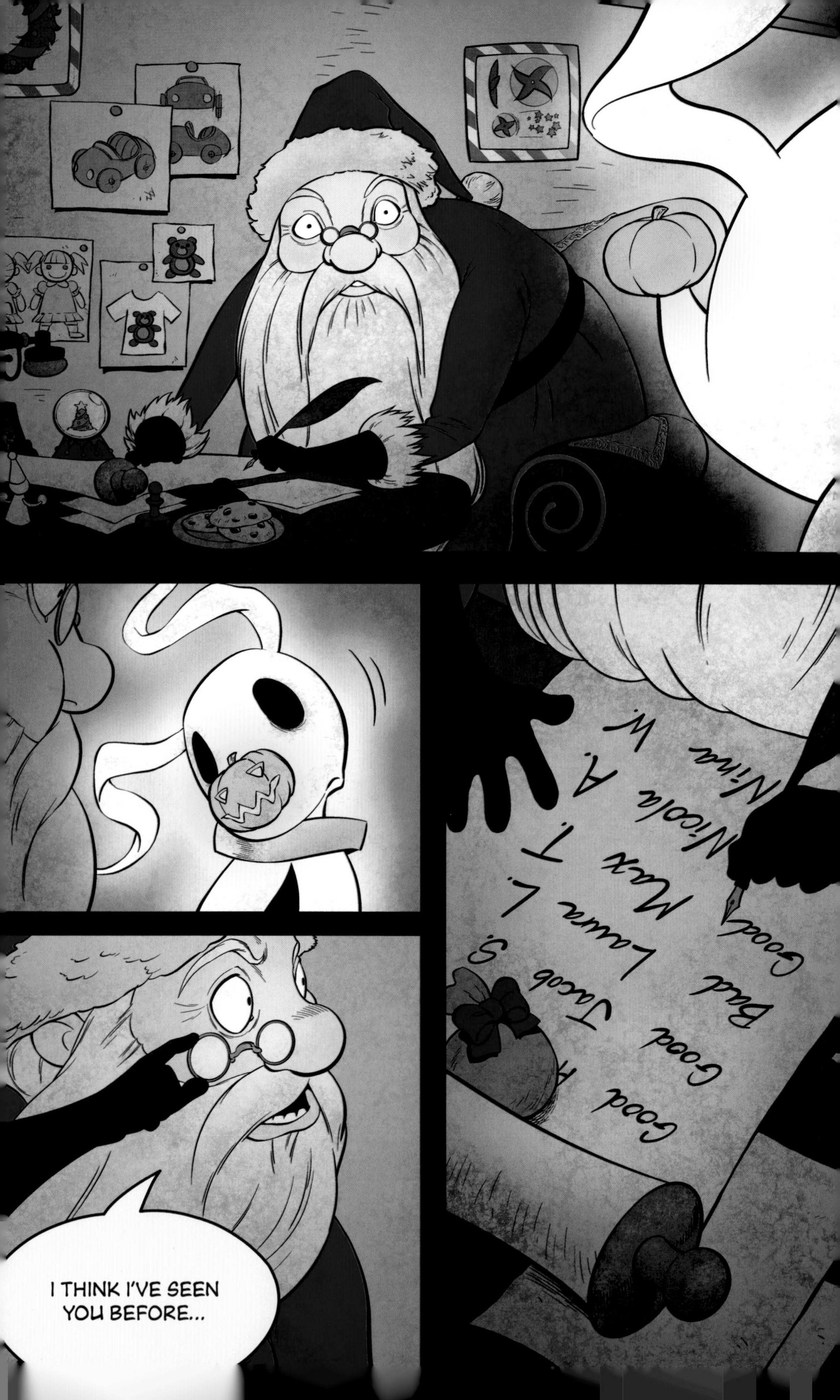
Good
Good Jacob S.
Bad Laura L.
Good Max T.
Nicola A.
Nina W.
I THINK I'VE SEEN YOU BEFORE...

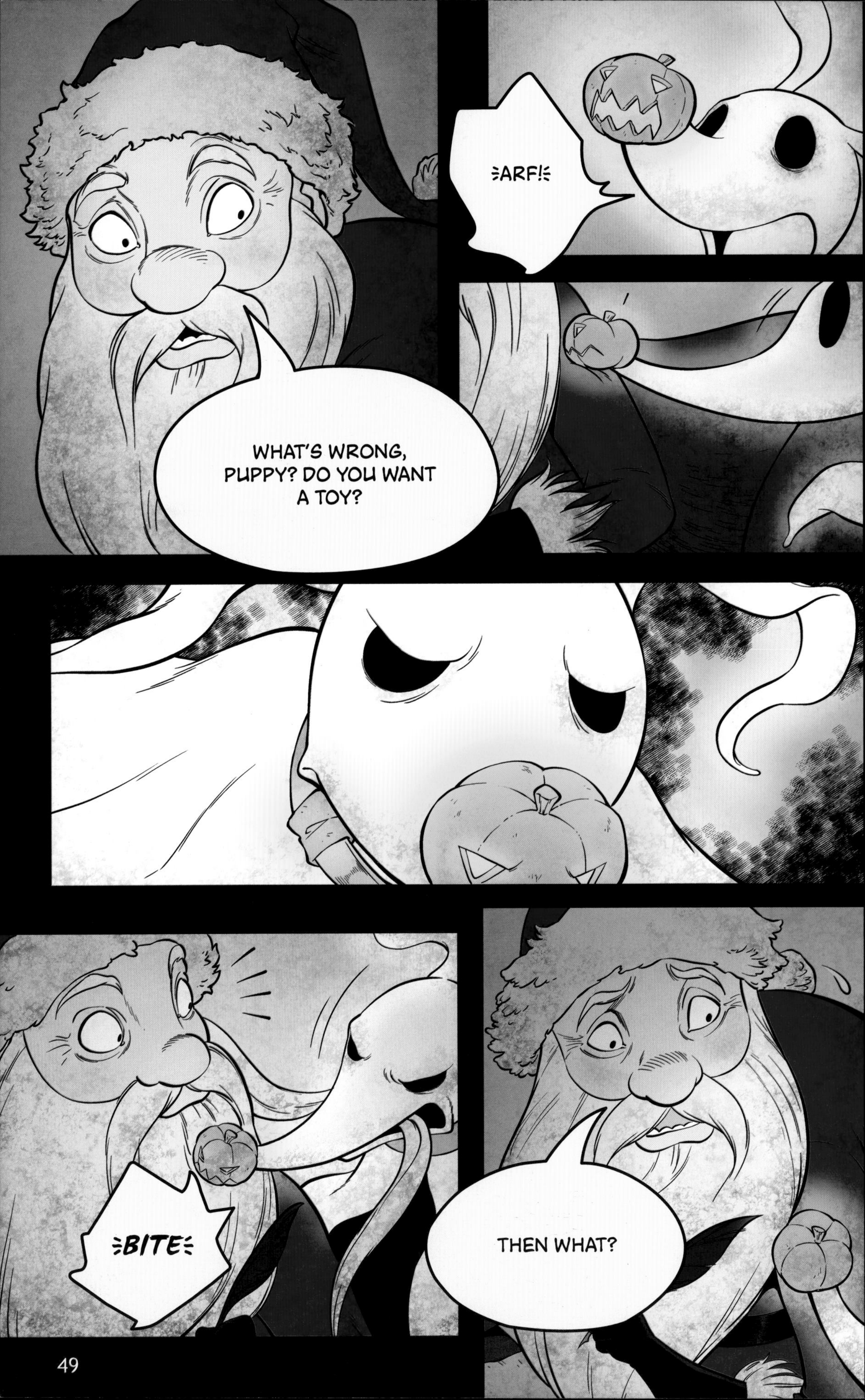
ARF!
WHAT'S WRONG, PUPPY? DO YOU WANT A TOY?
THEN WHAT?
BITE

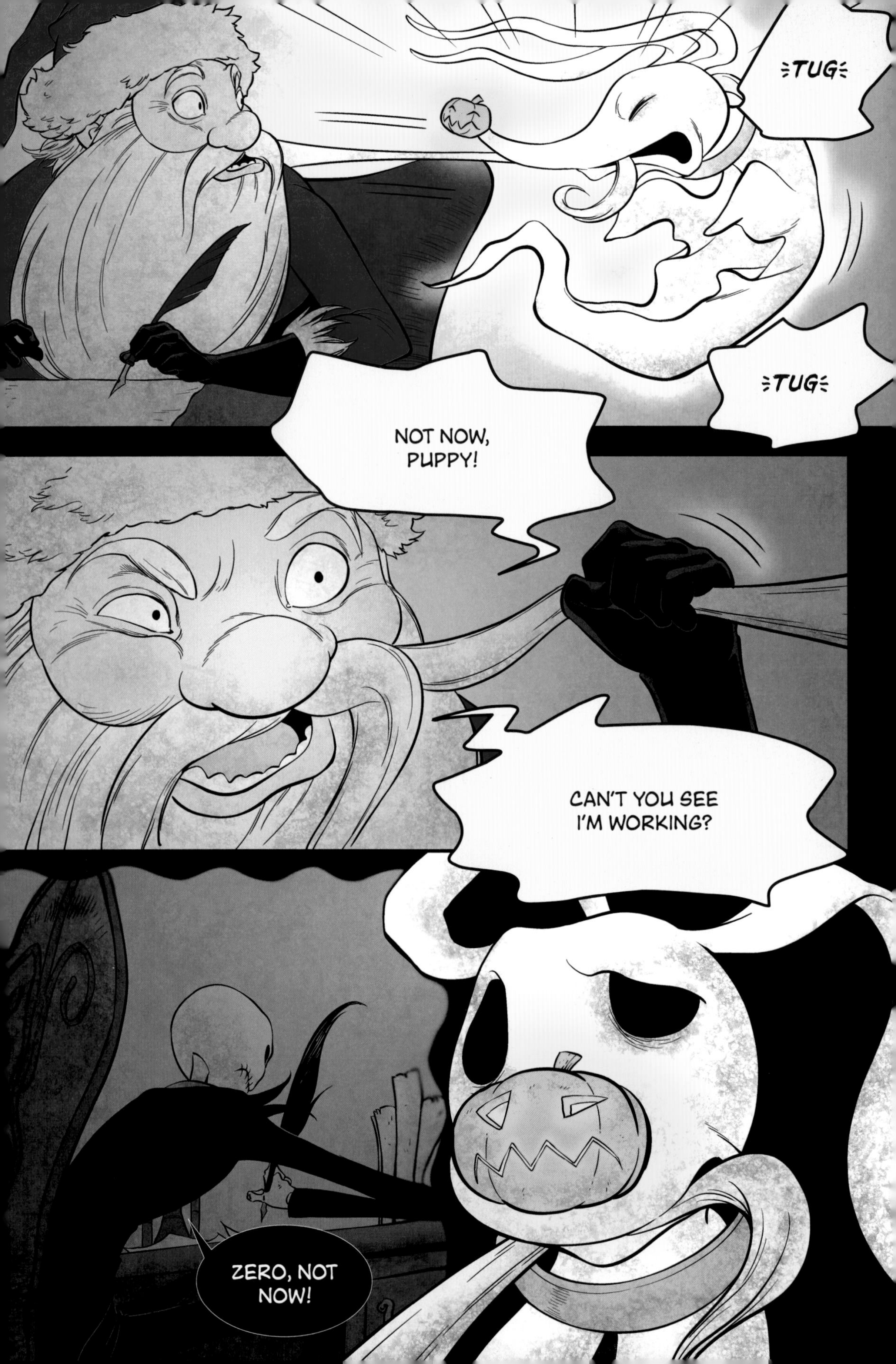
TUG
TUG
NOT NOW, PUPPY!
CAN'T YOU SEE I'M WORKING?
ZERO, NOT NOW!

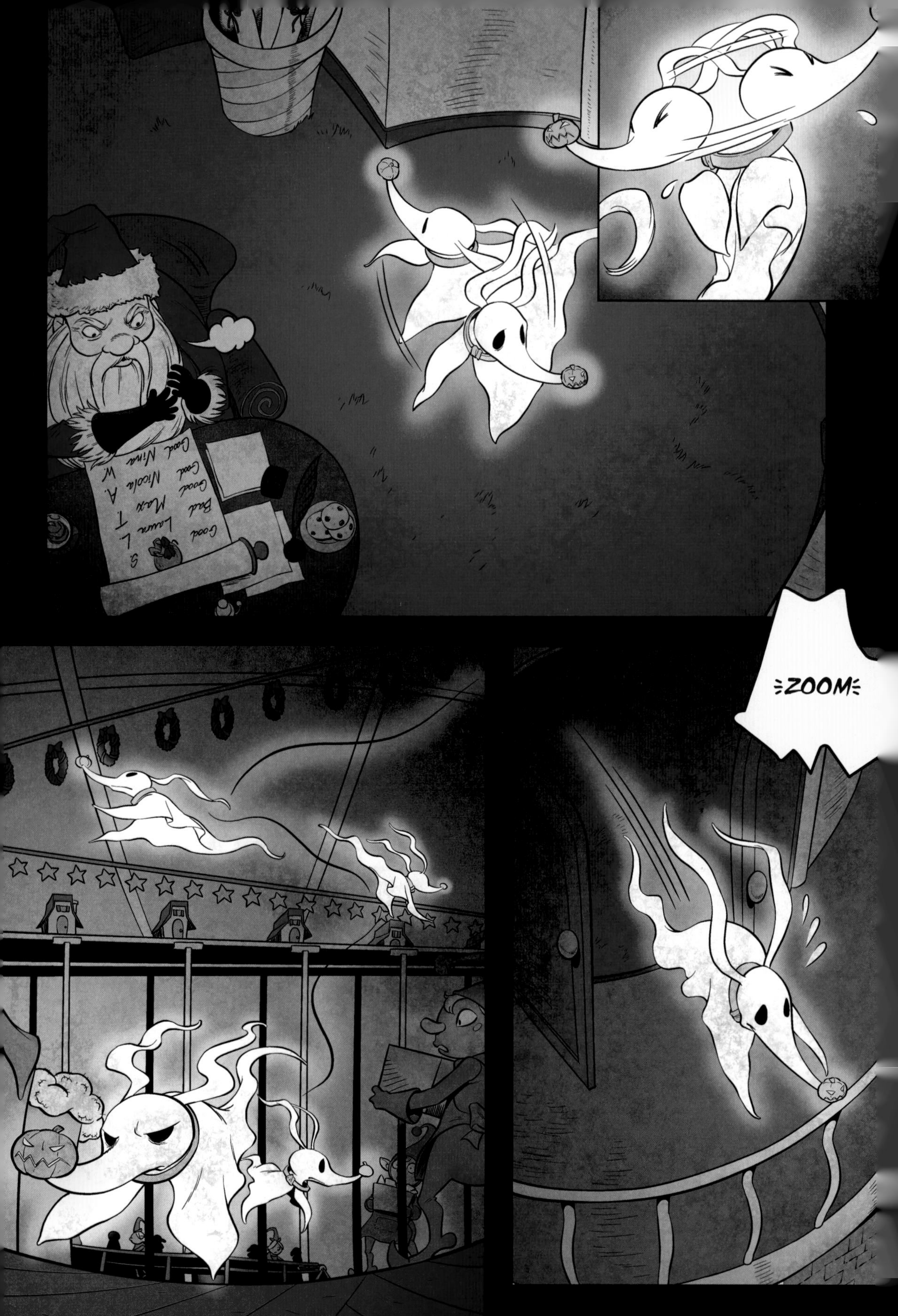
Good Laura L.
Bad Max T.
Good Nicola A.
Good Nina W.
ZOOM

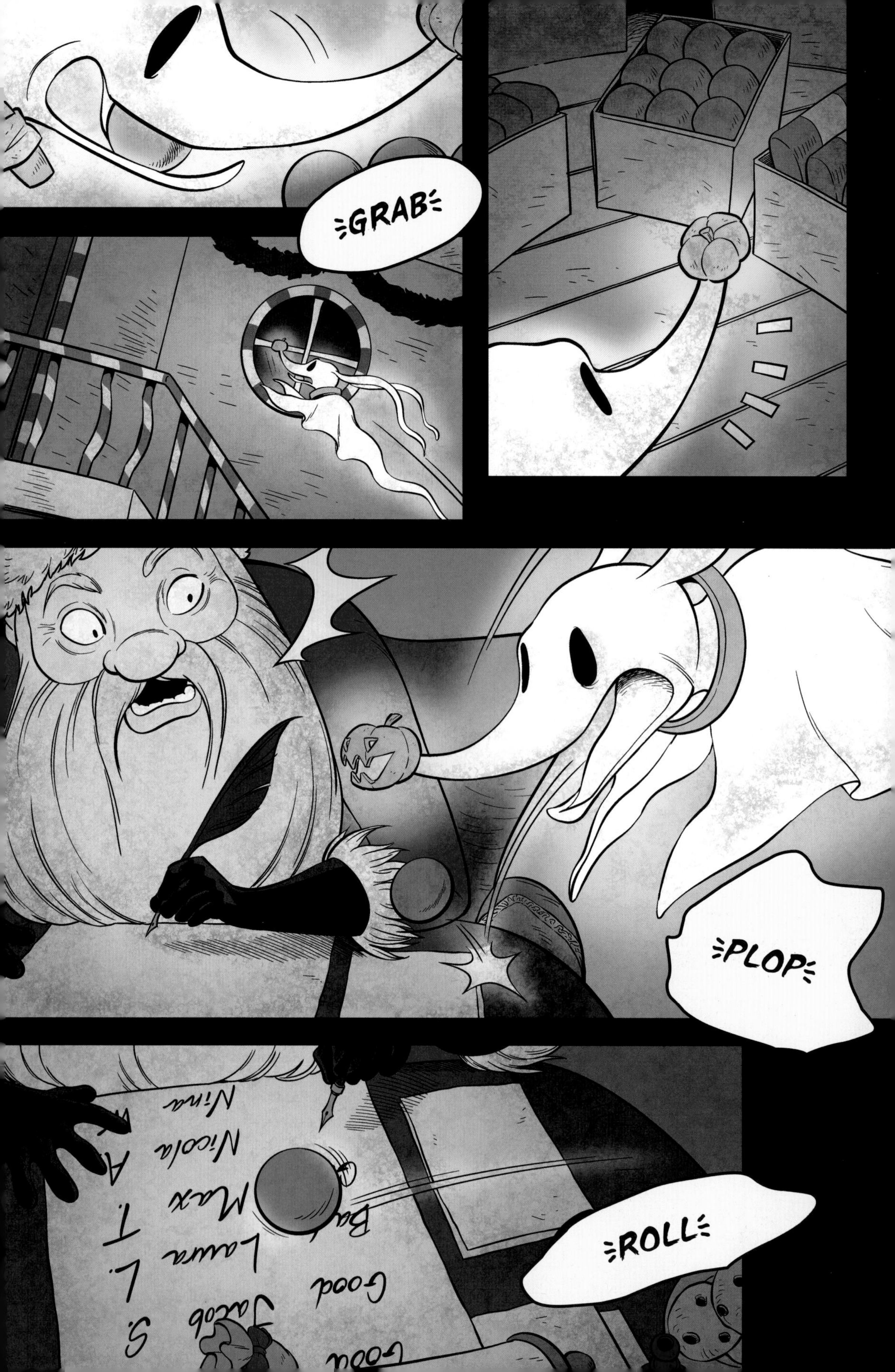
GRAB
PLOP
Good
Jacob
Laura
Max
Nicola
Nina
ROLL

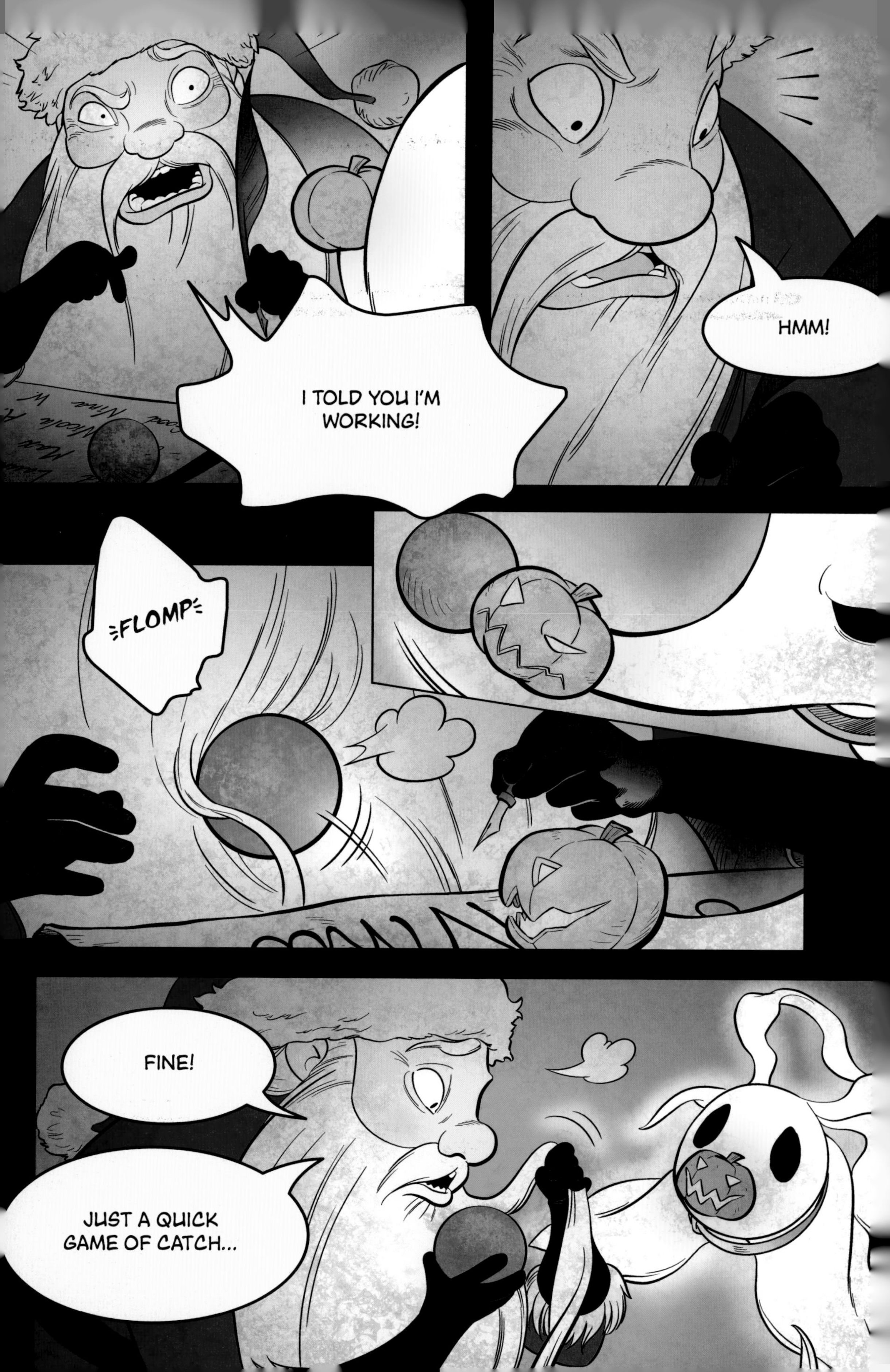
HMM!
I TOLD YOU I'M WORKING!
FLOMP
FINE!
JUST A QUICK GAME OF CATCH...

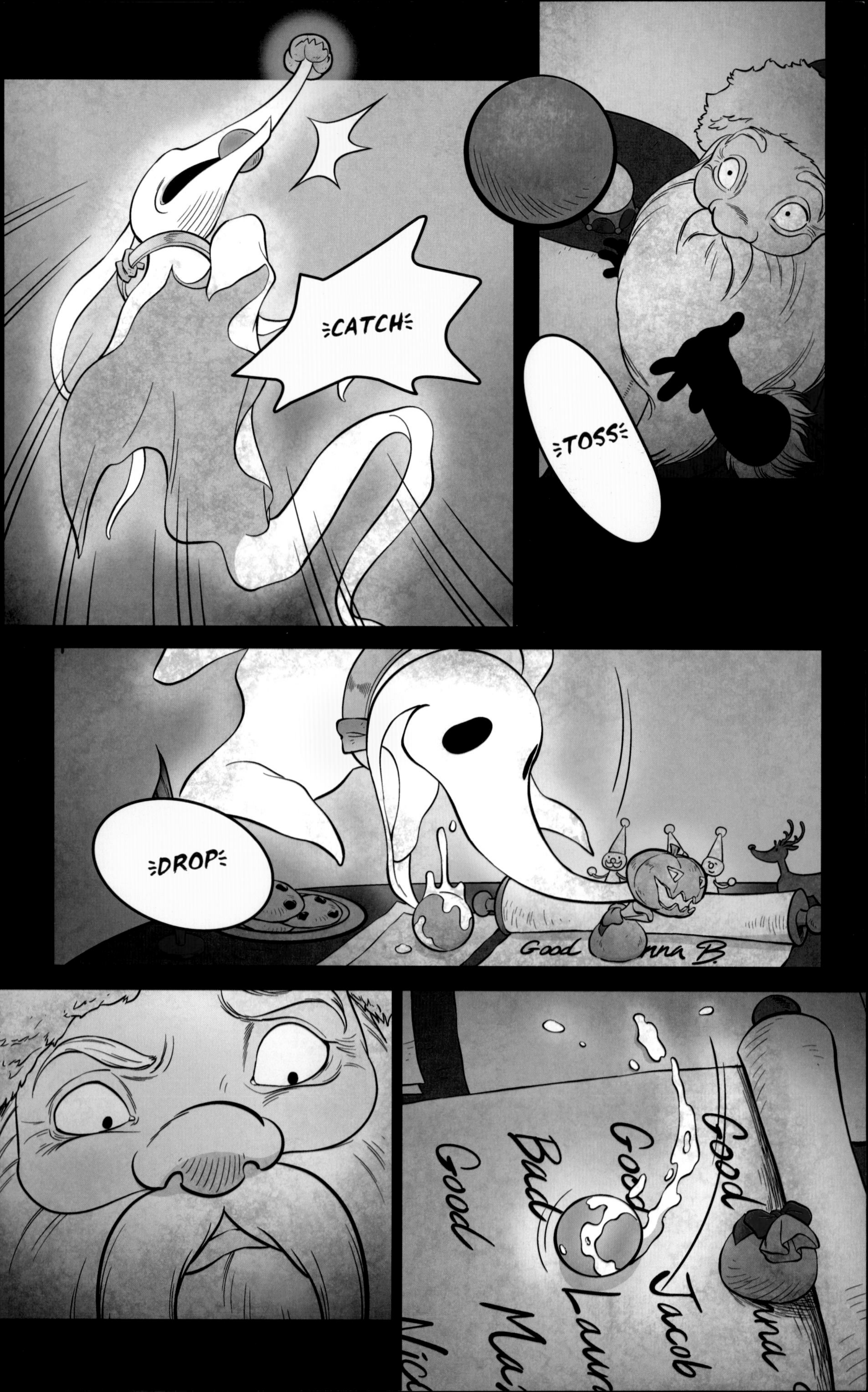
TOSS
CATCH
DROP
Good
Good
Good
Bad
Good
Jacob

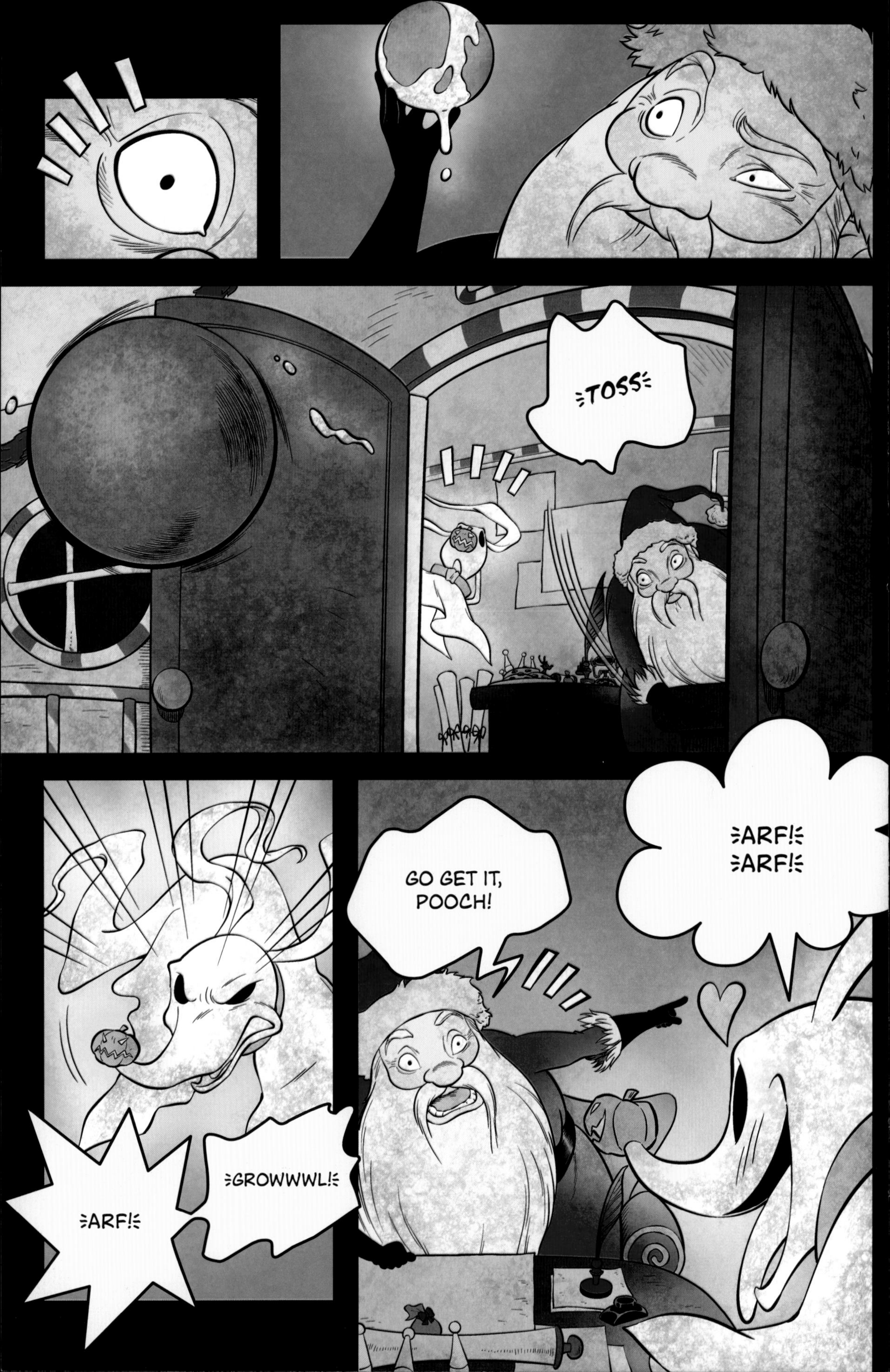
TOSS
ARF!
ARF!
GO GET IT, POOCH!
GROWWWL!
ARF!

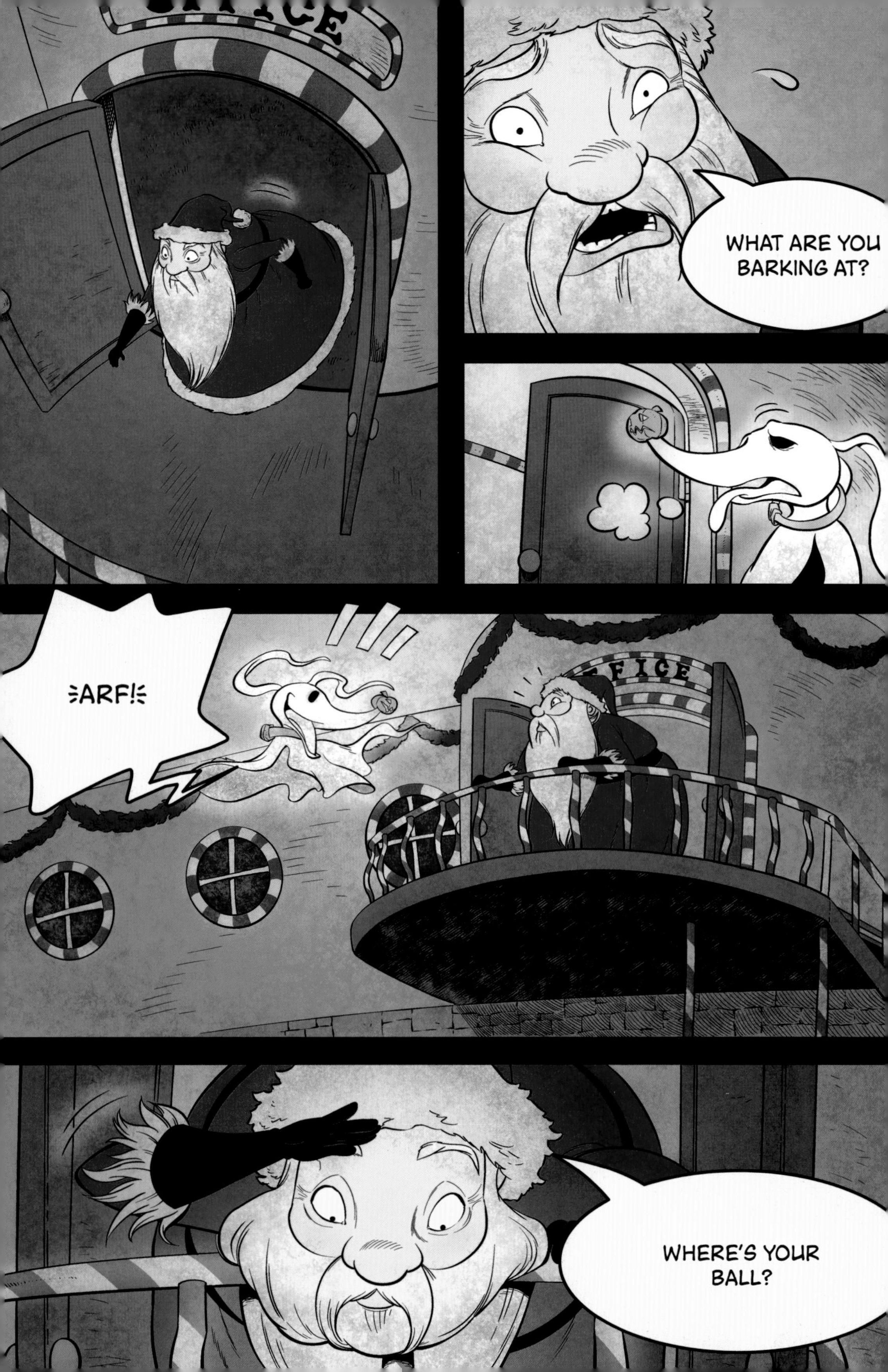
WHAT ARE YOU BARKING AT?
ARF!
WHERE'S YOUR BALL?

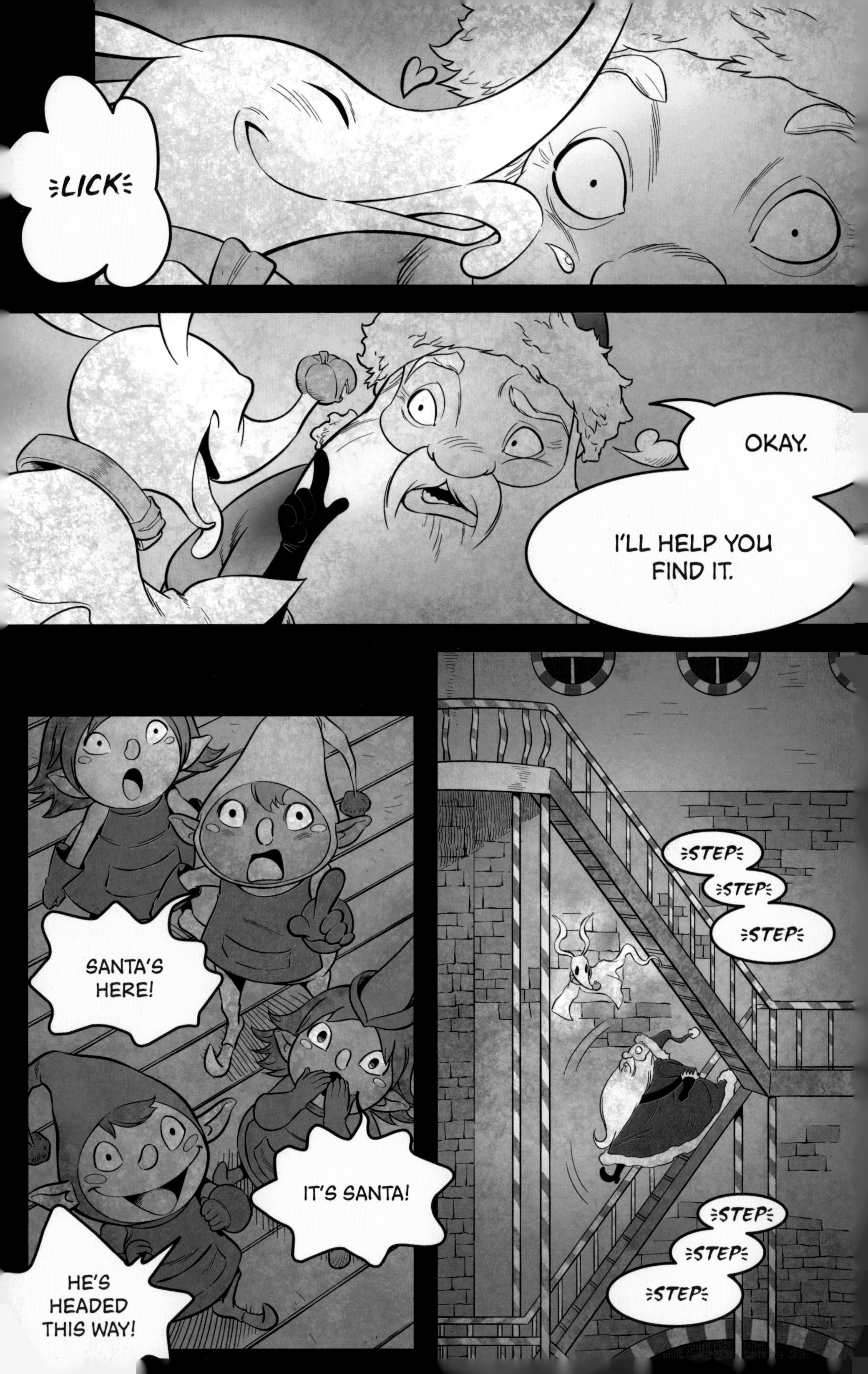
LICK
OKAY.
I'LL HELP YOU FIND IT.
STEP
STEP
STEP
STEP
STEP
STEP
SANTA'S HERE!
IT'S SANTA!
HE'S HEADED THIS WAY!

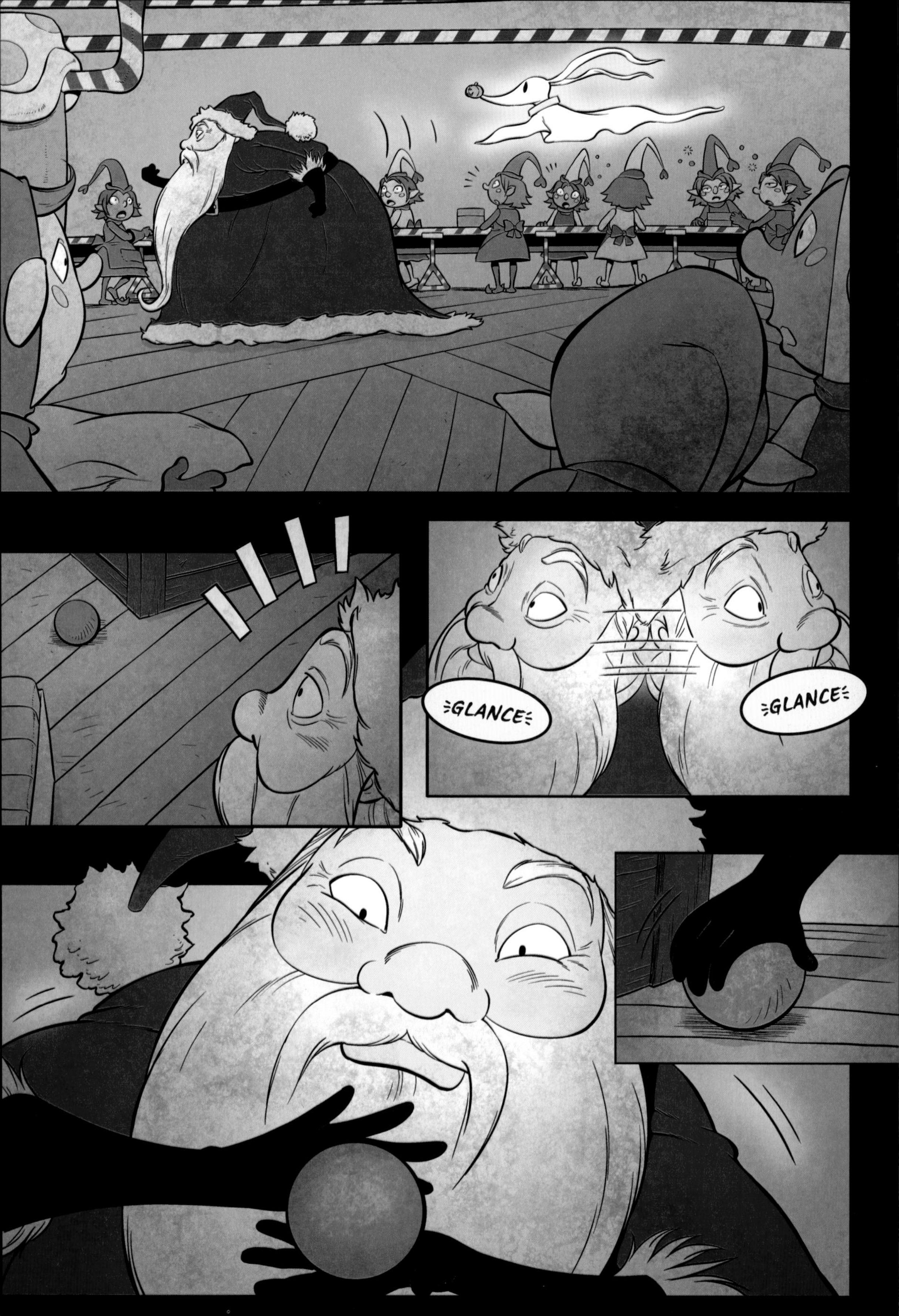
GLANCE
GLANCE

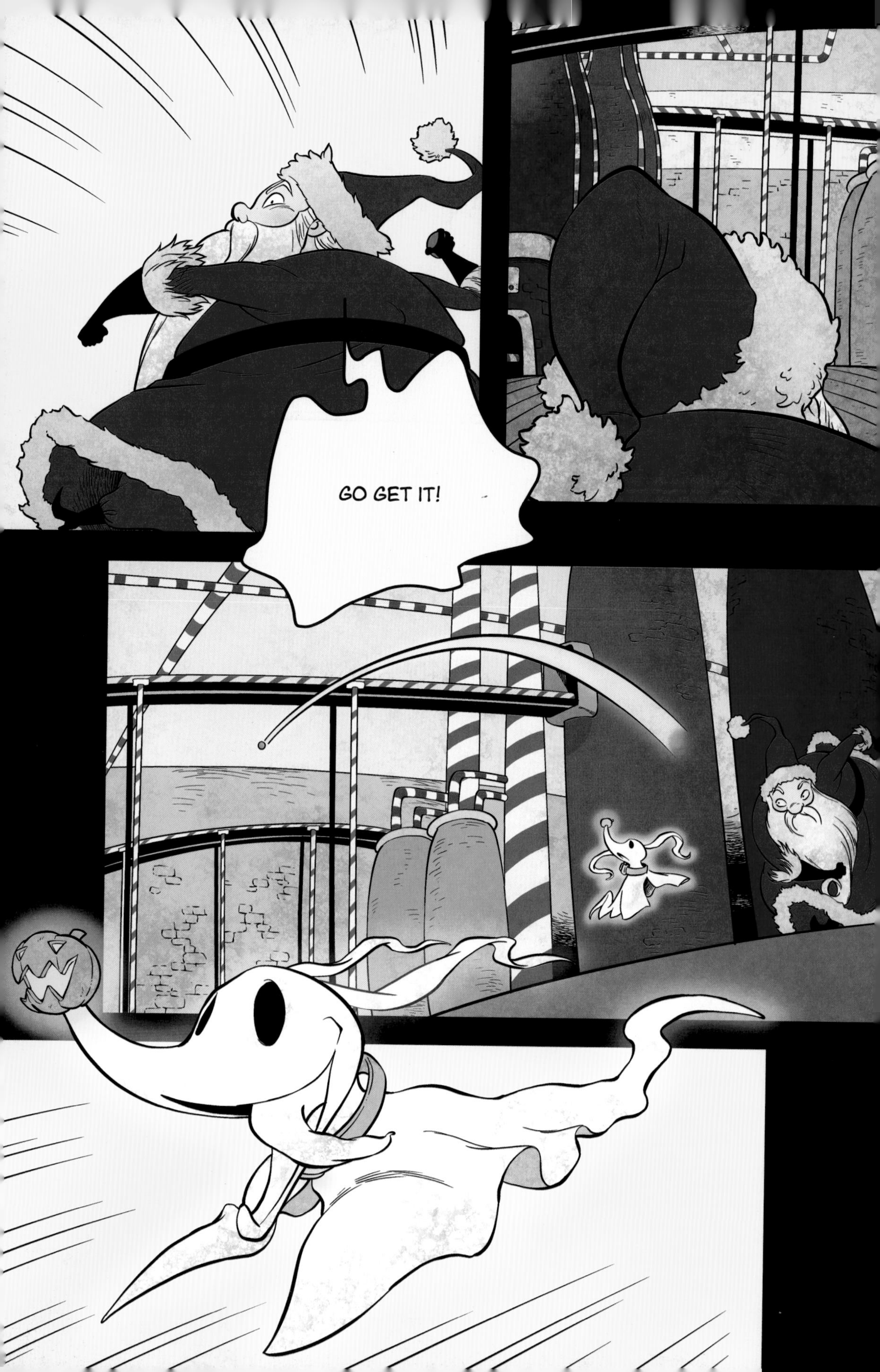
GO GET IT!

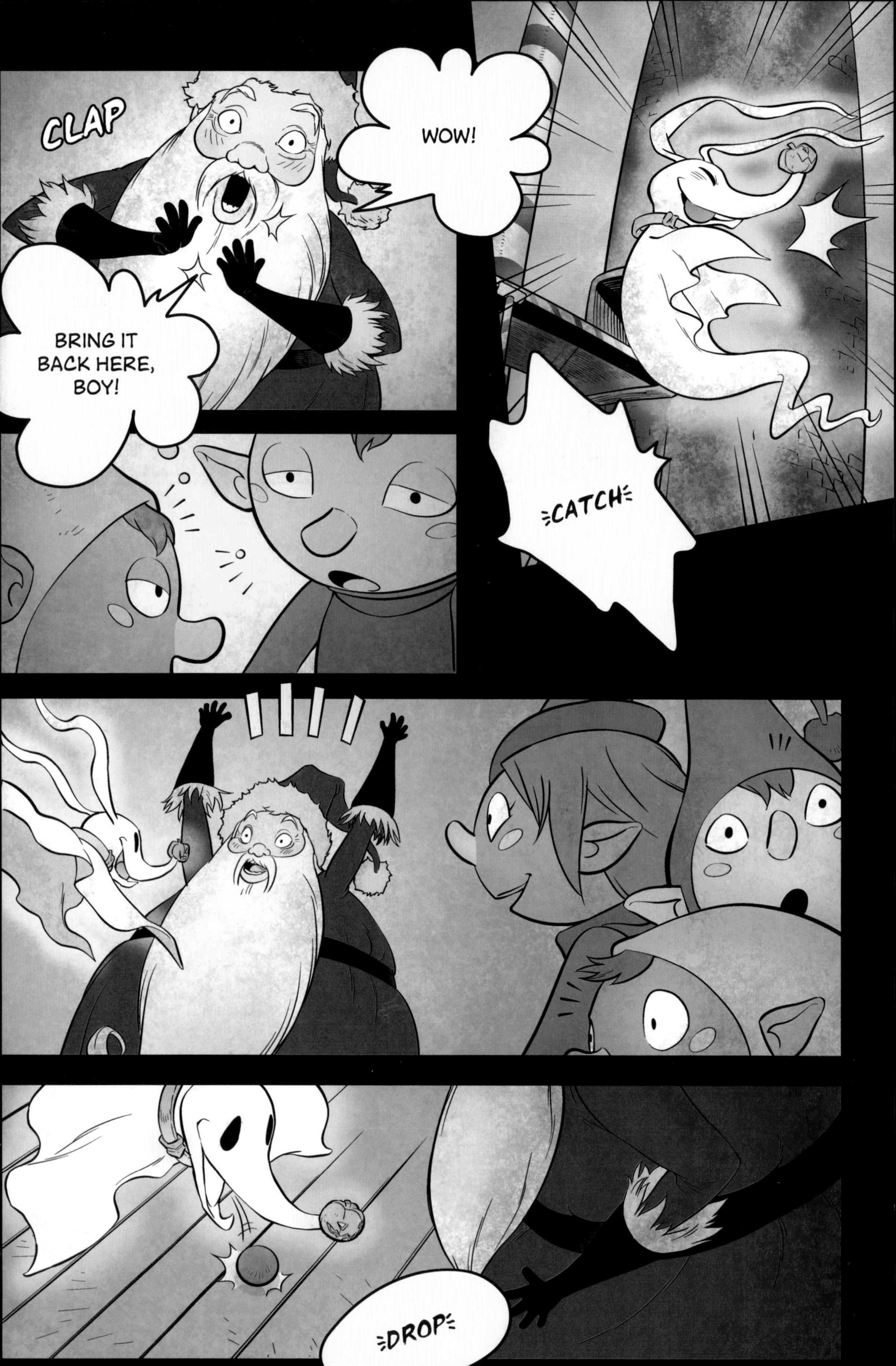

≈CATCH≈
WOW!
CLAP
BRING IT BACK HERE, BOY!
≈DROP≈

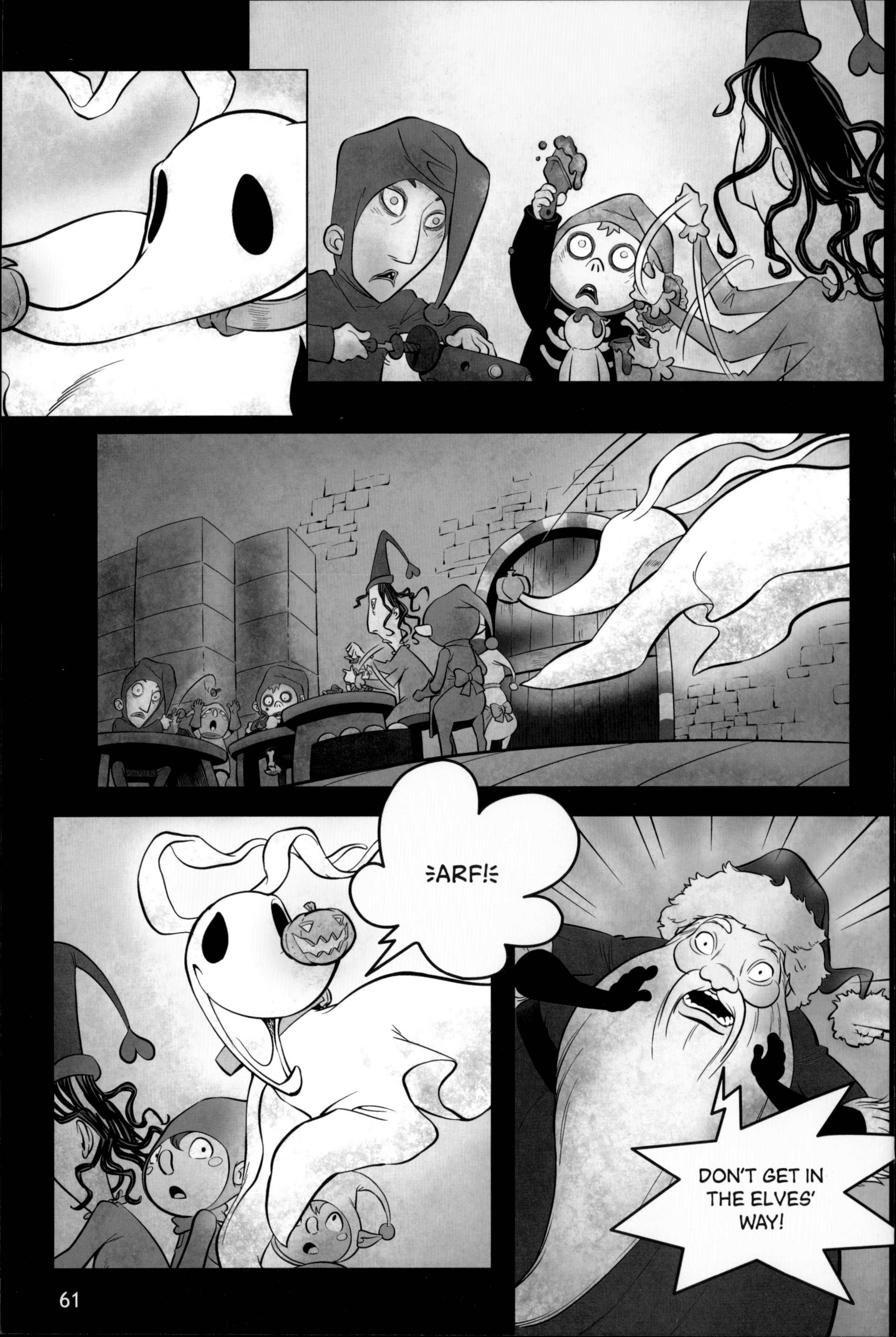
DON'T GET IN THE ELVES' WAY!
ARF!

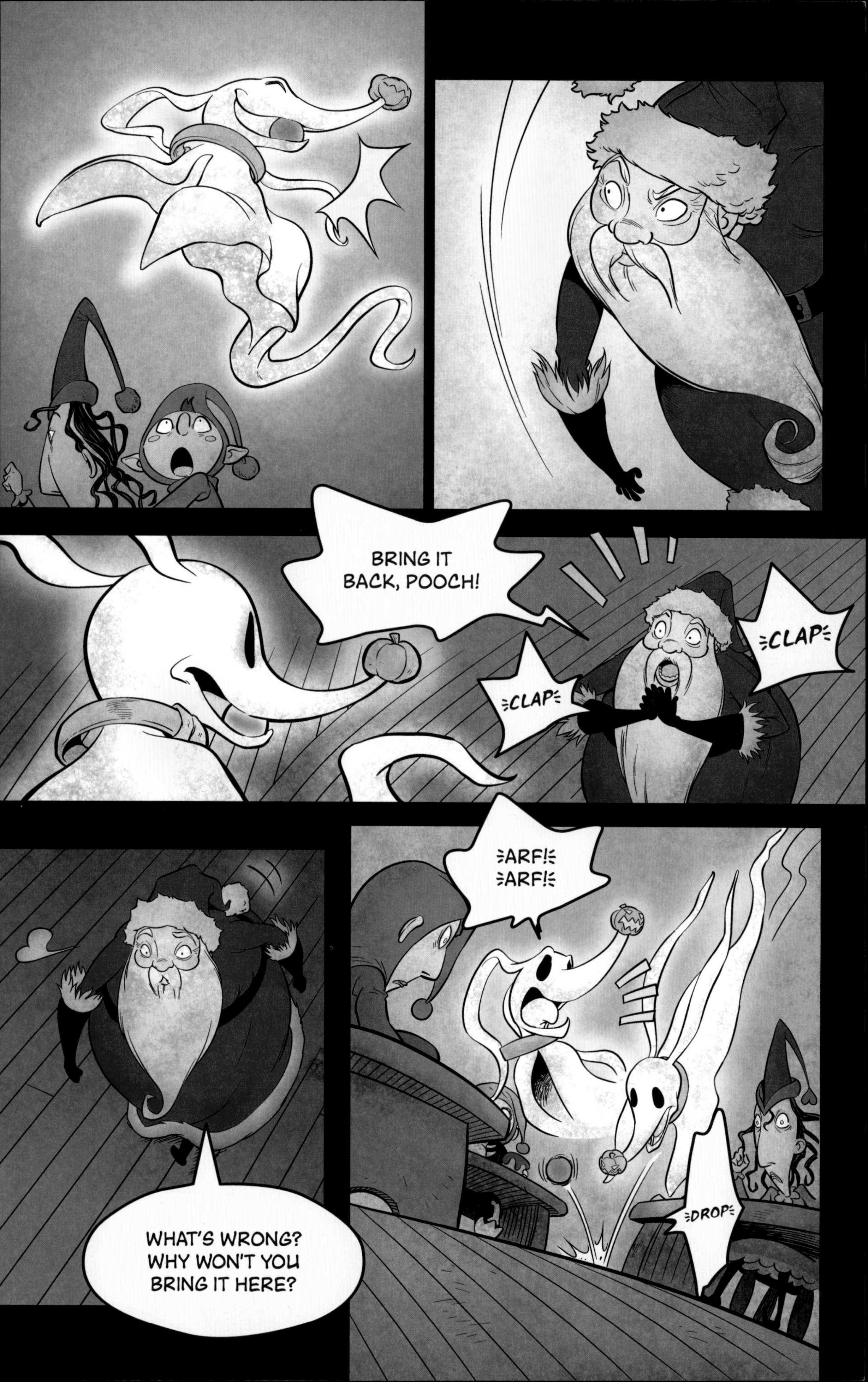
BRING IT BACK, POOCH!
CLAP
CLAP
ARF! ARF!
DROP
WHAT'S WRONG? WHY WON'T YOU BRING IT HERE?

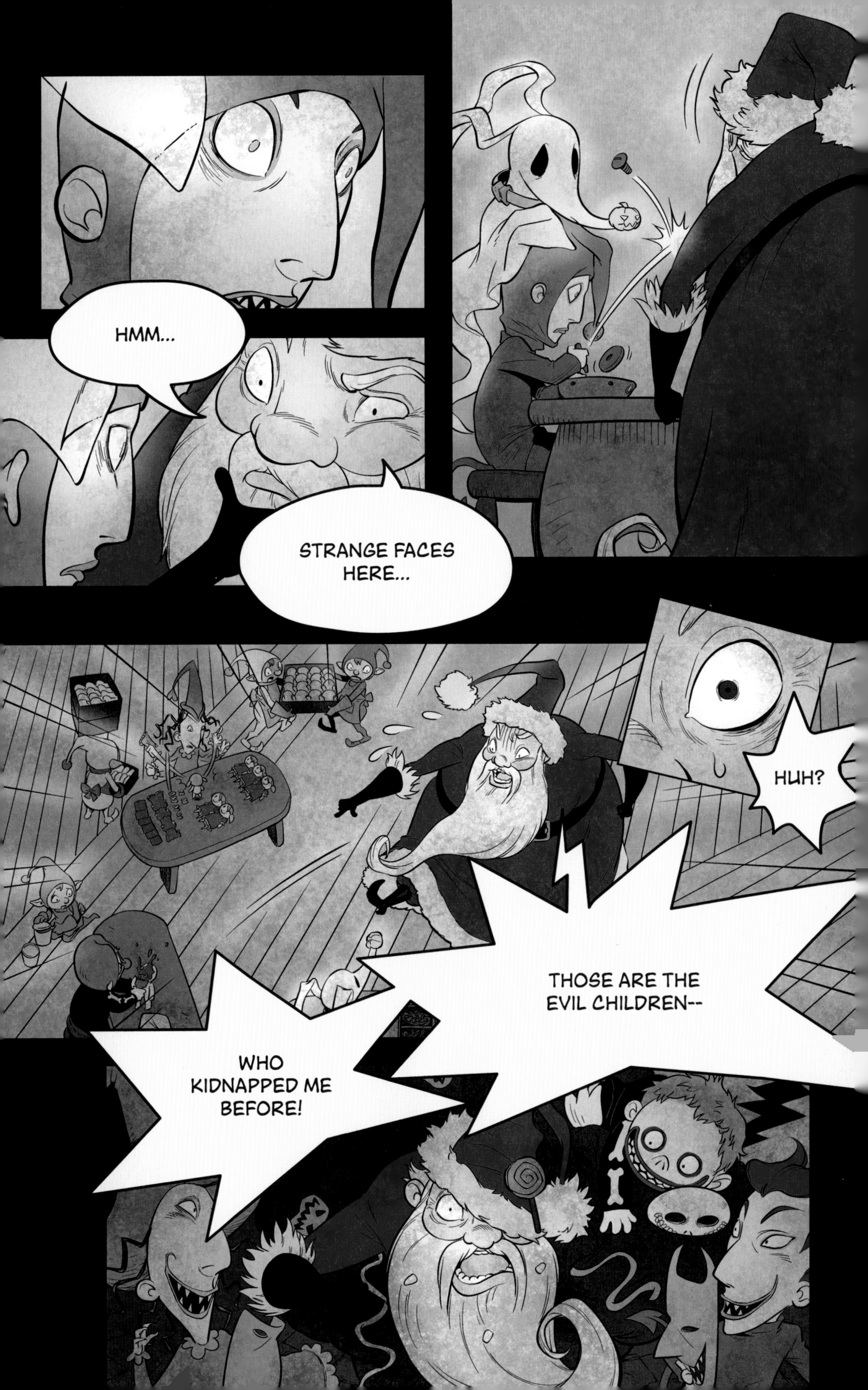
HMM...
STRANGE FACES HERE...
HUH?
THOSE ARE THE EVIL CHILDREN--
WHO KIDNAPPED ME BEFORE!

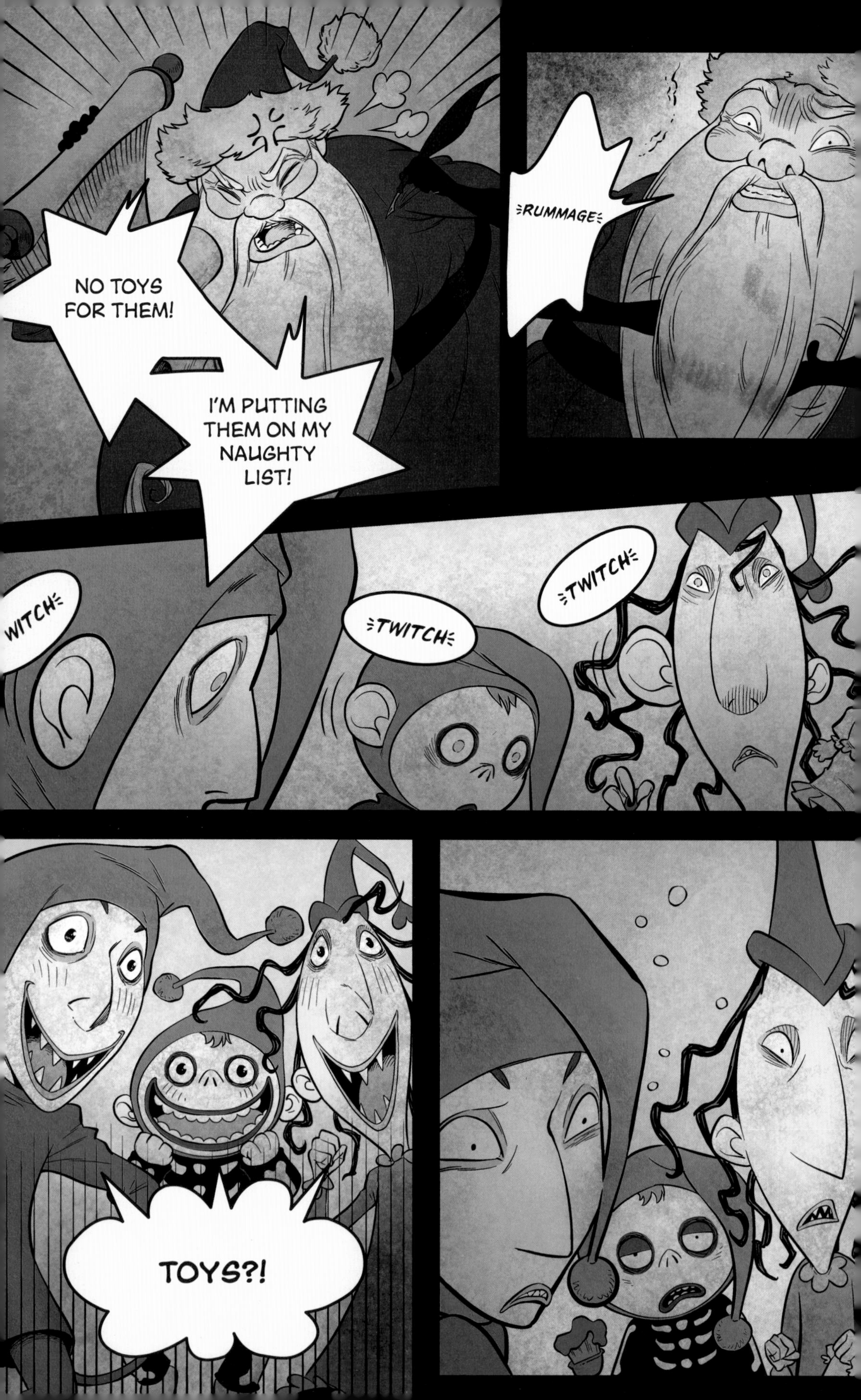
RUMMAGE
NO TOYS FOR THEM!
I'M PUTTING THEM ON MY NAUGHTY LIST!
TWITCH
TWITCH
WITCH
TOYS?!

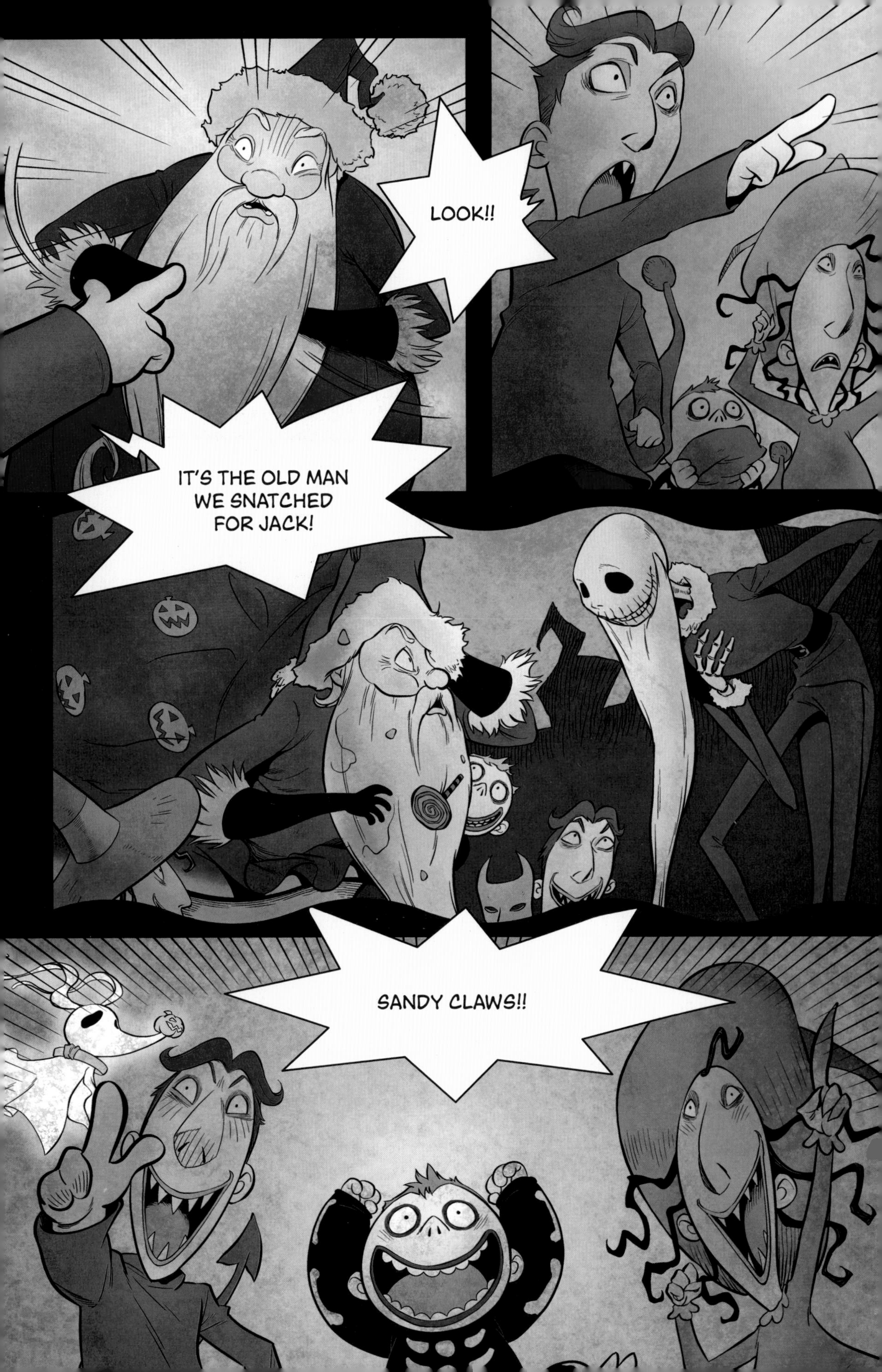
LOOK!!
IT'S THE OLD MAN WE SNATCHED FOR JACK!
SANDY CLAWS!!

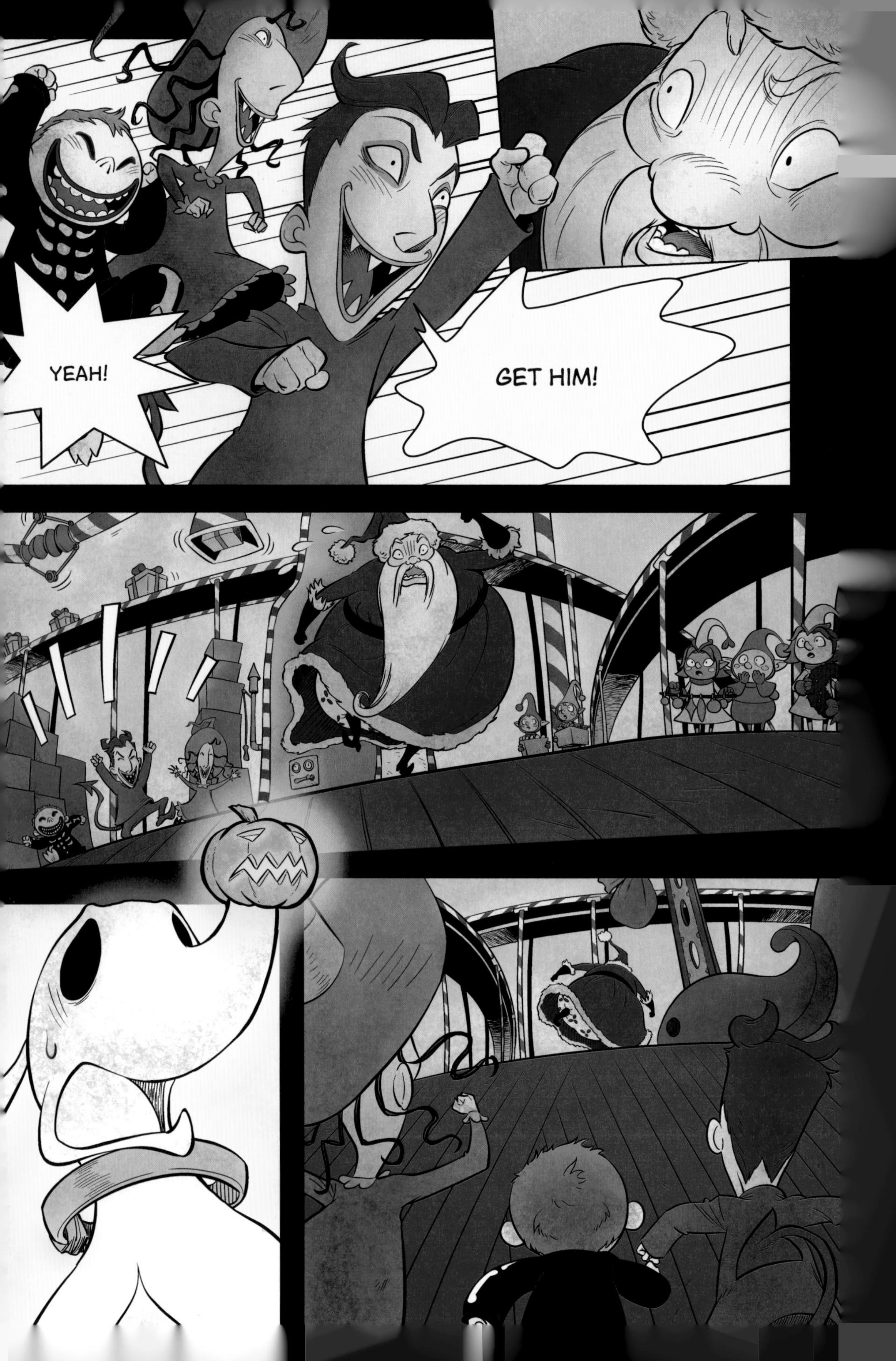
GET HIM!
YEAH!

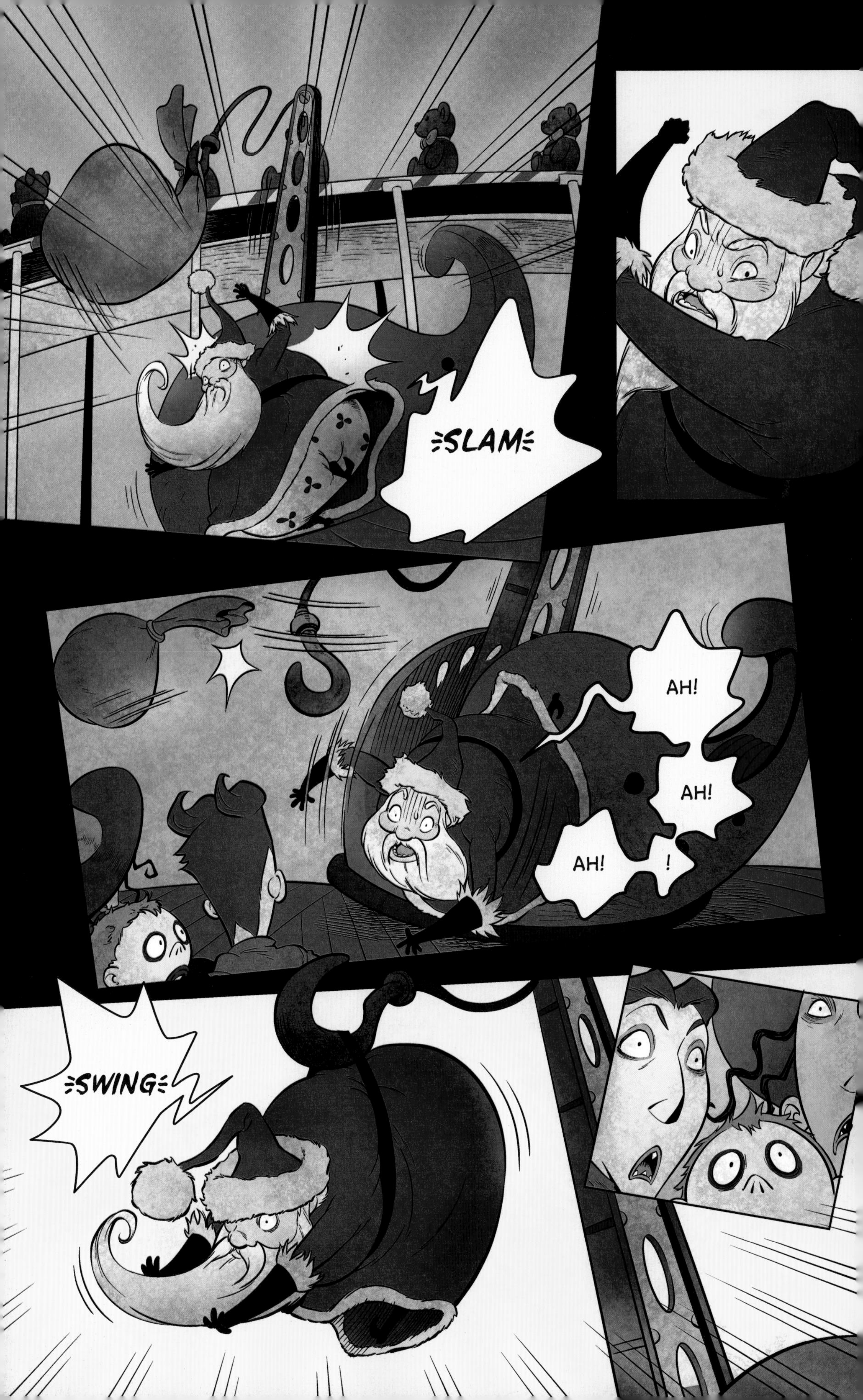
SLAM
AH!
AH!
AH!
!
SWING

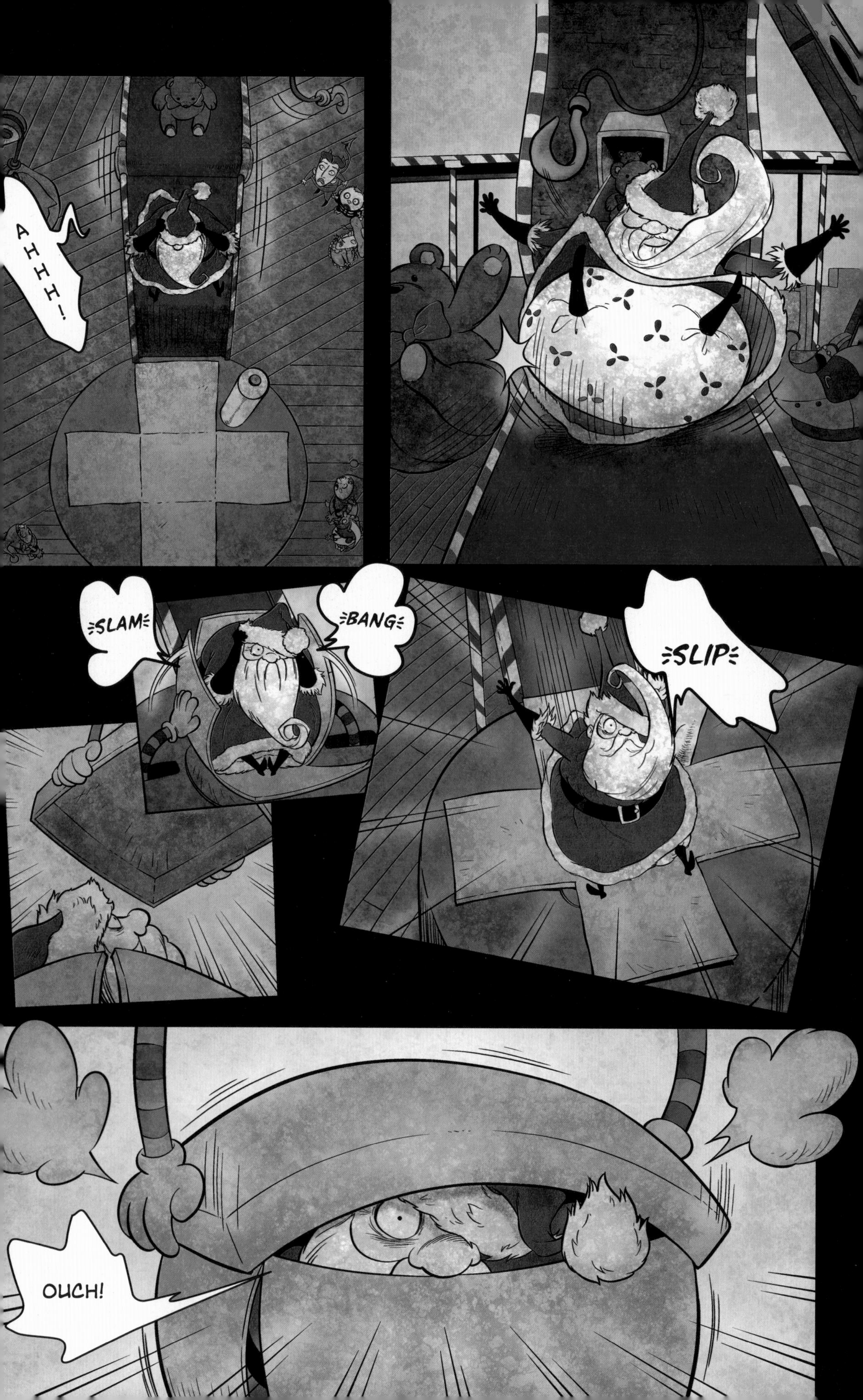
AHHHH!
SLIP
BANG
SLAM
OUCH!

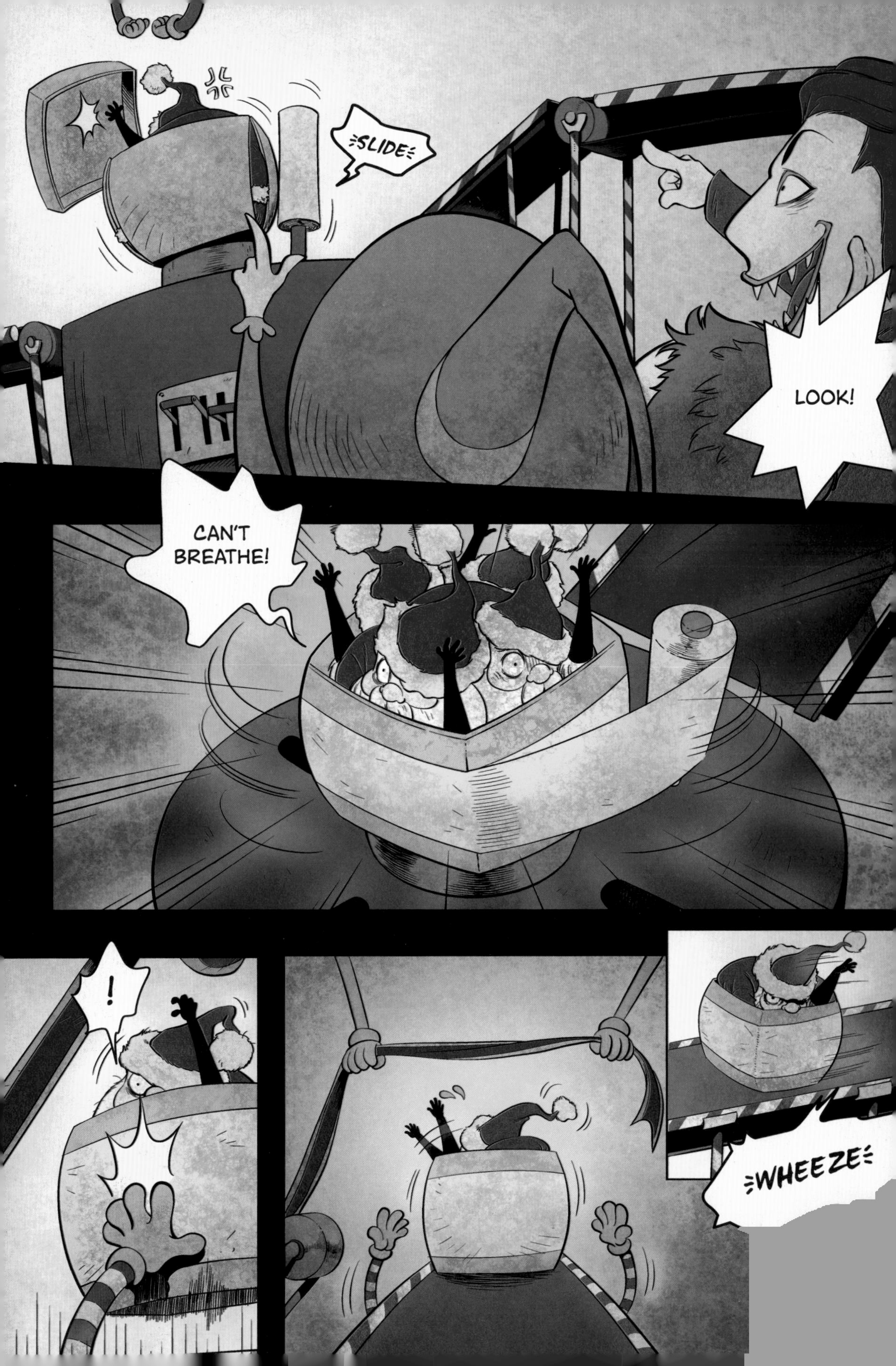
LOOK!
SLIDE
CAN'T BREATHE!
WHEEZE
!

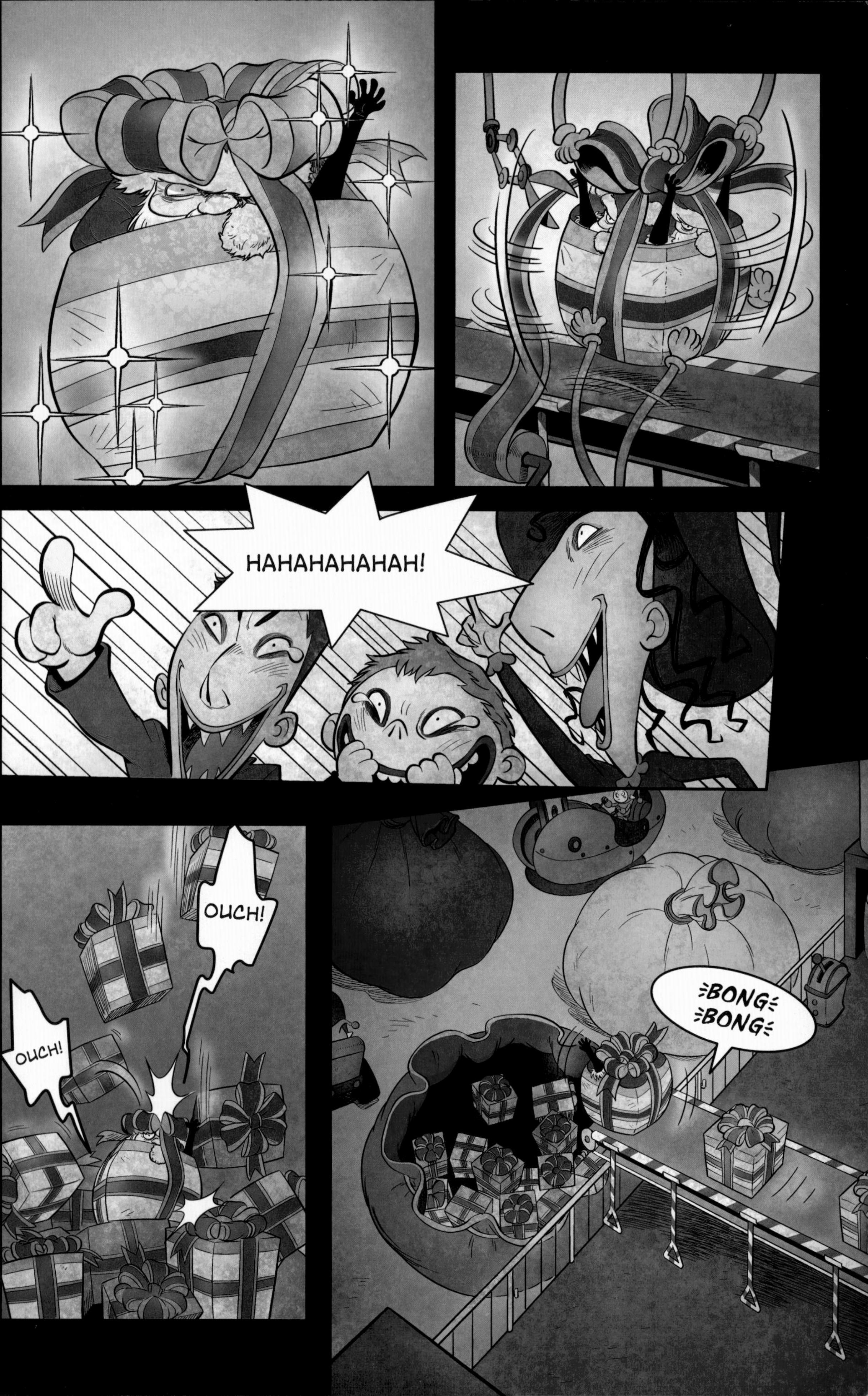
HAHAHAHAHAH!
BONG BONG
OUCH!
OUCH!

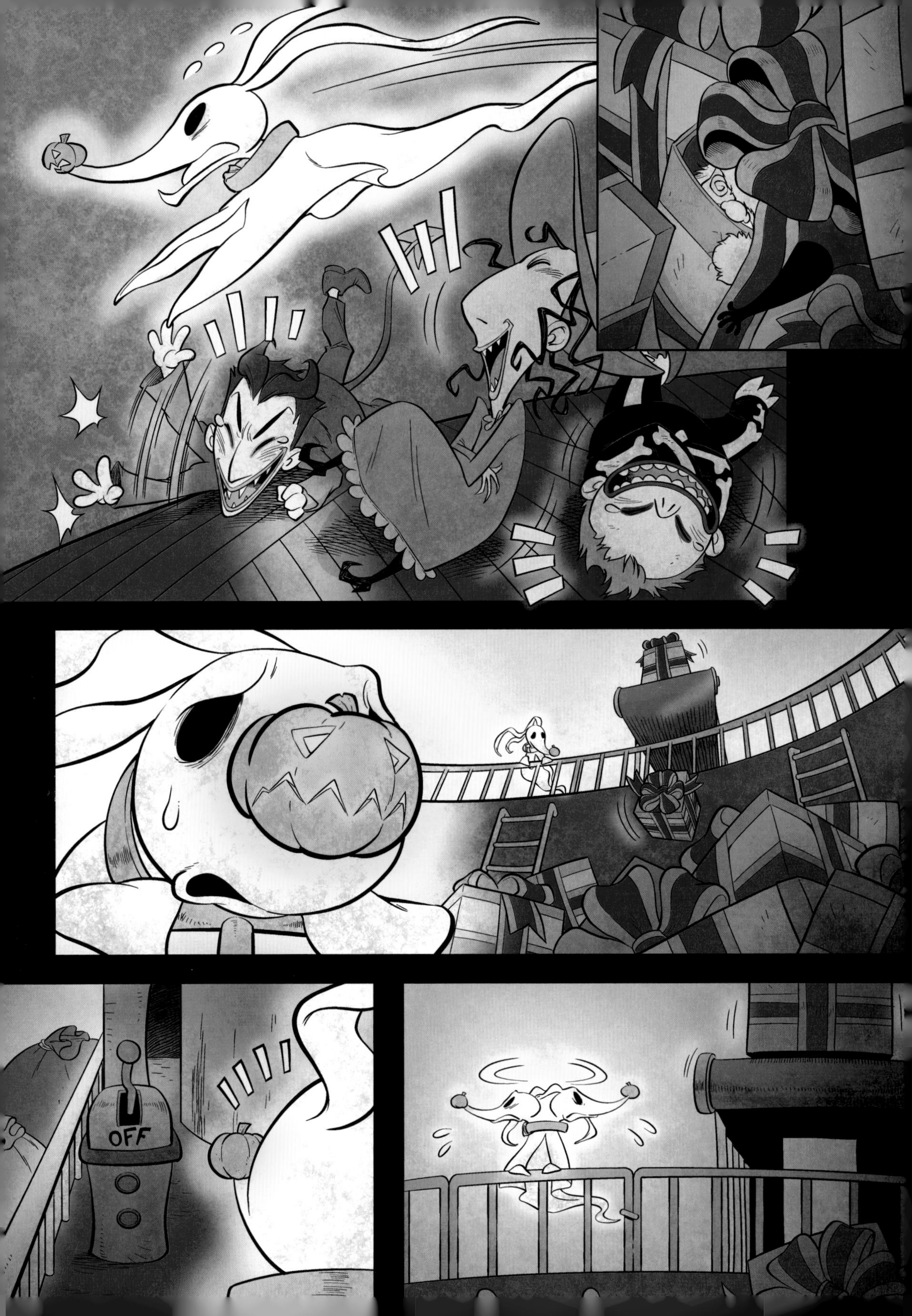
OFF

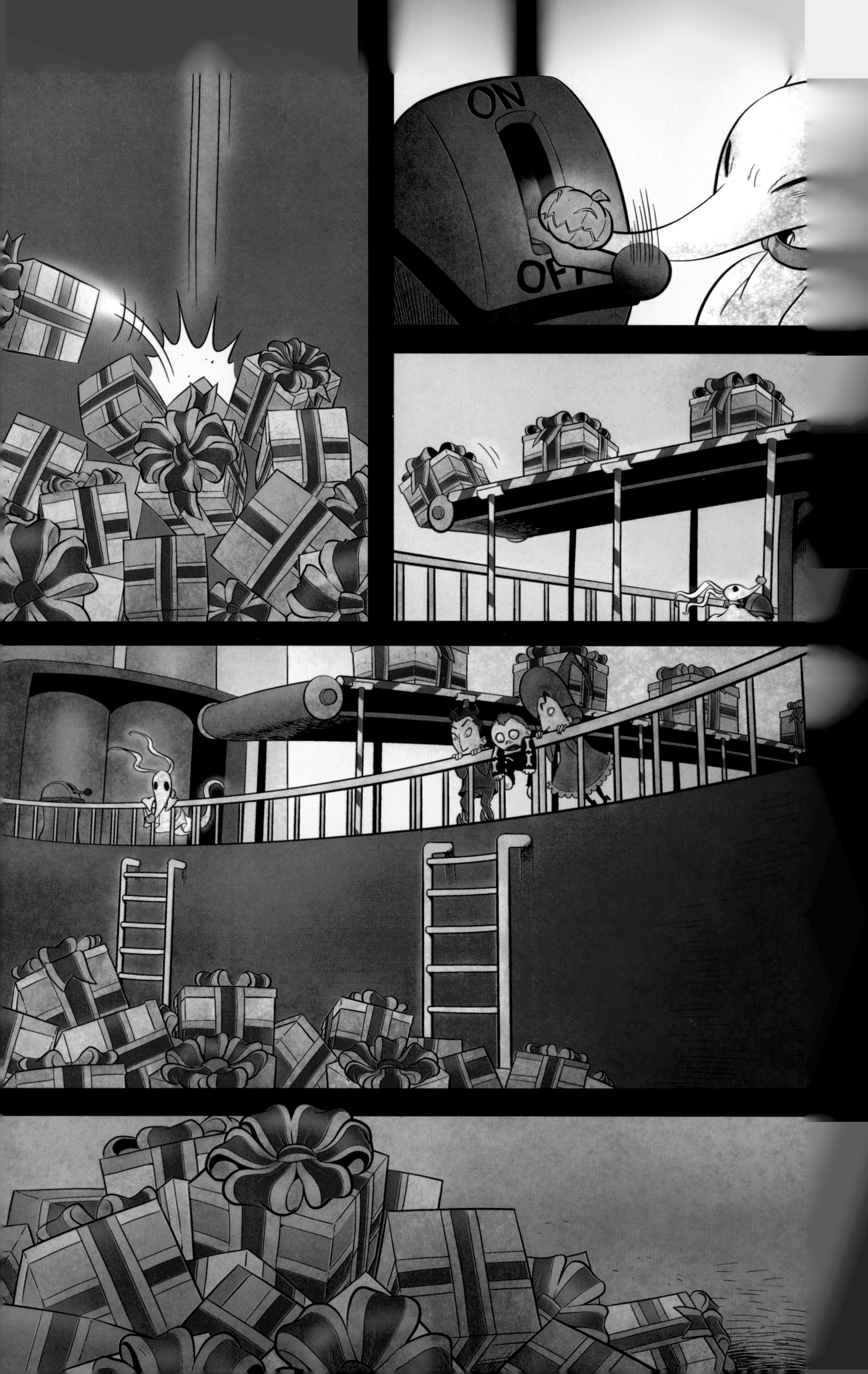
ON

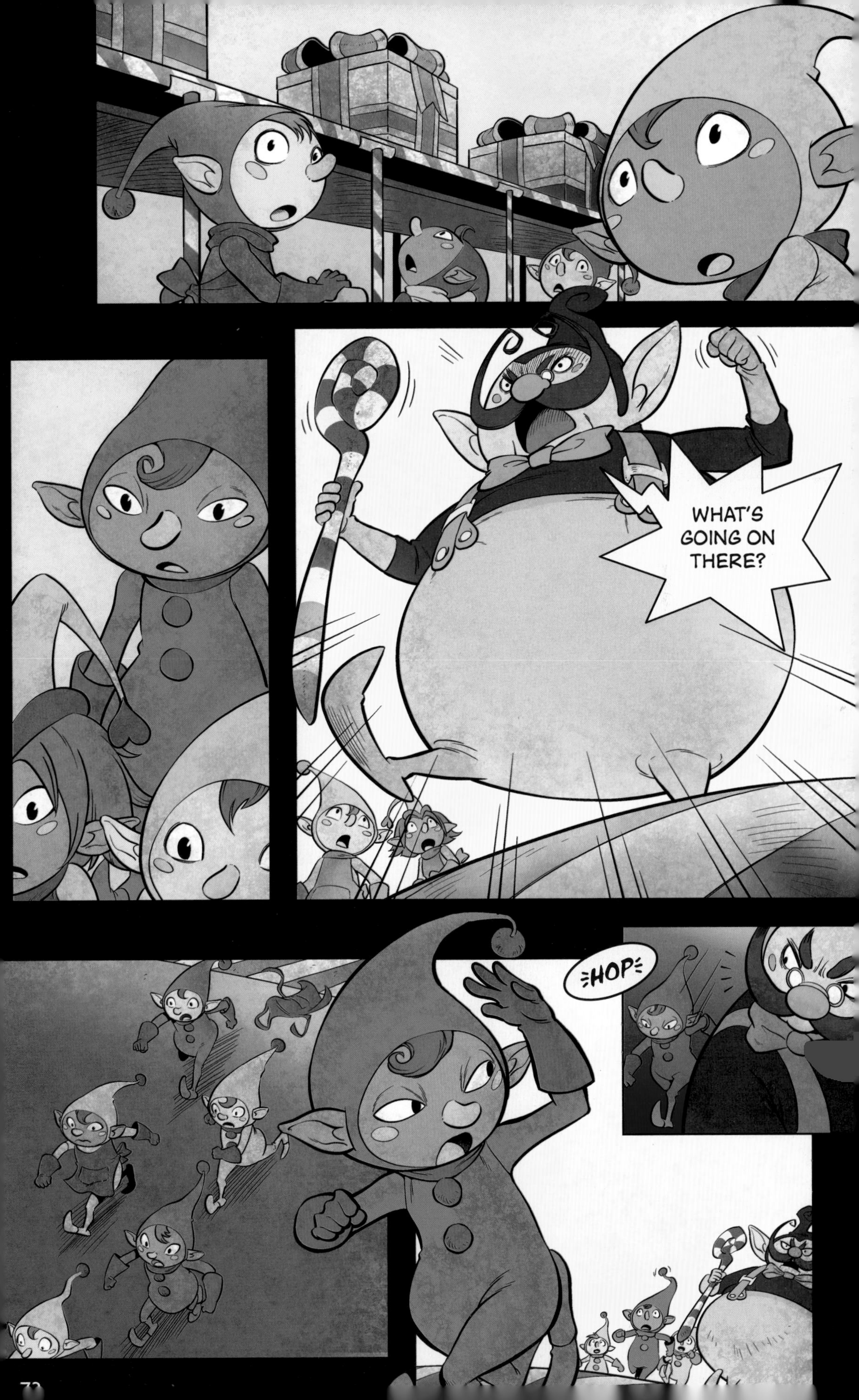
WHAT'S GOING ON THERE?
HOP

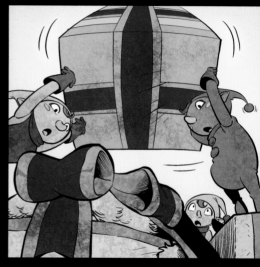

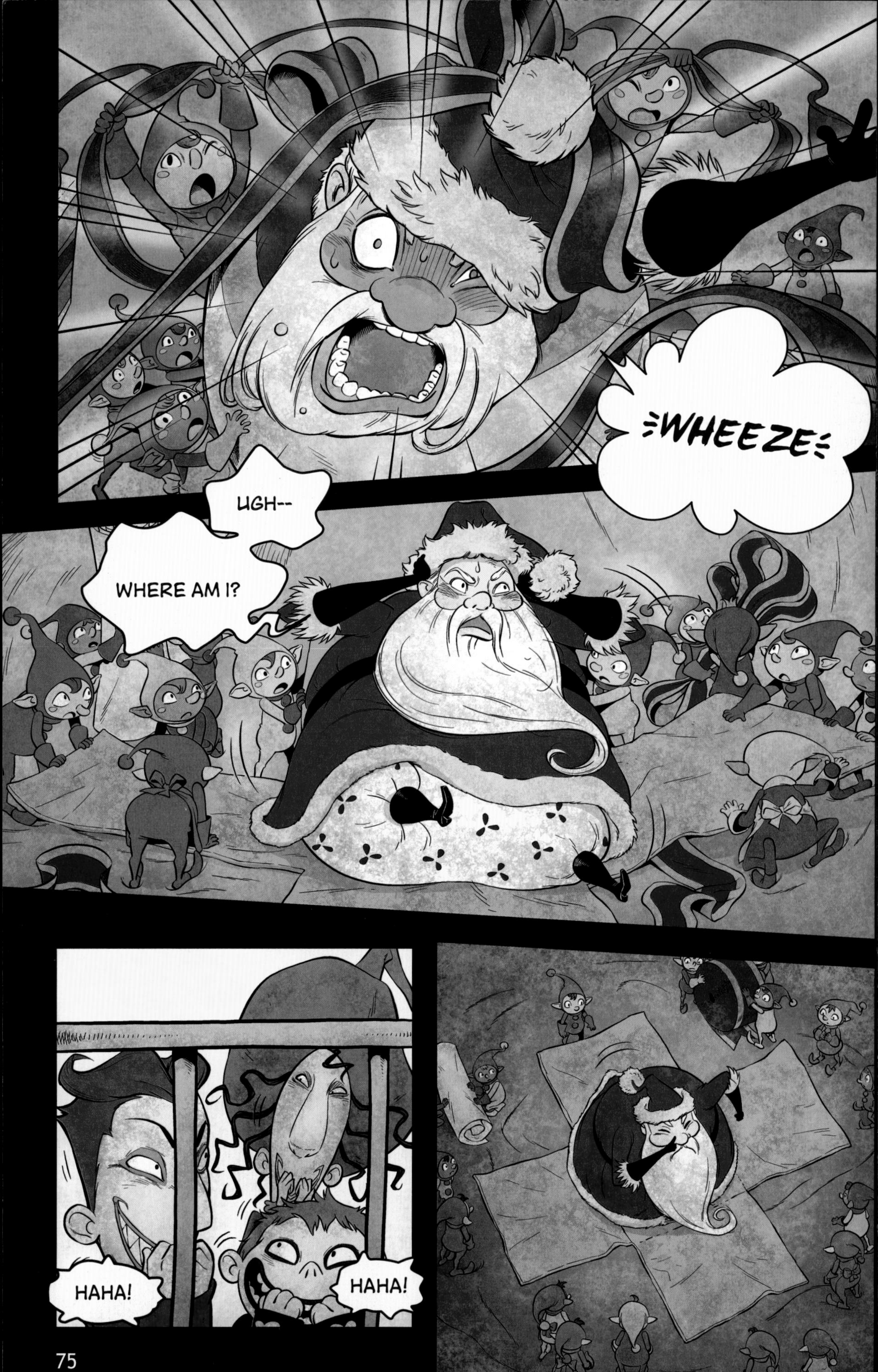
WHEEZE
UGH--
WHERE AM I?
HAHA!
HAHA!

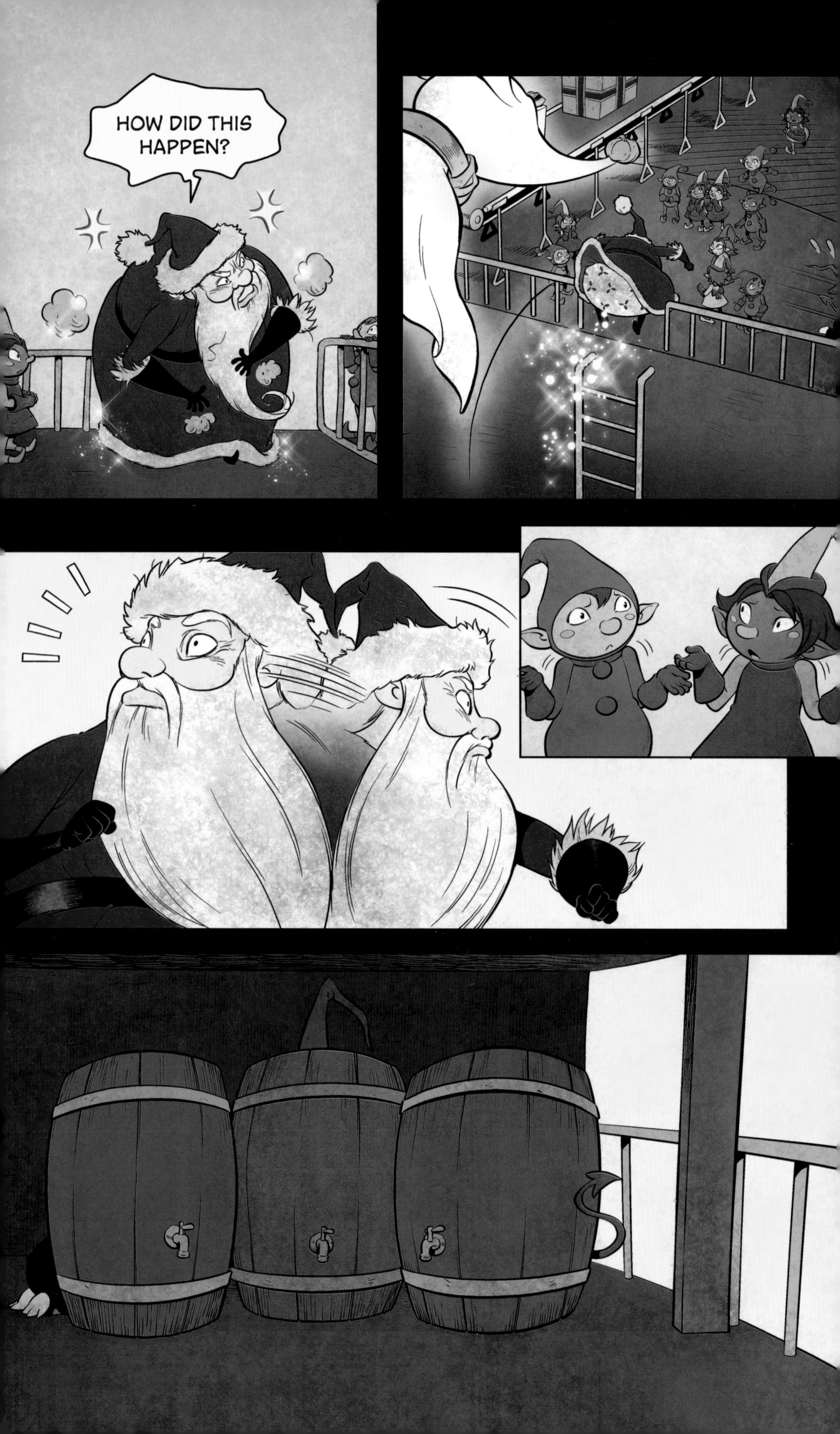
HOW DID THIS HAPPEN?

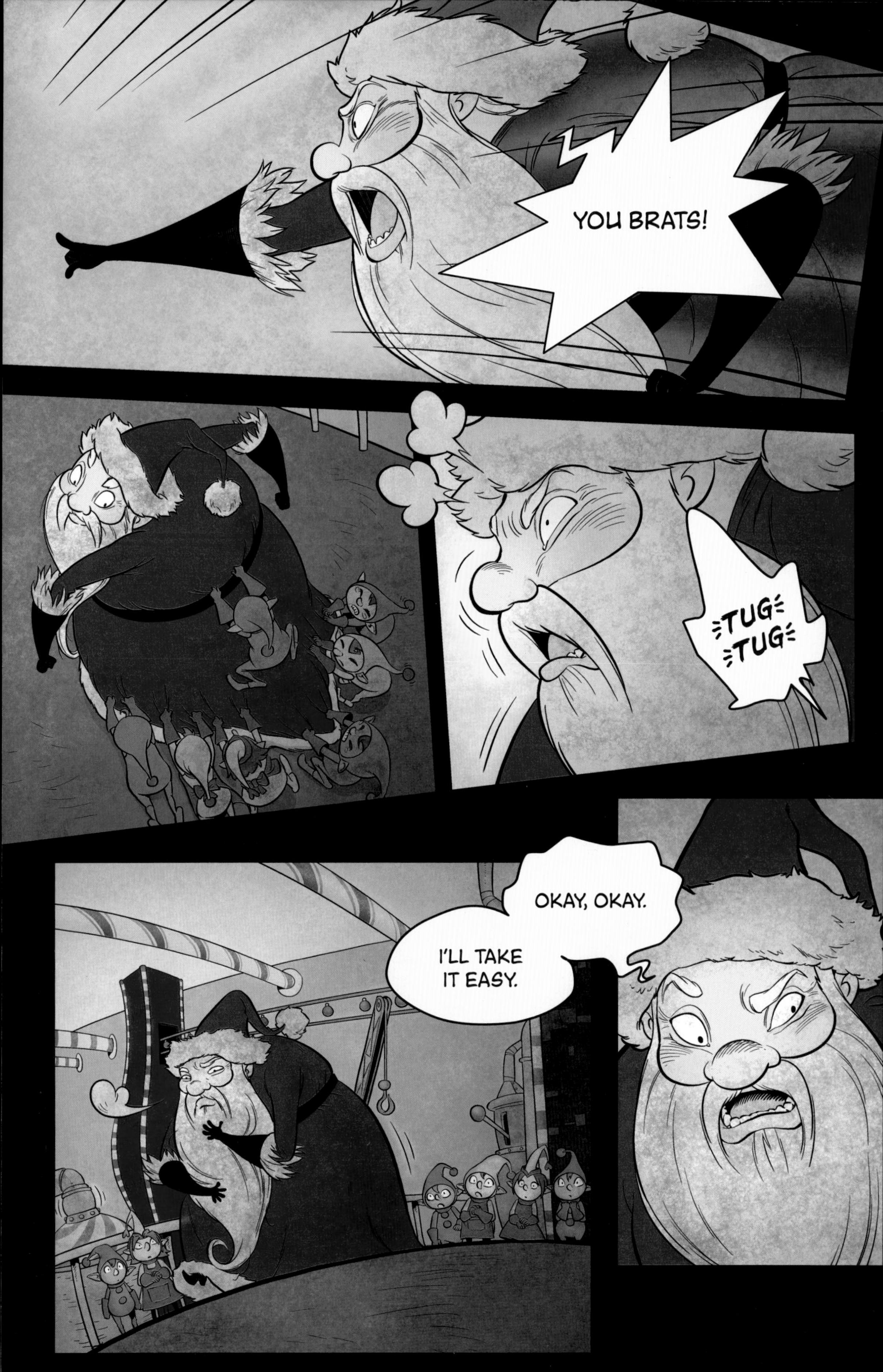
YOU BRATS!
TUG TUG
OKAY, OKAY.
I'LL TAKE IT EASY.

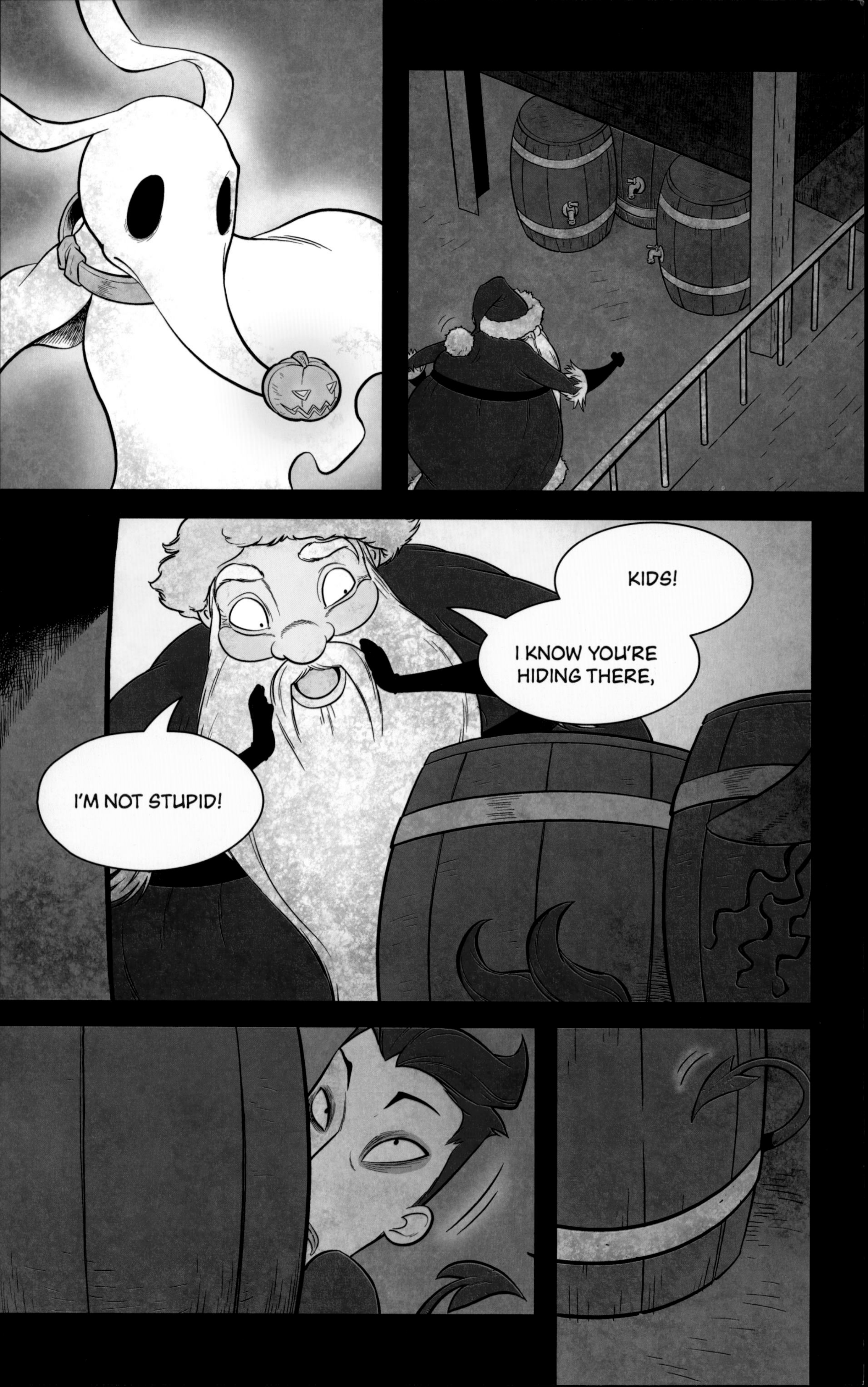
KIDS!
I KNOW YOU'RE HIDING THERE,
I'M NOT STUPID!

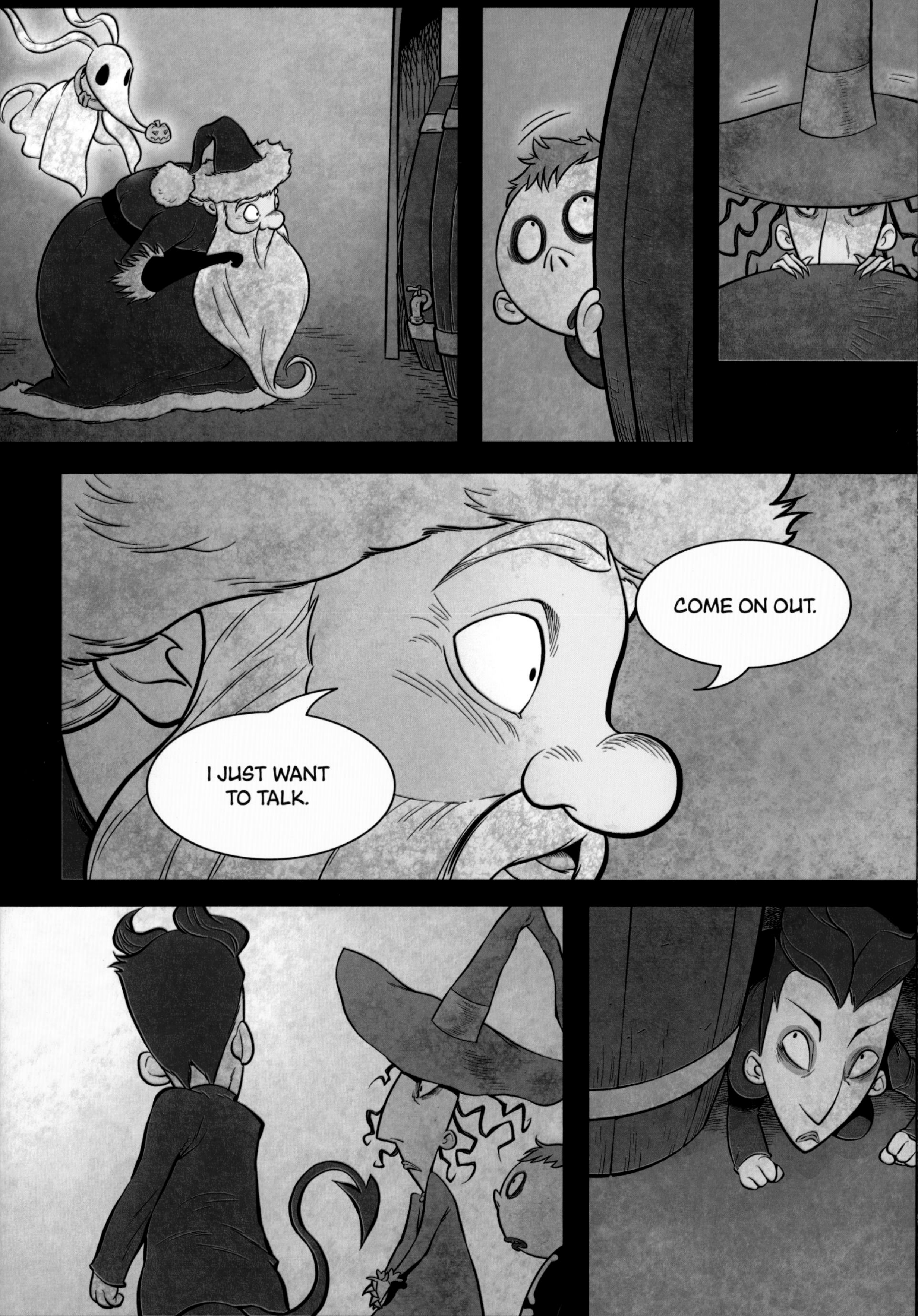
COME ON OUT.
I JUST WANT TO TALK.

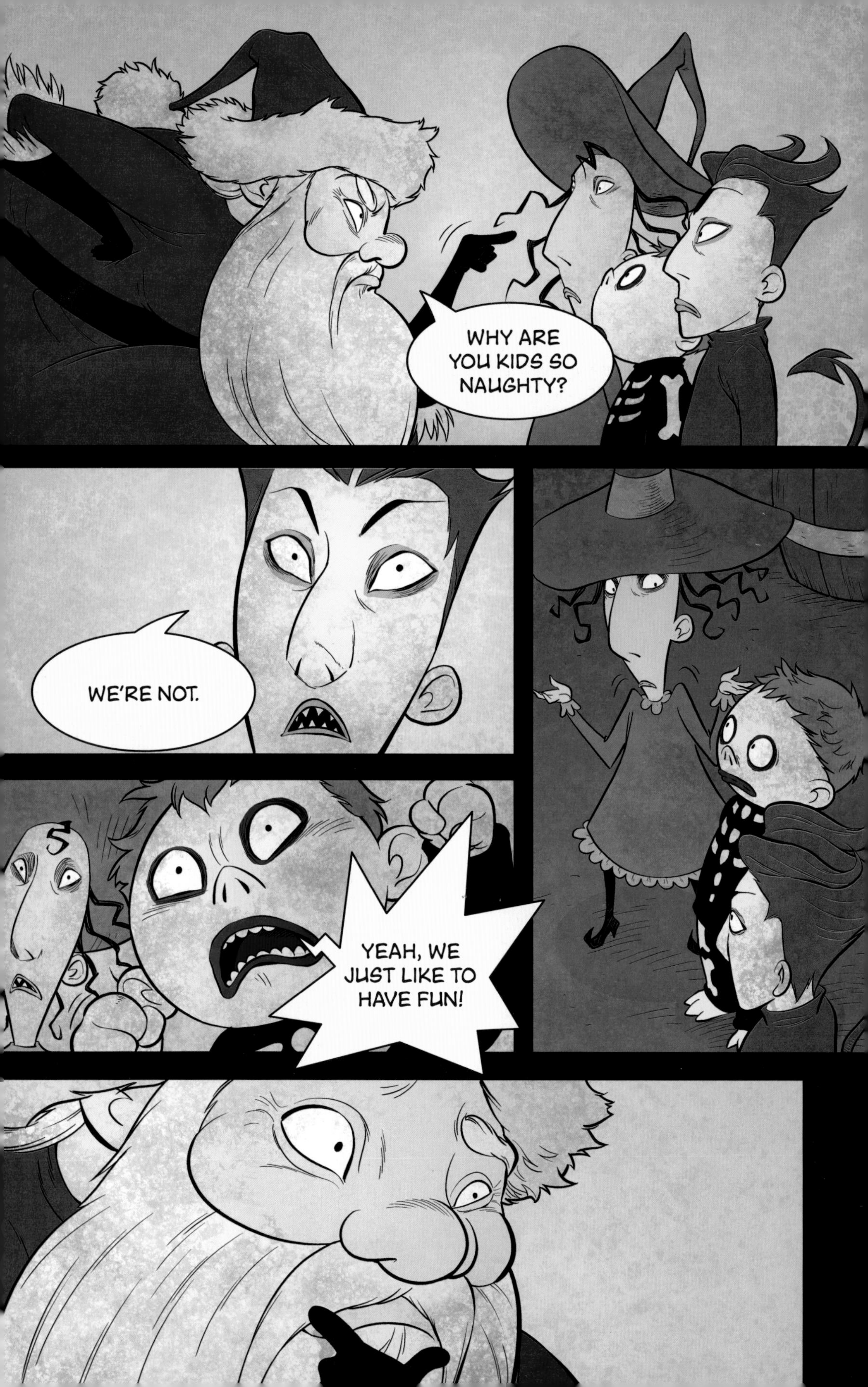
WHY ARE YOU KIDS SO NAUGHTY?
WE'RE NOT.
YEAH, WE JUST LIKE TO HAVE FUN!

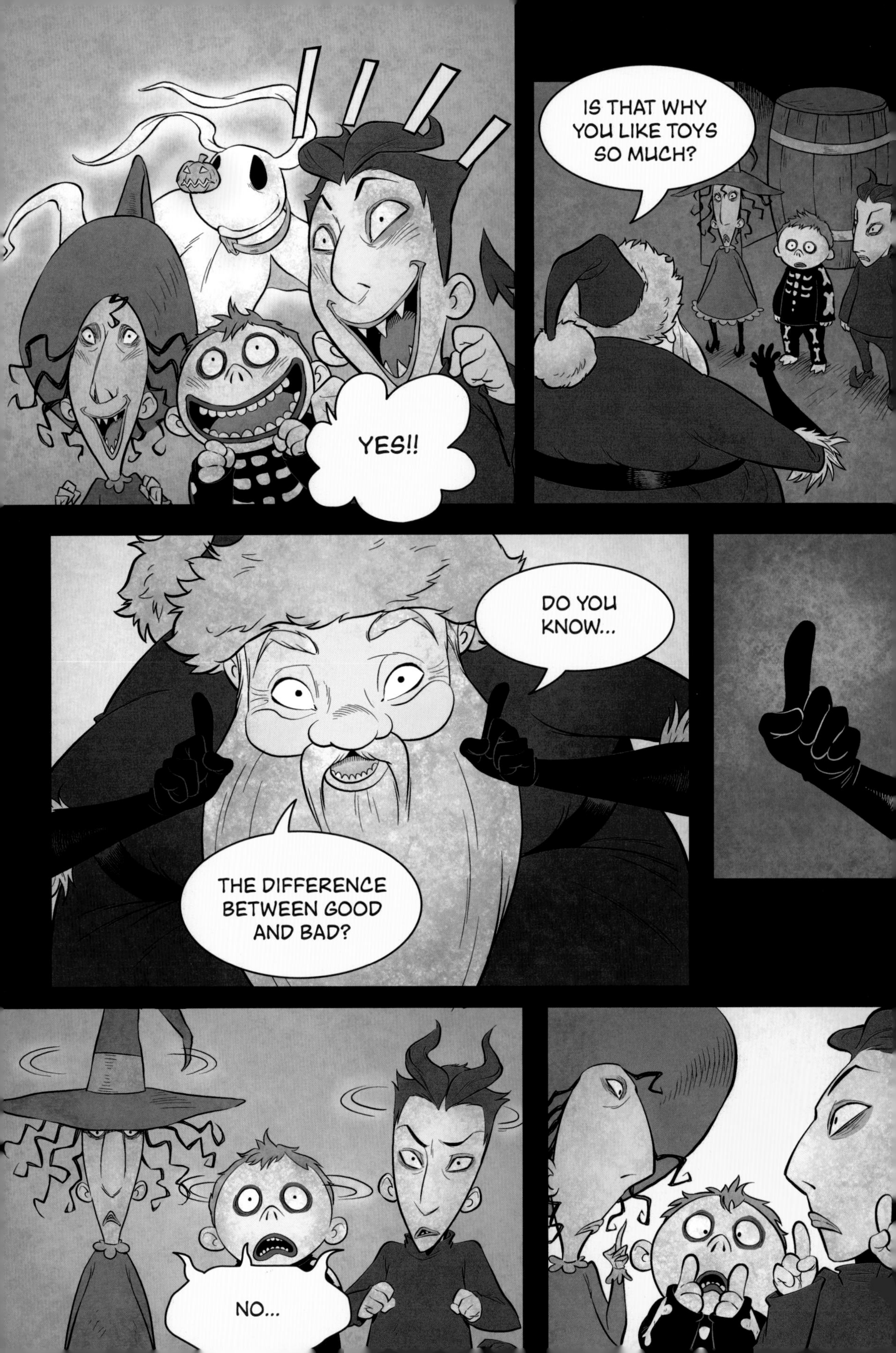
IS THAT WHY YOU LIKE TOYS SO MUCH?
YES!!
DO YOU KNOW...
THE DIFFERENCE BETWEEN GOOD AND BAD?
NO...

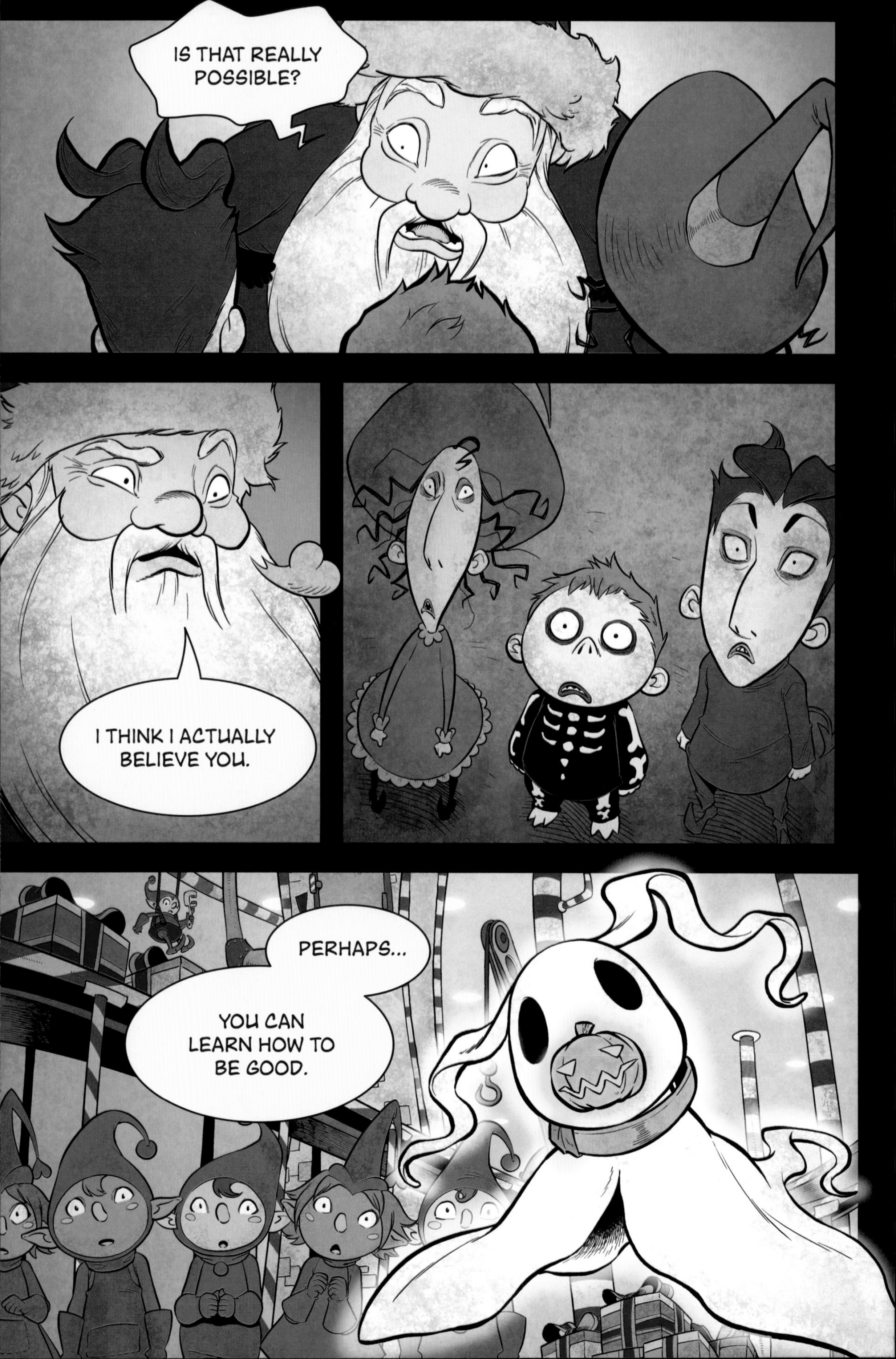
IS THAT REALLY POSSIBLE?
I THINK I ACTUALLY BELIEVE YOU.
PERHAPS...
YOU CAN LEARN HOW TO BE GOOD.

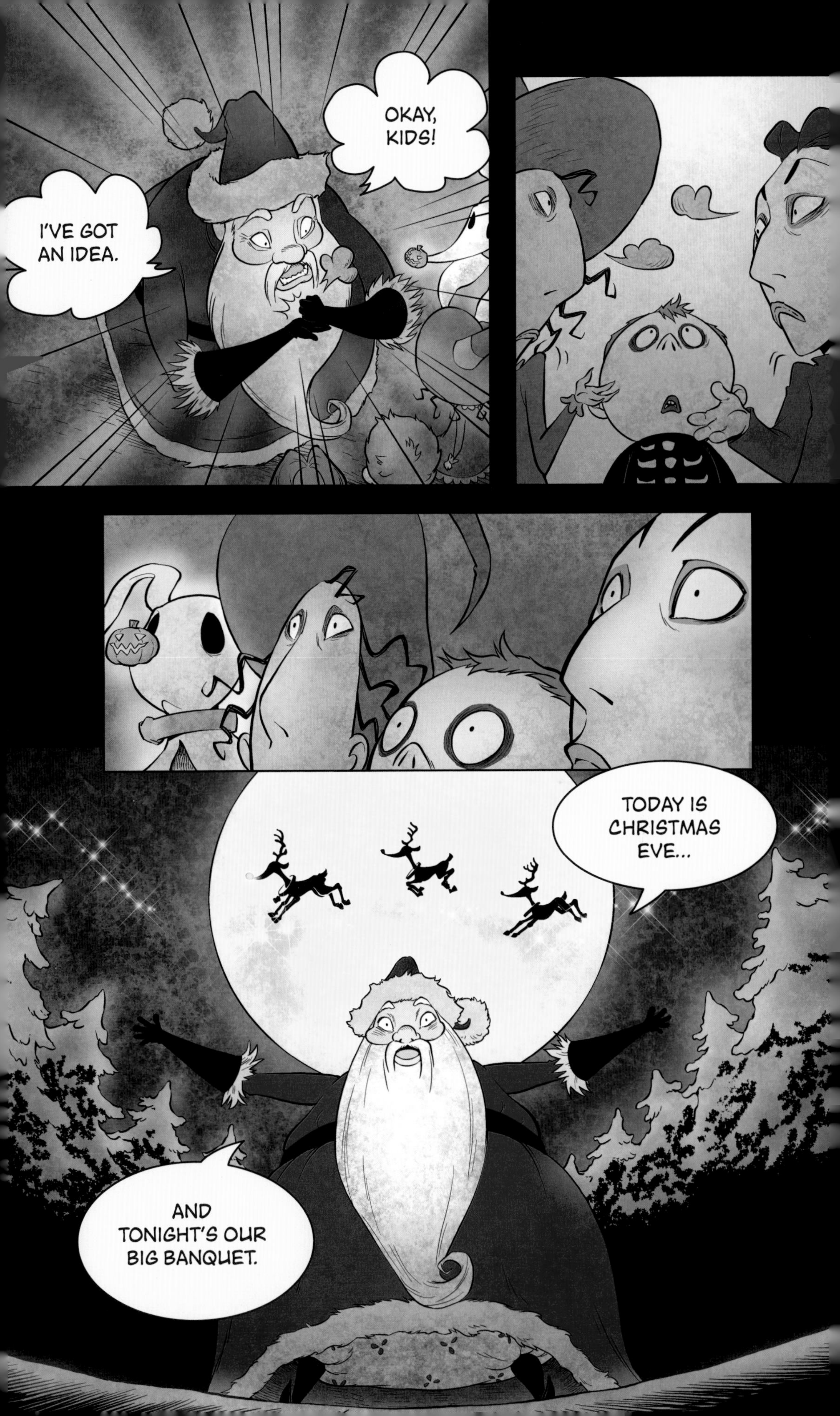
OKAY, KIDS!
I'VE GOT AN IDEA.
TODAY IS CHRISTMAS EVE...
AND TONIGHT'S OUR BIG BANQUET.

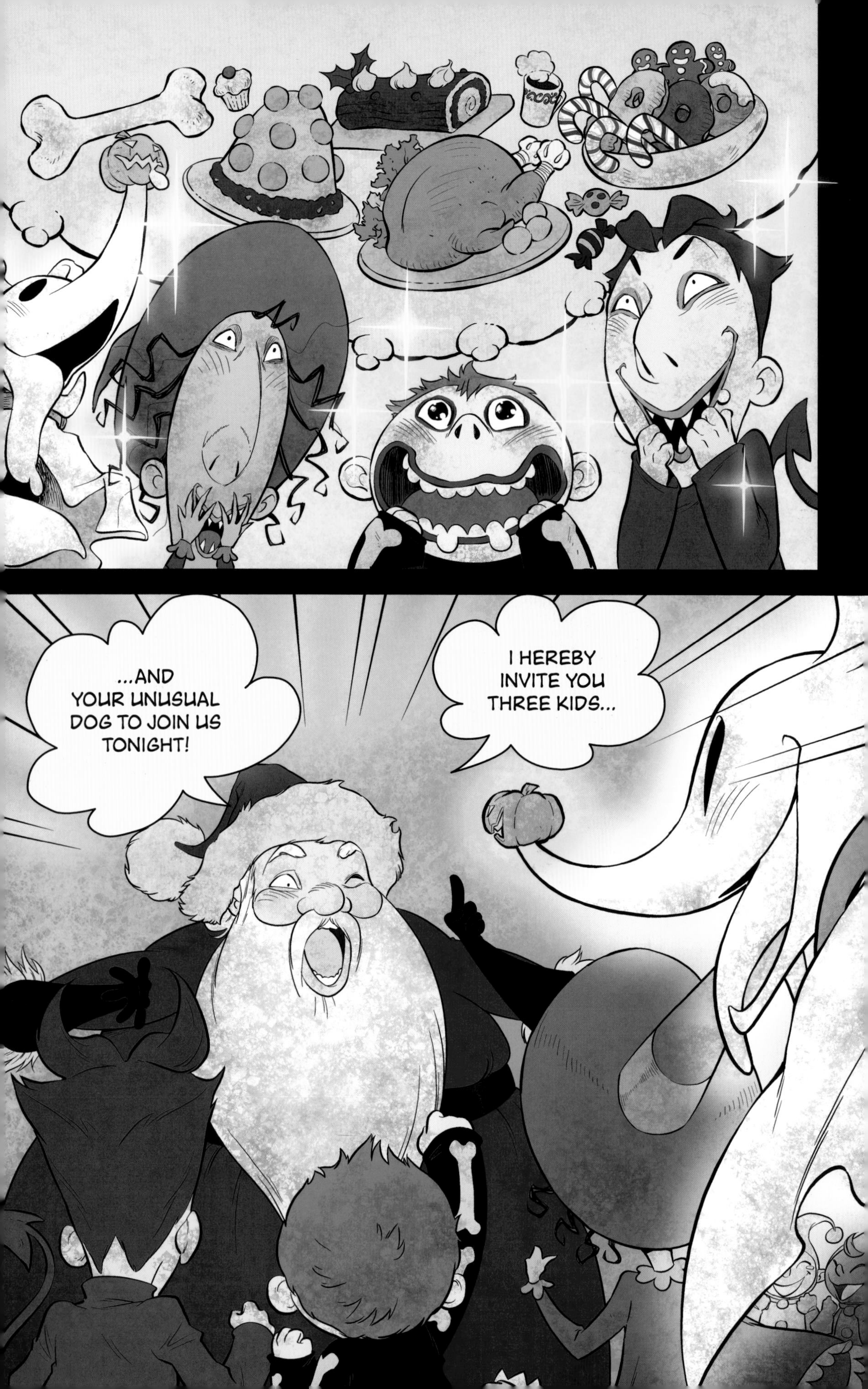
I HEREBY INVITE YOU THREE KIDS...
...AND YOUR UNUSUAL DOG TO JOIN US TONIGHT!

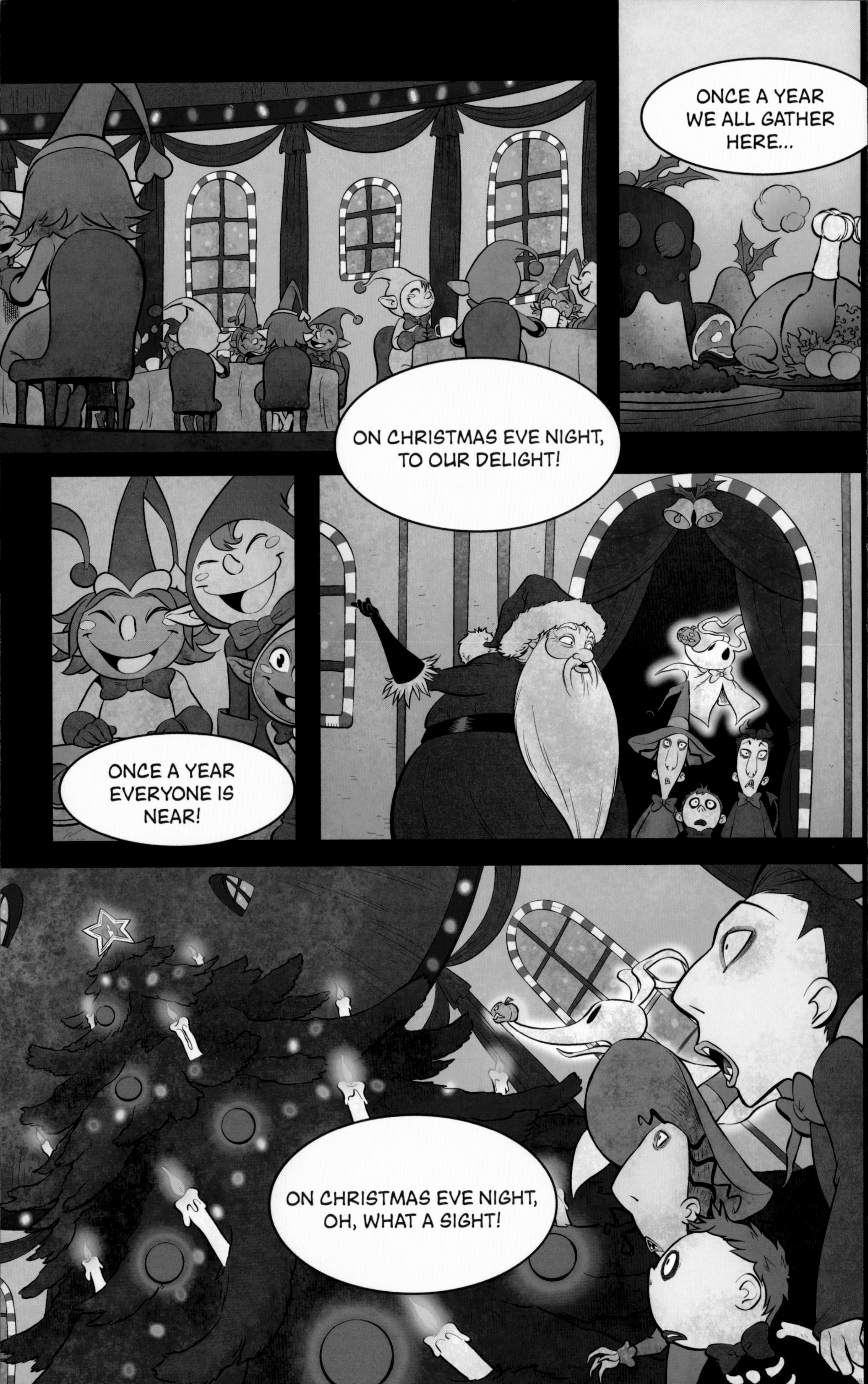
ONCE A YEAR WE ALL GATHER HERE...
ON CHRISTMAS EVE NIGHT, TO OUR DELIGHT!
ONCE A YEAR EVERYONE IS NEAR!
ON CHRISTMAS EVE NIGHT, OH, WHAT A SIGHT!

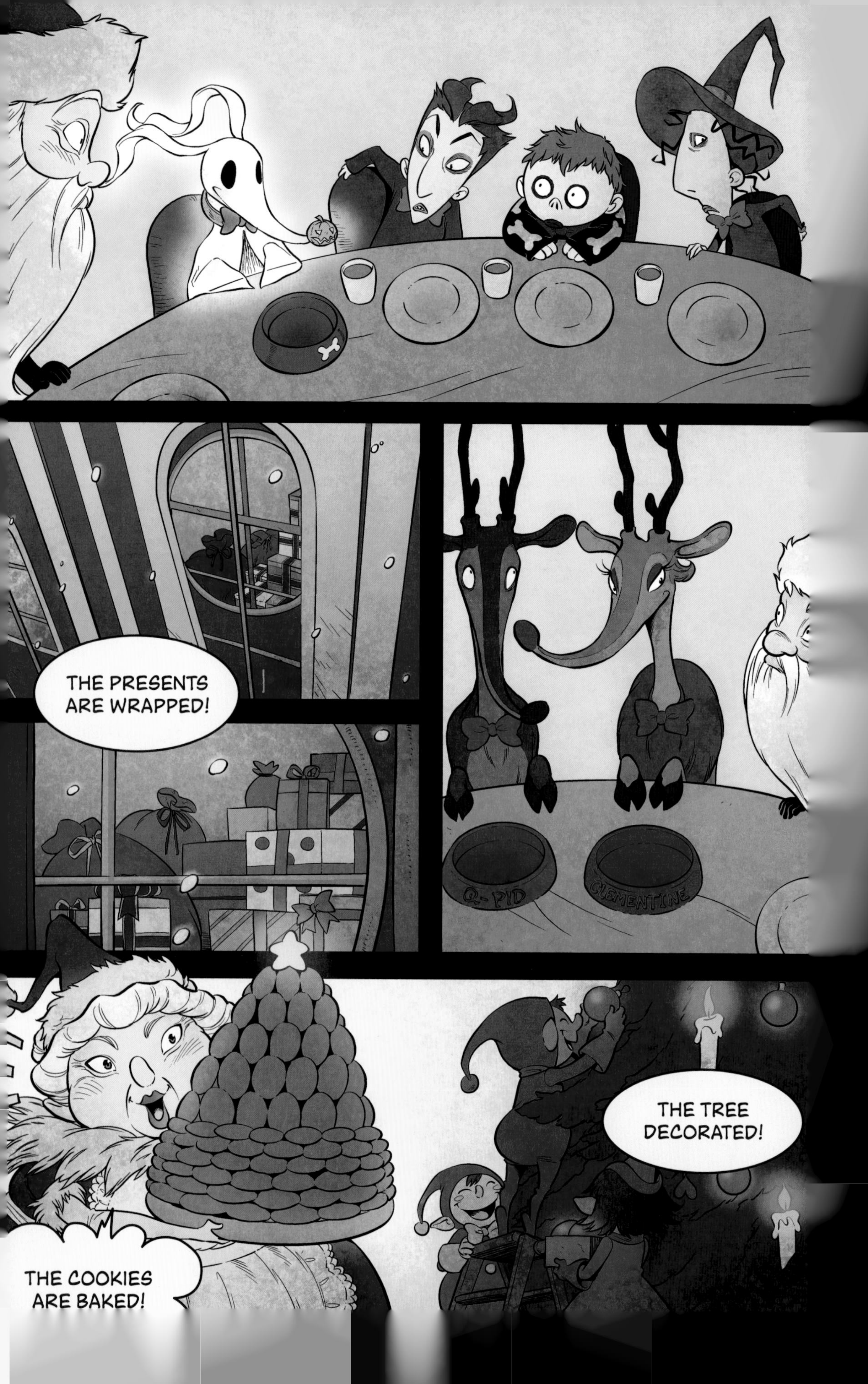
Q-PID
CLEMENTINE
THE PRESENTS ARE WRAPPED!
THE TREE DECORATED!
THE COOKIES ARE BAKED!

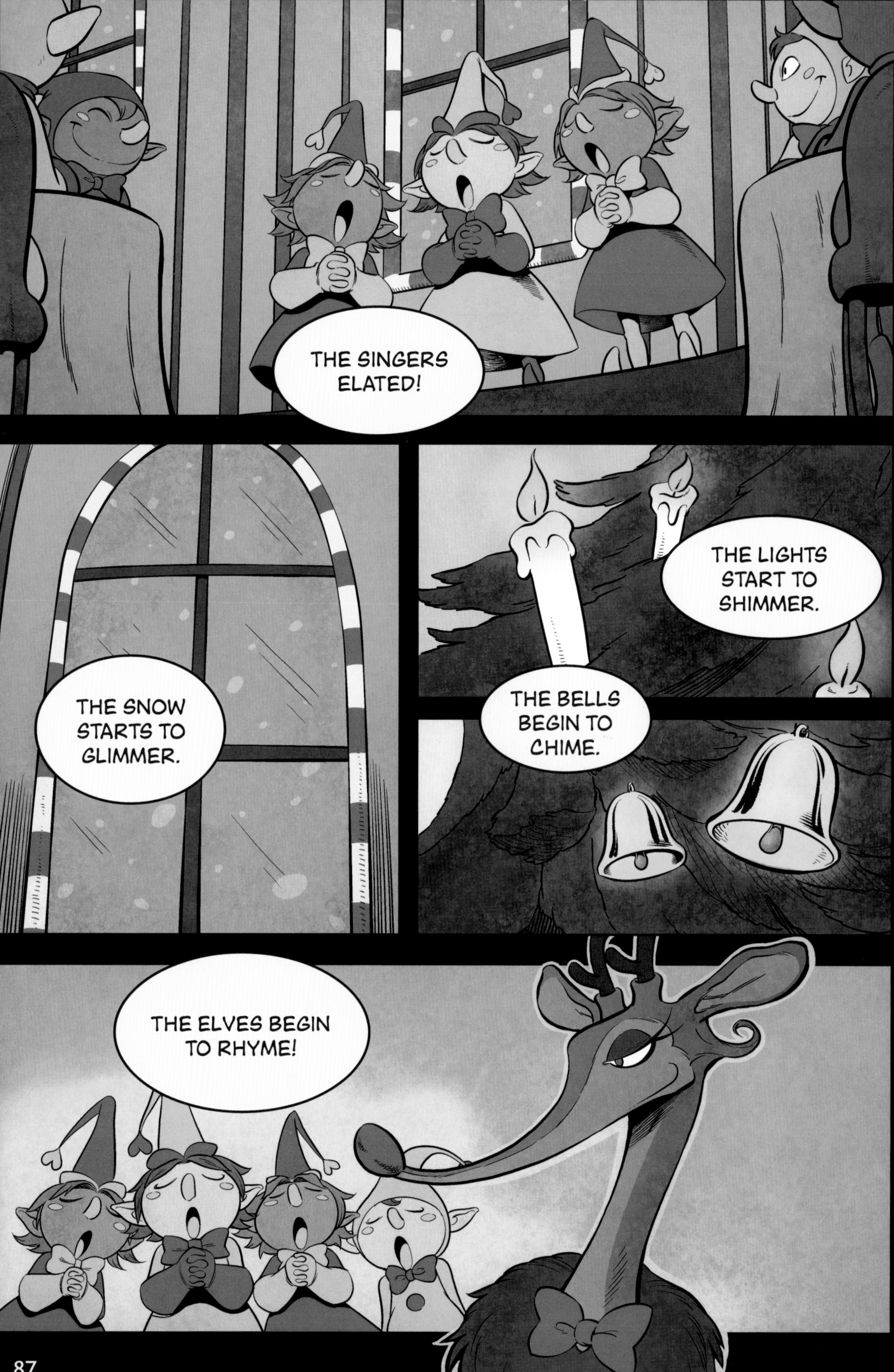
THE SINGERS ELATED!
THE LIGHTS START TO SHIMMER.
THE BELLS BEGIN TO CHIME.
THE SNOW STARTS TO GLIMMER.
THE ELVES BEGIN TO RHYME!

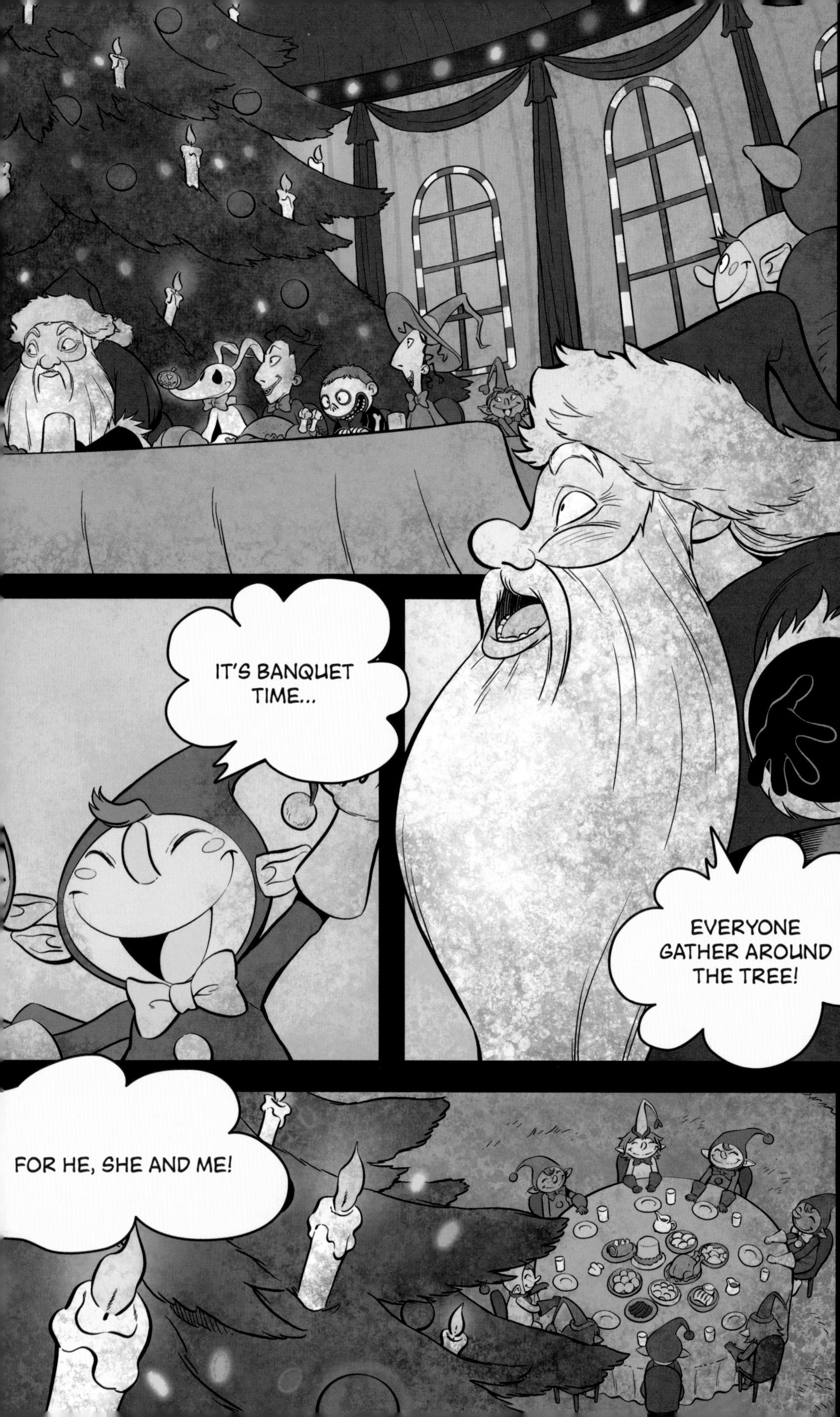
EVERYONE GATHER AROUND THE TREE!
IT'S BANQUET TIME...
FOR HE, SHE AND ME!

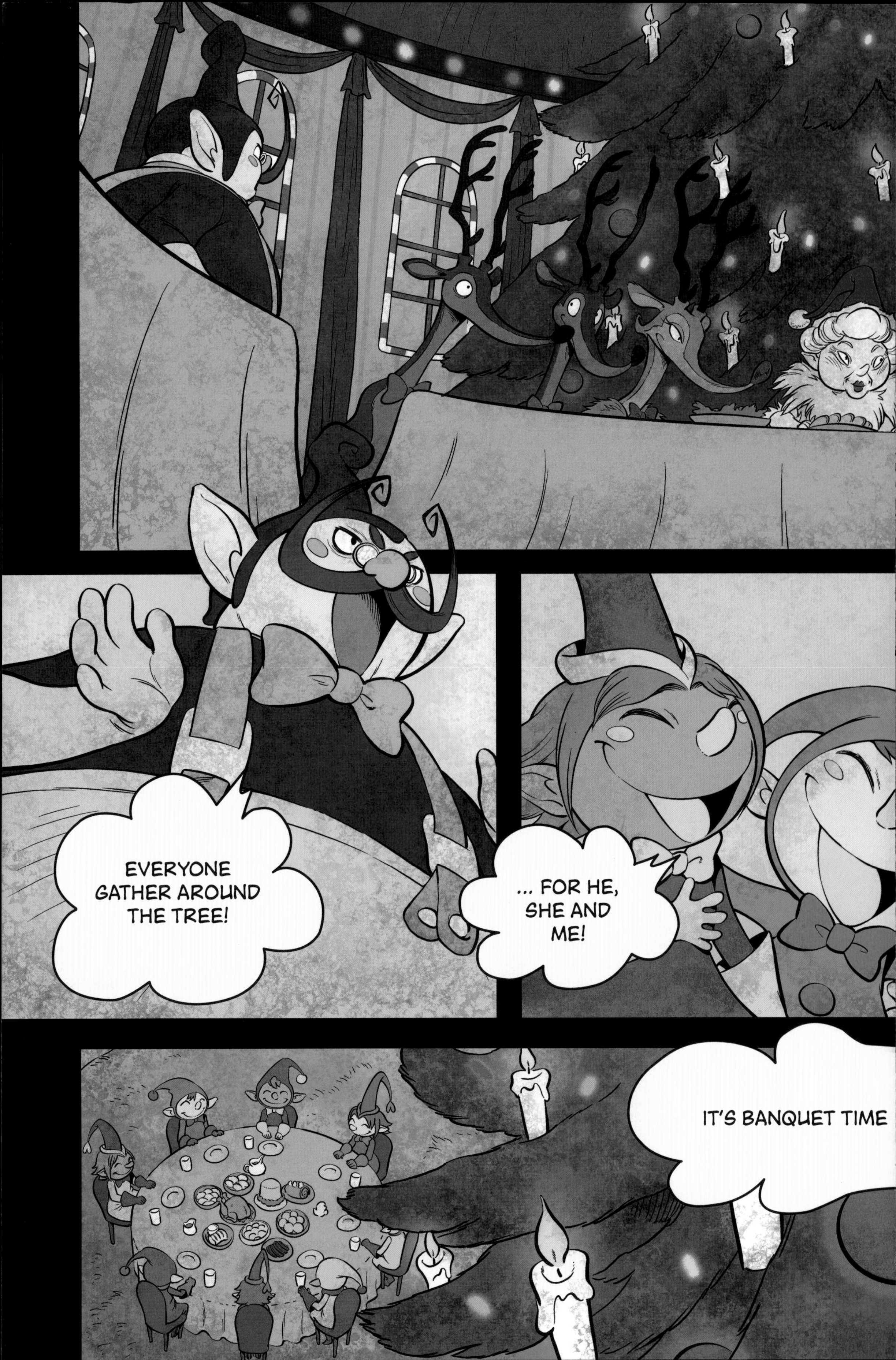
... FOR HE, SHE AND ME!
EVERYONE GATHER AROUND THE TREE!
IT'S BANQUET TIME

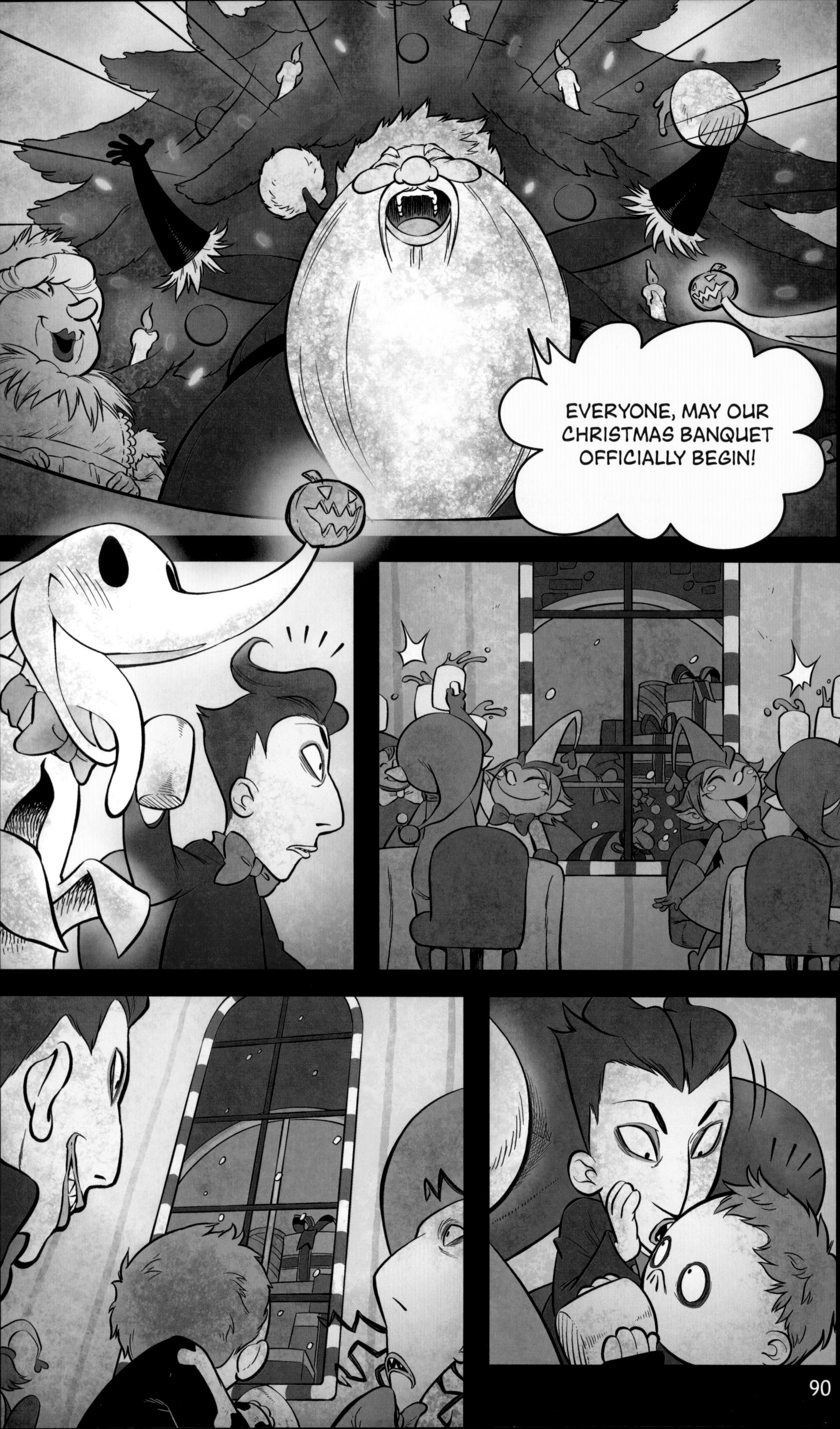
EVERYONE, MAY OUR CHRISTMAS BANQUET OFFICIALLY BEGIN!

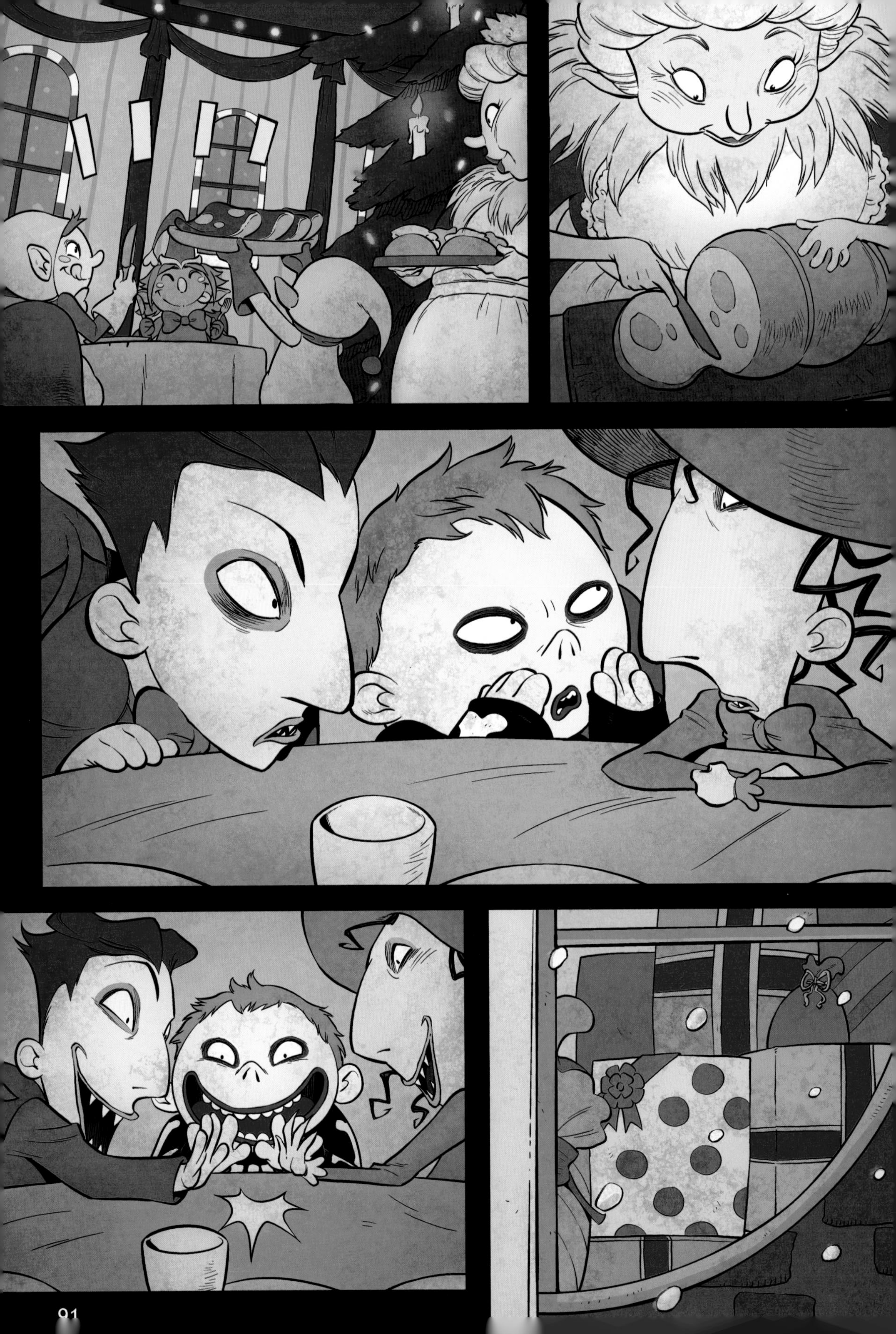

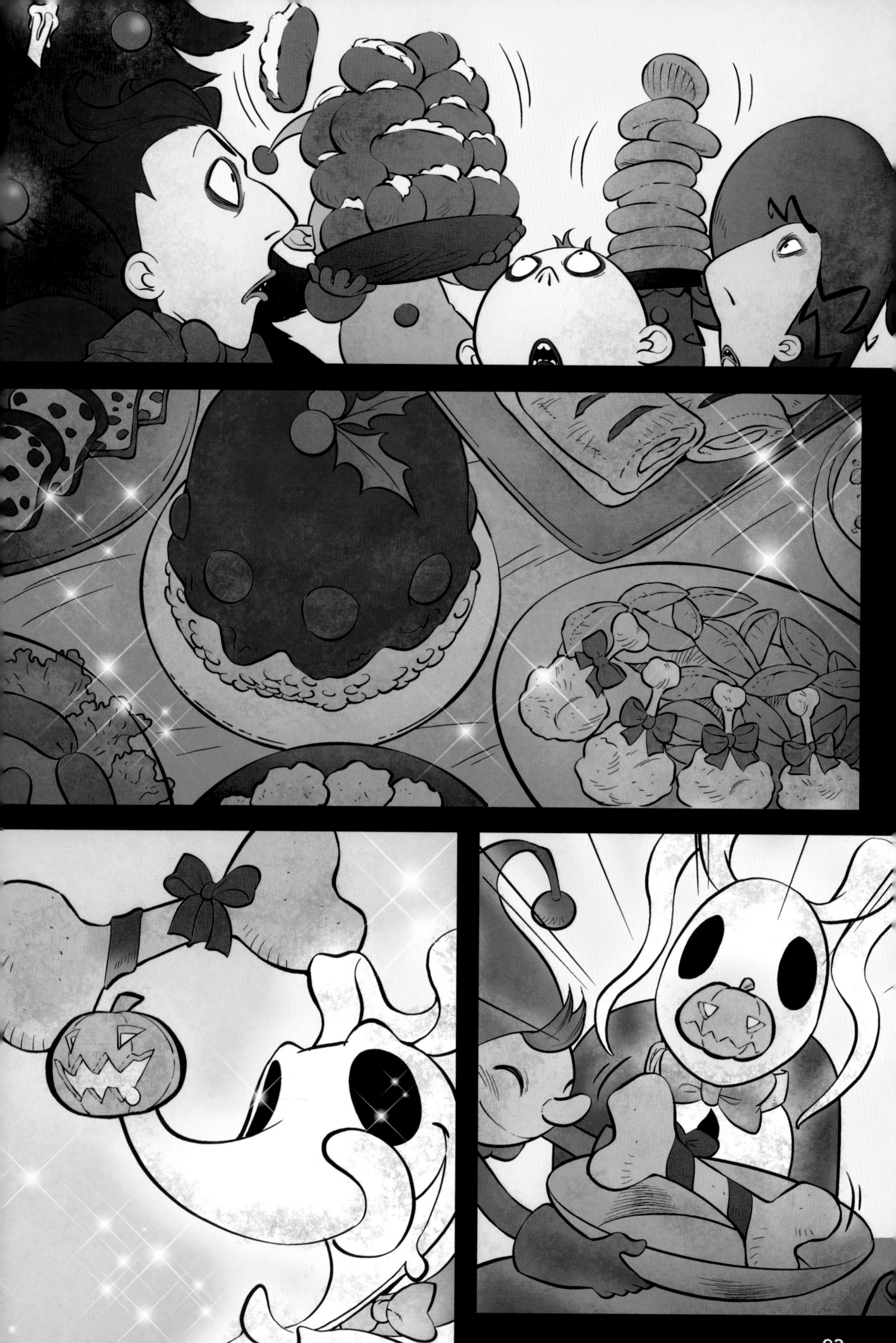

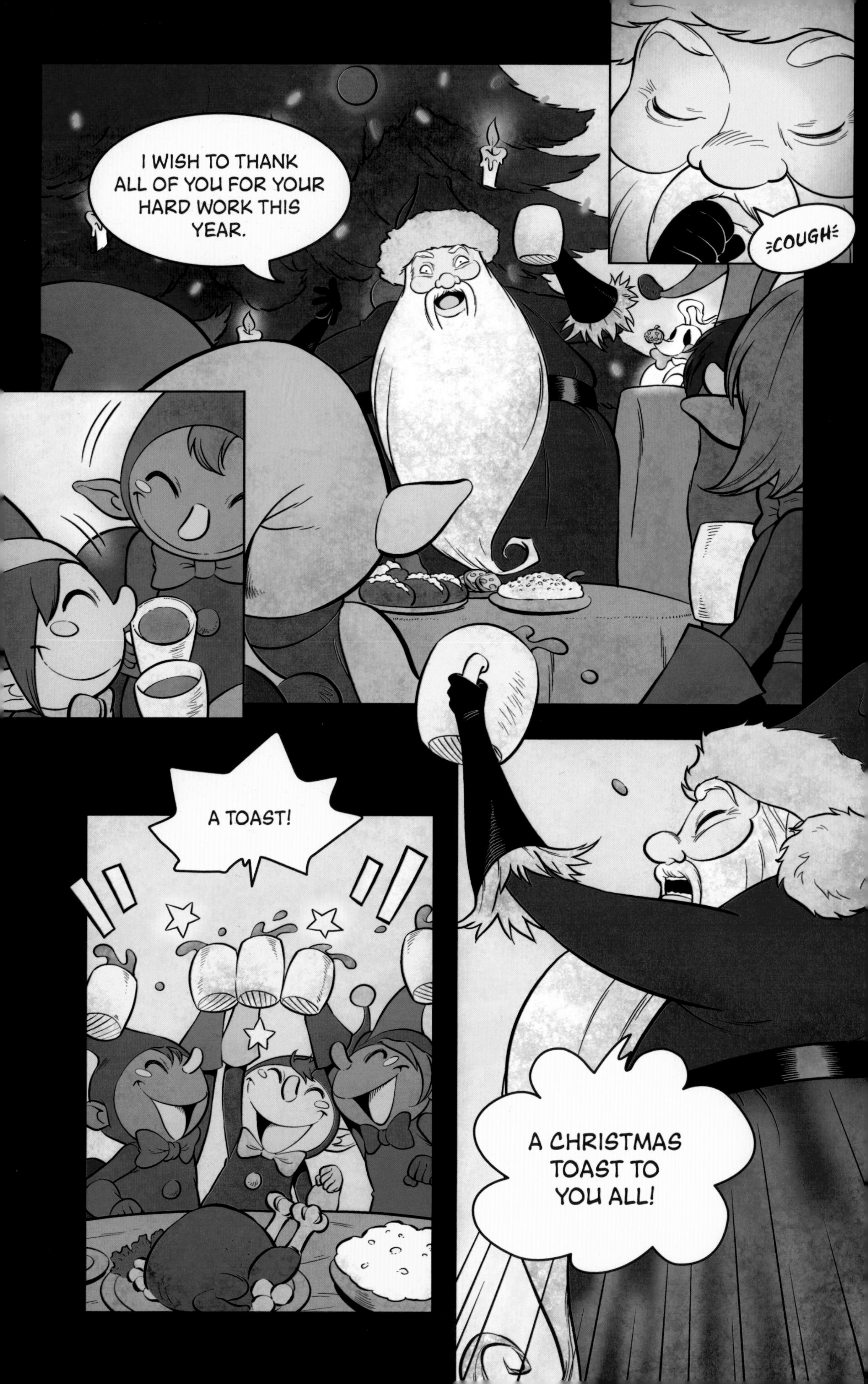
COUGH
I WISH TO THANK ALL OF YOU FOR YOUR HARD WORK THIS YEAR.
A CHRISTMAS TOAST TO YOU ALL!
A TOAST!

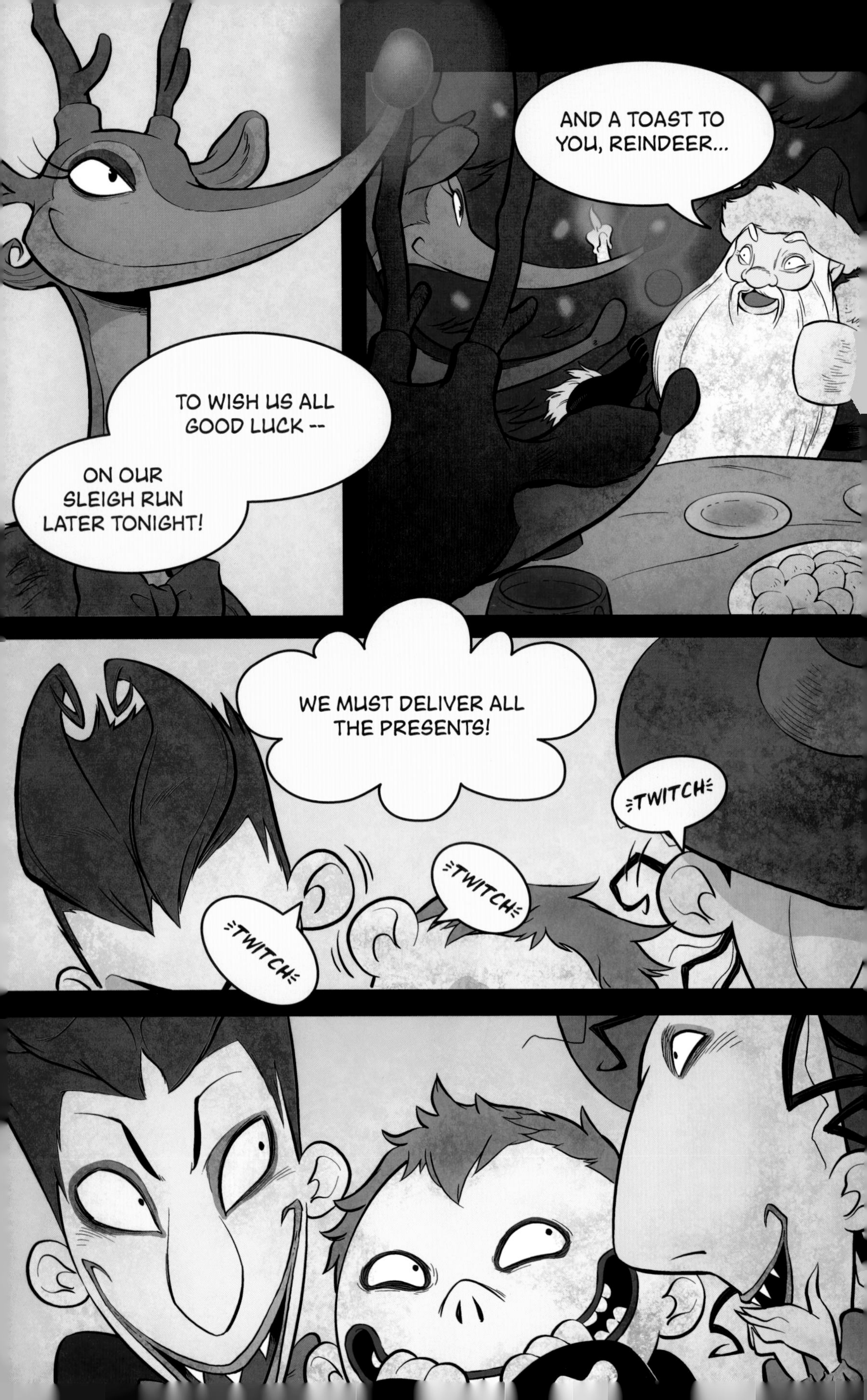
AND A TOAST TO YOU, REINDEER...
TO WISH US ALL GOOD LUCK --
ON OUR SLEIGH RUN LATER TONIGHT!
WE MUST DELIVER ALL THE PRESENTS!
TWITCH
TWITCH
TWITCH

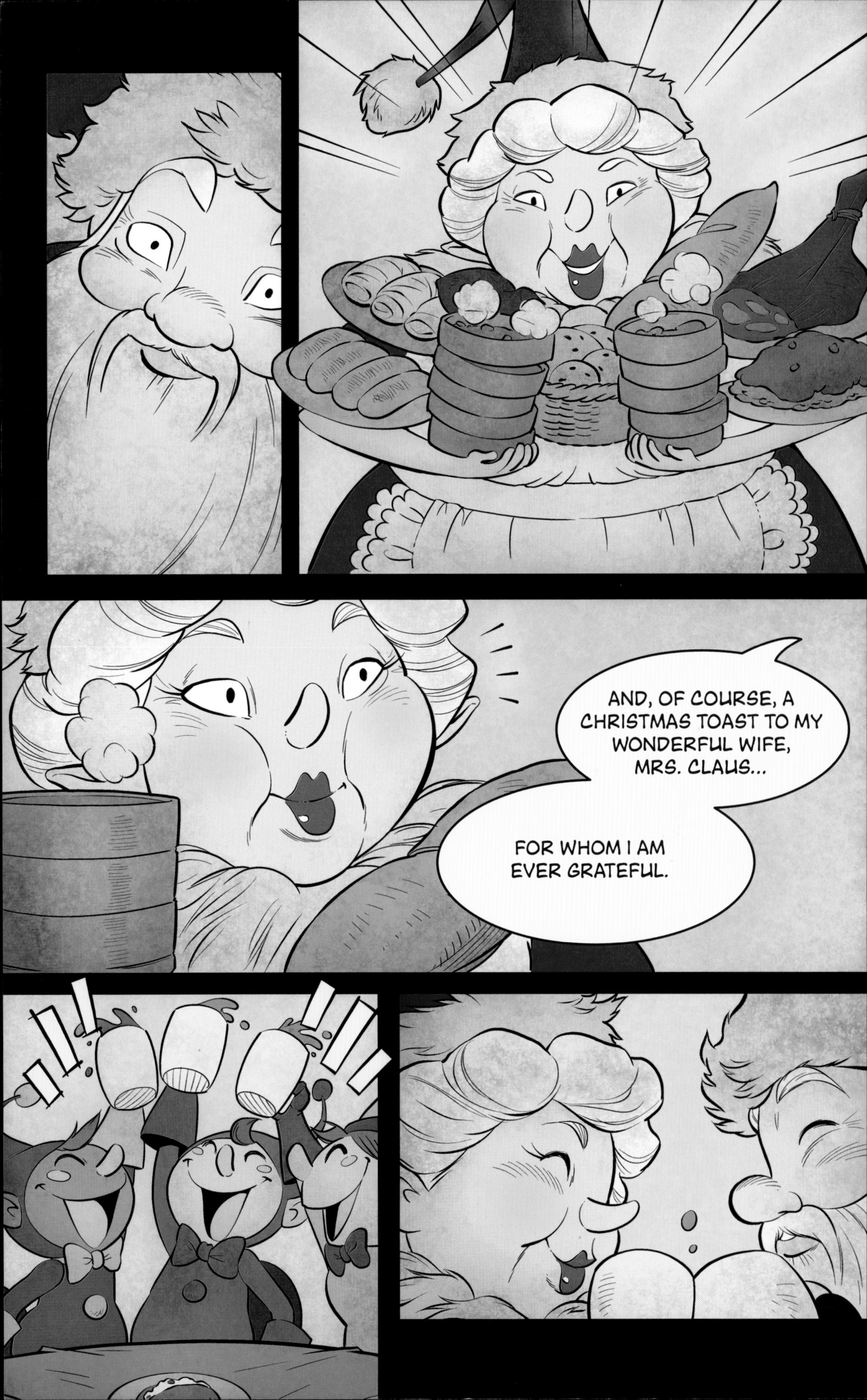
AND, OF COURSE, A CHRISTMAS TOAST TO MY WONDERFUL WIFE, MRS. CLAUS...
FOR WHOM I AM EVER GRATEFUL.

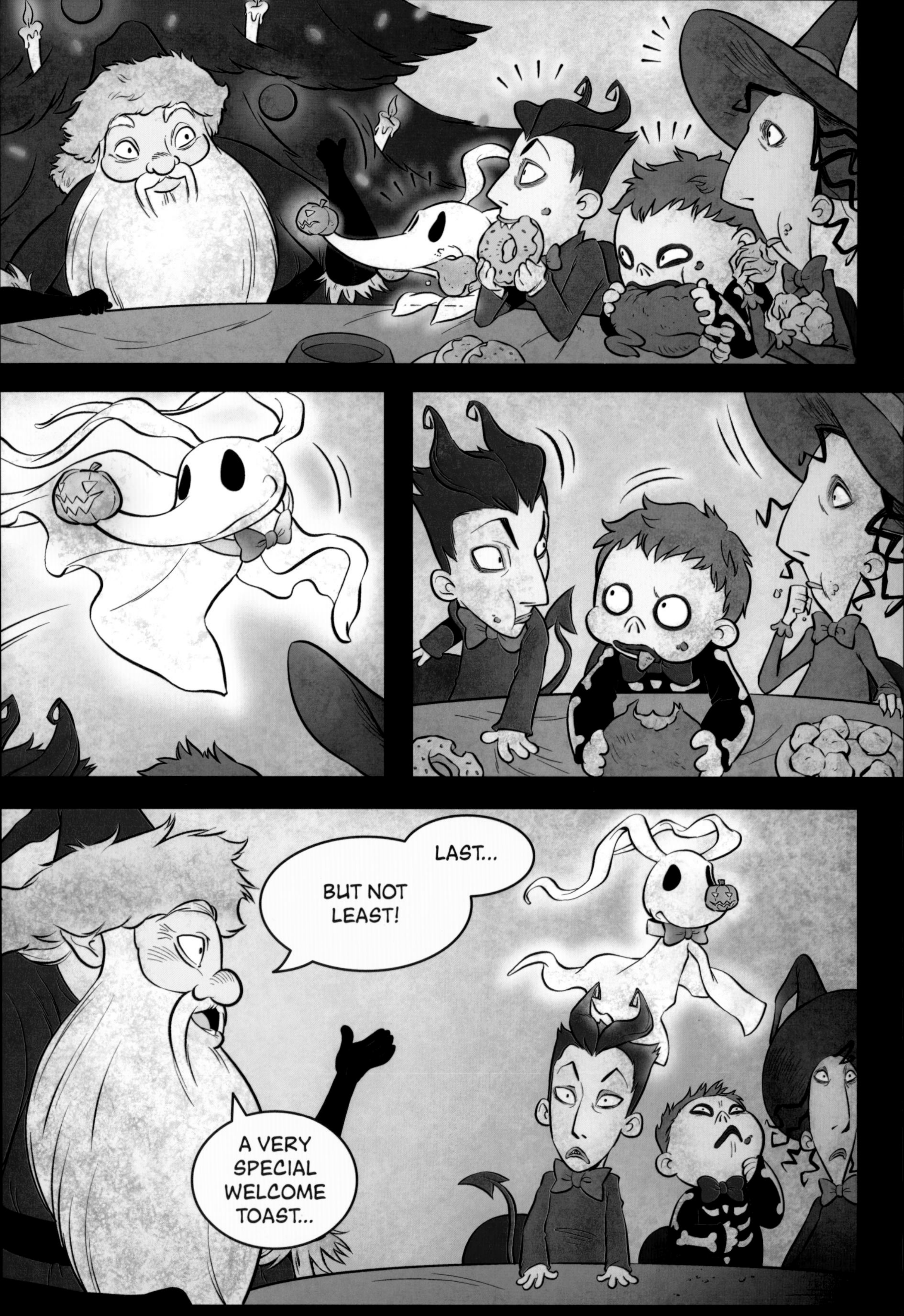
LAST... BUT NOT LEAST!
A VERY SPECIAL WELCOME TOAST...

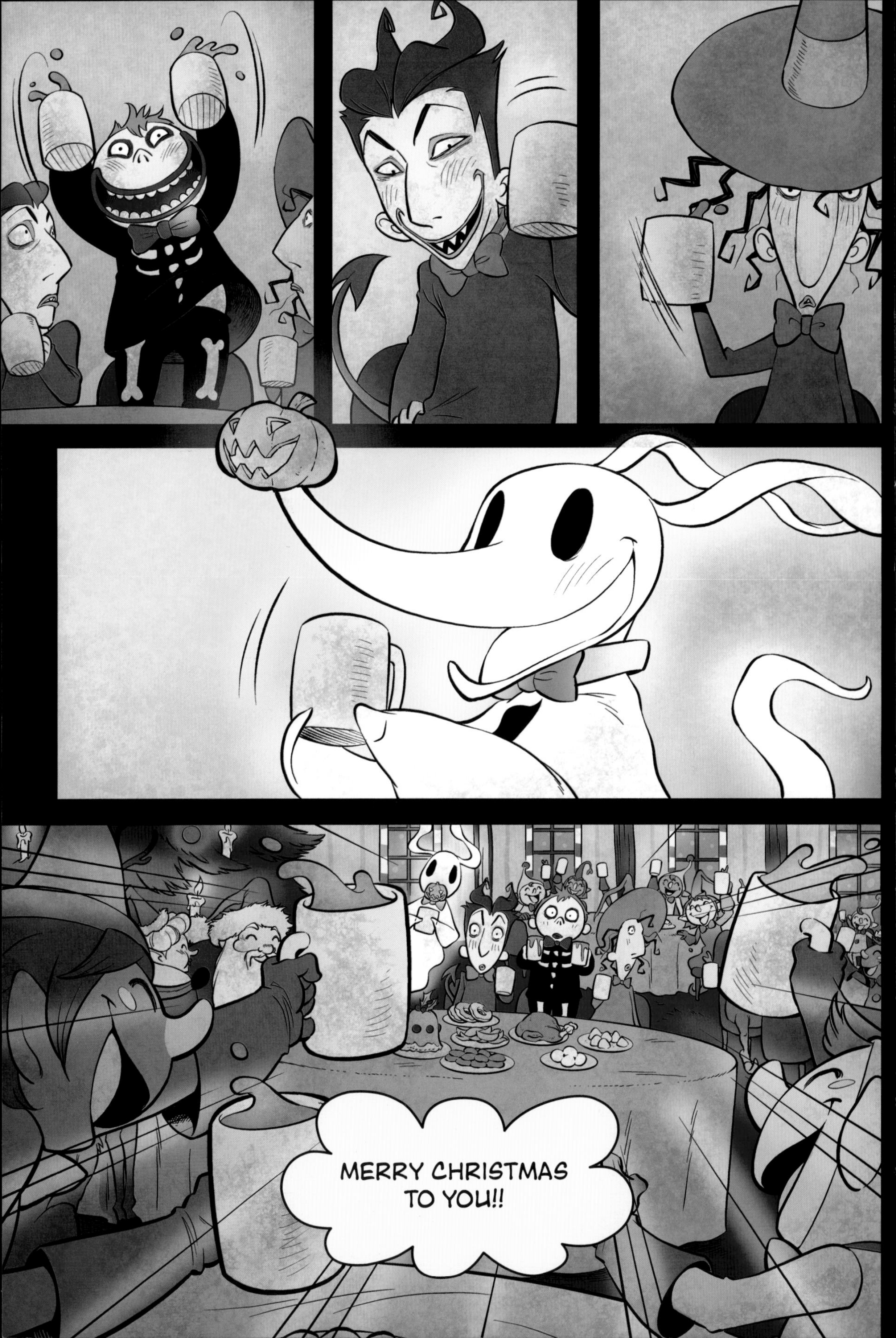
MERRY CHRISTMAS
TO YOU!!

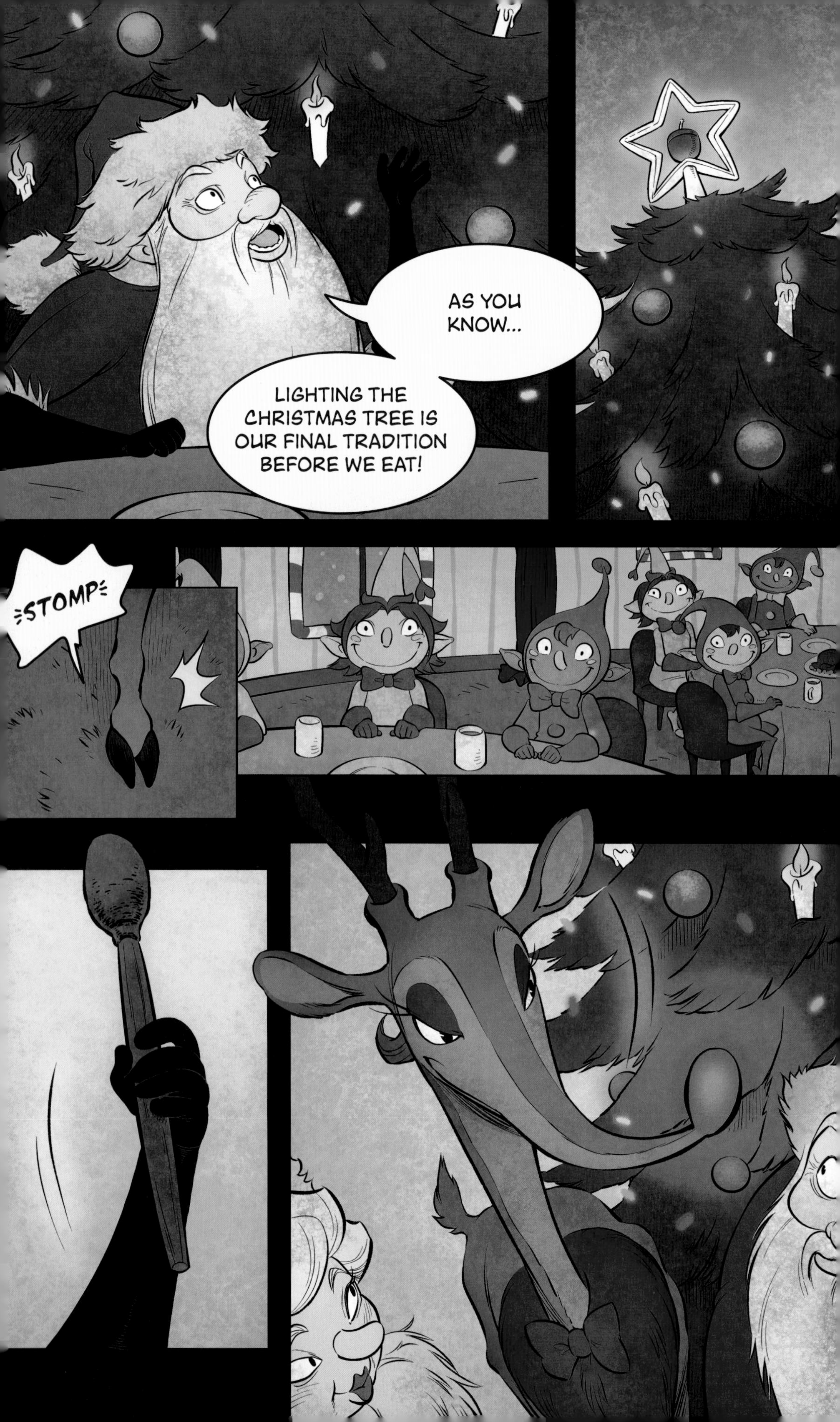
AS YOU KNOW...
LIGHTING THE CHRISTMAS TREE IS OUR FINAL TRADITION BEFORE WE EAT!
STOMP

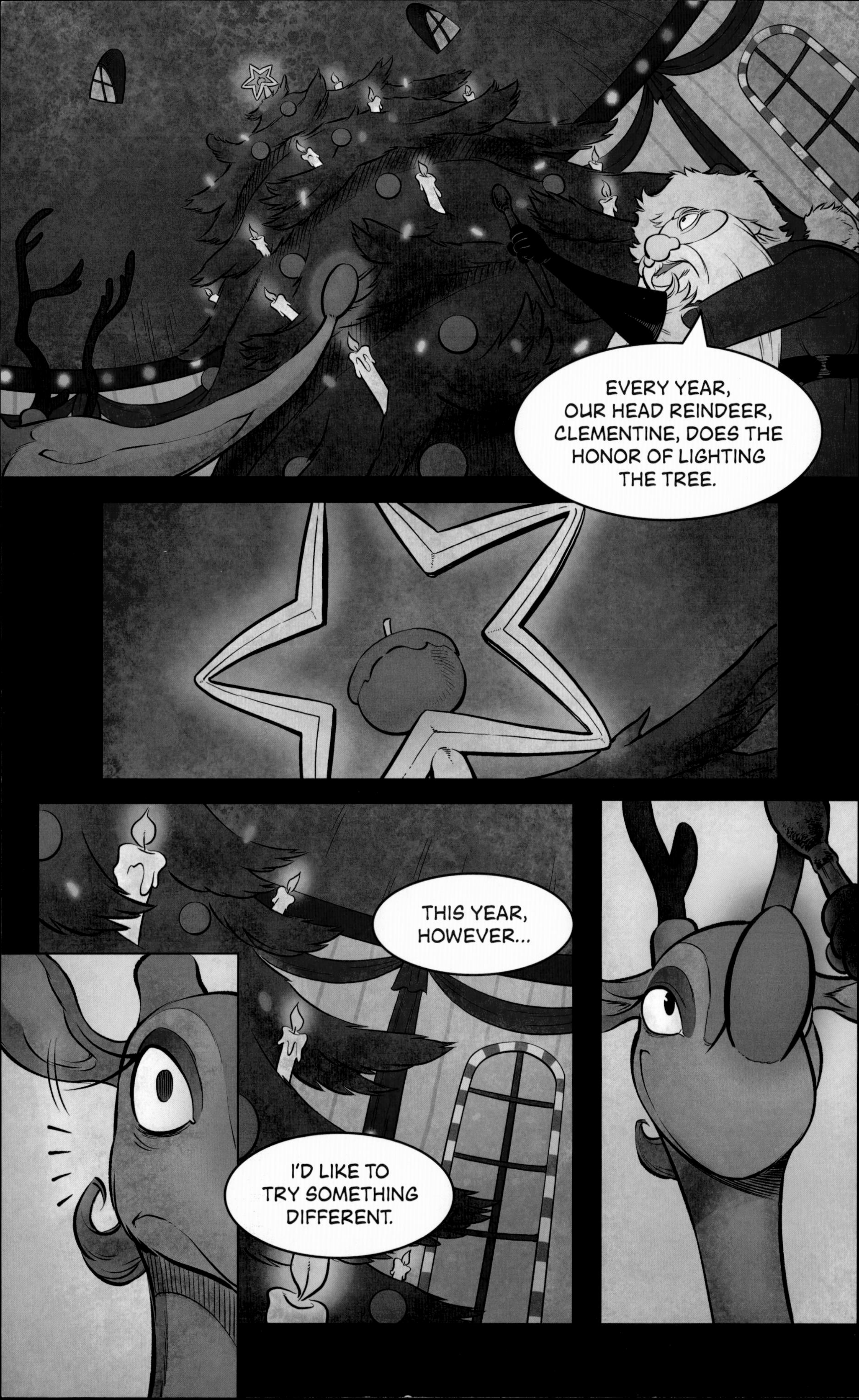
EVERY YEAR, OUR HEAD REINDEER, CLEMENTINE, DOES THE HONOR OF LIGHTING THE TREE.
THIS YEAR, HOWEVER...
I'D LIKE TO TRY SOMETHING DIFFERENT.

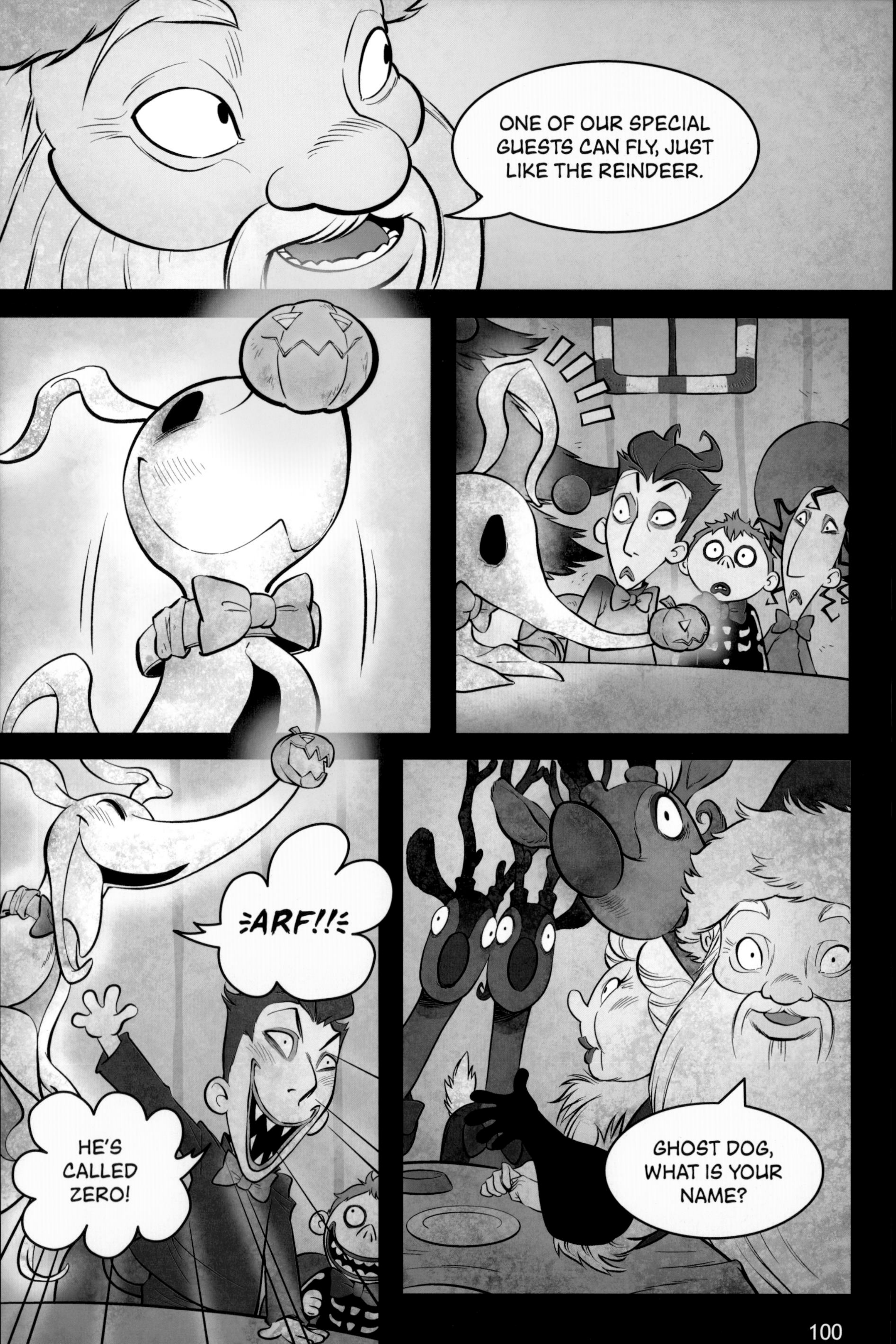
ONE OF OUR SPECIAL GUESTS CAN FLY, JUST LIKE THE REINDEER.
GHOST DOG, WHAT IS YOUR NAME?
ARF!!
HE'S CALLED ZERO!

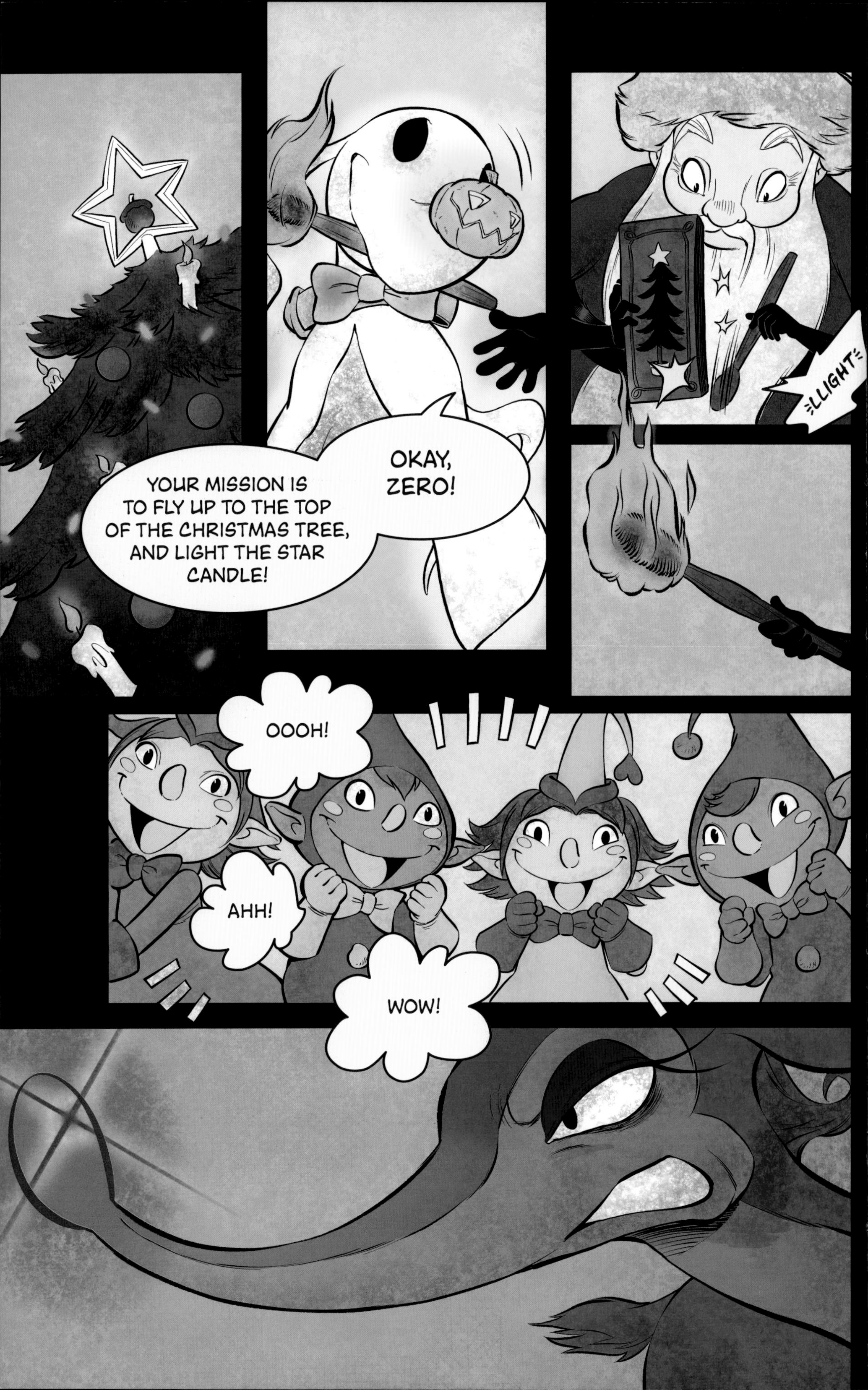
LLIGHT
OKAY, ZERO!
YOUR MISSION IS TO FLY UP TO THE TOP OF THE CHRISTMAS TREE, AND LIGHT THE STAR CANDLE!
OOOH!
AHH!
WOW!

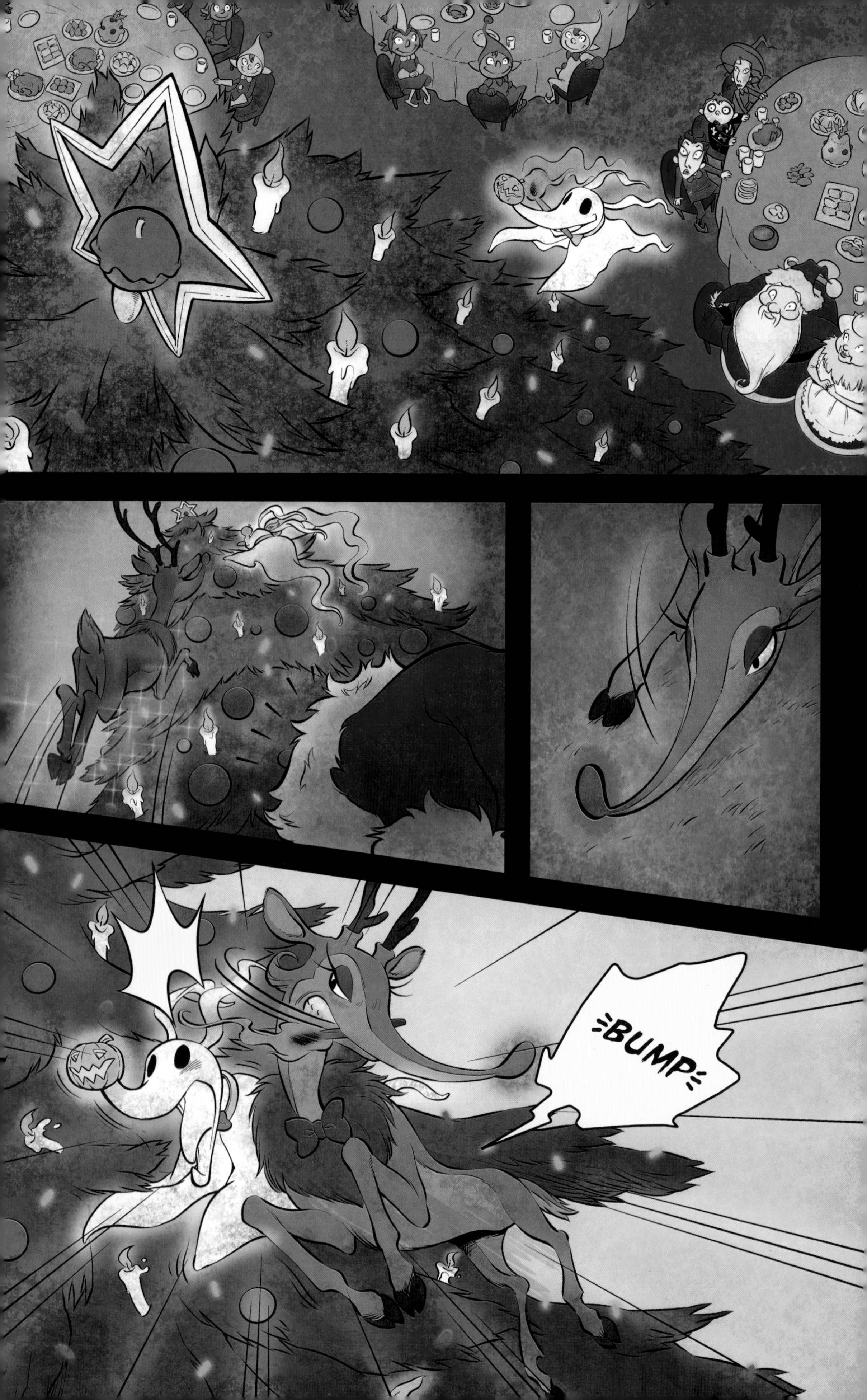
BUMP

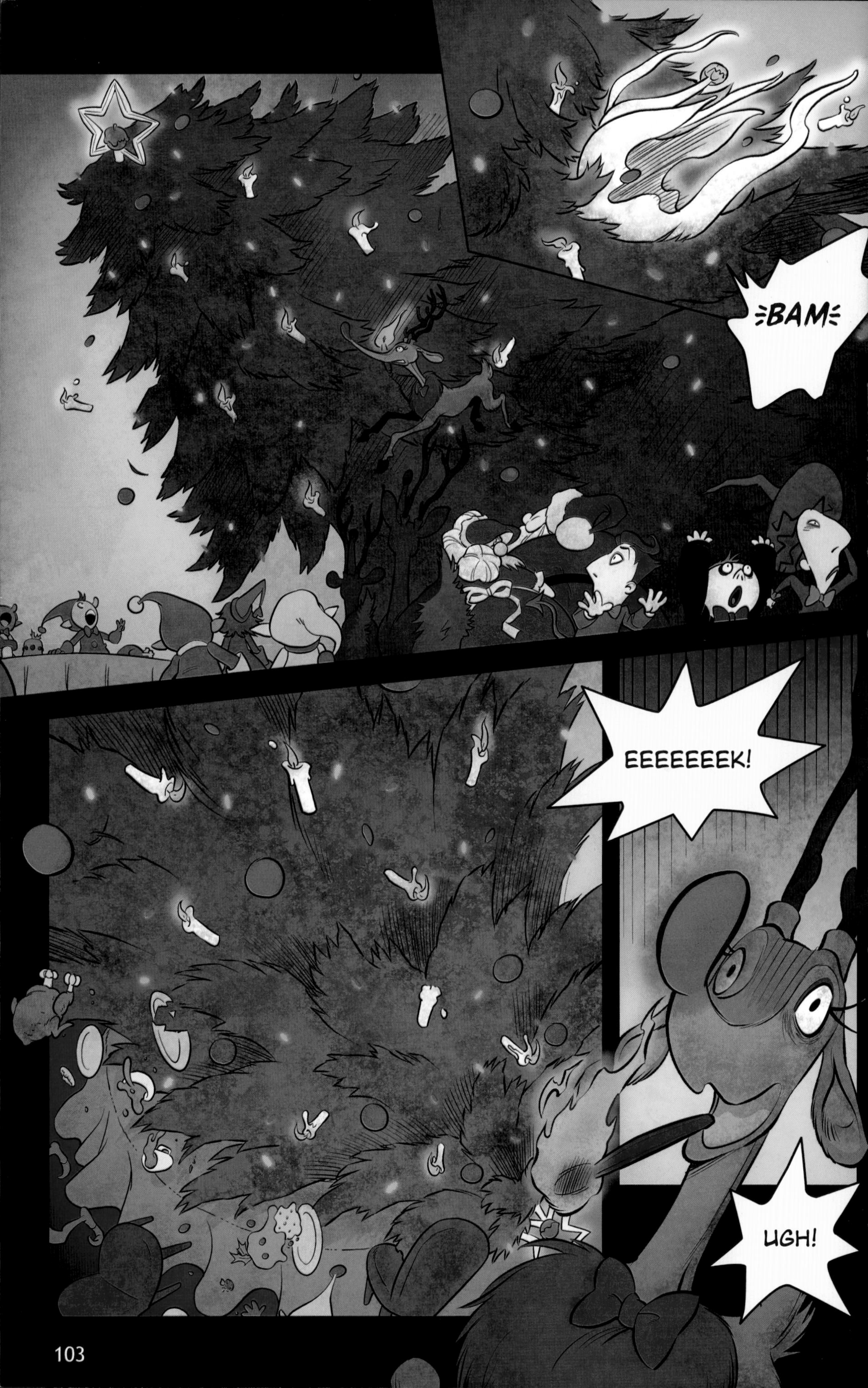
BAM
EEEEEEEK!
UGH!

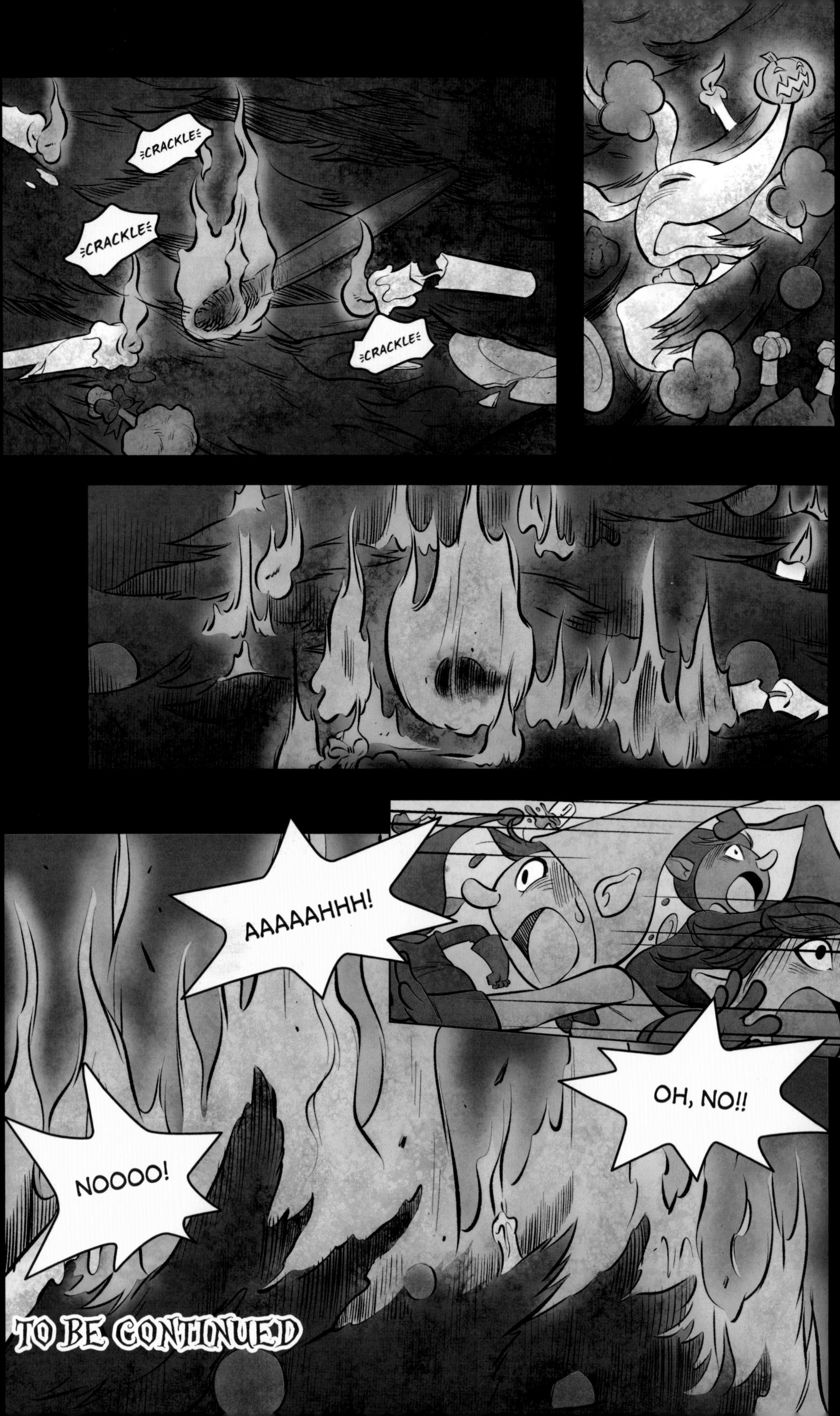
CRACKLE
CRACKLE
CRACKLE
AAAAAHHH!
OH, NO!!
NOOOO!
TO BE CONTINUED

COMING SOON

ZERO'S STILL TRYING TO GET HOME...

...BUT FIRST, CAN HE SAVE CHRISTMAS TOWN?

FOLLOW THE RELEASE SCHEDULE AND FIND OUT WHAT HAPPENS NEXT AT
TOKYOPOP.com/UPCOMING!

DISNEY

TIM BURTON'S THE NIGHTMARE BEFORE CHRISTMAS

ZERO'S JOURNEY

COVER GALLERY

ISSUE #10

FINAL COVER (KIYOSHI ARAI AND JUN SUZUKI)

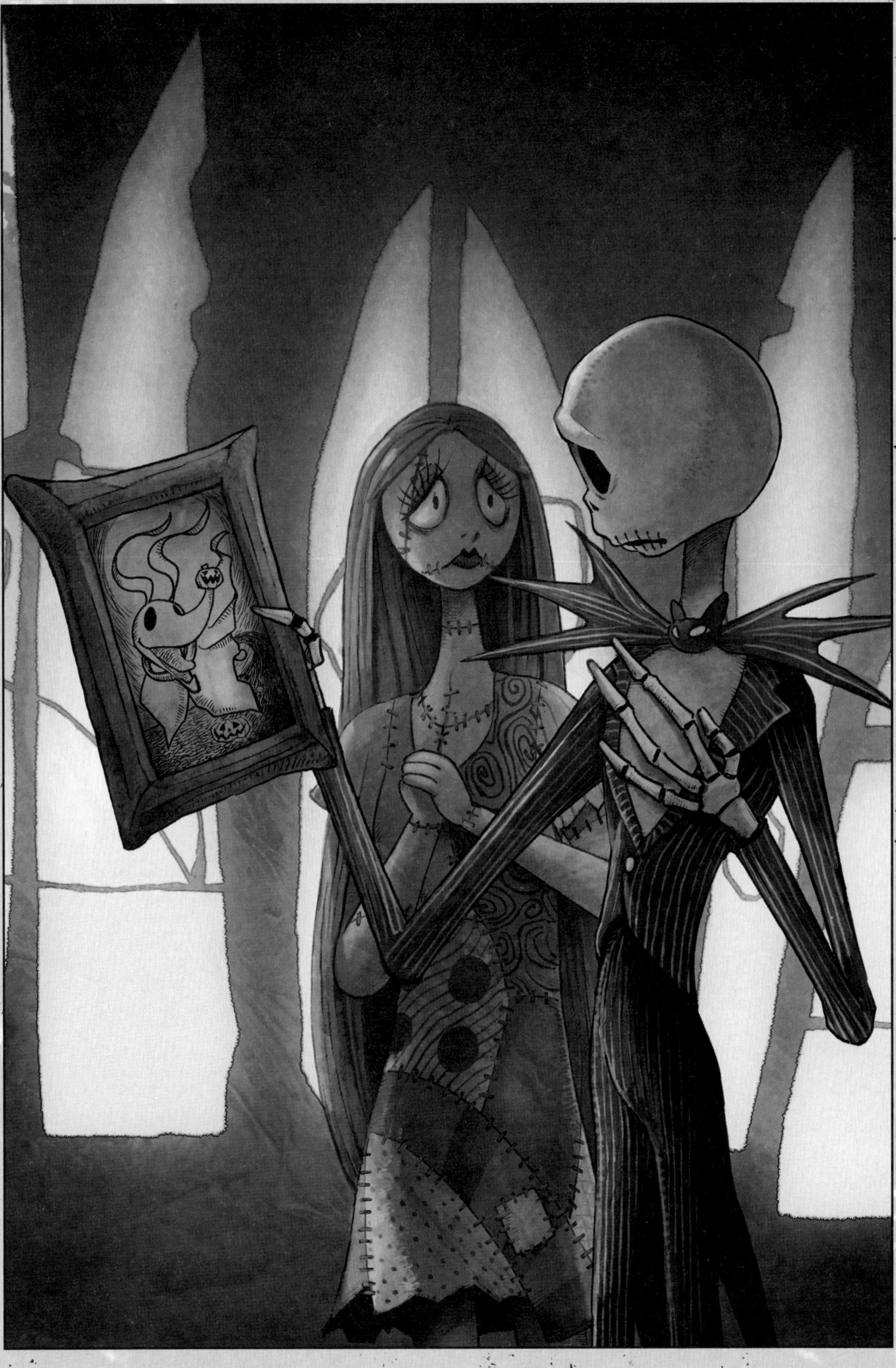

ISSUE #11

FINAL COVER (KIYOSHI ARAI AND JUN SUZUKI)

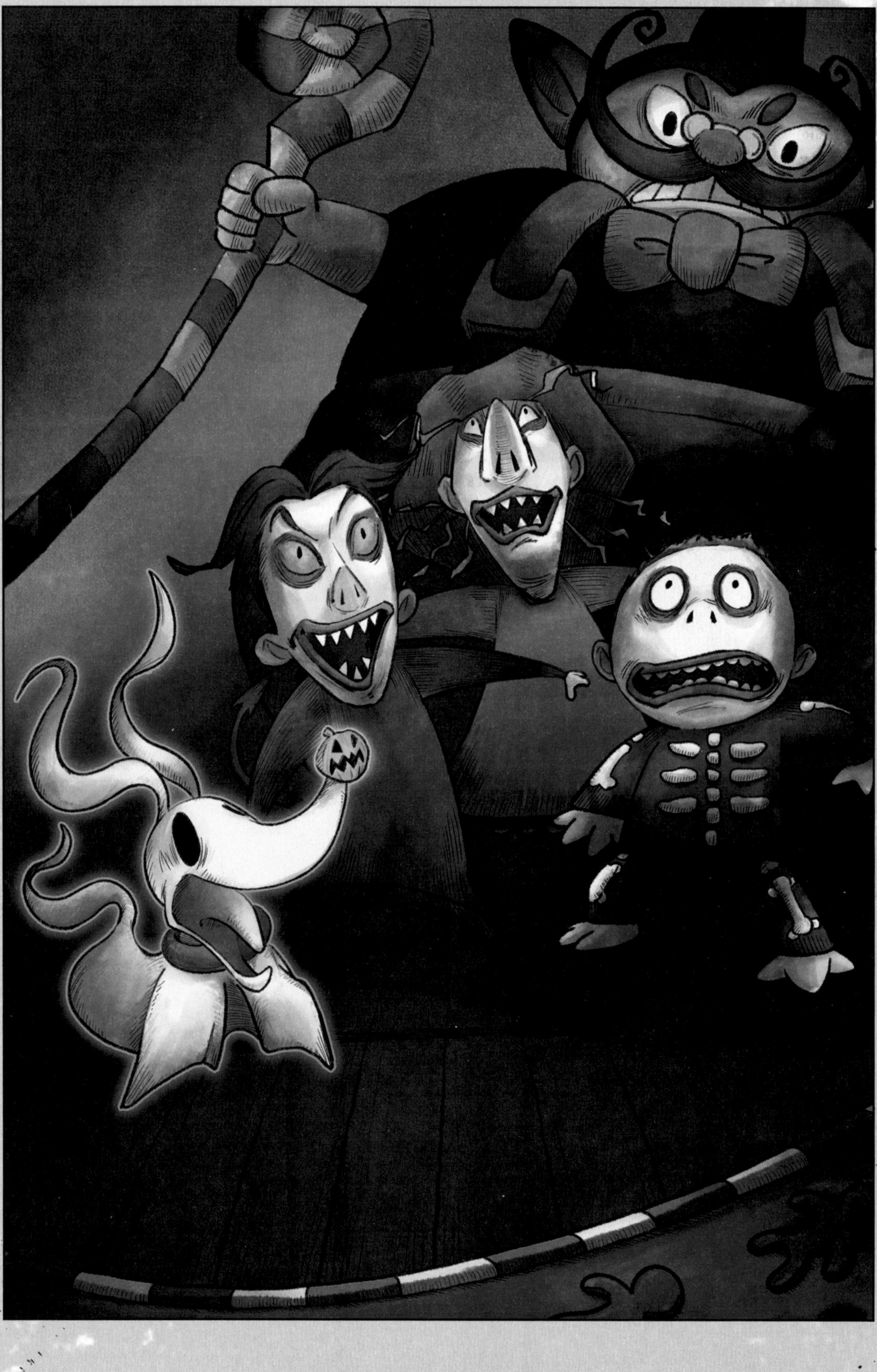

ISSUE #12

FINAL COVER (KIYOSHI ARAI AND JUN SUZUKI)

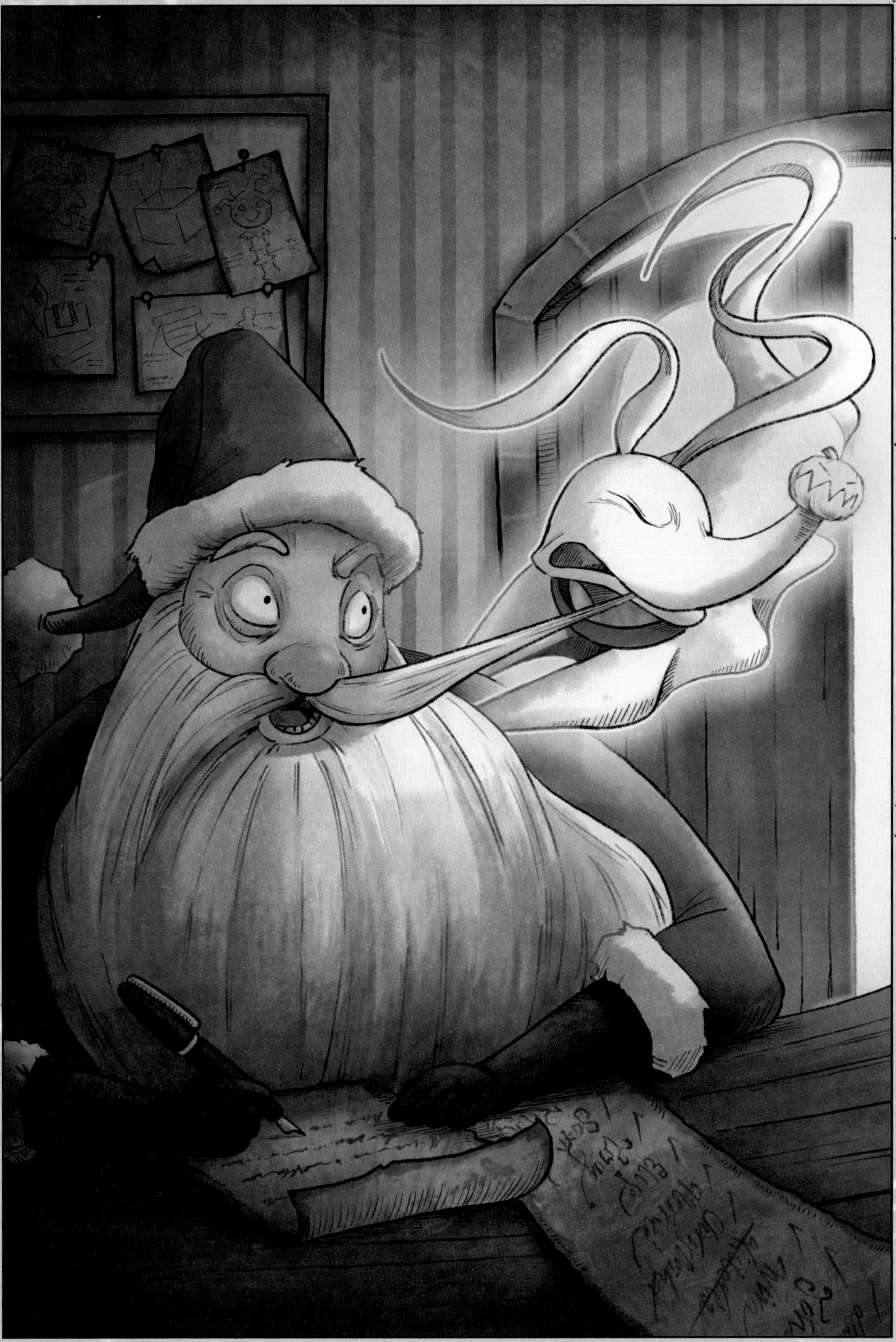

ISSUE #13

FINAL COVER (KIYOSHI ARAI AND JUN SUZUKI)

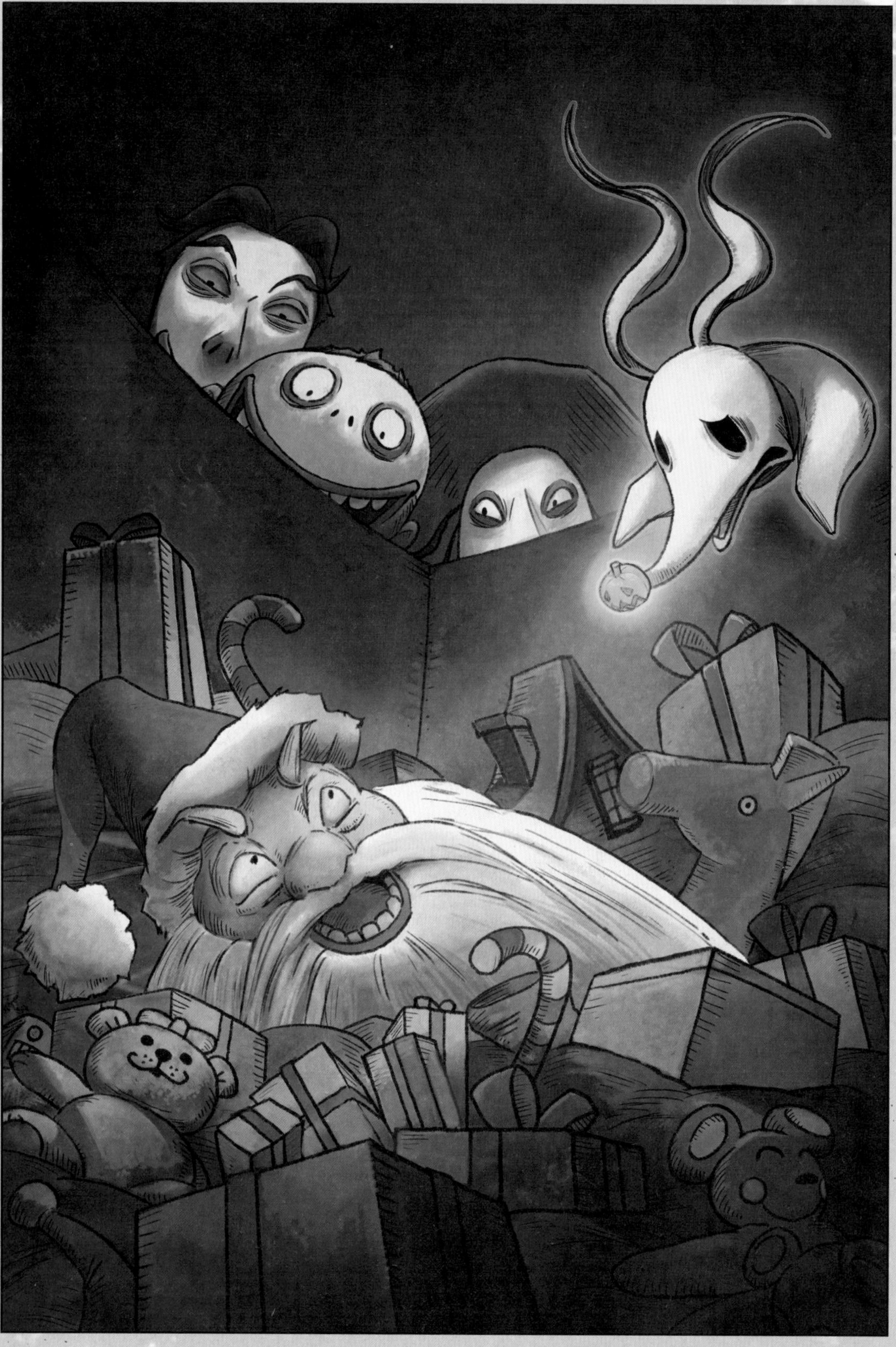

ISSUE #14

FINAL COVER (KIYOSHI ARAI AND JUN SUZUKI)

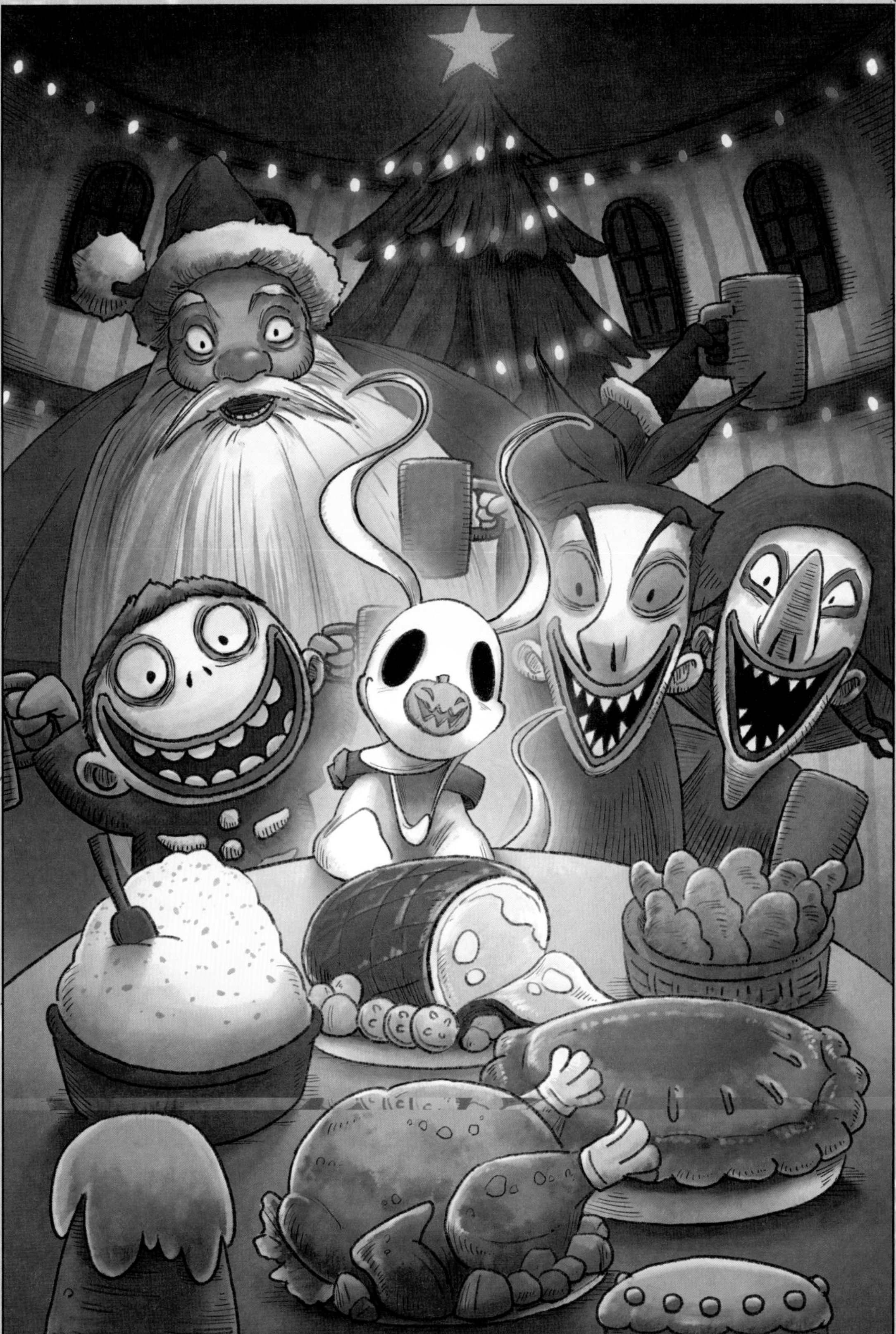

GRAPHIC NOVEL #3 — MAIN COVER

FINAL COVER (KIYOSHI ARAI AND JUN SUZUKI)

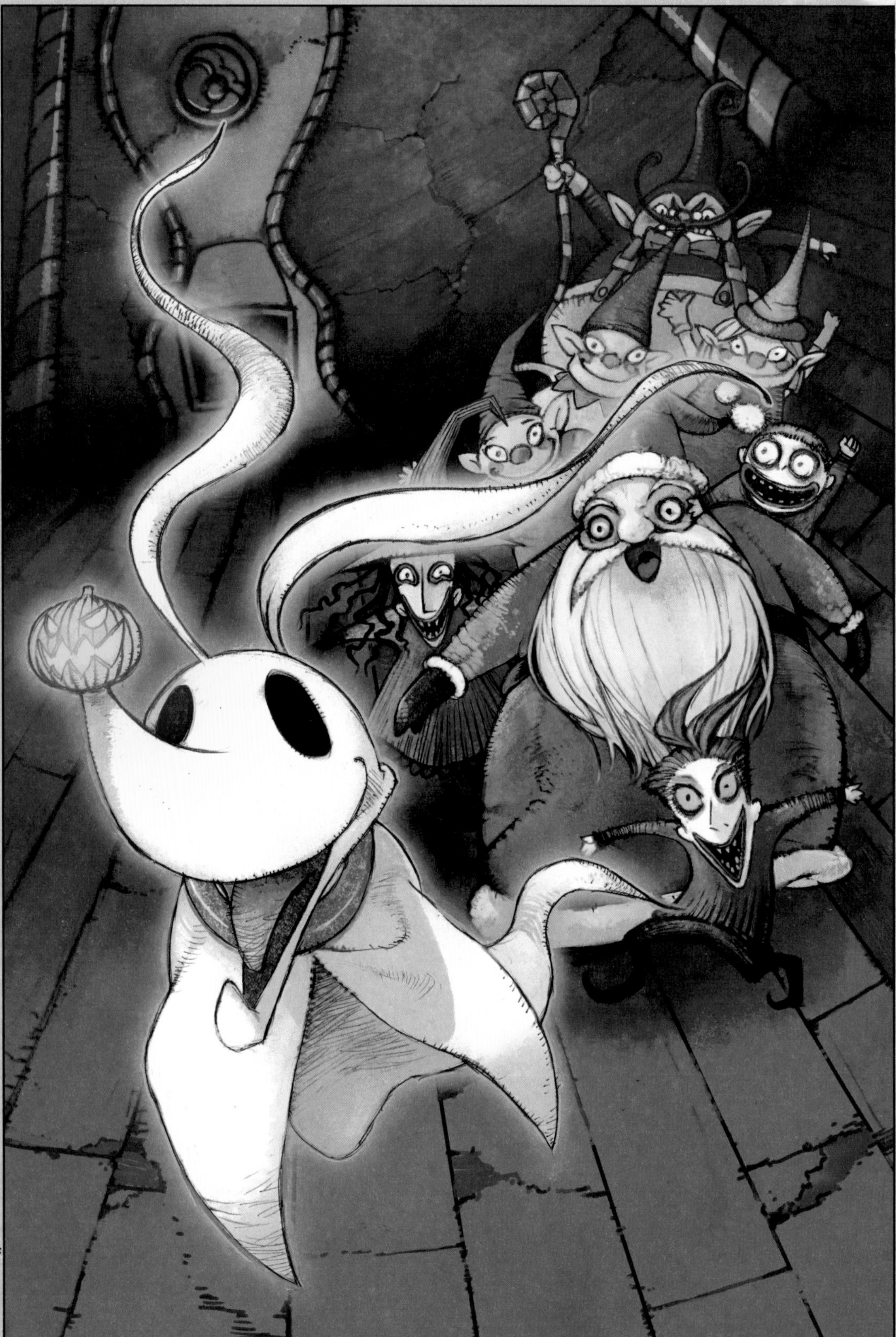

GRAPHIC NOVEL #3 — VARIANT COVER

FINAL COVER (DAVID MACK)

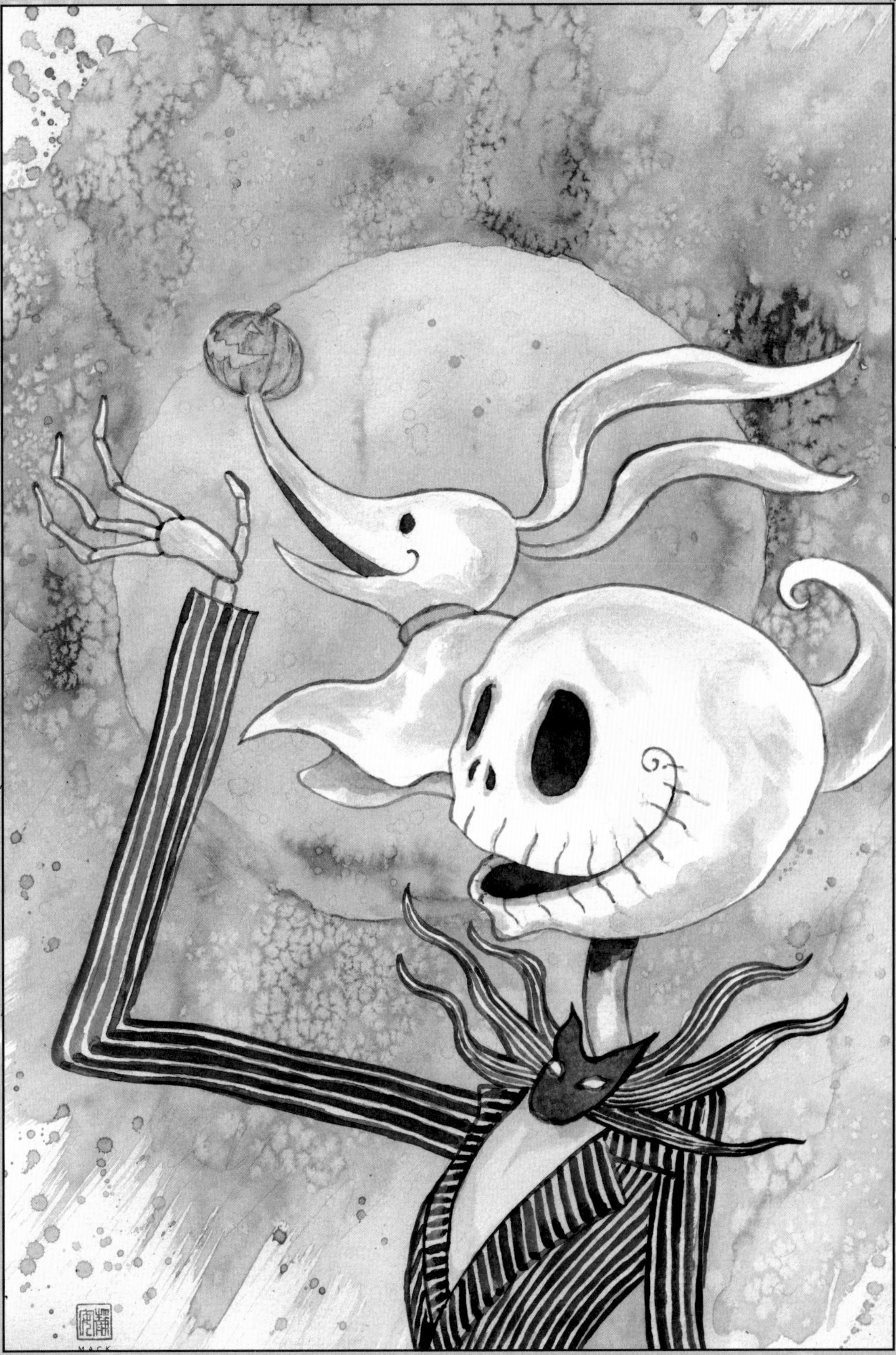

SINGLE ISSUE COVER SKETCHES

SKETCHES (KIYOSHI ARAI AND JUN SUZUKI)

ISSUE #10 COVER A

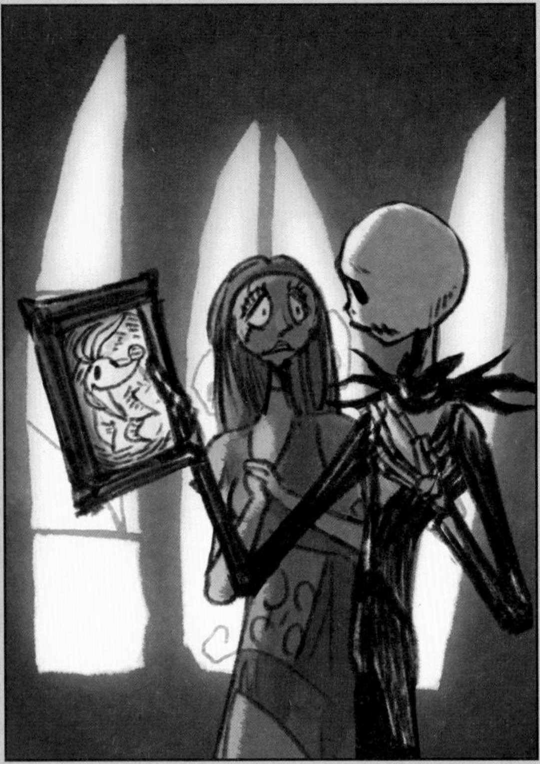

ISSUE #10 COVER B

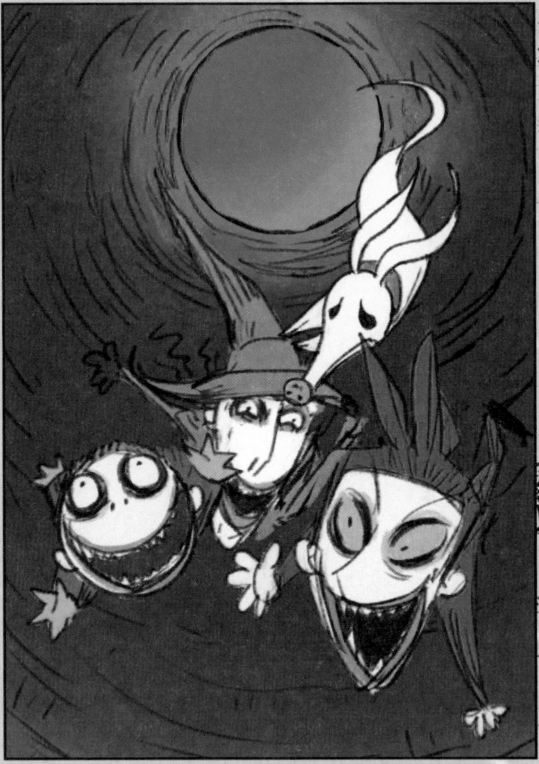

ISSUE #11 COVER A

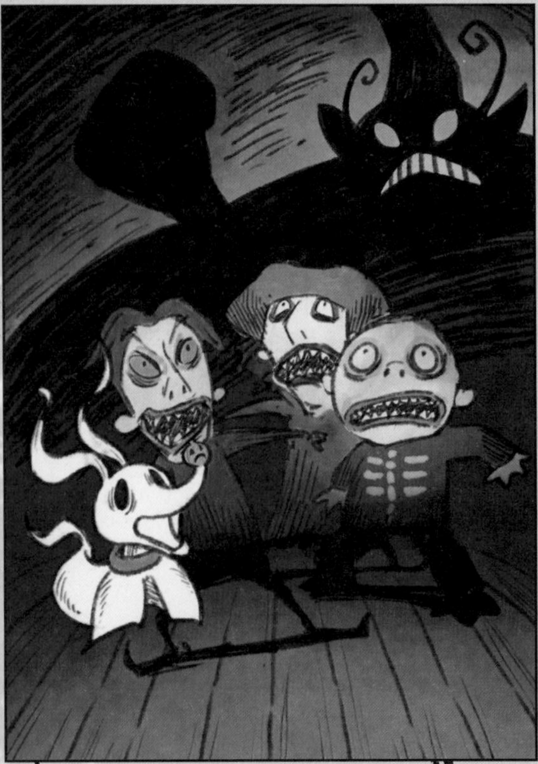

ISSUE #11 COVER B

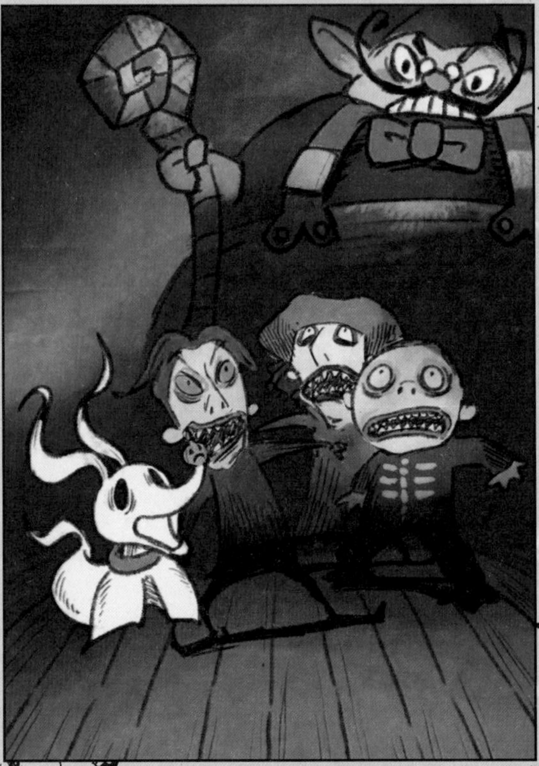

SINGLE ISSUE COVER SKETCHES

SKETCHES (KIYOSHI ARAI AND JUN SUZUKI)

ISSUE #12

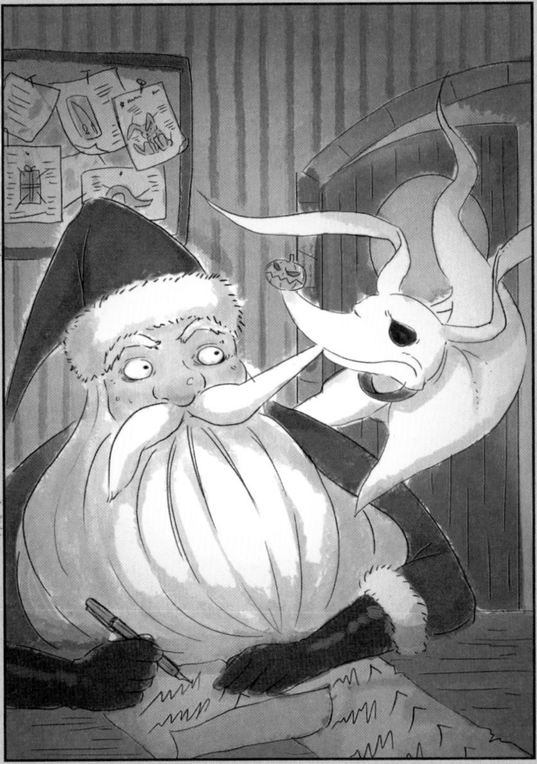

ISSUE #13

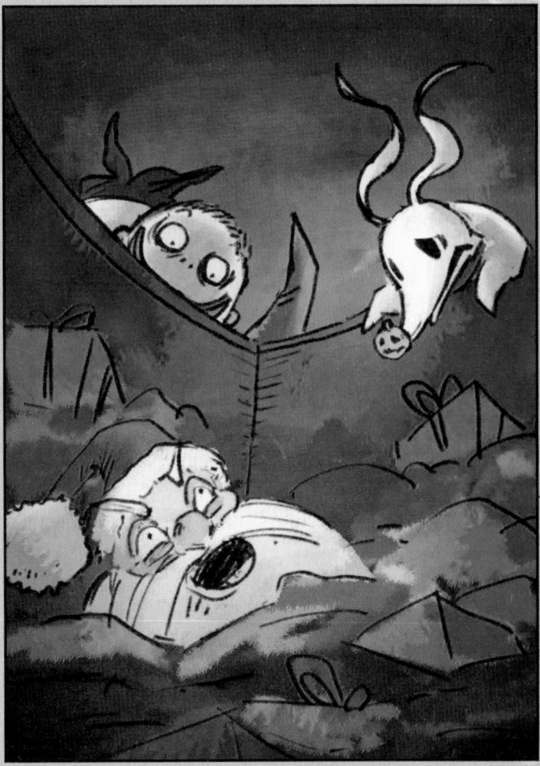

ISSUE #14

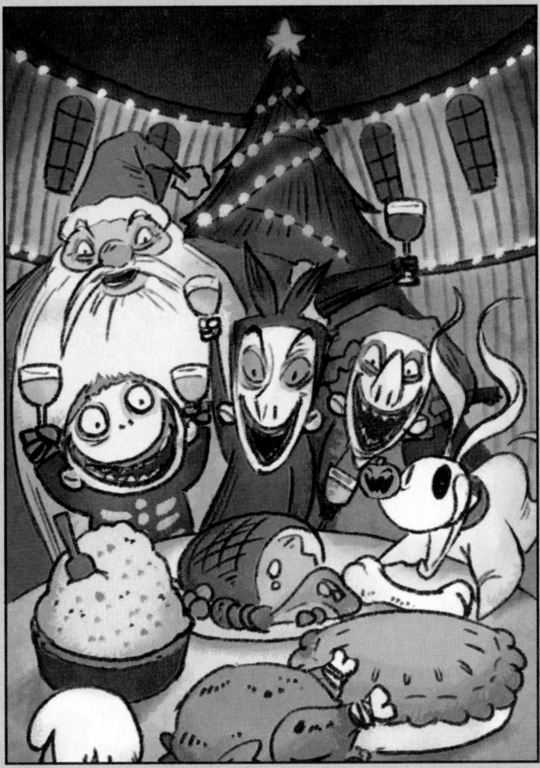

GRAPHIC NOVEL #3 — MAIN COVER A

SKETCH (KIYOSHI ARAI AND JUN SUZUKI)

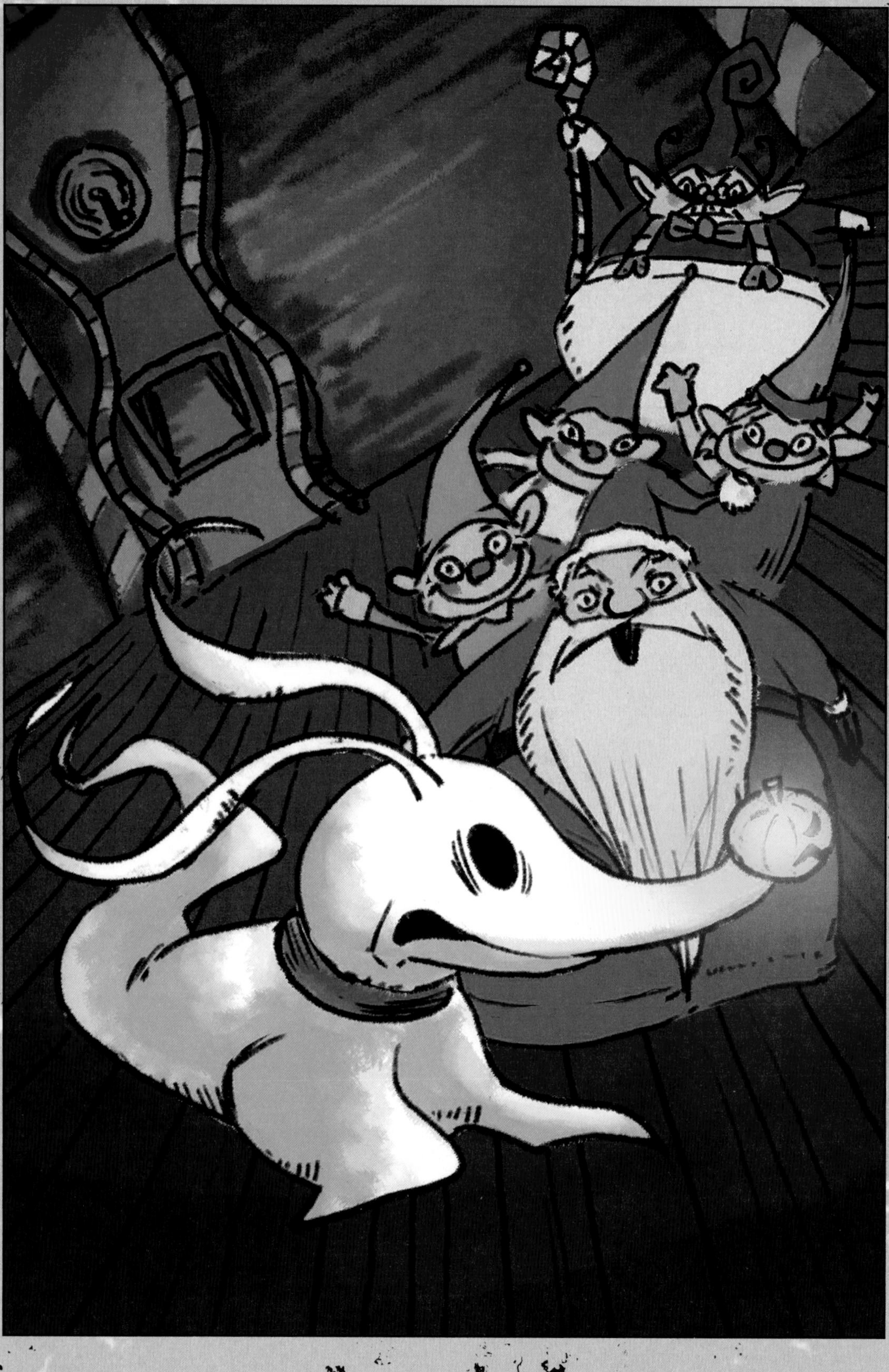

GRAPHIC NOVEL #3 — MAIN COVER B

SKETCH (KIYOSHI ARAI AND JUN SUZUKI)

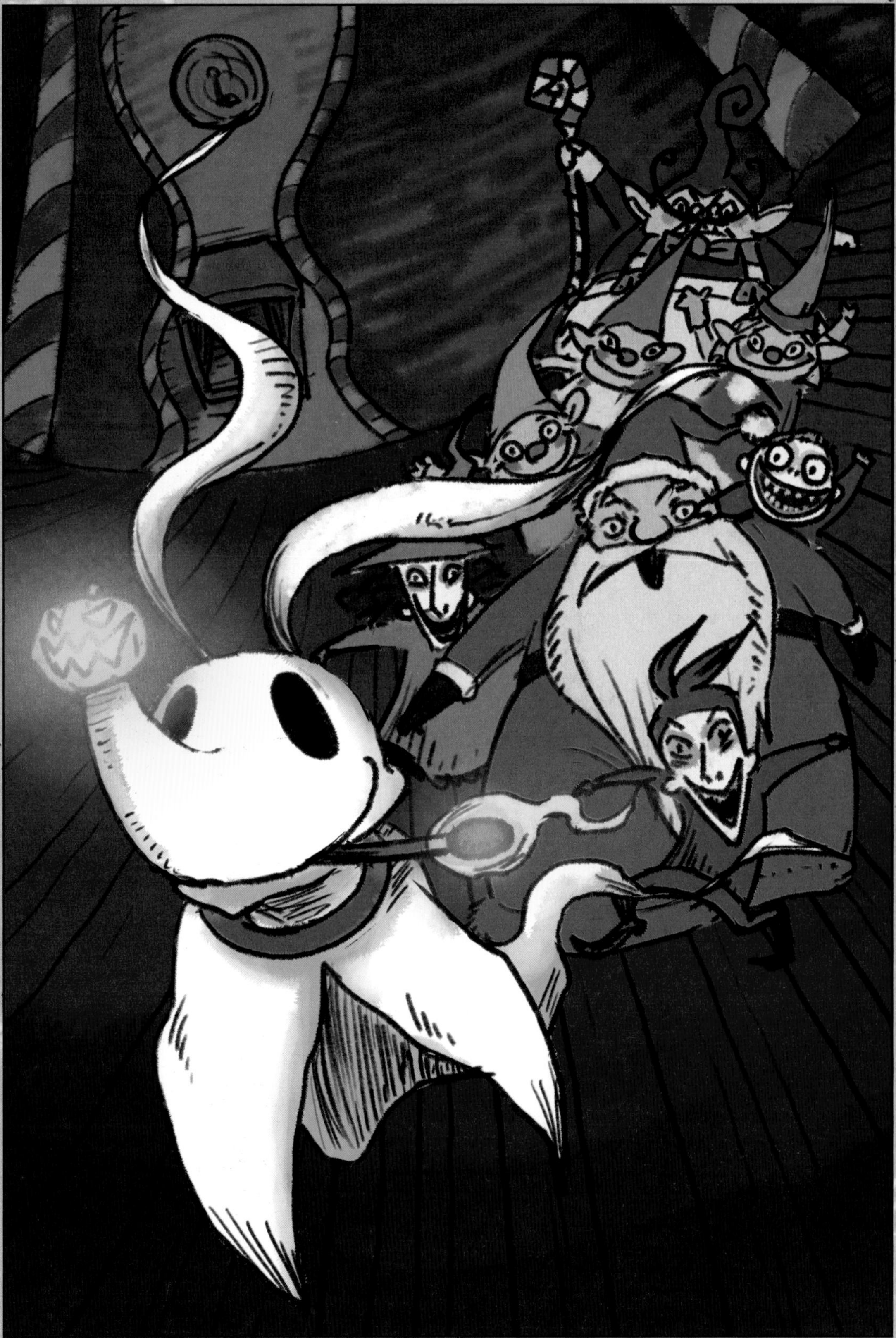

GRAPHIC NOVEL #3 — VARIANT COVER

SKETCH (DAVID MACK)

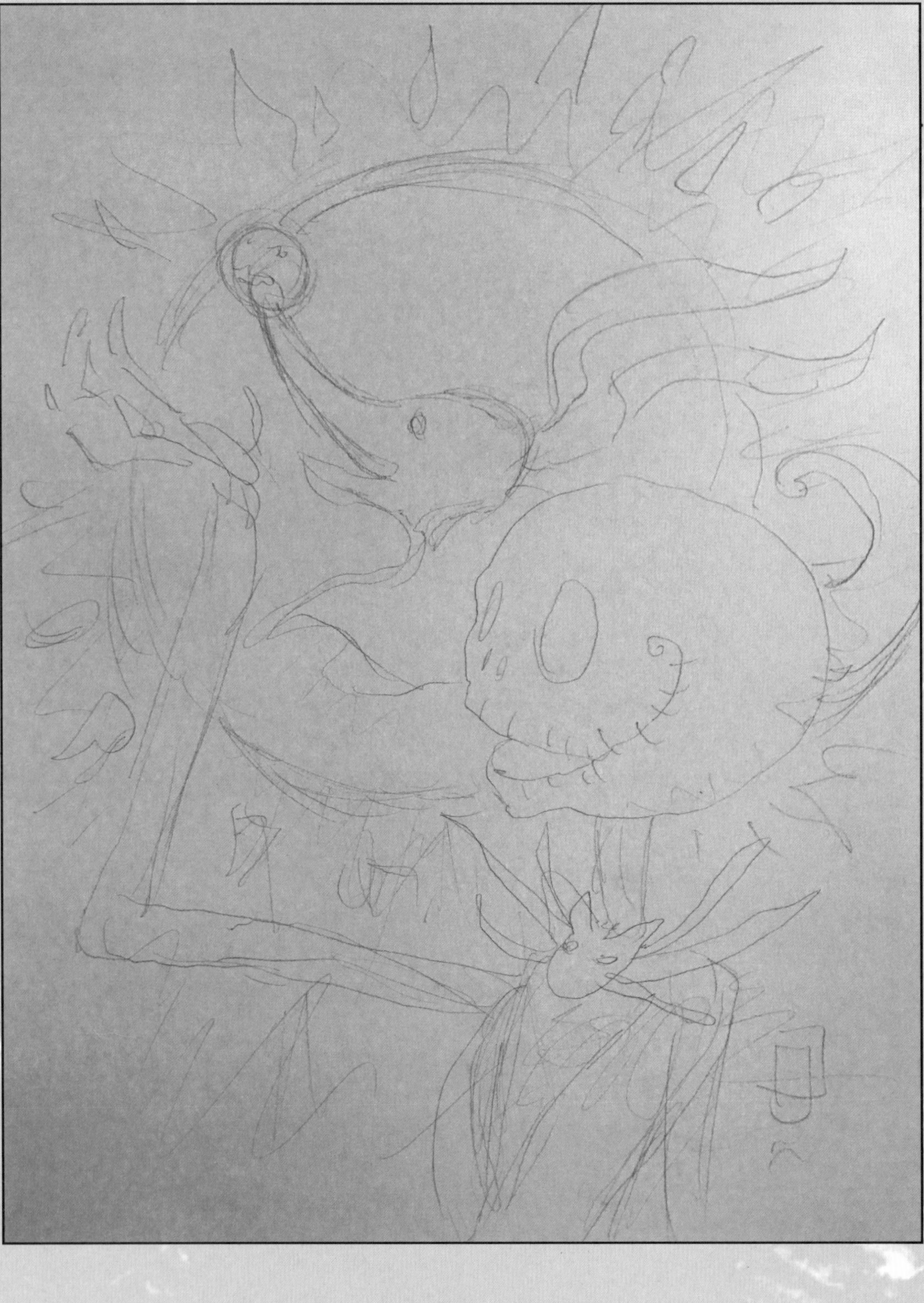

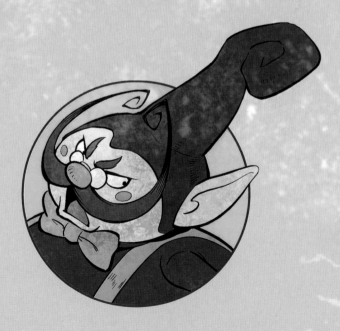

Disney Tim Burton's The Nightmare Before Christmas

Zero's Journey

CONCEPT GALLERY

LOCK, SHOCK, BARREL

CONCEPT ART (KIYOSHI ARAI)

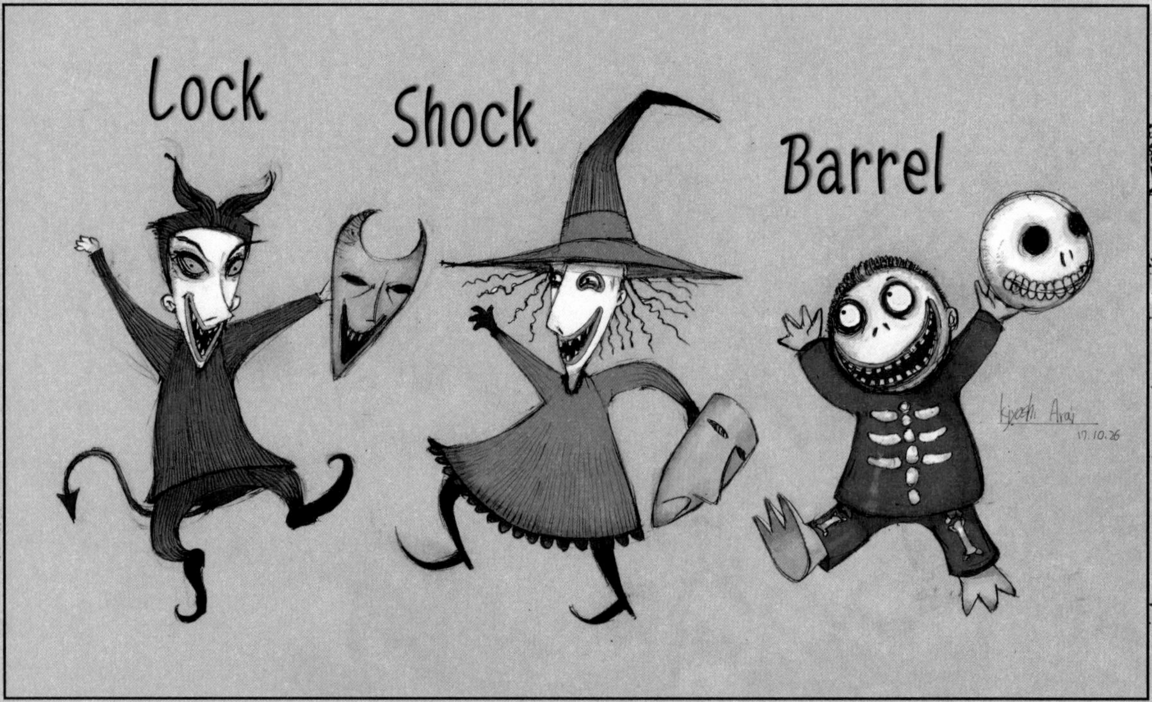
Lock
Shock
Barrel
Kiyoshi Arai
17.10.26

SANTA CLAUS

CONCEPT ART (KIYOSHI ARAI)

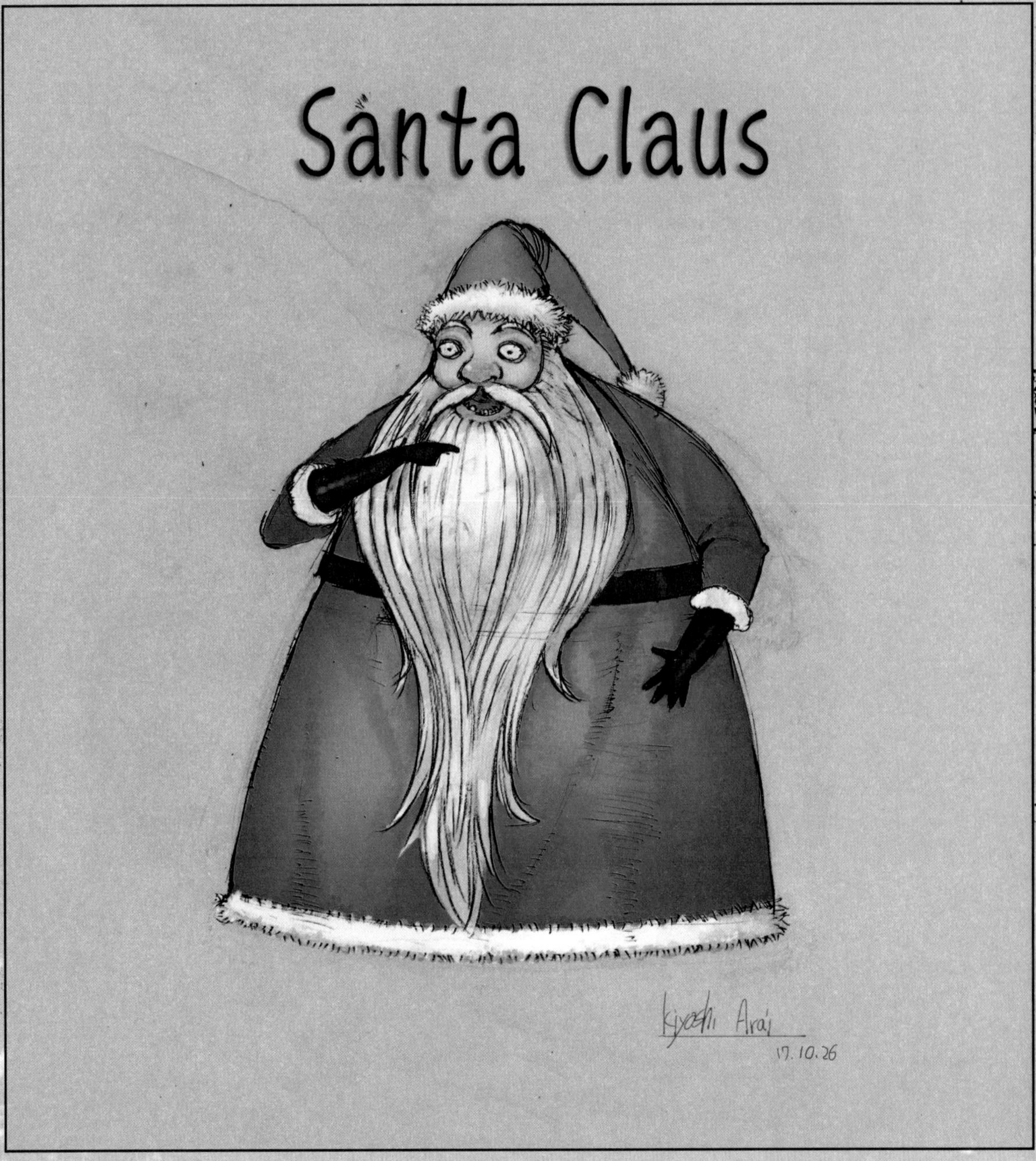
Santa Claus
Kiyoshi Arai
17.10.26

FACTORY BOSS

CONCEPT ART (KIYOSHI ARAI)

FACTORY's BOSS

BACK

2019.1.21
Jun Suzuki

CLEMENTINE

CONCEPT ART (KIYOSHI ARAI)

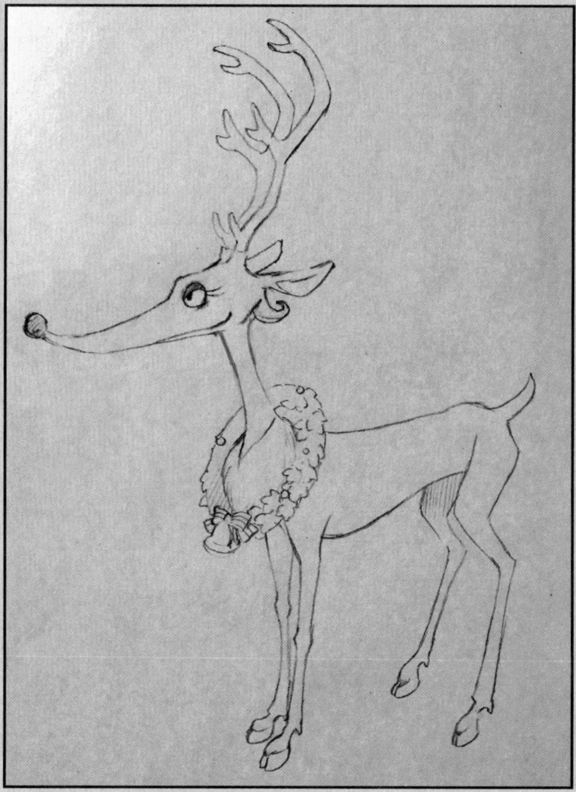

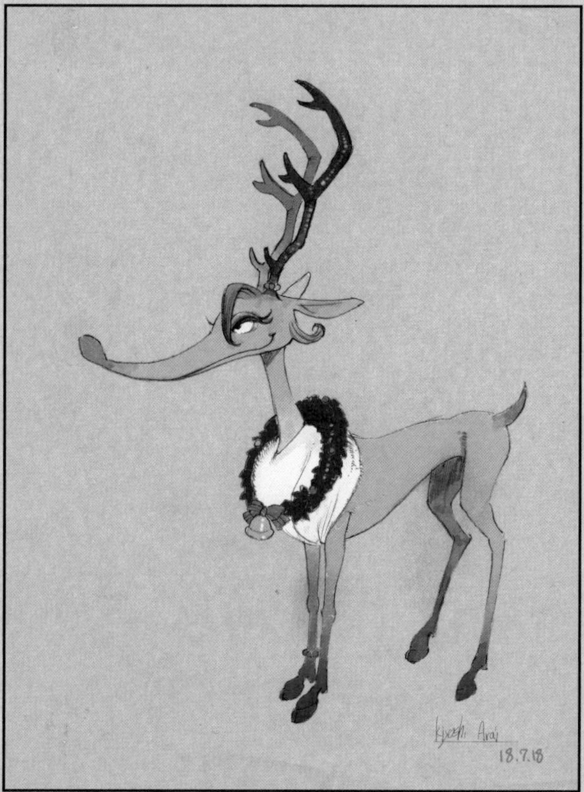
Kiyoshi Arai
18.7.18

REINDEER

CONCEPT ART (KIYOSHI ARAI)

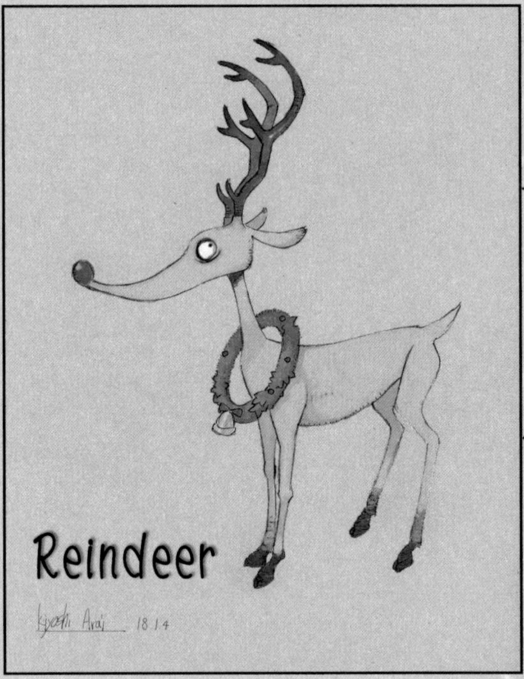
Reindeer
Kiyoshi Arai 18.1.4

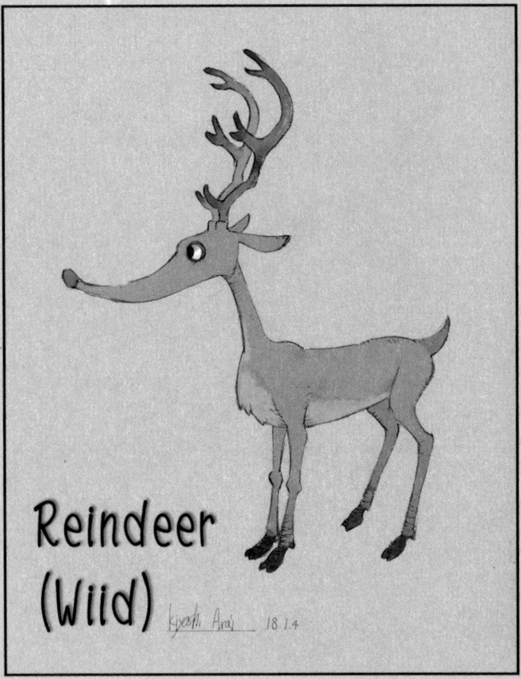
Reindeer
(Wiid)
Kiyoshi Arai 18.1.4

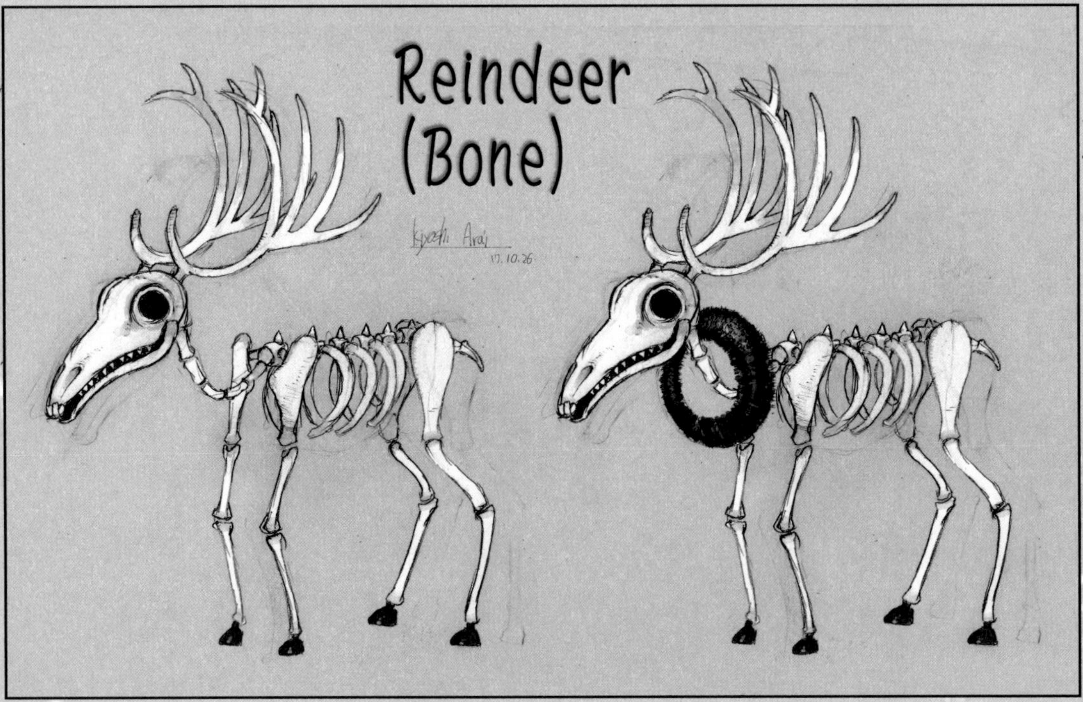
Reindeer
(Bone)
Kiyoshi Arai 17.10.26

SANTA'S WORKSHOP

CONCEPT ART (KIYOSHI ARAI)

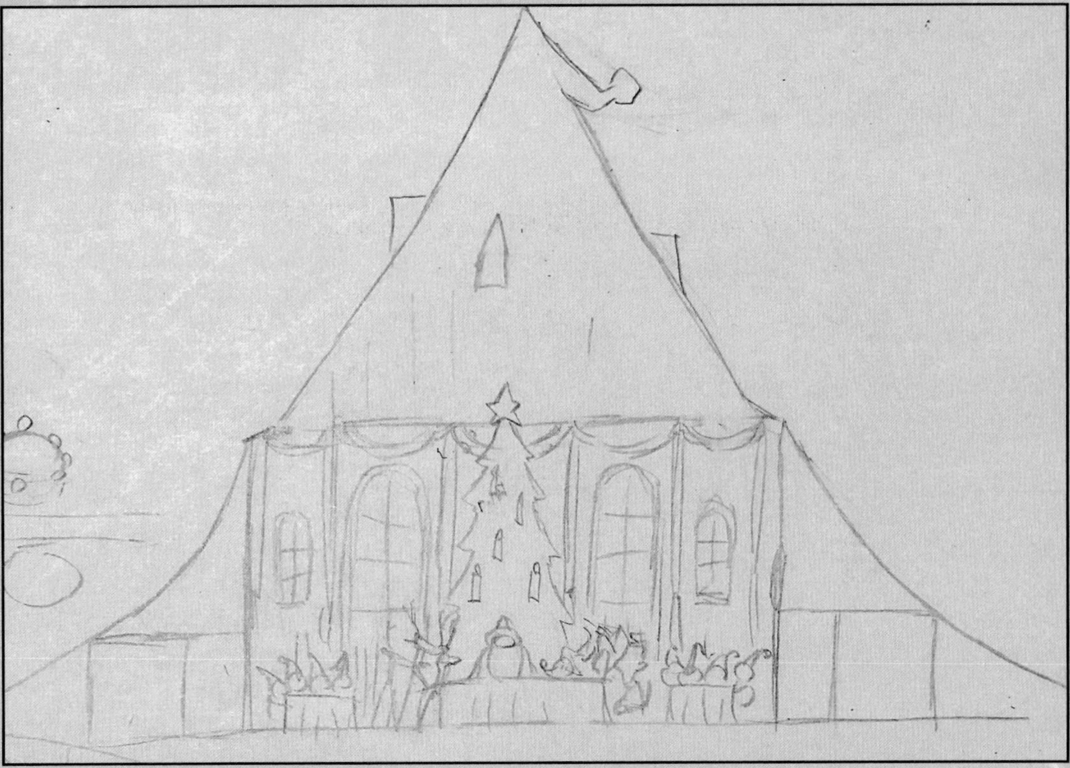

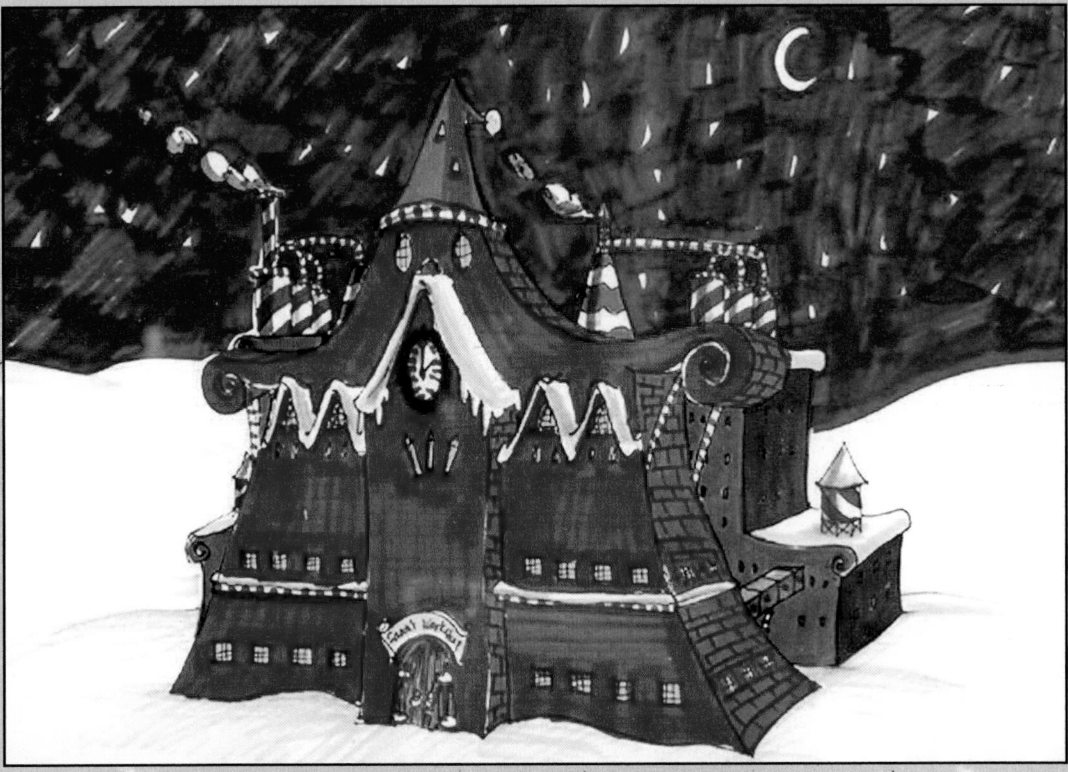

Disney Tim Burton's The Nightmare Before Christmas: Zero's Journey Graphic Novel Volume 3

Original Characters by - Tim Burton
Story by - D.J. Milky
Main Printing Cover by - Kiyoshi Arai & Jun Suzuki
Variant Cover by - David Mack
Character Design - Kiyoshi Arai
Concept Art - Kiyoshi Arai & Jun Suzuki
Storyboards and Pencils by - Kei Ishiyama
Inks by - David Hutchison
Colors by - Dan Conner
Color Flats by - Patricia Krmpotich

Editorial Associate - Janae Young
Marketing Associate - Kae Winters
Technology and Digital Media Assistant - Phillip Hong
Translator - Mayu Arimoto
Editorial Coordinator - Daisuke Fukada
Editor - Stu Levy
Copyeditor - Kae Winters
Graphic Designer - Phillip Hong
Retouching and Lettering - Vibrraant Publishing Studio
Editor-in-Chief & Publisher - Stu Levy

A TOKYOPOP® Manga

TOKYOPOP and 🌀 are trademarks or registered trademarks of TOKYOPOP Inc.

TOKYOPOP inc.
5200 W Century Blvd
Suite 705
Los Angeles, CA 90045 USA

E-mail: info@TOKYOPOP.com
Come visit us online at www.TOKYOPOP.com

f www.facebook.com/TOKYOPOP
🐦 www.twitter.com/TOKYOPOP
P www.pinterest.com/TOKYOPOP
📷 www.instagram.com/TOKYOPOP

Main Cover Printing ISBN: 978-1-4278-5905-1

Variant Cover Printing ISBN: 978-1-4278-6164-1

First TOKYOPOP Printing: August 2019
10 9 8 7 6 5 4 3 2 1
Printed in CANADA

Don't Get **LOST** Like **ZERO!**

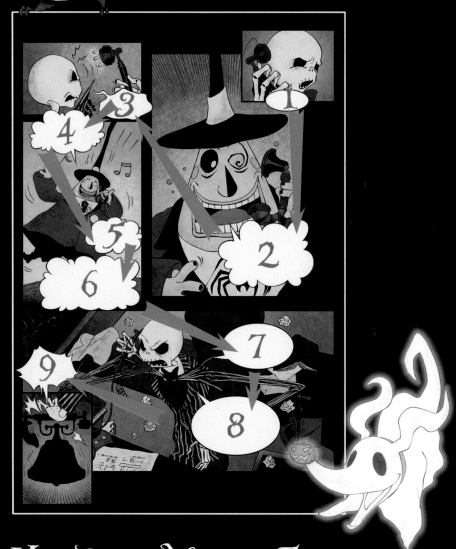

You Read Manga From Right to Left and Top to Bottom From Each Panel!